Praise for *A Botanical Daughter*:

"This book is the most fun a reader can have while
still gritting their teeth in fear! Enchantingly eerie and
upsettingly lovely, *A Botanical Daughter* is an intoxicating
hybrid of blood, botany, and old-timey charm."

Andrew Joseph White, *New York Times* bestselling
author of *Hell Followed with Us*

"Ripe, lush, and bursting with beauty and horror,
*A Botanical Daughter* will delight, amuse and terrify,
all while breaking your heart. Perfect for readers who
can imagine *Frankenstein* as created by the characters
of *Good Omens* in the Garden of Eden."

Delilah S. Dawson, *New York Times*
bestselling author of *Bloom*

"Macabre and magnificent. Horrifying and
hilarious. Oddly and unquestionably heart-warming.
A delightfully gruesome and rather brilliant debut from
Noah Medlock. A viciously violent Victorian romp that
would have Mary Shelley saying 'Damn!'"

Angela (A.G.) Slatter, award-winning
author of *The Path of Thorns*

"Medlock invites readers into a rich and sumptuous
world in a dark and charming novel full of macabre
delights. The perfect blend of classic science fiction and
horror, wrapped around a core of found family, love, and
heartbreak – this story hits all the right notes."

A.C. Wise, award-winning author of *Wendy, Darling*

# A BOTANICAL DAUGHTER

## NOAH MEDLOCK

**TITAN** BOOKS

A Botanical Daughter
Print edition ISBN: 9781803365909
E-book edition ISBN: 9781803365923

Published by Titan Books
A division of Titan Publishing Group Ltd
144 Southwark Street, London SE1 0UP
www.titanbooks.com

First edition: March 2024
10 9 8 7 6 5 4 3 2 1

This is a work of fiction. All of the characters, organizations, and events portrayed in this novel are either products of the author's imagination or are used fictitiously. Any resemblance to actual persons, living or dead (except for satirical purposes), is entirely coincidental.

A CIP catalogue record for this title is available from the British Library.

Printed and bound by
CPI Group (UK) Ltd, Croydon, CR0 4YY.

*For James*

# ~PART I~

## GERMINATION

# ONE

It is an unusual thing, to live in a botanical garden. But then again, Simon and Gregor were an unusual pair of gentlemen.

You might imagine that the vast greenhouse at Grimfern would be too stuffy for human habitation. You would be more or less right, though Gregor Sandys—that notorious botanist—had become accustomed to the garden's balmy climate. Grimfern's many brilliant glass surfaces were always covered in a sheen of condensation, so he developed a habit of carrying a handkerchief in every pocket for the sole purpose of wiping his spectacles. His sumptuous fruit trees and exquisite orchids required such moisture and heat that by the end of a hard day's gardening he could practically wring out his cummerbund. Gregor would swelter at any temperature though, cooking slowly like a steamed ham, for his precious collection of botanical curiosities.

In a house made of glass, the dazzling sun was a constant worry. An embellished wrought-iron frame held up countless artisanal panes, and if a denizen of the garden were caught off-guard by a passing sunbeam—or even by a particularly flamboyant candle flicker—he would be quite incapacitated by the light's furious beauty. Simon Rievaulx, the other resident at Grimfern, had set up his taxidermy workstation in the cool, dark basement of the glasshouse precisely to avoid this problem. Down there, beneath even the boiler, he could make sure that his compositions did not spontaneously *de-compose* by keeping his cadaverous creations, and himself, pleasantly chilled.

The immense roof of the central dome was a masterpiece of levity through structural integrity—a hallmark of Victorian engineering. The Grimfern Botanical Garden was a prismatic Hagia Sophia—a fountain of jewelled rafters. Even the great Crystal Palace in London would be jealous of its bespoke glasswork. Gregor had taken care to fill his glass mosque not only with greenery, but also with music; he had his mother's piano placed carefully under the great dome to achieve maximum acoustic effect. There he would sit of an evening and swoon to the excesses of French and Bohemian composers. Of course, the great glass roof made a great damn clatter when the storms hit, so even under its shelter Gregor's rhapsodies could be rained off. In addition, the heat and damp played havoc with the beast's temperament. Even the simplest étude became savage with its barbarous tuning.

The final complaint to be discussed here about living in a rococo conservatory is the sheer lack of privacy. Simon and Gregor, being confirmed bachelors, had no qualms about keeping each other's company. Well, they shared one qualm—that they should guard their own workspaces as sacred to themselves.

Simon never visited the west wing where Gregor conducted his research, and Gregor never descended the stone steps to Simon's refrigerated taxidermy practice. They slept, washed, and cooked in the east wing of the gardens, which was split up with luscious ferns and vines into smaller rooms. A playful device allowed for a bath or shower in amongst tropical foliage, with the jungle flora appreciating this steamy atmosphere.

An odd thing about this notionally see-through house was that barely anyone, except for the two gentlemen inhabitants, ever actually saw inside. It was set upon a commanding hill with a long, sweeping lane, stone steps, and terraces. It was ringed by a thick hedge and guarded by sentinel poplar trees. The wider grounds were kept by a squadron of villagers, handpicked for their discretion, or for their un-inquisitiveness. They trimmed the lawns, spruced the bushes, mucked out the horses, and so on, enjoying generous pay and limited oversight from Mr Sandys. But they were never to set foot, or even peer, within the topiary fortress where the masters lived.

The only villagers who even came close to the greenhouse were the post lad and the girl who dealt with the laundry. They would meet Gregor at the top of all those steps, where the privet reared up into an arch over an iron gate, to swap fresh mail for dirty clothes, and vice versa.

The story starts here at one such exchange, in part because the boy—Will—carried with him a long-awaited delivery: a crate marked with angry customs notices in both Dutch and Malay. But we also start here because the girl—Jenny—was entirely absent.

"Package for you, sir. Straight from Araby, by the looks of it!"

Gregor eyed the crate with ill-concealed glee.

"It is a specimen from Indonesia, in fact." He dropped his canvas sack of laundry and hefted the rough-hewn box from Will. "And it took more than a few well-chosen words in the ears of powerful people to get it back here."

The young man just smiled and shrugged, making the most of his time near the greenhouse to nosy around the patio. Gregor tolerated this indiscretion, as all he could spy on would be the meticulously spherical rose bushes. The view inside the greenhouse was blocked by emerald, sun-hungry leaves, thick and waxy against the steamed glass.

"I guess Johnny Foreigner doesn't like you nicking his plants."

"I didn't steal this, I discovered it. And it's not a plant. It is a fungus."

"Finding or robbing, flowers or fungus. Can't tell the difference, myself!" Will said with his cock-eyed smile. The corners of Gregor's eyes creased behind his spectacles, but he held his tongue. Now there was only the matter of the laundry bag, slumped on the floor between them. Both men stood there, just blinking at it.

"The girl—she isn't here?"

"No, sir," said Will, "Jennifer's not turned up today."

"Whyever not?"

The lad shifted his weight, his countenance darkening. "It's a sorry business, Mr Sandys. It seems—"

"Question withdrawn. She can pick up the laundry next time. Good man. Off you pop."

Gregor turned sharply and rushed his acquisition to the laboratory, dragging the laundry behind him. He dumped the linen sack in the entryway, with shirts and smalls spilling out onto the stonework. The post he cast carelessly near enough to a sideboard near the door. He had better things to do—there was botany afoot.

Simon emerged from his underground workshop, blinking in the full light of morning. His jaw was pale and sharp, and scrupulously shaven. He stopped briefly at the pile of clothes on the stonework floor, looked this way and that, then stepped clean over it with his gangly legs.

"Was there any post for me, Gregor?" he called into the west wing.

"Probably," might have been the muttered response.

The sideboard was empty. The sideboard which was placed there for the express purpose of receiving the mail. Simon tapped it. That was where the post was supposed to be. There was laundry on the floor and no post on the sideboard. The whole world was out of alignment. Such things irked Simon in a way that he had learned never to show.

"Where is it?" he asked back, in a practised, even tone.

"By the door!" came the distant, disinterested response.

By the door. *But not on the sideboard.* Simon turned a full circle before his doleful eyes fell upon a pile of envelopes, sticking out of a large terracotta pot. Barely a foot away from their proper place, on the sideboard, the sideboard put there to receive the post. He retrieved them stiffly (he wore his pinstripe trousers slightly on the too-tight side) and brushed off the potting soil.

One letter, addressed to him personally, displayed such lavish penmanship that he opened it hurriedly with a grin.

[Letter from Rosalinda Smeralda-Bland, dated Saturday 8th June 1889]

Dearest Simon,

A curse upon the botanist! Has he no love for me, the greatest (and presumed last) of his admirers (other than your own, dashing self)? The letters I have written to him, so carefully crafted, so stuffed with adulation, I fear have languished unopened upon his potting shed bench. So much love—so much stationery—wasted!

I implore you, darling Simon, when you next see the elusive gardener, to strangle him with his own watering hose. And after that, give him the news that I intend to visit Grimfern on Whitsun to see what botanical wonders he has in stock. I have been badgering him for weeks about it, and in the absence of a response, I shall take no 'no' as an invitation.

See you tomorrow, Simon.

Love to you both,

Rosalinda S-B

P.S. Fair warning—I shall have to bring Mr Bland, I'm afraid…

"Rosalinda's coming, Gregor, to buy some plants. On Whitsun—that's today!"

Gregor was finally interested enough to emerge from his laboratory, dressed in an apron and carrying a crowbar which he had used to open his Indonesian crate.

"Today? She can't come today. She didn't tell me!"

"From the tone of her letter, I think she rather did, in fact."

Gregor took the letter and skimmed it, squinting in the absence of his spectacles which were perched, forgotten, above his auburn hairline. "Shame about Mr Bland. It will be nice to see Rosie, though."

"But, Gregor!" Simon's large eyes were even wider than usual. "The greenhouse is in disarray! Plates and glasses here and there, post in the plant pots, clothes all over the atrium—"

"Oh yes, the girl didn't come to fetch the laundry."

The clothes sack could, of course, have been moved anywhere other than the middle of the floor, directly by the greenhouse entrance. It would be a chore of a matter of mere moments to place it elsewhere, but Gregor had not the drive and Simon had not the grace to do it now, themselves. As far as these stubborn fellows were concerned, the clothes would have to remain there for the rest of eternity.

"The girl—Jennifer Finch, isn't it?" asked Simon.

"Possibly. I—"

Just then, there came a thud from Gregor's laboratory in the west wing. There was nobody except for the two of them in the greenhouse. Gregor frowned, growled something about the wind, and disappeared behind screening vines to find out what must have fallen.

Simon chewed his lip and put on his black silk gloves. He happened to be planning a visit to Jennifer's father, who sold him animals of dubious provenance for use in his taxidermy works. He would go there today and ask after his wayward daughter. There was little-to-no hope that Gregor would do anything about the laundry issue, and perhaps by speaking to the Finch girl, Simon could resolve it without actually having to do any housework himself, either.

Gregor bounded back into his laboratory, the straps of his apron flapping behind him. It was a bracing, bright day, and there were cloud-shadows scudding along the brick floor.

Gregor's workshop was messy, but it was a human's mess rather than Nature's. In the great central atrium, he had meticulously planned and maintained Nature's chaos to resemble itself. Tropical plants were laid out in a riot of colour and shape—it was Gregor's scrupulous organisation and upkeep which kept it looking spontaneous. In his laboratory, however, careful filing systems and square trays of seedlings, which should have spoken of humankind's impulse towards systematisation, lay scattered and chaotic in Gregor's tempest of genius.

Gregor stalked around the various workstations, trying to spot a stray animal or a broken pane—the potential source of a bluster. But there was no sign of a further disturbance, nor even of anything having fallen to make the noise.

Until he looked back at his newly arrived crate.

No sooner had he prised the lid open, Simon had called him back to the atrium. Gregor had reluctantly left the crate slightly open, its lid just off-kilter. Now though, it was squarely shut.

"Who…" Gregor began, before holding his tongue. There was no one in the garden besides himself and Simon.

He pulled at the lid, but it gave more resistance than he expected. He finally wrenched it open and the contents released a puff of mildew, before shaggy tendrils of grey broke between the contents and the lid.

This was the precious specimen Gregor had imported, at no insignificant cost, from the Isle of Sumatra to his greenhouse in sleepy Buckinghamshire. Out there in Indonesia he had discovered this mycelium with miraculous properties. But had it… closed its own crate?

He looked at the torn threads between the lid and crate. Thin wisps looked almost white and cottony. There was a root system spread throughout the box—the aerial roots of an orchid, which sprouted into a small cluster of leaves, and bore a single, bell-like flower. The poor plant was nearly engulfed by the mycelium. Thicker globs of the fungus, a bulbous mass, were huddling up in a dark corner. Cowering, almost.

"You don't like the sun much, do you? And you have a little friend—what a pretty orchid. Wait—are you…"

Despite the unfavourable conditions, the orchid seemed to be flourishing. Its flower was firm and vivid, violet and green with spots of rich burgundy. The shape was florid and round, yet exquisitely pointed—as if it had been rendered in the Art Nouveau style. These kinds of orchid—*Paphiopedilum*—grew on the jungle floor, far away from any direct sunlight. This one was an absolute beauty.

"Are you protecting your pretty flower from the light?"

He placed the lid down in a diamond shape upon the square crate, then crossed the room to his experimental jotter. He scribbled some initial, unstructured thoughts and eyed the box carefully over the rims of his steamy spectacles.

After a few minutes, Gregor heard a scuffling coming from the box. The lid trembled, and so did Gregor's writing hand. Then, with a scrape and a thud, the lid slotted squarely back into position. Gregor scratched a blasphemy into his notebook, which will be left to the reader's imagination.

Gregor reapproached the crate with great caution. He wiped his spectacles and scratched his beard. Instead of opening the lid once more, he carefully removed a plank from the side of the box and peered inside.

In that murky cave, the mycelium had reached up like so many stalagmites to coax the lid back into place. That way, the orchid would only be exposed to the filtered light creeping in between the crate's thin wooden planks.

"You're a very motivated mycelium, aren't you," Gregor muttered, "and not a bad little gardener, to boot."

After gazing for a while at the miraculous contents of his delivery, he felt a tiny fleck brush against his cheek. He jumped and shuddered, until his eyes refocused on a slim finger of grey—a wormlike appendage scoping the surroundings. Before his very eyes, the thing was burgeoning out towards the intrusion of sunlight.

"Oh no you don't, you little bugger."

Gregor fixed the plank back onto the box and scribbled a couple of pages of notes. Then with his whole arm he slid his other, lesser, experiments to one end of the central workbench. The Sumatran mycelium would take pride of place, both in his workspace, and in his fevered mind.

# TWO

Simon saddled the grey mare and set off down the sweeping lane, leaving Gregor to his inscrutable research. Simon disliked riding horses but growing up in a forthright religious household had perfectly accustomed him to doing things he disliked, and not doing things he did like. He did not care for animals, for example—his profession was a mere accident of talent. It wasn't his fault he was good at stuffing God's creatures and posing them to lampoon the social mores of the day. He had tried sculpting in other materials—in clay, marble, wood, and bronze—but corpses were the only medium that really sang under his fingers.

The Finches lived in a ramshackle water mill on the edge of the village. The ride there was smooth enough through the sultry summertime country lanes, but his several layers of miserable black tweed quickly had Simon hot and bothered. Florence the mare was a stubborn horse, who would never let her fatigue show to her rider. Simon admired that. Together they suffered in silent dignity all the way to the little water mill.

He tied Florence to a post and wrestled with the gate to no avail. The catch did not want to budge, and Simon's over-developed sense of decorum did not allow him to rattle it with enough force to free it. He glared over at Florence, but she was not of a mind to help. At long last John Finch stepped out of the mill cottage, wiping his hands with a rag. He was a gruff widower of some muscle and little joy. These days he earned more through poaching than he did through milling, and Simon would often make the journey down from Grimfern to avail him of his catch.

"Oh 'eck, here's death come to take me at last," Finch mumbled, chucking the red rag into a bucket.

Simon looked over at him with his huge, dark eyes. The former miller's mouth was a perfect parabola, as if a child had drawn him 'sad'. In reality you could never tell what he was thinking, as he would always pull his mouth into that shape whether he was impressed or indifferent.

"Gate's stuck," was all the old man had to say.

Simon's voice was muffled as if coming from far away—he barely moved his mouth and kept his jaw firmly clenched. Ventriloquism is a side effect of social awkwardness. "Good afternoon, Mr Finch. I was hoping to enquire as to—"

"Yeah, yeah, I've got your stuff," growled Finch, batting away the words like so many midges. "Three hares and a pair of pheasants. Usual price."

Simon was really here to ask after his daughter but could not resist the lure of raw material—a blank canvas.

"And were they properly—"

"Killed in the right way, as you like them, lad."

Simon needed there to be no ugly scars or damage to the bodies of his subjects, and as such had exacting requirements as to the method of killing. John Finch didn't ask questions— as far as he was concerned, the money man was always right. He fetched the merchandise from their hanging spot in the doorframe. Simon paid him and loaded the carcasses into Florence's saddlebag.

"Ah, but the principal reason for my visit this morning… is your daughter. Or rather, her absence. Is she… How is your daughter, Mr Finch?"

Finch removed his flat cap and scrunched it up idly. Simon had never before seen the top of the man's head. The grizzled grey of his temples stopped suddenly where the brim of his hat started, and the roof of his head was bald as a tonsured monk.

"There's been some upset. Jenny's little friend. The Haggerston girl. Close as sisters, those two were. Gone. The way of all things, God knows."

"I'm so very sorry to hear that. How old was she?" asked Simon.

"Not old enough. Barely nineteen, I should think. But then again, nobody is ever old enough. My Mary, Jennifer's mother… Well, sod it. There's nowt to be said."

Simon could not allow the feeling of grief to seep into his emotional fortifications, or he would be overwhelmed then and there. He nodded in understanding and copied John Finch's stiff-lipped frown.

"In which case, Jennifer's absence from work is understandable. Please send her my—"

Casting the briefest of glances at the miller, Simon started. He was looking right at Simon, which made them both uncomfortable. Normally their business was conducted facing at right angles from one another, as befitted the awkward transaction of two dour men trading dead bodies. But now John Finch was looking straight at him, and Simon was obliged to attempt eye contact.

"Mr Rievaulx—Simon," the older man began, with a sigh in his voice, "you gents have got a big house up there, an't you. Lots of rooms and so on..." His sentence carried on into inaudible mumbling that couldn't escape his unruly beard.

"Not so many rooms, just one cavernous glass vault. What is it that you are implying, Mr Finch?"

"It's just—Jennifer, get out here, will you?" he bellowed over his shoulder, before returning to face Simon, piteously wringing out his workman's cap. Simon had never seen him like this before.

Soon Jennifer, Finch's daughter, appeared in the yard, her hair as wild as gorse. Her smock had many pockets, stretched from frequent use. Her boots seemed too big and her sleeves were too short, revealing bramble scratches all up her arms. Her freckled cheeks were red from a glut of angry tears.

"My Jenny's been looking for more work than she has now with your laundry. Idle hands, and all that. Keep her mind off... everything. Only, there's not much call for her in the village, and she's not got the temperament for the well-to-dos in town."

The young woman opened her mouth as though ready to summon a hurricane of indignation, but then couldn't seem to manage it. Grief can be a kind of exhaustion, after all.

"She's a blustery spirit, Simon, I won't lie to you. Got an air of her mother about her. But she could fit well with your… unconventional arrangement, and she'd work damned hard."

Jennifer raised her chest and gave Simon an attempt at a cock-eyed smile.

"What you're saying is, you want us to take her on, as a housekeeper?"

"That's the long and short of it. You'd be doing us a big favour, sir."

If you were to observe Simon closely at this point, you could just about make out a throbbing of his perfectly shaven jaw, indicating its repeated clenching and unclenching. Nothing else about the poised gentleman would betray his distress.

"You must understand, our travails require a great deal of secrecy and discretion. It is a working greenhouse. We have never employed a housekeeper before. We do the housework ourselves. Well, I do the housework. Most of it. Well…"

Simon drifted into a reverie of clothes piled high around wicker baskets, plates unwashed, beds unmade, floors riddled with moss and weeds…

John Finch moved closer to Simon so he could speak in such a way that his daughter wouldn't overhear. She was clearly unimpressed but looked away pointedly.

"Look, Simon," he said, a tremble in his voice, "I'm out on a limb 'ere. There's nothing left, no hope in the village for her, no life for her here with me. There's no money for any of it. I'm not expecting you to pay her a decent wage, I just need someone to look after her. I don't think I can any more."

Simon felt for the old man in his sorrow but had no idea how to comfort him. He simply patted him, rather stiffly, on the shoulder. John Finch smelled of fresh earth and dried blood.

There was not a real chance of Simon saying 'no' to all of this. Still, he built himself a framework of rationalisation that made it seem like his own idea. They did need help around the greenhouse, after all. Even if Gregor did not care about the order and cleanliness of anything that wasn't growing and green, Simon did. The living quarters' disorder truly irked him, but spending all day keeping it in check also left him with layers upon layers of resentment. So, Jennifer could tidy up and bring balance to the ménage in one fell swoop.

"What do you know about plants, Miss Finch?"

"Only what to eat and what not to eat."

"That will serve you in good stead. And what do you know of taxidermy?"

"Of what?"

"Excellent. Mr Finch, I will employ your daughter. We must return to the Gardens at once to make plans. Do you ride, Jennifer?"

Jennifer gave a *pffft* of derision, hitched up her skirts and swung herself up onto the grey mare, straddling it in a most undignified fashion. Simon's eyes were wide as teacups. John Finch wiped his nose on the back of his hand and beamed broadly. He quickly remembered himself and returned to his performance of eternal indifference.

Jennifer had nothing to bring along with her that wasn't already in the pockets of her pinafore, so they made their way back to Grimfern. Simon sat on the horse behind Jennifer and was obliged to hold on to her waist. He was thoroughly mortified.

[Extract from Gregor Sandys' experimental jotter, Sunday 9th June 1889]

*The damned fungus is a gardener!*

*No—I mustn't get ahead of myself. It doesn't truly understand the light requirements of the Paphiopedilum orchid. It must simply be entwined with the plant's root system in such a way that it can sense when it is stressed. It is in the fungus' interest to keep the plant alive, in order to continue drawing nutrients from it. So, when there is too much light, the mycelium closes off the box. Astonishing, yes, but fully explicable by natural science. It protects its precious flower as jealously as it would guard its own life. A biological imperative!*

*And what an orchid to guard. William Morris could not dream up a more perfectly sinuous specimen. By the ancient law of finders-namers, I shall christen it Paphiopedilum gregorianum. I assume the fungus won't mind.*

*To test my theory, I have set up a little experiment. Carefully shaded by a tent of muslin, I have transferred the orchid-mycelium symbiote to a pot under a trellis. At the top of the trellis is a spritzer, and by the orchid's roots is a miniature bellows. Once the mycelium is settled, I shall blow air across the root system, drying out the substrate and orchid. Will the fungus be spurred into action? Will it mist itself?*

*For now, I must leave it to acclimatise. Rosie arrives this afternoon. I wish I could show her this orchid—she would die for its colours. And then tomorrow, or maybe next week, the fungus will be put through its paces… And if the mycelium can look after an orchid, I may well be out of a job, what!*

Jenny was a dab-hand with horses. She had no trouble taking Florence the grey mare at a canter through the winding lanes around the village, twisting this way and that through snickets narrowed by June's green richness. The stubborn horse beneath her had been reluctant at first, but soon they were racing madly and freely together—Florence's grumpiness lost in the giddiness of speed.

Mr Rievaulx, at the rear, was more like cargo than a passenger. Tense throughout all his body, Jenny noticed that although he kept his hands near her waist where he should have been holding on, he didn't actually touch her at all. When the shaggy trees of her shortcut trail hung low she would bob down, but Simon could only stammer "I… I… I…" and get a faceful of bower for his hesitation.

They reached the boundary of the Grimfern Estate and Jennifer pulled Florence into a rearing stop. Simon finally grabbed her for dear life while the horse settled. Will, who was serving as doorsman for the afternoon, stuck his head out of the gatehouse, where he had been 'on guard' reading a Penny Dreadful. His open jaw sunk back into his neck in surprise at what he saw in real life however—Jennifer's arrival was apparently more salacious to him than the lurid contents of his periodical. When the horse settled Simon withdrew his gloved hands from Jenny's waist as if they had been burned.

"Good day, Mr Rievaulx—Jennifer." Will removed his cap and beamed up at her. "I thought you weren't coming in today? I told Mr Sandys…"

"Yes, hullo, Will. I'm here now, anyways. Tell you later. Oh, and it looks like there's moss blocking the gutters."

Will turned to peer at the roof, confused. As many times as she had been through this gate on foot, Jenny now barely recognised it. She could get used to this lofty vantage point.

"Sort that out, won't you, William," Mr Rievaulx muttered, not catching anybody's gaze, "and get the gate for us. Quickly, now."

Will fumbled for the latch and swung the gate wide. He stood there staring for just a little bit too long.

"What's wrong, Will?"

"Nothing! Just that… riding a horse looks well on you, Jenny."

"Oh naff off, will you?" Jenny said, laughing away the compliment.

"That will be all, William," said Mr Rievaulx in exasperation.

The post boy replaced his cap and closed the gate. As they headed off up towards the greenhouse, he kicked a stone into some bushes, probably a little harder than he meant to. Then he went back to his reading with a huff.

Jenny kept the mare at a trot as they rose along the sweeping drive. Groundsmen stopped their work to watch her go by—pairs of them, with rakes or shears, small against the rolling expanse of lawn. Jenny felt their gaze, and let it feed her determination. She had always been an oddball to the villagers—a girl of little daintiness, a young woman who refused to partake in the games of coyness and courtship. That is why she and Constance had such a fast friendship, and why the whispers of shame around her death clung to Jennifer also. She caught sight of one worker mutter something to his mate. The other fellow laughed hollowly and leaned on his spade.

Jenny shook herself and geed the horse a little. She couldn't let herself think about Constance, for fear of losing herself in the grief-rush. She couldn't let herself think about the snide villagers and groundsmen, either. Not now—not now that she had been elevated over the tattling masses.

They stabled Florence, leaving her with a hearty pitchfork's worth of hay. Mr Rievaulx let them through the iron gate under its topiary arch to the patio. Jenny had seen this part many times before, with its roses and stone urns, when she had clambered up with Will to swap the mail and laundry. Never before, though, had she crossed beyond the gate. She took care to place her steps squarely on the herringbone bricks, twisting her ankles in odd angles to achieve it. It seemed more proper for a first passage onto new territory not to tread upon the daisy-graced cracks.

Ahead, thick, dark leaves of trees Jenny could not name pushed against countless panes of glass, casting greenish shadows and hiding the interior from view.

"You had better come in, I suppose," said Mr Rievaulx, pulling at the door's ornate handle and opening up this crystal box for her.

Jenny was immediately buffeted by heavy, wet heat—the hottest day of Buckinghamshire summer was nothing compared to the steamy atmosphere of Grimfern. She stepped in slowly, mouth agape at the queer forest of wonder—the whole world's jungles compressed into one vivid grove. Jenny traced a strange path winding through the multicoloured underbrush, finding a large and placid pond bursting with water lilies. All around there were plump, shaggy bushes with flowers of purples and pinks, sprays of vines dripping from overhead walkways, tall palms lolling about above even these, and cream-painted pillars of sinuously wrought iron holding up the ceiling. And oh, that ceiling! Jennifer spun around as she took it all in, her heart rising to burst. A whole house made of windows!

The sky was so big and blue beyond the ceiling. A flock of birds swooped about beyond the roof. She thought of Constance, as she always did at the murmuration of birds, and the huge feeling of beauty in her chest threatened to overflow into grief once more. She abruptly sat herself down on the stone wall around the pond and focused on her boots. There was moss and lichen growing in the gaps between stones. Even these tiny greennesses were precious—with their tiny stalks and dew-drop eyes.

Mr Rievaulx approached her stiffly.

"Did you make all this?" she asked, breathless.

"Gregor did. Mr Sandys, that is. You might say he is quite skilled with a trowel."

"And then some," said Jennifer. "It's… it's… it's a whole world. It's *the* world. A world-garden in a box."

Simon looked around the atrium appreciatively. He didn't seem to disagree. He raised his deep, tight voice to call for Gregor, who called back gruffly from the east wing.

"I think, Miss Finch, you had better meet the great gardener."

Gregor had spent the morning prodding and poking his incredible fungus and scribbling down the findings in his jotter with a blade-sharpened pencil. He suspended a muslin canopy over the orchid and its fungal guardian, to shield them from direct sunlight. Then he broke apart the crate and set up a frame over it with a water reservoir and spigot. If the mycelium could moderate the light, could it also manage the orchid's water intake?

Finding the prodigious gardening abilities of the Sumatran mycelium had given Gregor a mad spark of that determined inspiration which fuelled many of his most outlandish breakthroughs. In his youth, one such spark provided the energy to imagine the most unlikely of graftings, which had won him a plaudit from Kew. Right now, it wasn't only Kew that he was aiming to impress, but the whole Royal Horticultural Society. In fact—stuff the RHS. They wouldn't appreciate Gregor's incredible endeavour. This would impress the Royal Society! Julian Mallory and the RHS could go lick a nettle for all he cared. Gregor had already succeeded in encouraging self-preserving motor function in a fungal specimen. What leaps would be required to develop in it an animal's instinctive reasoning, or a human's rationality? At what point could a non-animal be empirically described as 'conscious'? After scribbling the word repeatedly in his jotter, crossing it out, circling it, and underlining it until his pencil blunted and his page became heavy with lead, he wandered reluctantly over to the small library in the east wing.

It was perhaps generous to refer to it as a library—the book nook was a series of shelves surrounding a floridly carved desk and chair. The moisture of the botanical garden wreaked havoc on the books themselves, which became yellowed and curled and even mouldy within a season of being bought new.

Amongst the musty novels and grizzled encyclopaedias lay a token number of philosophical texts—largely Simon's purchases. Simon would leaf through these tomes, occasionally giving out an *aha!* or a *fascinating!* But Gregor knew they were largely for good show and aesthetic value. Gregor cared not for the great philosophers, even the Greeks. Why digest another man's pages when you could be writing your own? The *Book of Gregor* would be written by his own hand. Still, it couldn't hurt to check what the old boys had come up with regarding matters of the mind.

He had hitched up his trousers and was trying to sound out the title of an Ancient Greek text on the bottom shelf, when Simon's call came from the atrium. Gregor harrumphed back and waited for him to appear and inevitably scupper his ironclad focus.

When he arrived, Simon's back was unusually stiff—even for him—and his tie was slightly off-kilter, which was virtually unknown for the strait-laced taxidermist. Gregor withdrew a book at random and let it fall open, so it would seem that he was perusing its contents.

"Got a new project on, Simon, old boy. Trying to get a head-start before Rosalinda gets here. Kindly sod off, won't you, my love."

"Under normal circumstances, I would, of course, but, um—"

"Whatever's the matter with you?" Gregor asked.

"We have a housekeeper."

"No, we do not." Gregor snapped the book shut, deciding he was very glad of his prop and resolving to carry a slim volume with him at all times in the future for the purpose. "Grimfern hasn't had a housekeeper since the house burned down. What's the point of a housekeeper if one doesn't have a house?"

"Perhaps she can be the greenhousekeeper, then." Simon's usual vocal gravitas deserted him as he squeaked, "Miss Finch!"

A girl with a plain dress and heavy boots emerged from behind an over-weighty clematis, which formed part of the library wall. This was Jennifer—the laundry girl whose absence had caused such a fuss this morning. Her freckled cheeks were rosy and her hair fell in tangles like a hanging fern.

"I could be a groundskeeper, or a gardener, if you like?" she offered with a self-effacing shrug.

"I am the gardener!" Gregor bellowed. It was quite against the natural order of things at Grimfern to depend upon anybody except the residents. Anything Gregor couldn't do fell to Simon, and vice versa. Bringing in this stranger would ruin the sanctuary of their intense partnership.

"Or anything, really—please, sirs, I really need this job. My father…" The girl had a feisty expression and clenched fists, but tears were welling up in her eyes.

Gregor interrupted to avoid such a breach of protocol. "No, no—stop that. Simon, I think I see now that this is already a *fait accompli*. On your head be it. Miss Finch—you will keep your duties to the central atrium and the east wing only. I regret deeply that you have already been admitted to the garden. Simon's compassionate heart has rather got the best of him. I must stress that you are not under any circumstances to enter the west wing, for it is my laboratory, or the basement, for that is Mr Rievaulx's workshop. Is that clear?"

"Yes, Mr Sandys."

"I need to lie down for a bit," sighed Simon, retreating in relief to his underground sanctum where he kept a divan expressly for the purpose.

"And I have much important work to do. You can start with the atrium—we have to get ready for our visitors. Good day to you, Miss."

With that, Gregor disappeared into his laboratory with an angry flourish. Once out of sight, however, he squeezed the philosophy book tight to him, placing it next to his cloaked experiment. It wouldn't do to let anybody see the mycelium just yet. Not until he could be sure of its abilities. Rosalinda and Simon, discreet as they were, might mistake the thing for a mere parlour curiosity, which would break Gregor's heart.

And then there was this accursed Miss Finch, newly admitted to the garden, what of her? She probably wouldn't understand it, even if she did see it. But the less she knew, the better.

# THREE

Gregor's business was plants. It was his parents' fortune which had provided for the glasshouse on their rambling estate, and it was their ill-fortune which had burned their actual house to the ground. Gregor had been a young man when he watched the conflagration from the safety of the isolated botanical garden. That was the night he inherited the Grimfern Estate, sans manor house. He had left the charred foundations to be reclaimed by the wild woods, and instead developed the garden's reputation as a centre for botanical research, attracting wealthy and learned individuals from across Europe. Gregor traded successfully in horticultural rarities, which only he had the deftness of touch to nurture in Britain.

Though the garden was decidedly closed to the public, a select cabal of scientists and socialites could correspond with Gregor to arrange an appointment. Of course, very few people had his details in the first place—his address was a valuable commodity amongst the horticultural set in London. This morning—the 9th of June 1889, Whitsun Day—one welcome repeat visitor had made the arduous carriage ride out of the city to visit Gregor and his plant emporium.

"Goodness, this heat, Gregor," she purred. "Don't you know how many layers I'm wearing?"

Mrs Rosalinda Smeralda-Bland was a sumptuous woman of continental extraction. Her interest in plants was part aesthetic, part empathetic; since she herself resembled a pomegranate so ripe it was bursting juicily at the seams.

"I'm afraid the heat is required to preserve the most exquisite of the hot-house flowers," said Gregor, suddenly erupting into a beguiling grin, "yourself the first amongst them."

Gregor's accent was showing—his rolled 'r's were calligraphic embellishments for his plum-honeyed words. Rosalinda pursed her moist lips and struck him playfully with her fan.

"Oh, I'm always treated well when I come to visit my boys. Where *is* Simon?"

Gregor called his name, stamping on the brick floor. Soon the baleful figure of Simon emerged from his cellar. He air-kissed Rosalinda with all the solemnity of a Byzantine funeral and stood with his hand on Gregor's shoulder.

"Simon has just been out for supplies. There's a man in the village who provides him with pelts and what-not. He came back with rather more than he went out for, in fact."

Jennifer popped her head out from behind a *Camellia japonica* and frowned.

"How are you finding that piece you bought, Rosalinda?" Simon drawled, casting a sideways glare at Gregor's passive barb.

"Oh, she's just delightful. She has pride of place in the parlour—all my friends love her. Mr Bland of course has a mortal fear of owls"—here she dropped her voice to a jaw-clenched confidence—"but that of course was the primary reason for her purchase."

Just then, Mr Bland staggered through the conservatory door with a pile of empty hat boxes for his wife to fill with plants. The trio's easy rapport was destroyed by his presence. Simon removed his hand from Gregor's shoulder and they stepped apart. He knew—*he must know*—but still. Mr Bland's excruciating plainness served to accentuate his wife's zest—a vibrant butterfly shines when stapled to plain card.

"Good afternoon, Mr Sandys, Mr Rievaulx." He shook their hands without meeting their eyes. "My wife is so looking forward to touring your establishment. She has mentioned it quite a bit. All week in fact—"

"Well then, we'd better start looking around! See you later, Simon." Gregor kissed the taxidermist on his prominent cheekbone in an act of social defiance. Rosalinda bit her lip, pleasantly scandalised. Mr Bland looked at the floor, which Simon used to make a quick getaway of his own, down to the secrecy of his basement workshop.

Gregor whisked Rosalinda around the central dome of the greenhouse. "We've had a lot of new stock in from Nepal, and you'll just love this season's chrysanthemums…"

He had become adept at showing his visitors exactly what they were looking for, even if they themselves did not know what that would be. Every bloom was loved and well-cared-for, but not one leaf in this section was sacred. Gregor was an artisan as much as a researcher, and, when required, a salesman beyond even these. Any of his specimens could be parted with for a price.

Soon, Rosalinda had filled her hat boxes with Nepalese rhododendrons, Japanese chrysanthemums, and Gregor's signature orchids: a variety so frilly and pale they seemed like fanciful splashes of water. Mr Bland, who had to transport the living cargo around this floral warren, was taking a breather. He stood wheezing and still, watching the haughty business of some caged birds of paradise. Rosalinda and Gregor were leaning on the balcony of a gallery which ran around the atrium, looking down at the queer forest of incongruous blossoms.

"That's quite a haul you have there, Rosalinda," said Gregor, languid against the banister. "We've given poor old Mr Bland quite the run-around."

"He needs the exercise," she quipped, "and I need the beauty provided by your botanical prowess. And yet—"

Here she looked far into the impenetrable distance, like Isolde yearning for her Tristan. Gregor saw the wistful sadness on her lovely face and his resolve almost faltered.

"I know you possess wonders that are yet unseen. You have many secrets in your heart, Mr Sandys. And in your laboratory…"

"I don't allow clients into my laboratory, Rosie," Gregor mumbled.

"Client? *Zut!* Which of your clients knows the ins and outs of your practice as well as I? Which of them is more well-read than I on the gardens of Pairi-daeza, or of Lebanon, or of Moorish

Spain? Which of them hosted the salon at which the noted botanist first ensnared a budding taxidermist? *Really*, Gregor, how long have we known each other? How many secrets have we shared? It's not so much a question of clientele—"

"Alright, what do you want to see?" he snapped but smiled at Rosalinda's teasing. "One thing, Rosie, I'll show you one thing in my lab."

"Then let it be the wildest, most unusual specimen you're working on. I don't care about beauty, not for this. I want to see something unimaginable."

There was, of course, only one experimental pot that would sate her wild inquisitiveness. The pair snuck down a wrought-iron staircase to the ground floor, taking care to not let Rosalinda's husband catch them escaping. Gregor removed his cravat and used it to blindfold his guest, who was positively thrilled at the gesture. He led her by the hand through an ivied partition into the west wing, where rows of workbenches strewn with soiled books and bizarre plants signalled that this was Gregor's workshop. Here the smell of soil overpowered the smell of flowers.

Gregor led her over to a bench which was sheltered from the sun by a thick muslin drape. He raised it to bring both of them inside, then trapped them like children in a fabric fortress. The sun bled through the muslin, casting a golden glow. With stifled giggles he removed her blindfold and watched her face, hungry to read her every reaction.

She was initially disgusted with what she saw—this pleased Gregor no end. A shallow glass bowl about a foot in diameter contained an inch of soil and a seething mass of sinews. These tendrils caressed and cocooned a gorgeous orchid, dainty but flushed with colour. Above the bowl on a tripod was a device that would release sugar water when pressed in a certain way. Fungal threads already wound their way up the legs of the tripod and caressed the sluice gate above; spotting this made Gregor squirm. The smell of mould and decay was overpowering.

"You'll have to explain quickly, Gregor." Rosalinda was breathing shallowly into her petticoat. "You've forgotten that I have a delicate lady's constitution!"

"Please." He screwed up his face. "I know you well enough— your curiosity beats your feigned sensibilities."

She dropped the fluttering act but could not shake a profound dislike for the gelatinous tendrils before her. "Go on, then, what is it? Fungus, no doubt, but why have you trained it up the tripod like an English ivy?"

"That's just it—I haven't." His wild eyes drank in the filmy sheen of his gelatinous glob. "It did that itself. There's sugar water in the tank which it can use for nourishment. But if it opened the spigot all the way, it would become waterlogged. Now I suppose we shall see if it has learned how to water itself. Watch—"

He took up the miniature bellows that lay beneath the bench and blew dry air across the specimen's many brandished feelers. This caused dust and spores to rise, which in turn caused Rosalinda to manually close her nostrils. After a short bout of desiccating wind, Gregor stopped pumping. The thin wisps of the fungus, however, continued to jostle as if in a light breeze. The wriggle became concentrated at the spigot of the water tank, and sure enough it turned, allowing a fine rain of sugary dew to fall. Once the thing had had enough, the jostling began again, this time to turn the tap off. Rosalinda looked at the botanist in wonder, but he was still watching his discovery in terrible glee.

"Wherever did you find it?"

"The original mycelium—that's the word for the fibrous mass of the thing—was taken from an overgrown ruin on Sumatra. It displayed unusual characteristics indicating the transmission of information through itself, but nothing like this. I had to persuade the Sultan that it had hallucinatory properties so he thought I was just extracting it for pleasure. I believe he took some—I hope he wasn't adversely affected."

Rosalinda hit him again with her fan.

"When I finally got it back to Blighty it made a concerted effort to remain in its crate. Protecting its orchid, I suspect. And now, it seems, *watering it.*"

"So it's… alive?"

"I mean—yes, it's alive. All fungi are alive, until they're dead."

"But is it conscious? Does it know we're here?" she whispered, as though afraid it could hear them.

"It doesn't know we're here. All it knows is water and light, and the absence of those things. Is it conscious? It's hard to say. Plants grow to face the sun, but does that mean they know where it is? Deciduous trees shed their leaves in autumn—does that mean they understand the calendar? There are carnivorous plants which sense the best time to strike at their prey…"

Rosalinda took another terrified glance at the many-tendrilled monster. Gregor just shrugged.

"But I'm a botanist, not a philosopher."

He raised the cravat-blindfold and Rosalinda acquiesced. He escorted her back to the atrium where Mr Bland was still playing with the birds—he was poking his fingers through the bars to stroke their colourful plumage, but they kept pecking at him. As the pair approached, Gregor made a great show of retying his cravat and straightening his shirt. Rosalinda was looking singularly satiated.

"Well, if you two are *quite* done, we'll leave with these wretched plants."

As Mr Bland hurried her back to the carriage, Rosalinda made a gesture to Gregor as if to say her brain had exploded out of her temples. She then took the exploded brain matter and blew it across to him in a kiss. He caught it with one hand and held it to his heart, touching another finger to his lips in a playful warning. He hadn't intended to show anybody his mycelial discovery, but he was glad to make an exception for Rosalinda—so full of vitality and curiosity.

# FOUR

That evening, once Jennifer had been dismissed, the men sat by candlelight in their verdant atrium, drinking port. Simon was in a smoking jacket and velvet fez, although he didn't actually smoke for fear of damaging the garden. Gregor was in his undergarments and a robe, as was his wont. The only person who would witness his indecorous dress would be Simon—and that didn't matter one bit. Gregor had kept a pile of philosophical treatises close by him all through supper, as if proximity would transfer their teaching to him through the æther. He continued to jot ideas down in his notepad, even though none of the books he had flicked through had dealt with non-human consciousness. He decided on his own criteria for consciousness:

- *Reaction to external stimuli*
- *Flow of information through the organism*
- *Demonstrable self-awareness*

All this posed an ethical problem. Supposing he did develop a fungus which could recognise its own self-hood, what would the organism *be*? To his knowledge, no animal other than humans and their immediate ancestors was capable of such selfish introspection. Furthermore, organisms in the plant and fungus kingdoms were so unthinking they were largely sessile—they didn't even move around. Yet Gregor's cultivation of the Sumatran mycelium had brought it to the point of passing his first two requirements for consciousness: it reacted simply to its environment by intentionally sending thoughts from its core to its tip. It was as clever as some simple insects. If his skill was as great as he feared it was, and he did create a fungal entity that was a throbbing nervous system in its own right, what kind of autonomy would it demand—what inalienable privileges? What of suffrage? What of its soul before God?

"Simon, what do you understand to be the nature of a soul?" he said suddenly.

Simon was staring darkly into the endless distance. He didn't refocus his gaze to reply.

"That part of us which cannot be destroyed."

Simon always got metaphysical when he drank port. Gregor considered the answer carefully. Candlelight danced in his cynical eyes.

"And what of creating this indestructible element—the soul? Is such a feat accessible to mankind?"

"Humans do it all the time—we reproduce. We create more consciousnesses, more minds, more souls. And these in turn create more and more."

Gregor stood up in excitement, clutching his jotter. His thin dressing gown fluttered around him.

"So, artificially creating a consciousness isn't immoral?"

"No—an artificial soul is simply a child."

A child.

Gregor had long suppressed such a dream—children were not for men like him. He had come to terms with a life dedicated to botany, and to the sallow features of the inscrutable Simon Rievaulx. But a mycelial consciousness would be a life—a life of his creation. He registered his own emotional excitement and put it to one side. There was science to be done.

"Simon, my dear, I have something to show you."


Simon was taken by the hand and pulled towards the west wing by the wild-eyed botanist. If either of them had let go the other would have toppled over, such were the forces in either direction. But that was how this relationship had always worked.

Simon had rarely set foot in Gregor's laboratory since he had moved in. There was that one time Gregor had snipped his flesh with his secateurs and swooned at the sight of his own crimson juices, and the other time Gregor had suffered an allergic reaction to a Peruvian specimen and called for Simon's aid. This time was entirely different. Gregor wanted him there to share in his research—Simon felt like an exalted guest. He used the opportunity to absorb every detail of the workspace: the bare roots growing in glassware, the illegible scrawl of Gregor's labels, moss growing around the drainage grilles.

Gregor lit a gas lamp on a workbench next to a strange tent of muslin. He placed one hand at its opening, pausing like a ringmaster to build a sense of occasion. He cut quite a figure, with his intense visage and his revealing flannels. Simon fastened the tassels of his smoking jacket.

"I put it to you that there are three hallmarks of consciousness. One—that an organism can sense, and react to its senses. This distinguishes, say, a plant from a rock. Two—that said organism can transmit information about itself and commit certain signals to its memory. This distinguishes animals from the lesser kingdoms: plants and so on. Three—that an organism is aware of itself thinking. Are you with me?"

"Gregor, what is this about? What have you done?" Simon's voice was urgent, but the great botanist showed no signs of having actually heard him.

"Now, consider this entity," Gregor said briskly, whisking off the muslin sheath to reveal ghastly grey threads winding about a tripod like some Stygian wisteria. Beneath it was a mere slip of an orchid, jealously isolated from the world by those strands of grey.

Simon balked at the sight, but was well-versed in controlling his disgust, given that he gutted woodland critters for a living. That said, the good feeling he had for his companion dissipated immediately.

Gregor continued, "It is a mycelium—a mass of fungal threads—extracted from Sumatra and encouraged to tend to the orchid. Observe."

Taking up the dainty bellows, he replicated the same

self-quenching impulse he had demonstrated for Rosalinda. The mycelium dutifully watered itself and its flower.

Simon was unmoved by the cleverness of the specimen—he could criticise a dancing monkey's two-step. But what this represented for Gregor's endeavour was incredible—this stringed monster was a fungus as clever as a fly. It satisfied the first two of Gregor's definitions of consciousness. Simon now understood his companion's bizarre line of questioning earlier.

"You are wondering what it would take to bring it to complete consciousness," Simon said flatly.

"The organism needs to be more complex by several orders of magnitude. Think about our own brains, which regulate all sorts of organs and limbs. This mycelium simply needs more orchids to look after. Simon"—he grabbed Simon's arm hard enough to leave finger marks—"it's a rudimentary brain!"

The botanist's cheerful ravings faded in Simon's mind. He was caught off-guard by a mortal horror at the word 'brain'. Suddenly, Gregor's plans became terrifyingly plausible. Simon's own consciousness—in self-defence—shut down any fretful imaginings of the implications of non-human subjectivity. His own brain just couldn't think about it, or about anything else for that matter. So, in something of a fugue, Simon allowed himself to be danced around the garden by the excitable man in his underwear, and plied with port, and kissed and kissed, and taken to bed.

The next day, Simon stood perfectly still for hours in his subterranean workshop. The piercing gaze of his unsold stock—unsold due to his taste for the macabre—would have unnerved another man, but Simon was anchored by his silent pets. By late afternoon he emerged from his catatonia and set about the creation of a new anatomical specimen; one that hadn't been ordered, but that he would like to possess for himself.

He took one of the rabbits purchased from Mr Finch, and with a fine saw opened its skull, making sure to leave the brain undamaged. He took great care to remove the cerebrum with as much of the spinal cord as he could manage. He had an unnaturally steady hand and only the finest equipment, but rabbits' brains are delicate and really quite tiny. He usually just plopped it out with a teaspoon so it wouldn't fester in situ, but now it was the focus of his work. Once freed of its corporeal prison, Simon suspended the brain and cord in aspic in a glass jar. He placed it on a special display at the far end of his cellar. The curved glass reflected his face with grotesque distortions as he inspected his handiwork.

*There. Now I don't have to think about it any more.*

# FIVE

[Extract from Gregor Sandys' experimental jotter, Monday 10th June 1889]

*The intent: to create* consciousness *in botanical matter. "That which cannot be destroyed."—S. R.*

*The background to this lies in my three articles of cultivated consciousness: that the organism be sensitive, reactive, and self-aware. A fourth article could be added to describe human-level consciousness: reflexive self-awareness, a philosophy of mind within the mind itself. This would be a dream to cultivate, but for now I reserve my efforts for the development of an organism which follows the first three articles.*

*I approach this endeavour with certain pre-existing resources. I have already encouraged mutually self-preserving behaviour in a species of fungus native to the jungle caves of Sumatra, and the newly christened* Paphiopedilum gregorianum. *In monitoring the symbiotic relationship, I have observed the transmission of information—of thought—through the mycelium. The experiment is limited by the* subject's relative simplicity. There is not all that much it can do, so it cannot be taught to do much with intention. In order to achieve higher cognitive function, the subject requires a more sophisticated set of corporeal functions.

One path I have considered is to develop the fungus's intrinsic complexity, but the botanical techniques for such an endeavour are beyond the imagining of our wildest horticultural experts, myself included. A mushroom prancing about on puffy hyphae—such a thing could only happen in some absinthe-soaked delirium! I have concluded that it would be impossible in practical terms to encourage ambulatory motor function in this subject.

It is well known that plants and fungi have incredible capacity for sensitivity and reaction, but usually each species is highly specialised. A flytrap senses the fly with a dedicated whisker, then snaps shut accordingly. It cannot choose to snap shut around, say, a pencil to write its name. But, if the flytrap's mechanism were monitored, regulated, and operated by a nervous system which also controls the movement of an arm, the holistic system could manipulate the pencil to write a name. That holistic system would be the entity—the flytrap would be its hand, the mycelium would be its nervous system (dare I say, its brain?).

Therefore, my proposal is to create an ecosystem of cooperating flora and fungi which, when taken as a unit, performs functions with a complexity approaching that of an animal.

Proposed sensitive flora: Mimosa pudica, the great mimic, which closes its leaves in reaction to touch. Mimicry is the first step to mastery. Morning glories (Ipomoea vars.) sense the sunrise to open, and Hibiscus vars. close at night. Bellis perennis, the common daisy, is seen to sense the coming rain.

Proposed reactive flora: Codariocalyx motorius, the dancing plant. Its hinged leaves provide great freedom of movement. Dionaea muscipula, the Venus flytrap. Its jaw-like movement could be used for grasping.

Proposed substrates: Most of the species listed above require mutually exclusive biomes in which to flourish. Many practical choices, then, will depend upon the choice of substrate—the foundation to which the macro-organism adheres. A terrarium of agar would suit the fungal elements of the creation, as seen in my previous experiment, but would not suit the more complex members of the plant kingdom. A terrarium of soil would suit all, if sufficient nutrients were provided. A series of terraria could be envisioned, separated by glass and connected by the mycelium. Ultimately, these proposals are entirely unmoving. A frame with hinges could be designed—a kind of trellis doll—upon which the colony of flora could grow. Perhaps in time the dancing plant could operate the limbs…

The hour is late, my mind is racing. My dreams are greater and more vivid than even this botanical effigy. The hypothetical functions of my design are endless—if the community of plants and fungi can operate its trellis frame, will it be able to walk? If its light-sensitive elements become sophisticated enough, will it be able to see? And grasp with fingers, and sense the weather, and know the world and sing its beauties? Will I have created philosophy from the buzzing of chemical instincts?

*And what of the meeting of minds? I will have created an 'artificial' intelligence, although I hesitate to use that word. I will have brought together naturally occurring phenomena in a commune of self-knowledge. Instead, let me call it 'cultivated intelligence'. When this cultivated intelligence encounters my own spontaneous intelligence, what will be discussed, what will be shared? I swear I will see the day when humans fully understand the botanical kingdom,* and the botanical kingdom fully understands us.

Simon closed the soiled jotter and thought carefully. There was birdsong from somewhere beyond the greenhouse. He didn't catch Gregor's eye, even though the other man was watching him intently. He was glad Gregor had shared his work-in-progress with him. It was difficult, sometimes, for the pair to share their uncompleted works, for fear of criticism. It was a special occasion for Simon to be asked what he thought of Gregor's write-up, so special that he didn't mind it interrupting breakfast. Now would come the difficult part, however—providing honest critique. Simon buttered another slice of toast and tried to choose between the rainbow of jams he had prepared using fruit from the garden.

"It is a remarkable document."

"It's a remarkable idea." Gregor had not come to bed last night. His eyes were red and swollen, his manner curt.

Simon could not deny the boast that the text contained an astounding proposal. His reservations lay in its feasibility. Reading Gregor's outlandish predictions made him doubt the morality of the enterprise. But if his objections centred on the practical, then he wouldn't have to insult his companion with objections metaphysical.

"What of the substrate? As far as I see it, that is the next thing you need to decide upon. Everything else falls into place after that decision."

Simon saw that he had poked at a weak spot. Gregor harrumphed and folded his arms. Good—if he got himself stuck on the practicalities, they would not ever have to discuss, and therefore disagree upon, the moral question.

"The multiple terrarium scenario is the most achievable," Gregor muttered, "but is incredibly unwieldy. It's such an inelegant concept. To develop complexity akin to human physiology would require countless tanks, and the entity would still be incapable of self-propelled movement."

Simon selected a dark damson jam and spread it thickly on his buttered toast.

"Then what of the doll concept? How large would that have to be to achieve human complexity?"

"Vast. A towering Ozymandias. Dash it all—the whole thing's preposterous."

Simon's lip curled slightly. It was a shame that Gregor's idea would never see the light of day. But it was better that their lives remained uninterrupted by sentient flora. He took as delicate a bite as one can with toast and jam, savoured the damson, and spoke to console the despairing Gregor.

"Such a shame. I suppose nothing will ever rival an actual human for complexity, in thought or action."

He took another delectable bite, feeling very proud of himself. With the toast still in his mouth he froze—Gregor had that look. That wild look, that joyous look, that dark look. That look which usually said Simon was about to be ravished. Not at breakfast, surely. This morning, the look heralded a sickening logical leap.

"I suppose you're right, darling," Gregor said at last, his face contorted in grim glee. Normally Gregor spoke with the rarefied public-school elocution of his father and peers, but now, as always in times of great emotion, the subtle Scottish lilt he'd picked up from his mother revealed itself. "Nothing will ever rival a human for complexity."

"What. What are you—"

"The substrate should be integrated into the system. Of course! How efficient! And why not use an existing system as the substrate? How elegant!"

"Existing system—you mean an organism?"

"I mean a human. You can grow square tomatoes if you give them a mould. I shall grow a consciousness by giving it a model to follow."

"No person in their right mind would subject themselves to such a monstrous operation!"

"You're right again, darling." Gregor was on the edge of laughter. He had bounded from his seat and was pacing around, shaking his hands with each stressed syllable. "No man alive could tolerate the process. So we won't take a man alive. A body is all I need, not a live one. Recently dead would be preferred. How quickly the carrion feeds the worms!"

Simon was profoundly disgusted. He dealt with death every day—corpses were his medium, after all. But his work existed precisely because of the taboo of human death. Incapable of confronting their own mortality, his clients revelled in the spectacle of aestheticised death. The thought of a dead human turned his stomach. He jabbed his jam knife as he spoke, threatening Gregor with sugared fruit.

"Reanimating the dead! Desecrating a corpse! This experiment has gone too far before it's even begun!"

"Who are you to accuse me of desecrating a corpse? And it's not reanimating. The person is gone—what's left is merely a plant pot. Being devoured by necrophores, that's the best we can hope for underground, why not achieve something along the way?"

"Because it's wrong to use a human being as potting compost."

"Tell that to the daisies in the churchyard."

"There's nothing I could say to stop you now, is there?" said Simon, astonished.

"I have to do this, Simon. And if you don't help me, I shall probably be arrested."

This was the lowest of low blows, and both of them knew it. Simon glared at his partner with apocalyptic fury. Their relationship—their existence—depended on a careful balance of trust. They trusted that the other would never leave, despite there being no formal declaration before God that they wouldn't. If their relationship were to end in acrimony, an injured party could destroy both their lives by divulging their activities to the magistrate. They lived a happy and relatively stable life day-to-day because of plausible deniability—two bachelors could live together for convenience, and intense male friendship was a Classical ideal. So what if Rosalinda knew, or Mr Finch, or Jennifer. If anybody accused them, they could deny it. But, if one of them were tried for a separate crime, all this would come out in court, and there would be no escape. Gregor had played his ace—support him now, or face Reading Gaol.

Simon thought this through. He imagined a pair of scales with which to balance the matter: his moral objections stacked on one side, as prim and coherent pucks of measured weight. The other side, however, was amorphous—fear and devotion and excitement. It was an octopus that wouldn't stay put on the scales. It slobbed and sucked at the balance, growing and transforming at will. Horror of the many-tendrilled monster soon effaced the image of the stacked weights.

"You'd better know what you're doing."

"I'm confident in the plan. I just need the substrate."

"You'll need me for more than just procuring a body. My sutures are the best outside of Harley Street."

"I was hoping you'd lend your taxidermical skills to the endeavour. But first," Gregor leaned in and kissed Simon's forehead, "a body."

# Six

That morning, Jenny was late for work. Even with a relaxed starting time—the boys needed a bit longer to be dressed and decorous in the open-plan greenhouse—she'd still managed to stuff it up, getting bloody distracted *like she always did* rambling out by the Wycombe Road. She bounded past the gatehouse as fast as she could go, but then slowed to only walk as fast as she dared, stiff-limbed and head-down, to avoid the judging glares of the groundsmen. *I know, I know, I know…*

She spotted Will coming back down from the greenhouse with two sacks. She didn't fancy a catch-up there and then, but there was nowhere to hide on the wide open pathway. His bright grin showed he had seen her anyway. He called her name cheerily—she winced out a smile.

"Hullo, Jenny! They've got me doing both the laundry *and* the post now. I blame you for this!" He slumped the sacks down and shook his fist at her playfully.

She wince-smiled a little more and nodded.

"Nah, but not really. I don't mind. Though I mean—*it is* because you got that new job that I'm now landed with two. But I'm fine with it. Glad to, er, glad to help out."

"Cheers, Will. Look, I'd better—"

"So what's it like, inside the greenhouse? I heard they keep a tiger in there. Makes it really a jungle, right? And that's why it's all so hush-hush. They could have brought it from Injah. Do they, Jenny? Do the fellers keep a tiger in the greenhouse?"

"Will Taylor, you wouldn't know a tiger if it bit your head clean off."

"Would too! Just that exact thing happened in my last Penny Dreadful."

"Listen, Will, I've got to go, I'm already late…" Jenny started backing up the drive.

"Been to see Connie?"

Jennifer reeled from hearing her name. Ceasing to be a figment of the world, Connie now existed only in her innermost, private thoughts. Jenny didn't like hearing her name on other people's lips. She had, in fact, been to see her this morning, under that twisting tree, by the Wycombe Road. It was why she was late. She brushed stray petals from her dress, sniffed, and nodded curtly.

"Next time you see her, say hi from me, won't you."

"Of course. Thanks, Will. I'll—"

Jennifer turned and near sprinted the rest of the way to the greenhouse. The faster she went, she felt, the less likely her eyes would betray her with tears.

Letting herself through the iron gate and doorway with a heavy set of keys, all was accompanied by the clinking, scraping, clanging of metal against rusty metal. She threw an apron on and noticed how mucky her fingers were, giving them a good scrub in the quaint little kitchen in the east wing. She pulled her frizzy hair up and back—this heat was ridiculous. Then she huffed and looked around—what on earth was there to clean in this house of plants? The wonders of Grimfern glistened in the summer sun. The little library was nestled within trellises of flowering climbers, the bathroom hidden away behind wide-leaved palms. The bedroom—just one bed—was bedecked with thick wisteria and lilacs. Maybe the sickly-looking Mr Rievaulx slept in his basement?

There was a cluster of glasses on one of the night stands. Nightcaps of Mr Sandys', perhaps, long forgotten with dry puddles of brown and plum in the bottom. She picked these up and returned them to the kitchen sink.

Then she spied another huddle of drinking vessels—brandy glasses mostly—on a mirrored side-table near some wing-backed chairs. She popped these, too, in the kitchen sink.

The hairs on the back of her neck prickled. Scanning the underbrush, she saw the bearded and bespectacled face of Mr Sandys glaring at her from the central atrium. She half-saluted a silent greeting—what else could she do? He squinted back at her and withdrew into the foliage.

There was more glassware and crockery than Jennifer had ever seen in her life dotted around the garden. She went about the queer forest like a pixie picking mushrooms of crystal and porcelain, finding tumblers and teapots, saucers and even silverware. When these treasures were nearly all back in the kitchen and washed, there wasn't enough room in the cupboards to store them all.

The last forgotten hoard of cups was by the piano in the very centre of the greenhouse. As she approached, Jenny became aware of Mr Sandys watching her from the balcony which ran right the way round the central atrium. He was misting a green-and-purple hanging plant, or at least pretending to.

Jennifer held herself tall in defiance of his scrutiny, and made for the coffee cups, which sat on both sides of the open piano. But on seeing their contents she recoiled. Each one, being left with an inch or so of coffee however long ago, had grown white-blue with mould. She peered into one, its pale crust cracked, revealing brown slime beneath. Her breath caught the powdery surface which threw up a whirl of damp uncleanness, and she retched. When she looked back up accusingly to Mr Sandys, he was gone.

Back in the kitchen, Jenny set the kettle to boil, thinking it best to destroy the mould with heat. On reflection, she extinguished the stove and threw the cups straight into the dustbin.

"That's one way to keep things clean."

Mr Sandys was right behind her. She stifled another recoil.

"I wouldn't want to drink out of them if I was you, sir."

"Quite so."

In the long, still silence, there was the pitter-patter of tiny feet on the glass roof above them. Half a dozen small birds had alighted upon the panes, hopping around before their next pleasure-flight. Jenny was enraptured by their playful business.

"You like birds?" Gregor asked, not taking his sharp gaze away from Jennifer. She shrugged.

"I like all God's creatures. But flocks of birds, sir... I'm sorry. Connie and I used to watch the murmurations over the meadows. The sky can be so big out there, Mr Sandys. Bigger than anything. But the birds would seem to fill it on those certain, special days. Great clouds of birds, swinging this way and that, rolling and rising... And we'd be so far away from the village, and all that expectation. Free—me and Connie. Just us and a storm-wind of birds."

The much smaller flock above them seemed to have had enough of pecking at the roof. They took flight once more, flitting bizarre circles above the greenhouse.

Mr Sandys was still watching her, though his eyes had softened. The lines around them now spoke less of scientific scrutiny, and more of fatherly indulgence.

"After you left yesterday, Mr Rievaulx mentioned your circumstances to me. I was sorry to hear of your loss."

"Please, I—"

"No, when Mr Rievaulx explained it to me, I was deeply moved. And this led me to surmise that I may have overreacted to your new position. And, for that, I apologise."

"That isn't necessary." Jennifer turned away to the bulging cabinets of crockery, trying to close the cupboard doors along with the conversation. Sometimes, the last thing a grieving person can tolerate is kindness.

"How did she… go?"

Jenny scrubbed at the glasses. The hot, stringent water felt good against her skin. Welcome surface pain to distract from that deeper ache.

"I'm afraid I'll speak out of turn, sir. I'm to know my place, Father says."

Mr Sandys leaned against the tiled worktop, fixing her with that intense, unflinching gaze of his. He spoke softly, but with great firmness.

"Miss Finch, on certain matters the correct time to speak is 'out of turn'. And as for knowing your place: I want our garden to be a sanctuary for all its inhabitants, flora and fauna alike. So this is your place, Miss Finch. You are free to speak your mind here."

Jenny's shoulders lowered a notch.

"Forgive me, sir, but what they're saying about Connie isn't true at all. It isn't right." She jabbed a soapy, freckled hand in the direction of the village. "I knew her better than anyone. She would never do that to herself."

Mr Sandys didn't react, but Jennifer was sure her words had landed with him. Had she found, at last, someone to confide in? She daren't hardly believe it. And yet it was so easy to speak in this man's unjudging presence.

"Were you at the funeral?"

"They wouldn't put her in the graveyard, not a 'suicide'. Although I know different, of course. Her father, George Haggerston—d'you know the carpenter from the village?—he buried her under the twisted hazel tree by the Wycombe Road. I've been visiting her of a morning, laying wildflowers. That's why

I was late, actually. We used to ramble wherever the wind took us, finding the most dapper wildflowers to braid in our hair."

At the memory of it, Jenny touched her tousled locks. A few petals fell loose from where a garland had been hastily removed.

Mr Sandys replaced his spectacles. His eyes had a strange glint to them.

"Come with me."

He led her through the botanical garden to a stone bench sheltered by a trellis arch, from which sprays of colourful flowers cascaded. Foxgloves and kingcups—a riot of colour, like someone had taken an entire English meadow and squashed it into six square feet, which of course was exactly what Gregor had done. There were even sharp thistles and stinging nettles for authenticity. Jennifer looked around appreciatively as he sat her down on the stone bench. Above them still was the modest murmuration of tiny birds.

"I want you to take one flower to braid into your hair."

Jennifer hesitated and looked around. There were enough flowers around her to bedeck a May Queen every day from now until Michaelmas. Eventually she chose a modest, waxy white trumpet, a bindweed, which grows so commonly in hedges. Mr Sandys snipped one off with enough vine left to secure it to Jenny's russet curls.

"I have a new instruction for you," Mr Sandys said, returning to the emotionless delivery of a severe taskmaster, "a modification to your uniform. Each morning you are to arrive with wildflowers in your hair. I shall brook no refusal."

"Yes, Mr Sandys." Jenny was happy with her quest.

She set about sweeping up any fallen leaves, put away the mountains of cups as best she could, then turned her attention to the duvets.

Mr Sandys returned to watering his extensive horticultural collection, and eventually withdrew to his inscrutable workspace in the west wing.

⁓

[Extract from Gregor Sandys' experimental jotter, Tuesday 11th June, 1889]

*Under the twisted hazel tree by the Wycombe Road...*

⁓

Simon held the reins as the grey mare led them through pitch-black country lanes on their way to the village. He had attached the hansom cab, which gave him and Gregor quite a comfortable ride, though the main reason for this luxury was that a third passenger would be joining them for the return trip. A 'passenger', so to speak, who wouldn't exactly be of a mind to ride a horse. It was slow-going on the winding routes lined with thickets, and their oil lamp struggled against the overbearing darkness of Buckinghamshire.

Once they reached the village, they were obliged to extinguish the oil lamp, meagre as it was. Gregor gave up squinting at his jotter and clutched a spade close to him. Simon slowed Florence down to a crawl—the carriage wheels would be quieter that way.

Eventually they reached the other side of the village, ventured out along the road to High Wycombe, and lit the oil lamp again. Simon caught a glimpse of Gregor's face in the odd light. His heavy brows and sunken eyes gave him a hollow look.

In time, they came to a mossy pillar which marked the edge of the parish. Just beyond was a bleak hillock, the remnants of a dry-stone wall long sundered, and a gnarled tree, silhouetted against the stars.

"This is the place," Gregor whispered.

They tethered the grey mare just off the road and approached the grim tree. Its corkscrew contortions were such that it seemed to be in agony—each wind-blasted branch was a shriek, each thorny leaf was a sob. This was the tree Jennifer had mentioned, the twisted hazel which served as her best friend's headstone.

Simon held the oil lamp as his partner inspected the ground around the tree's bitter roots. Gregor soon found a clutch of picked wildflowers, and Simon swung the light around to illuminate the murk—sure enough, there was a section of bare soil, a freshly covered grave. Gregor removed his jacket, allowing his shirt to billow. It was a humid night after an extremely hot day. Both of them took sweet air into their lungs and held it as Gregor brandished the spade. Finally, he brought it crashing down and split the crumbling earth.

When Gregor was a foot deep, he wiped his brow and proffered the spade to Simon. The taxidermist didn't know what to think. Somehow he hadn't appreciated that the primary business of graverobbing was, in fact, *digging*. The plan was spiralling out of control. First it was the audacity of the experiment itself, then the acquisition of a human body, and then the insistence that they dig up Jennifer's closest friend. Now he was here in the dead of night at a suicide's grave, spade in hand. While Simon fretted, Gregor took a draught of water and rolled up his shirtsleeves. His skin was wet from exertion, his chest heaving. Simon cursed himself and stepped into the grave.

It wasn't long into Simon's shift when there came a sickening crunch from the spade. Gregor dropped to his knees and removed some dirt with his bare hands, uncovering heavy sackcloth. Simon dropped the spade and stumbled backwards into the darkness.

"What have I done… oh no, no—"

"Simon, get here now. I think it was her leg. You weren't to know. Devil's blood—what kind of father buries his daughter in a two-foot grave?"

They uncovered the rest of her by hand. The corpse of Constance had been wrapped in the roughest of sackcloth and covered with a paltry volume of earth. They carried her over to the hansom and sat her in the passenger's seat.

Filling the hole again posed a problem—without a body, the refilled hole was still a foot deep. To avoid drawing attention to their activities, they took it in turns to collect soil from a little way off and carry it back to the former grave. Once restored, Simon placed the bouquet of wildflowers that Jennifer had left back where they'd found them. Gregor, who, unlike Simon, quite enjoyed riding horses, swung himself up onto the grey mare, his jacket slung over his shoulder. Simon climbed into the hansom next to Constance and found himself nodding to her in gentlemanly deference. Gregor squeezed his thighs and the four of them started off back to the village. Constance's head bobbed carelessly, which horrified Simon's Catholic sensibilities.

"I say—do you suppose she'll be alright back here?"

"She'll be fine. Weigh her down with the spade if she needs it. We have to get used to thinking of her as a 'thing', not a person. She isn't Constance any more. *She's the substrate.*"

# SEVEN

[Extract from Gregor Sandys' experimental jotter, Wednesday 12th June 1889]

*My plants could hardly ask for a more pristine pot in which to grow. We have it in Simon's basement, where the cool temperature will keep it from decomposing too rapidly. It is right for it to be there, in his crypt, surrounded by rigid animals as if it were in an Egyptian tomb. Yes—much more respectful a repose, even, than the hardscrabble roadway where it was before.*

*The substrate has suffered three injuries, here listed. The damage to the skin around the neck consists of rope marks from the hanging— but Simon, with his knowledge of the effects of death upon the tissues, insists that the damage occurred post-mortem. Be that as it may, these abrasions are the least of the three injuries. The cause of death, according to Simon, was the puncture to the substrate's abdomen, which ruptured several vital organs. Jennifer did doubt that the death was self-caused. Simon's work seems to corroborate her account.*

The absence of dried blood on the skin suggests the substrate was washed clean. Grisly. But the damage to these organs is irrelevant to the experiment, as they will be replaced with plant roots and communicative channels.

The one injury that does affect the process is the broken femur caused by Simon's unhappy spade. As it will not be able to stand as-is, I propose the removal of the femur and its replacement with a hardwood splint.

The next stage will be to create a frame around the substrate's body, so that when the flesh loses its integrity—as it shall over a period of being decomposed—the floral community will still receive structural support. Hopefully by that time their roots and the mycelium will also keep the entity together. For the frame I propose flexible hazel, both for practical reasons and as a tribute to the plant-host's penultimate resting place.

After that I shall begin the afforestation of the virgin soil. This will involve the simple propagation of mosses on the surface. An emulsion of chopped moss and agar will get the thing blooming quickly. Obviously, I will need access to the interior of the substrate at later times, but the sooner flesh becomes soil the better.

Beyond these initial steps, the plan will be to embed first the reactive plants, then the sensitive plants, then the mycelium to connect them. I have already taken a cutting from the initial specimen. In a way, this small mould is the entity already—certainly more so than the plantbed is. This strand of fungus will turn out to be the child Simon envisaged. A rare thought that. A child for one such as I. My calculations are steadfast and yet I still feel awe for the undertaking, and for the result: A Botanical Daughter.

Jenny finally opened the stiff spigot and a tremendous noise greeted her—the astonishing roar of water hitting the bottom of a metal watering can. She wasn't used to all this, but Mr Sandys had reluctantly entrusted her with some basic watering duties. He quite plainly doubted her abilities to perform even this menial task, which was why she had to get it absolutely right. When the can was nearly full she tried to close off the creaking tap again, but it took her so long the water overflowed.

*No matter. Keep at it.*

She went to pick up the watering can, but its sheer weight caught her by surprise. She had to hold it with both hands, dangling it between her legs as she waddled over to the east wing.

Jennifer had been given some simple watering duties in the living quarters, since Mr Sandys was spending so much time this summer in Mr Rievaulx's basement working on some inscrutable project. Mr Sandys made it very clear that he resented losing even a slight amount of control over his garden, but whatever it was down there demanded every scrap of his attention.

Jenny hefted the watering can over to the bathroom—a clearing in the forested east wing guarded by walls of lush climbers. The plumbing was elegant, with a clawed tub, shower, sink, and W.C. all in bright ceramic and dark iron. The floor here was tiled in charming black and white checks, though currently the effect was spoiled by piles of used Egyptian cotton towels. With some difficulty, Jennifer watered the bases of the plant-walls, trying hard not to drown them, as per Mr Sandys' instructions. They had such vivid, shiny leaves, and dotted across them were flower spikes of vibrant orange.

Once the walls were watered and the various dangling orchids were misted to the best of her ability, Jenny set herself to the normal business of cleaning a bathroom. She wiped down the ceramic surfaces and scrubbed hard at what needed to be scrubbed. She scoured the limescale from around the faucets—something the boys had apparently never thought to do. As she went about collecting up the discarded towels to be changed, a sudden movement in the corner of her eye caused her to start.

It was a clutch of small brown birds, swooping upwards beyond the glass and vines. They fluttered up and lighted upon the roof, pottering about between the panes.

The wind-rush sent Jenny momentarily off-balance. It transported her, instantly and completely, to the wide-open meadows around the village, where she would run, run as fast as she could, laughing, with Constance just ahead of her, and the birds—the birds! So many birds overhead they seemed like a cloud. And Jennifer's heart lifted in her chest to be part of the flock, her toes barely touching the earth, her fingers reaching for Constance's, and each girl yearning for the sky. They were one with the birds in the freedom of their flight, falling in the wildflowers and rolling, laughing. Their hair falling in tangles. Broken petals strewn across cotton dresses.

Jenny shook herself. It was just a clutch of small brown birds, hopping upon the glass roof.

"Not now, meadowlarks," Jennifer muttered. She left the bathroom hurriedly, scooping up the towels, holding tight to their cotton softness.

She followed a trail of further towels, shirts, and smalls through the dappled east wing to what she suspected was the master bedroom. Mr Sandys must use this as his sleeping quarters, as you could see his flourishes everywhere about it— the miniature trees potted in tea canisters, a bare-root peace lily in a crystal decanter, and the flowering climbers winding around the four-poster bed. Mr Sandys could grow anything where it wasn't supposed to grow, it seemed.

The other tell-tale sign of the botanist was the piles of clothes, towels, and personal particulars all around the floor. Jennifer gathered these into one great laundry mound, as you might if you were raking leaves to burn. Then she started to turn down the bed.

*It mustn't be very comfortable for Mr Rievaulx to sleep downstairs in the basement like a mole. Why couldn't he have a clearing of his own in the east wing?* It struck Jennifer as deeply unfair.

Grabbing the pillows, she spotted that there were piles of books on both bedside tables. One side had them all at odd angles, the other perfectly square. Maybe Mr Sandys was a voracious reader. And slept on both sides of the bed?

Once it was clear, she fetched fresh linens and spread out a bedsheet with one great waft. Out of the corner of her eye, through the bed canopy of wisteria and lilac, she spotted them— the small brown birds. The little buggers had followed her over from the bathroom.

"Oh no you don't. I'm just getting on with my business. I don't need you bringing your bad news to me wherever I go."

She was proud of herself for her mental resolve. There was no need to dwell on anything that made her upset. She was well put-together, in-control, and focused on the task in hand. She shooed the grief-birds away with a flick of the bedsheet.

The larks bristled briefly and lit again upon the greenhouse roof—tapping now upon the glass with their tiny beaks.

"There's nothing to eat up there, silly birds."

She kept on making the bed, with the larks pecking away above her all the while. On the far side of the four-poster, the orderly pile of books was accompanied by a black tie, neatly folded. One such as Mr Rievaulx might wear. The silk of it was so soft under her fingertip. The bed linen sent sensations through her too—and the tapping, the birds' tapping—and suddenly it was Constance's hand brushing her own. Their fingers intertwined. Jenny scrunched her hand up in the duvet. Skin to golden skin could touch and bring with it such happiness. And then such suffering.

And those bloody birds kept up their tapping overhead, pecking away at her brain.

Jennifer buried her face into the fresh pillow and screamed. Then she flipped it over, straightened her dress and marched, stiff-armed, out of the east wing.

Struggling to find something to do which would keep her mind away from Constance and the feathered menace, Jenny settled for taking out her pent-up frustrations by beating a rug. She hung a faded Persian one from the east wing out on the patio and struck it over and over again, till great plumes of dust sprang from it and her freckles blossomed in rosy exertion.

But the meadowlarks were not done with her. They gathered nearby, peering at her from the topiary bushes before hopping nearer onto the garden table. Jennifer brandished her wicker beater at them, but they were ever more insistent.

"Leave me alone!"

Jenny's cry managed to scare the birds, but they simply turned a circle in the air. One brave lark came and perched right upon the hanging rug. She pointed her beater at it. One tousle of reddish hair had fallen down over her furious eyes.

"What do you want from me?"

The small bird cocked its head but did not reply. The question conjured its own answer in Jennifer's heart.

That evening after work, when the sun was less warm though still golden, Jenny traipsed a very long way back to her father's mill. She kept to the winding side-snickets, some of which were known to only her. She burst her way through a buddleia which seemed to be growing out of its hedge sideways as much as upwards and came out onto the wide expanse of a wildflower meadow.

Their meadow.

The light here was just as she had remembered it—honeyed and dazzling. Flowers of every colour blended into each other across the fields—a haze of hues broken only by haphazard fences and deep-green becks. Heavy-laden trees sagged in their summer richness. And the sky stretched away—limitless. And empty.

There was not a single bird out there that night in the meadow. Not above, nor below, nor singing in the trees.

The golden light coalesced into the silver of early stars. Jenny perched upon a stile, searching the horizon for her cloud of birds—any birds at all—just one bird? But there, amongst the kingcups and daisies, she was truly alone.

Simon pulled the thread taut and tied it off, removing the excess with a tiny pair of sprung scissors. All of his taxidermy equipment was as small as it could possibly be made and was of endlessly reflective silver. It felt blasphemous to use it on a human. He pushed away the wheeled stand which supported his various large magnifying lenses. There was no need for the small ones which slotted over a monocle, since he was instructed not to focus on aesthetics. Still, he did as decent a job as he could, and Constance's abdomen was repaired as well as any surgeon could hope for.

It was an abhorrent injury. A serrated blade had been inserted and pulled six inches up. This was certainly what killed the poor girl, but then what to make of the neck abrasions? Simon shifted his stool and brought the lens frame over to re-examine. They were certainly rope marks, but the pattern of bruising definitely implied that she was already dead when the hanging took place. Plus there was no sign of a broken neck—that could just be luck, or bad luck, if she had done it herself. But who rises from the grave only to hang themself? No—it was Simon's strong opinion that Constance had been killed, and that the hanging was a setup. But what could be done about it? They could not involve the constabulary now that they had her corpse in their basement. Poor girl. Simon felt that he had both uncovered a terrible crime and prevented it from ever being solved. He wiped the remaining debris from the skin around her suture and draped her with a muslin cloth.

Returning to his desk he flicked through some notes he had made for his taxidermy projects, but he couldn't concentrate. Looking around, all the woodland creatures seemed to be staring at the body, keeping vigil as they would for a sleeping nymph. How could he work with Constance in the room? His sanctuary had become a morgue.

He peeled back the fabric and observed her mottled face. Simon knew what the issue was: she was incomplete. It would take weeks for the plants to settle according to Gregor, and perhaps months for the mycelium to take. All the while Constance would remain in a state of unending becoming. That rankled Simon's perfectionism and occupational discipline. A wonderful thing about taxidermy is that it transforms the chaos of life and death into perfect stasis. When captured in art, the subject ceases to be a creature of unpredictability, of yearning to one day be. It becomes fixed and finite. Its 'becoming' is finally and permanently completed. Gregor's work in botany, by contrast, dwelt entirely in spurts and changes. The interminable adolescence of living things, variously bulging up and fading away. Gregor's masterpieces were never done, never whole, because they would always continue to change.

To settle his nerves and ground himself once more in the truly static, Simon took one of Mr Finch's pheasants from cold storage. Without washing his equipment after use on Constance, he split open its torso and extracted its entrails. Some cultures would use this to scry the future. Simon would use it to annihilate the present. He isolated the digestive system, the oesophagus, stomach and intestines, and held them tightly to thaw. He then suspended them in a glass jar filled with aspic, leaving it to set. He placed it next to the rabbit's brain he had encapsulated the other day. It was a wonderous specimen, very fine and clear details in the digestive tract. There—now nothing would turn his stomach ever again.

[Extract from Gregor Sandys' experimental jotter, Saturday 15th June 1889]

*With the surface of the substrate now moss-primed and reinforced, I have moved on to replacing its interior systems with floral and fungal counterparts. Simon performs the fleshy side of the procedure, since he is a master of the mortician's art; I practise my version of this with roots and soil, then he returns and unites skin with plant matter.*

*I began with the joints, replacing the ligaments of her shoulders with my adapted Codariocalyx motorius. I have encouraged its growth so that its hinges could be used to operate the arms. The stems of its leaves are ingrained tightly into the moss of the subject's upper arms, and pinned securely to hazel rods so that the hinges may have purchase once operational. In this way I have nurtured Codariocalyx in her shoulders, wrists, knees, and ankles. I do not believe the plant species will have the strength to operate the hips, nor the precision to operate the finger joints—further research is required for these.*

[Extract from Gregor Sandys' experimental jotter, Tuesday 18th June 1889]

*I must work more quickly—the joints of the Codariocalyx are softening with the lack of sunlight. I can't move the substrate upstairs into the light yet, though, for fear of chaotic decomposition. We have attached the flytraps, each an inch long when open, to the inside of her finger joints. Simon did most of the fine sewing; my hands tremble terribly. Now, when a joint is artificially triggered by an outside force's double-tap, say Simon with a wooden spill, the finger closes in one-tenth of a second. Although these joint systems are unconnected, it is heartening to see the fingers move of their own accord.*

*We have obscured the substrate's face with cloth. Until the leaf-coverage thickens as the foliage matures, it will bear a sickly, mossy resemblance to the girl.*

[Extract from Gregor Sandys' experimental jotter, Wednesday 19th June 1889]

*We have added the Mimosa pudica to the substrate's hands. A thin canopy of the delicate leaves spreads itself from her wrists to her fingertips. We know that her sensory and motor functions are working independently, but already the illusion of agency is clouding our minds. Simon delicately stroked the pad of her ring-finger and her whole hand recoiled from him as if he had tickled her! Clearly his touch had simply caused the Mimosa to curl up in a ripple along the hand. As chance would have it, the bustle of leaves caused several flytraps to trigger, closing her fingers into a fist. Simon had quite a fright and took some calming down with tea and birdsong in the atrium. It is sometimes odd to be upstairs in the heat of the sun—our lives are spent underground this summer, germinating our strange daughter.*

# EIGHT

A small ritual which Simon performed daily was the reading of a chapter and the consumption of tea. This occurred well after the ordained time for High Tea; in summer he took it as the fires of the afternoon started to smoulder, no earlier than six p.m. It was one of those aspects of life at Grimfern in which he could revel in freedom from social pressure. Imagine what his mother would say if he had tea after five.

The literature he chose for these occasions was heavy and obscure—he had inherited a strong sense of self-sacrifice from his parents, such that even when unnecessary his instinct was still to make himself suffer. Thus he struggled through ill-translated texts of Sufi mysticism; dry accounts *of the accounts* of the court of Elizabeth I; and the winding, tortuous sentences of contemporary Romantic poets. The content of the reading material did not matter, although he made a good performance of erudite interest. What mattered was that he *was reading*, with tea.

The location was also important, so he chose the high gallery running around the central atrium, from which you could observe the canopy in all its emerald foliage. Gregor had planted up a section of the wrought-iron balcony with bushy ivies and pendulous vines, creating a shady nook on high. This was the perfect place for Simon. In it, he felt like a tree bird observing the forest, refusing to partake in sylvan fancy.

On this particular day, he prepared the verdant outlook with a deckchair and located his reading glasses. He extracted a tome from the bookshelf in the east wing (he returned them after every reading session) and nestled it onto a nearby glass table. He boiled water in the kitchenette, and carefully carried the tea things to his perch. Each trip required the crossing of the garden, the climbing of a narrow spiral staircase, and the crossing of the gallery. The plodding, inefficient back-and-forth was part of the process—part of the summoning of tranquillity. He was just settling into the deckchair, bringing the first cup of steaming tea to his lips, when he heard an indistinct voice from below.

"I say, who goes there?" he enquired.

The mumble returned, this time accompanied by the rustling of leaves. Simon let out the longest of breaths and staggered to his feet.

"Gregor, are you down there?" Simon peered through the thick vine leaves to the weird woods below. A section underfoot shook—there was a woodland creature in the bracken. Simon sharpened his beady eyes. Finally a pair of hands separated the branches of two potted trees, and a befreckled face peeped through, framed by a halo of auburn frizz.

"Miss Finch, what are you still doing here?"

"I was just finishing up. Trying to tell you that I'm off now, sir!"

"Miss Finch, please come up here to speak to me. I won't tolerate being wooed from the bushes."

Jennifer set off at a sporting jog through the undergrowth. Simon could see her progress snaking along Gregor's winding paths by the displacement of the canopy—she was a squirrel darting through the greenery. She bounded up the spiral staircase, pulling her body up with her arms as much as her legs, and skidded to a halt by Simon's nest. He could see from her fidgeting that she was full of energy and keen to get off out into the countryside and home. Very few people could work a full day and still have more energy than they knew what to do with. Jennifer was one of those people. If Simon described her as a lively rodent, it would be with the deepest respect for rodentkind.

"Now, Miss Finch, what is it you wanted to say to me?"

"Only that I'm done for the day and was heading off."

That morning she had threaded daisies through her upknot, as per Gregor's instructions. Now, after a long day sweeping and dusting, there was more hair outside of her bun than in it. Some daisies remained, broken and squished, littering her locks.

"Heading off home?"

"Yes, sir, only dawdling probably. I'll go up and round by Kingswood. My father won't be back until sundown."

"How is your father?"

"Same old. He's bought a gun but doesn't know how to use it, bless him. He's still a miller at heart, even if he pretends to be a poacher."

"Business must be good, then, if he's acquiring new equipment?"

"Not really, sir." She puffed out her cheeks in the manner of freelancers everywhere at the discussion of money. "You're still his main customer. But with the money you pay me as well, he had enough for it. It's a rusty old thing, I'm sure."

"Has he shot anything with it?" Simon was worried about the state of pelts and corpses if the critters were extinguished with grapeshot.

"Has he bonkers. But he takes it with him whenever he goes out for game. I think it makes him feel more like a real hunter, and he has been catching more stuff. So it's worth it, I guess, over all. Blimey—I mean, what's he gonna shoot here in Buckinghamshire, squirrels?"

Simon was horrified at the thought, not least because Jennifer resembled a squirrel herself. He worked very hard at not letting her see that he was fond of her. He bid her good day and thanked her for her work. Returning to his book, he found himself imagining her sojourn through Kingswood, dancing through bracken, pressing wildflowers to her chest. Would she kneel and weep, laying garlands on the grave of her friend—a grave Simon had himself emptied? He shuddered the thought away, but it returned with the sight of every petal of the garden—each one now seeming to him like a misplaced graveflower. He resolved to visit Jennifer's father again and buy up anything he had in stock. Perhaps she deserved a raise, too. Or a nice taxidermy piece…

After his very-high tea, the sky above the greenhouse was orange and pink. He strolled through Gregor's forest with his jacket slung over his shoulder. His partner the genius was a small wonder with a trowel. But as well as practical skill for botany, he had an aesthete's eye for magical moments. He hadn't just created a garden, he had created this exact moment—the heat, the sweet scent of nectar, the honeyed light of evening, all framed by the most exquisite plants on this fair earth.

On his way past the staircase to his cellar, Simon heard a strange melody. Enchanted by this plainsong, he drifted down into his workspace. Maybe Gregor was singing a ditty whilst working on the experiment, humming whilst propagating mosses or feeding its flytraps. What he saw wasn't completely different from that, but a trifle more disconcerting.

Gregor, in loose shirtsleeves and open collar, was standing over the agar dish which contained his protean nervous system—the knotted threads of his oriental fungus. His head was bowed, his glasses having slid to the end of his nose. He was pouting at the thing and cooing softly. Simon stayed at the foot of the stairs, silently watching the usually cynical man singing to the grey mycelium as if it were a baby. The tune was 'Mary, Mary, quite contrary'—the words were half-remembered and largely mumbled, but his voice was pure and soft. Gregor's hair fell down across his face, but didn't obscure the gentle smile on his lips.

Simon was deeply moved. He trod carefully across the room and placed his hands lovingly on Gregor's cocked hips. Gregor pushed back into the embrace until they were touching from knee to shoulder.

"How does your garden grow?" Simon whispered into his ear.

"She's nearly ready," said Gregor, before twisting his neck and shoulders so that they could kiss on the mouth.

"She?" teased Simon. "You usually refer to 'the experiment', or 'the substrate.'"

"Ah, but this!" Gregor released himself from the clutch and gestured to the dish. "This is the true vessel of the being's soul. It will become a conscious entity, a person perhaps. It can't do much yet, but what week-old child can? That doesn't stop it being alive, it doesn't stop it being our daughter."

Simon looked at the mess of tendrils on the workbench. He had not shaken the idea that what they were doing was wrong, although he could not yet articulate it. On top of that, he had never seen Gregor so enraptured and paternal. Perhaps this was indeed their shot at the joys everybody else took for granted. This was their shot at a baby.

He hugged Gregor so tightly that he could have grabbed his own elbows. The buttons of their shirts caught and rubbed. Everything was blossoming happiness and constricting fabric.

# Nine

A few days later, Jenny was scrubbing the brickwork floor by hand. She didn't mind it. Hard work, scrubbing floors; honest work. It was a thankless task, since the bricks themselves weren't particularly dirty, but the grouting benefited from a good scrub. That way nothing unexpected could grow in the cracks. Jennifer was the first line of defence against dandelions.

Mr Sandys and Mr Rievaulx were outside for breakfast today. The sun was strong but there was a refreshing breeze, which meant that the temperature outside was much milder than the sweltering greenhouse. The gents were taking a leisurely breakfast. Jenny didn't mind working hard while they lounged about. After all—she was getting paid for it. She did wonder how they made their money. She left her father's house at daybreak and returned at dusk, spending the intervening hours scouring and sweeping, folding, polishing... Whereas these men of knowledge wafted through the day with a book in one hand and a cup of coffee in the other, always half at work, always half at rest. Well. Wheat grows in the field, bluebells grow in the shade.

She continued scrubbing but her mind started to wander. Tranquillised by the repetitive motion, her vision blurred and made hazy space for her imagination. Mr Sandys' impossible interior forest shimmered in the heat. She wondered idly if wheat could grow in the shade as well as bluebells. The gaps between the herringbone bricks gaped as she became dizzy. It was so hot in here. Her tongue was heavy, her jaw, her eyelids—

Nodding back to reality, she found herself lying like a child in the pool of soapy water. She sat up and shook herself, wiping her face on her pinafore. She was still woozy and couldn't stand, her mouth still too numb to cry out. The masters outside probably couldn't hear her—they were still snoozing in the sun with their breakfast things in front of them. It wouldn't do to stay here in the strong light of the glass roof. Jenny crawled to the staircase which led down to Mr Rievaulx's cellar. She was forbidden from both the masters' workspaces, but surely they wouldn't mind her escaping the midday sun. She lowered herself down the first of the steps. Against her palms, the stones went from hot to cold rather sharply.

She was in the belly of Grimfern Botanical Garden—the mechanical monstrosity that was the boiler. Jenny had never seen it working, having started her occupation here in the heat of early summer. She didn't care to see it going, quite frankly. She had seen the locomotives at High Wycombe, heard their noise, smelled their peculiar inhuman smells. This boiler reminded her of those metal monsters—a large furnace with a gaping maw for shovelling in the blackrock, and pipework shooting out of it at horrendous angles. Disjointed. Threatening. Looming large over her as she dragged herself down the staircase. She felt a faint building up inside her, or was it a scream? Everything about her was dark metal menace. Finally she reached an archway at the foot of the stairs, which signified the very bottom of the greenhouse. She slumped against a pillar, her eyes slowly adjusting to the queer darkness.

Jennifer knew what Simon Rievaulx did for a living. She knew what he bought from her father. She knew that he made funny little sculptures with dead animals, and she had heard that some people paid a lot of money for such things. She hadn't been able to imagine what a finished product would look like, but she was fairly certain that she wouldn't enjoy looking at it. After all, the magic of animals was in watching them play, darting about, hiding in hedgerows and up in the branches of trees. What was interesting or clever about looking at corpses as if they were works of art?

Well, now she need wonder no more. The workspace was surrounded—guarded, perhaps—by a multitude of woodland animals. Jenny was struck by how *alive* they looked. Each creature was poised and posed; each seemed to want something, and each seemed to know how to get it. Her curiosity took control of her, and the heatstroke was overridden by intrigue.

She walked slowly around the room, observing each work, trying to imagine what the thing was feeling. There was a hamster-bishop, with a shining mitre and a great crosier. His visage was focused and determined, but his free paw was clenched in a ball. She decided he was an ambitious young clergyman, determined to bring the light of God to all the furry heathens.

There was a pair of kittens dressed as bride and groom— and Jenny would be damned if the she-kitten wasn't the loveliest bride she had ever seen. Her dress was fondant satin, her bouquet sublime. The look on her face, as she regarded her husband-to-be, was demure but full of anticipation.

*Good for you, kitty—good for you.*

The largest tableau was a funeral scene outside a miniature church. There was a hamster-vicar, perhaps one of the bishop's underlings, standing at the head of an open grave, prayer book in hand. An owl in horse-riding gear turned her face away from the scene, overcome with emotion. A raven stood next to her, with a high collar and tie like a provincial schoolmaster. Mr Rievaulx had given him tiny spectacles to balance on his beak. Leaning over to peer into the grave, Jennifer recoiled sharply. At the bottom of the shaft was an open coffin with a convincingly half-decomposed dove. The poor, pure bird had been shot and mangled, or so the artist would have you believe. Jenny hoped he was very good at his craft, and not just a vindictive bird murderer.

On the worktable in the centre of the room was a long mound of earth, covered in moss and strange plants. Jenny wondered if this was what the masters had been working on, down here, out of the sunlight. Maybe this was a particularly sensitive flower arrangement, using plants that only grew in caves and such like. There was no accounting for taste, and that wouldn't be the queerest thing about the two gentlemen who lived together in a greenhouse.

Just before leaving, Jenny's eye was caught by a stringy blob in a dish. She had never seen something so ugly and so beautiful at the same time. It was a disgusting mucus-green colour, but with a slimy sheen which was yellow and purple as you moved your head. The wild colours entranced the young woman, but revulsion at what was clearly mould kept her at a distance. The sheen made the clump seem wet—it was probably soft and cool, and so pretty. She reached out a pale finger and touched its slimy core. The thing shuddered, but Jennifer read pleasure rather than fear.

Surely, of all the things in Mr Rievaulx's basement of curiosities, this was the best and most wondrous. Jenny understood why she liked the kitten, for instance—it was just like a cat and just like a bride. It was funny, and hopeful, and romantic, and human. This, however, was thoroughly inhuman. It was abstract and ugly, but so, so beautiful. She had been mesmerised by it instantly—she could read its heart and hoped, somehow, it would read her own and find her beautiful, too. What a masterpiece! He had made her fall in love with his creation, a creation which didn't even have a face.

Returning to the surface, she picked up her brush and resumed scrubbing. The men were still at table on the patio. With the oil-slick rainbow shimmering in her mind's eye, the work went by like a psychedelic dream.

[Extract from Gregor Sandys' experimental jotter, Friday 21st June 1889]

*For years, we in the scientific community have considered plants to be relatively simple organisms—static and unfeeling. My own research, and the work of others in the botanical sciences, is starting to take apart that myth, exploring ways in which flora and fungi are complex and sensitive.*

*The single major obstacle to their sophistication is their lack of movement. "Who can impress the forest, bid the tree unfix his earthbound root?" Macbeth was firm in his belief that Great Birnam Wood could never crawl up to meet him in battle—but he was wrong. With movement comes the possibility for individual adaptation, for growth not along the set template for one's species, but for spiritual, emotional growth. Accordingly, I have given the substrate capacity for movement, but how to encourage Birnam Wood to rise to high Dunsinane Hill? With all the various hinges and senses I have bestowed upon the substrate, how am I to inspire and coordinate movement?*

*For this I turn to my nervous mycelium. It shall transmit impulses through the corpus to organise motor function. It shall connect the various 'root-brains' (I borrow the term from the indefatigable Darwin), turning a series of discrete shrubs into a flowerbed—a collection of units will become one supra-organism. Many creatures are known to form symbiotic relationships. A colourful fish cleans the anemone, which in turn protects it from attack. The lichen is formed of fungal and photobiotic life working in tandem. Microorganisms live in our guts, helping us digest our food. My dream goes a step further—many individual plants could become sociable organs of the whole. The 'mind' emerges from the intricacies of the brain... So too may it arise from the intricacies of the forest.*

*After this comes the question of intelligence—will we have created a gestalt consciousness? I yearn to proceed with the process, not least because the foliage detests Simon's dungeon. There are signs of chlorosis in the Codariocalyx, nasty yellowing which I take as a personal, horticultural failure. I must get the fungus ready for its new host. Soon... soon.*

[Extract from Gregor Sandys' experimental jotter, Sunday 23rd June 1889]

*Disaster. I intended to transplant the nervous mycelium into the substrate's skull, thus replacing her brain. Simon practised his art and sliced the bone smoothly so that the top of her head came away in a perfect hemisphere. With a few choice snips from my secateurs, I removed the rotting brain matter from its pot. Then, turning out the mycelium and agar from its dish onto a plate (in the manner of an upside-down cake), I transferred it to the substrate's skull. Simon reattached the pate with the addition of a minute hinge, so that we would have ready access to check on the progress.*

*Alas, two days later the mycelium had not taken to the spinal column. I had hoped for it to rush down the cord like a hungry vine along a wire. It just squatted there in the darkness of her brain cavity, sulking.*

*Simon, who is always sensitive to my moods, locked the liquor cabinet and decanted my brimming whiskey glass into one of his own. After a few mouthfuls we grew used to the alcoholic fumes, and Simon made one of those leaps of logic only possible for creative types. The substrate's anatomy, he reasoned, is not a perfect analogy for the supra-organism's. As such, we do not need to replace its human nervous system with our fungal one. Instead we could use the human physiology more creatively: and train the mycelium through the cardiovascular system, the ready-made tubules of the veins and arteries. She was empty of blood; Simon had seen to that. All it would take would be to flood the circulatory system with fungus-favoured nutrients and replace her heart with the plantbrain.*

*Simon used his collection of woodworking equipment to saw down her sternum. He turned her torso into a cabinet; hinged, like her skull, for easy access. Her rib cage now opens like a wardrobe. Inserting a nozzle with a hand-operated pump, we filled the veins and arteries with unset agar jelly. Once set, I shaved off the top section of the substrate's heart, exposing the four chambers and removing the valves. I then arranged the mycelium in such a way that the tendrils were aiming for the main thoroughfares out of the heart. We closed her cupboard-thorax and fastened the ornate latch. Now all we can do is hope, pray, and water.*

# TEN

Simon set out his array of miniature implements in a row alongside the greening plantbed. He had various sizes of forceps and syringes, bone cutters with ivory handles, and a brain scoop presented to him for his sixteenth birthday. He had silver hooks of every size attached to strong, thin chains. In an elegant storage box, he kept beeswax, taxidermical soap, and various shades of enamel paint. Along with the recent addition of hinges and other ornate metal titbits, Simon introduced a screwdriver and lemon-soda brass polish to his usual roster of equipment.

He gave the girl a quick check all over, although it was Gregor's job to tend to her foliage. She was already beginning to 'take', and it showed in her burgeoning plant matter. Perhaps when people ask, "How are you in yourself?" they are asking if the roots of your component mosses are firmly embedded, if your stalks are hale and hearty, if your limbs are operating in each other's best interest, and if your organs are forming a coherent unit. The plant-girl's precocious growth spoke of something more than *wellness*. It spoke of sheer life unbridled—an unshackled and concerted flourishing.

After tightening her cranial screws and polishing her various hinges, he moved on to her face. Her skin had been preserved with formaldehyde, so that her features would not wither as the mycelium encroached upon them. For the very surface of her face, Gregor had shown Simon how to grow a thin layer of moss. It is a relatively straight-forward procedure, to propagate moss. He took a spongy green batch from the cobbles outside and whisked it together with buttermilk and honey from the garden's own bees. He then applied the paste to her face as if he was painting a doll's foundation, only this dolly was swamp green.

She was so still, so serene, this child. The young woman's father had planted her in the thin soil by the twisted hazel. Simon and Gregor ripped her from the earth to replant her in richer mud. This way she could germinate anew, and blossom in a way she never could have done in her first life.

And would she carry within her the shade of Constance, like a word may carry with it an archaic meaning? Amongst the darkened arches of the crypt, Simon could sense her spectre, her implication, her connotation. Constance lived in the ghostly realm of metaphor, now—her presence merely inferred by the outline of her former existence. The word of her body had taken on a new meaning.

It would not do, however, to dream of reanimation. Constance would not be brought back to life by their act. But her body would be the host of this congregation of plants and fungi. It would be an abandoned cathedral, once more filled with spirit. The artistic process took on a religious significance for Simon. He swabbed the orifices of her face so they would not seize shut and found himself intoning the Mass. This is her body, given for you. We are all one, because we all share in one bread. A floral transubstantiation was taking place under his hands—he was a scientist-priest, the workbench was his altar, and the mycelium moved amongst them like the Holy Ghost.

He finished his mosswork and placed down the chalice of emulsion. She looked so restful on the altar, her planthands resting on her sternum. Candlelight granted her the illusion of breathing. Simon searched in his cupboards for an old taxidermy piece of his—another hamster-vicar, this one holding a human-sized thurible. Finding the furry clergyman, he lit incense in its ornate holder and placed it with the Host on the table. He bowed his head in prayer.

The smell transported him back to his grim youth as a fearful altar boy, horrified and fascinated by the suffering of Christ, the agony of Job, the fires of Revelation. The grinding of a detuned pipe organ. The choir master's fury, the weight of his robe, the smell of incense so strong that it became a taste. Finally, a nightmarish hamster-vicar rang a bell and Simon jolted back to the room, breathing shallowly.

The candles were burning low, the windowless basement was shrouded in darkness. Only the outline of the substrate could be seen, her foliage picked out in the amber light. Her hand was moving—or was it a trick of the light? No—her hand was slowly closing to a loose fist. Simon's own hand was trembling. Perhaps the flytraps had been triggered by something. He moved closer to inspect the plant-hinges for signs of a snared insect, but there was nothing in her grip. Her five digits opened once more, then closed. The action was mesmerising, like an anemone wafting in a reef—but in the depths of the glasshouse basement, there was no breeze to cause such motion. Simon's knees betrayed him, and he lowered himself onto a stool. The hand continued moving, isolating the fingers one by one. This was conclusive, this was proof. Simon staggered up the stairs to find Gregor.

It was dark upstairs in the greenhouse even though it was early evening, as a thick bank of cloud squatted over Buckinghamshire. The atrium was damp at the best of times, but the wet pressure of the weather made the feeling unbearable. Gregor was slouched at the grand piano, his shirt loose and his hair ruffled. He was playing a series of half-diminished chords with no regard for tonal relation—possibly Wagner, possibly existential angst. Simon approached him and opened his mouth to speak, but could not find the words. His partner looked back at him with tired eyes. Gregor was always completely devoted to his work, but this experiment had commandeered every waking thought and every fever-dream for nearly a fortnight. His beard was frazzled and his skin no longer seemed to adhere to his bones. Gregor squeezed the bridge of his nose, his spectacles thrust up into his stress-slicked fringe. Simon forgave the lack of affection in his gaze, as he was so achingly tired. But now— the breakthrough. If only Simon could get his blasted tongue to function. No matter how hard he tried he could not find a way to express what he had seen without sounding pathetic.

He held his hand out to the slouching pianist, closed and opened it repeatedly. The action sent a flood of emotion through him—happiness and exhaustion and fear. He sobbed a little. Gregor took him by the shoulders and stared intently into his teary eyes; Simon hoped upon hope that Gregor would understand his gesture.

The dark expression on Gregor's face erupted into a smile. He cupped Simon's cheeks and laughed, grabbed his own frizzy hair and turned right around in a circle. Finally, he took Simon by the hand and they rushed down to the crypt.

The corpse of Constance was lying on the workbench, pulsating with gentle signals. It was like a tree dancing in the wind, moved by an unknowable force. Simon was sure that the motor functions were increasing in intensity. What had they done? Their sacrilege was clear to him now. He brushed aside his religious paraphernalia which now seemed obscenely blasphemous. Gregor, the eternal materialist, had his cast-iron gaze welded tight onto the experiment—Simon knew that nothing could break the chains of his attention in this state, so despite his disgust he resigned himself to watching the watcher circling the dancing plant.

"Does it know what it's doing?" Simon asked.

"It is a plant. Or, a series of plants. It knows what it's doing, only in the sense that it is trying to live. It will do whatever it takes to achieve that end."

"Oh God—"

The tempo of the plantbed's movements was certainly increasing. Faster and faster her joints opened and closed. Even the heaviest of limbs were being manipulated now, her shoulders caused her arms to flail, her hips operated her legs. It was beginning to turn into a fit. Simon desperately wanted to do something to help her, but fear of the shivering corpse held him back.

"It's the mycelium, I'm sure of it," said Gregor, "it's testing out its motor functions. I'm going to encourage it to focus on one area."

He picked up a small wooden taper, felt its lack of weight between his fingers, and put it back down. His glance at Simon betrayed his naked ambition, but was there a touch of fear? Simon shook his head emphatically—whatever new horror Gregor was planning, Simon hadn't the strength to witness. Knowing the botanist, he'd run headlong into hell if there was a chance of a scientific leap.

Gregor reached his hand towards the specimen's, taking care to keep his body as far away as possible. He took the hand as if to shake it—palm to palm, with thumbs interlocking. Simon saw the flytraps press into the botanist's flesh without breaking it, the delicate *Mimosa* caressing his fingers. The rest of her body relaxed and returned to a placid repose. The hand, meanwhile, closed around Gregor's, testing his strength. The ecosystem was conscious and in control of its movements.

"Good evening, I am Gregor Sandys, botanist. I am your creator."

"Gregor," Simon cried out, "it is a dead body. This is Constance. You can't go about introducing yourself to a cadaver!"

"This is not Constance," Gregor hissed, "this is the mycelium coordinating a system of plant hinges."

"This is a girl's dead body. Saint Michael and all Heaven—what we've done is unholy!"

"Unholy!" Gregor roared, turning round as best he could whilst still holding the substrate's hand. "How dare you. You, who desecrates corpses in the name of art. Here we have created a life! The sanctity of the girl is still intact—enhanced, even. She has given herself so that this being can live."

"She hasn't given herself, Gregor! We took her. We stole her body and now here you are shaking hands with it. I'm sorry, Gregor, but I'll have nothing more to do with your putrid experiment!"

With that he ripped off his apron and hurled himself up the stairs and out into the moonlight.

Gregor turned his attention back to the substrate. He released himself from her grip, stroking her palm up to the tip of her finger. The hand sent its fingers probing for Gregor's, so he held it flat for it to find. It tapped its way around his digits, then stroked his own palm from wrist to fingertip in a shaky echo of his own gesture. Gregor's eyes moistened despite himself.

"You impossible beauty. The Royal Horticultural Society won't know what to do with themselves."

# ~PART II~

## CULTIVATION

# Eleven

[Extract from Gregor Sandys' experimental jotter, Sunday 14th July 1889]

*I have named her* CHLOE. *It is not the name of her body, which was, is, and will always be Constance Haggerston. It is not the name of her component parts—*Mimosa pudica, Codariocalyx motorius, *and so on. Those Latin names fail to describe her spiritually, in the same way that the word 'ventricle' fails to describe a lovesick heart. The Sumatran mycelium is no longer her sole identity either, since it has become so embedded into Constance, and so syncretic with her foliage. Thus I have given the entity a name, perhaps to speak it into existence.* ΧΛΌΗ. *An epithet of the goddess Demeter—she of new life emergent from the Hadean earth. Greek is better than Latin or English to invoke a mystic nymph.*

*Her physical growth has been astounding, perhaps due to the absence of sunlight in the basement. This phenomenon, where plants hurry to reach the light, is similar to 'forcing' vegetables by* reducing their access to the sun. There's a long way for her to grow before she reaches the surface from her cryptic rest, but hopefully we will be able to bring her up before she expends all of her nutrients in the attempt. The shoots that spring from her—inspiring her classical name—are slender and pale. If she were a normal plant specimen I would rush her to the light, sickly as she seems. I cannot wait too long, but I must use any available time to understand her interior development, before we unleash the full power of the sun upon her sheltered leaves.

Using tests copied from family doctors, I have determined that her nervous system is profoundly rooted and connected. I am only playing at being a doctor, but at this stage I am the only botanical physician of the only botanical patient. Part of me wishes I could perform more comprehensive experiments, but as CHLOE is so precious to science and myself we must proceed with a general ethic of non-invasiveness. So, a gentle tap on the knee with a soft mallet produces an instinctive jerk across her whole leg, showing the interconnectedness of the various plant and fungal systems. Holding her hand causes her to reciprocate. I cannot truly consider this to be communication without more evidence, although it gives me cause for giddy hope that consciousness is developing in the infested heart-brain.

So what of the articles which define consciousness? She is reactive and stores information—at least in her ability to copy my gestures on her palm. This memory is exceedingly short-term, a small leap from the Venus flytrap's ability to 'remember' one disturbance of its sensitive feeler, so that only a second disturbance will trigger the trap. It has to remember for a short time that the trap has been *triggered, and in a sense it 'counts' to two.* CHLOE *can remember a pattern of movement in my hand and replicate it herself, although so far there is no evidence that she has remembered it long enough to initiate the communication. Thus I conclude that she has too little sophistication on article two (memory) to allow a leap to article three (self-awareness).*

*Simon hasn't been down to visit* CHLOE *recently. He hasn't even been down to work—I think he abhors the presence of this child. Perhaps she is an abomination in his eyes. I cannot extract from him the nature of his aversion. For the good of both of them—the sunless sprout and the displaced mole—their locations must be reversed. I will take* CHLOE *upstairs to begin lit development in my workshop in the west wing. A strong dose of sunlight on her leaves will encourage a physical flourishing, which might force the fungal brain to adapt. I just hope the substrate will survive the balmy temperatures above ground without breaking down irrevocably. Simon will also be able to regain his natural habitat, the cool darkness of his aesthetical morgue. I have enjoyed my time in his domain, but I am happy to relinquish it to its rightful occupant.*

*I care for Simon in such a way that I would never want him to come to harm—the protective instinct of the family unit. I see now that my feelings for* CHLOE *are similar. How easily this creature becomes a member of our pack. I must guard myself against this feeling of familial affection—she remains an unpredictable experiment. Sometimes, while I am holding her hand and stroking her ivy-hair, I imagine her turning to me and requesting a bedtime song. I sing to her and she dozes. "Goodnight,* CHLOE*," I seem to whisper. "Goodnight, Father."*

Simon turned the shower off and emerged with some difficulty, given that he had to step around various jungle creepers and duck under the vines. Showering along with half the Amazon was one of those little costs of living with Gregor. Up here in the east wing, there were plants in every nook and cranny. Half-blinded by his long wet fringe, Simon fumbled past a *Monstera*, reaching for a towel.

Normally Simon would have some respite from the floral kingdom when he spent his days in the dusty, cool basement, where nothing grew, nothing changed, and all his taxidermy pieces remained in perfect stasis.

But now that *thing* of Gregor's was festering down there— bulging, spasming. Simon had not ventured to his sanctum since its hand gripped Gregor's. He could not even entertain the idea. But now he was trapped in the glass upperworld while his partner blocked off the down-below with his ghastly experiment. Simon shook away the frightful memory and dried his face on the towel.

Looking up, he jumped to see Gregor in the archway of the bathroom. He was blowing gently on an over-full coffee mug, respectfully, or awkwardly, averting his eyes. Simon covered himself with as many towels as he could muster.

"In God's name, Gregor."

The botanist took a sip, presumably his first of the day, and sucked the froth from his bristles. "It's time for CHLOE to be moved. She desperately needs the light. And I need... your help."

Simon, of course, wanted nothing more than to be rid of the body and the botanist in his basement. But he had no desire to see the dead girl again, much less to move her, and still less to help Gregor in any way while they were in the middle of a tiff. Simon's frantic mental calculations expressed themselves physically as a complete *lack* of movement. Eventually, the lure of the crypt won out over his own stubbornness.

"Maybe after I have dressed. And breakfasted, of course."

"Please, Simon. We have to get CHLOE up to the west wing before Miss Finch arrives. She must never see the substrate."

Horror at the thought of Jennifer coming face-to-mossy-face with her deceased best friend brought a throb to Simon's temple.

"Gregor, leave me be. I want nothing more to do with this."

"Simon, you're being thoroughly unreasonable."

"I stand here before you, wet and tired, wearing nothing but a towel, and you are asking me to move a cadaver. I am not the one being unreasonable here."

"You'll have your basement back."

A sullen drip fell from Simon's wet black fringe.

"That is the one reason—the only reason—I will help you with this."

They both nodded curtly.

"Let me get dressed," Simon continued, "and have *something* to eat at least. Then we shall get this done."

"I'll put some toast on." Gregor almost smiled, catching Simon's eye for the briefest of moments. "You'll need some toast."

Coffee and toast was elaborated upon with a nice pot of tea. Politeness forbade them to keep absolute silence, even Simon wasn't that petty, but the awkward density between them left little room for expression. When two people feel quite differently and share their thoughts, their similarities outshine their differences. When two stubborn gentlemen differ in silence, their differences loom monstrous in their imaginations. After the pot had been refilled and drained once more, and they had run out of idle things to say, Simon and Gregor set about the task in hand.

CHLOE's various stalks were pale and leggy. She had grown upwards from the table, which gave her the impression of a movement-smudged daguerreotype. They rolled her onto her side to slide a sackcloth underneath—her back was riddled with rhizomes like a root-bound potted plant. She undulated softly, as if she were a reef caressed by a South Sea tide.

Having wrapped her in burlap they tried to lift her from either end, but her tissues were too loose and she wriggled in apparent discomfort, so they were obliged to cradle her awkwardly up the stone steps, past the boiler and out into the bright central atrium.

"Good morning, Mr Sandys, Mr Rievaulx."

The men jumped and dropped their precious cargo. Gregor nearly uttered a blasphemy, which he saved at the last minute.

"Jee—ennifer Finch. There you are! You made me drop my, my—"

"—garden waste." Simon straightened his shirt cuffs.

"Yes, thank you, Simon. My *garden waste*. But, Miss Finch, you're here early, what?"

"Actually, sir, I'm a little late. It's a quarter past the hour. I'm very sorry, sir."

"Don't you fret about that now," said Gregor in a great show of insufferable largesse, though his eyes were unnaturally wide. "How about you make a start with the east wing and I'll get this *garden waste* safely back in the western one."

Gregor lifted the sack-shrouded corpse onto his shoulder, trying to ease it gently and rest it on its back-roots, though it twisted disconcertingly. With a pointed look back at his partner, the botanist disappeared into his laboratory.

Simon motioned for Miss Finch to stay a moment. He examined the bright yellow wildflowers secured to a single thick braid in the girl's hair. Grave flowers—as good as. The pit dropped out of his stomach. What they had done to Jennifer in her grief was truly ghastly.

"Was there something you needed from me, Mr Rievaulx?" Jennifer near whispered and shrank away from Simon.

Perhaps his hand had lingered too long by her braided hair. Or perhaps, being rather tall, he had loomed over her. He had this effect on people, of making people uncomfortable, and hated himself for it. But he could never tell until it was too late that he was comporting himself inappropriately. He took a long-legged step away from her.

"I suppose," said Jennifer, fiddling with her fingers, "if Mr Sandys is removing garden waste from the basement, his work down there has come to an end?"

It was Simon's turn to recoil.

"How do you…"

"Just with him being down there all the time and you being up here. World went topsy-turvy for a fortnight, eh?"

Ah—the broad smile, even as Jennifer fumbled awkwardly with her hands. Her chatter amounted to *small talk*. He had learned that people perform this when they are nervous. Simon displayed his teeth. He had learned that people like it when you do that.

"Topsy-turvy indeed it was, but no more! I have a feeling that everything is going to be rightside-up from now on. And everyone shall be in their proper place."

*Except Constance.* Simon winced.

Just then, Gregor emerged once more from his laboratory, wiping his hands on a rag.

"Yes, thank you, Miss Finch," he said. "The east wing, if you please."

Simon stayed her with a firm gesture. "Miss Finch and I were having *a conversation*."

"Were you now?" Gregor purred, his 'r' rolling dangerously. "Simon, please come and take a look at the… garden waste."

"I think that's rather your domain, don't you, Gregor?"

They both looked at Jennifer, who was caught between them like a badminton umpire—Gregor with incredulity, Simon with pride at his little joke. Miss Finch clearly hadn't the foggiest. Gregor approached the gangly taxidermist and craned to whisper harshly in his ear, sending intolerable sensations through Simon's spine.

"Some of CHLOE's sutures have come undone in transit. You might want to take a look at her."

Gregor and Simon were almost cheek-to-cheek.

"You might want to learn how to sew."

Simon had done it now. The sky had fallen and the ground had shifted irrevocably. There was no outward sign, of course. Neither party could admit to either pain or satisfaction in front of Miss Finch. Gregor withdrew from him, blinking and lost in thought.

But Simon had one further, spiteful impulse.

"Why yes, I was just speaking with Miss Finch," he began, unnaturally loudly, "admiring her beautiful braids. Graced with buttercups, I assume?"

"Kingcups, sir." She touched her petalled hair.

"And where did you find them?"

"Out by the Wycombe Road. Not far from… the twisted hazel." She looked at the floor.

"By the twisted hazel! Yes, I think I know the spot. Charming flowers—charming girl. Since it was I who hired you, against the botanist's wishes, I reserve the right to make a small addition to your duties. I would like to officially rescind my interdiction on your access to my workshop." Seeing her frown he rephrased himself. "I am letting you go into the basement whenever you like. It could do with a dusting every now and then, nothing more. I keep the actual station spick and span myself."

"Why, why thank you, sir," she said, nodding furiously, "it shall be a wonder to see your basement. For the first time, I mean. I'll get to dusting it after lunch."

She nodded some more, causing a gentle fall of yellow blossom, before hurriedly tying her apron and bustling off to the east wing. Simon swung his cheekbones round to glare at Gregor, who was still standing with a hand-rag at the entrance to his laboratory.

Some couples can finish each other's sentences. Some couples can share their innermost thoughts without fear of reprisals. Some couples know what each other needs without even asking. Simon and Gregor were not quite like any of these. They had the uncanny ability to know how to hurt each other without lifting a finger. Simon's gesture had thrown down a gauntlet. He had declared that CHLOE was not his concern, but also that Jennifer *was* above all else. It was as if he and Gregor were medieval princesses, favouring rival knights with their handkerchiefs. Jennifer and CHLOE were now in direct competition, although they didn't know of each other's existence; one sponsored by Simon, the other by Gregor.

Gregor clenched his jaw and withdrew into his laboratory. Simon retreated to his basement lair. He wandered around, reacquainting himself with the pieces on display, stroking the dark wood surfaces, breathing in the cool, fetid air. It felt good to have his own space again, and with it a touch of autonomy in the ménage. Now he wasn't Gregor's assistant any longer.

On the central workbench, usually supernaturally clean, there was a layer of potting soil and occasional smears of moss emulsion. Simon felt the earth and moss between his thumb and forefinger. CHLOE, of course, was the price of his outburst. He couldn't help seeing the pile of plants as something infinitely more precious, and more personal. But no—it was foolish to project a relationship onto what was ultimately a rotting corpse. Gregor could have her, as far as he cared. He had plenty of other aestheticised cadavers to please him in his taxidermy collection. Plus he had Jennifer, who unlike CHLOE had the virtue of being unequivocally sentient.

Simon rooted around in his cold storage. He wasn't of a mind to break his rut with a simple rabbit. He pulled out the whole chest of a sheep—a discarded anatomical project. He cracked open the ribs and shimmied the lungs out, before making delicate tapered slices across the main arteries and veins of the heart, to remove it in one piece. He held the frosty organ in his hands to thaw it and blew on it gently. Then, following the same procedure he used with the brain and the digestive tract before, he suspended it in a glass with preserving fluid. He placed the heart in his dark wood cabinet with the other specimen-like pieces. What made them art—he wondered— rather than scientific works? His sheer will as creator was one thing, but since he also made up one hundred per cent of the audience he had complete control over their reception. These organs were *art*. That uncomfortable feeling for CHLOE... affection? It would no longer clash against his distaste. Now that there was a heart in the curio cabinet, his own wouldn't betray him any more.

Gregor stormed into his garden laboratory. How dare Simon play power games with something so serious? CHLOE would be Gregor's greatest achievement, and now Simon was declaring that he wanted nothing to do with her. Heartless—that's what that was. Cynical. Let him have Jennifer—the girl didn't know her heucheras from her hellebores. CHLOE contained multitudes within her and was entirely mutable at his hand.

Gregor had a long list of people who inspired him to be the best that he could be out of sheer spite: his teachers; his late father, forever frozen as the disapproving parent of a teenaged boy; his rival, the detestably dashing Julian Mallory; and the whole damned Royal Horticultural Society. Now he added Simon to the list of people who did not believe in him. The joke was on all of them since every individual's disbelief made Gregor's self-belief that much stronger.

"It's just you and me now, child," he whispered. "You're going to make me very proud."

She was calm now at least, compared to her fulsome flailing during that first night. She flexed and relaxed constantly, rippling with sinuous movement. Quite a few of her overgrown fronds had snapped and now dangled helplessly. Every part of her except the right arm, damaged at the shoulder, danced like a curtain in the breeze. Her squirming made the transport awkward from dungeon to glasshouse, but from her pleasurable shivers now Gregor could tell she was thrilled with the sunlight.

He stroked her shoulder, luscious and verdant and active to his touch. Through a gap in the leaves, he saw the tear in the sutures—the connection between substrate and *motorius* plant had come loose. Damn it—Simon should be the one doing this. He was so much better than Gregor at needlework. There was no use thinking like that now, though. As poor as his sewing skills were, Gregor was now the only person available for the operation, so he surged himself up with a sharp inhale and set about repairing the cadaver's plant-shoulder.

It was a botch job which bore little resemblance to the fine work on the other shoulder, but it had clearly worked because CHLOE's right arm soon joined the left in its pulsating dance. However, the movement of the right arm was elbow-led, not unlike an impish child imitating a chicken. On closer inspection, CHLOE's right hand was fused to her hip. The sensitive *Mimosa* of her hand and the tight vines of her waist had intertwined and were unwilling to part. Gregor tried to tease them apart gently, then a little harder. Without intending to, he broke a small number of tactile leaves clean off from their stalks by her fingertips, which liberated the hand from its snare.

Gregor was horrified. He had pruned plants many times before, pruned them back hard. But this was entirely different; he felt as if he had ripped his own child's fingernails out. He scanned her face for signs of pain, forgetting that to the mycelium the face was just another surface for vicarious photosynthesis. CHLOE seemed unaffected by the accidental deforestation, so he resolved himself to begin her pruning. Those shoots which were long and sickly and those leaves which were blighted by lack of sun were soon removed. With a practised hand he trimmed the weakest parts of her, from bushy head to root-bound toe. She did not recoil from his cutters, except for the gentle undulation of her hypnotic dance.

# TWELVE

Jenny bit her lip as she sidled down the stairs after Mr Rievaulx. She would have to think fast and persuade him that she had never seen the inside of his taxidermy workshop. She had a reputation for brutal honesty in the village, but in reality she was just a terrible liar, meaning that there was no point in even attempting to tell a mistruth. She would summon all her faculties to give the impression that she was seeing all his pieces for the first time. An *ooh* and an *aah* would suffice—and the appreciation wouldn't be a lie. And if she saw that strange slime once more...

She had often thought about the greenish blob sitting in a glass dish. She daydreamed about stroking the goop and it shivering in gratitude. She imagined pressing her cheek to it, even allowing a tendril to fall into her mouth. She imagined wearing it as a cape, then as a duvet, then a cocoon...

"...to make sure that the climate is carefully controlled," Mr Rievaulx droned. Jenny snapped to attention. They were standing in the middle of the basement room already. Her mind had wandered, as it always did when she thought of the shiny squidge. "It slows the rate of decay, you see."

Jenny had missed the start of his tour, but ventured a nod, which appeared to be the correct response. Mr Rievaulx gestured to the sideboard which carried his prized yet unsold specimens. Jenny made a show of inspecting the hamster-bishop.

"This figure is my representation of the Bishop of Oxford, Samuel Wilberforce," said Mr Rievaulx, "famous, of course, for debating Thomas Henry Huxley on the matter of Darwin's theory of evolution."

"Of course," Jenny said, nodding sagely, "Darwin's theory. Is the hamster for or against?"

"Oh, most certainly against." Mr Rievaulx chuckled. "Soapy Sam asked Huxley if it was his grandfather or grandmother who was descended from monkeys. He is one of those people who see fit to mock you with their wilful ignorance."

"Did he appreciate the likeness you made for him?"

"My gift was declined by the bishopric. Blasphemous, I suppose. I thought it amusing."

Jennifer smiled and looked at the little rodent with fresh eyes. Its balled fist of determination seemed foolish now. She allowed her own fist to squeeze—she was doing great at this deception.

"This next piece was done on the request of a soon-to-be-married couple. You see, the bride—"

"You mean this is based on a real couple?" Jenny blurted, despite herself. "Oh, Mr Rievaulx, they look so happy together! And the dress—is it based on her actual one?"

"Yes, yes, the dress is a miniature reproduction of the bridal gown. It's actually made from scraps of the real one, because—"

"It's just perfect! The little darling thing wearing her mistress's gown!" Jenny was gushing, partly with genuine ardour, but partly exaggerated for Mr Rievaulx's benefit. She was giddy on the charade, and on the kitty's optimistic smile.

"If you'll permit me, Jennifer," said Mr Rievaulx, his tone severe. "The outfit is made from scraps because the real thing was never worn. The groom received a wedding present from the bride's brother—a fine horse. He was thrown from the beast days before the wedding and never recovered. I returned the fee and kept the piece. I assume she wouldn't have wanted it around."

Jenny's mouth was slack and her guts had frozen over. She had overplayed her interest in the piece and now seemed incredibly boorish. She looked into the cat-bride's glassy eyes as she pondered her next move. The cat did seem thoroughly elated.

*Oh, puss-puss. Oh, Jennifer.*

"She is a rather fine specimen, though," Mr Rievaulx whispered, grinning, "don't you think?"

"Oh yes, but the poor thing lost her groom!"

"It is a tragedy to lose one's love and continue to live. But these lucky felines are both quite dead. She has her fellow right by her side and will do forever."

Jenny sniffed a little, rubbed her face on her apron and shook herself. She might just have survived detection once more. She steadied herself by the kitten wedding, poking her own sternum to remind herself to breathe. Mr Rievaulx drifted over to the third tableau, the funeral scene with the schoolmaster raven and the owl in riding gear.

"And this is my most complex scene to date," he said. "*The Death of Innocence.*"

"Oh, with the dove?"

Jenny knew she had really stuffed it up this time. Her chin stuck tight to her sternum and her freckled cheeks flushed pink.

"How could you see the dove from over there," Mr Rievaulx asked, "given that it is at the bottom of the grave?" His lips were barely moving. Neither of them knew where to look.

"No, no, I can see," she professed, "innocence, isn't it. The dove."

"But—"

"Yep, top-notch work that, sir." She mechanically peered over the grave in a great show of active looking. "Quite dead-seeming. I mean, what artistry! You really do believe the dove was alive, but now is dead."

"It was. It is."

"Genius. Beyond compare." Jenny swung her fist in a gentlemanly gesture. "But tell me, sir—do you have any pieces which aren't made of animals?"

"How do you mean?"

"Anything with, say, plants? Or lichen, or…"

Mr Rievaulx's brow gained a half-dozen more furrows. Jenny was dancing on the edge of acceptability, but she needed to see the beauteous slime again, if only to prove to herself that she hadn't dreamed it last time in the crypt. To stroke it once more, to take it between her thumb and forefinger…

"I can't imagine such a thing," he said finally. "It sounds like something frightful Mr Sandys might knock up."

"I shall ask him about it, then."

"Don't—" Simon clamped his jaw shut. Perhaps he caught himself about to utter something emotionally truthful and thought better of it. He leaned on the sideboard as if to support himself.

"Is everything well, Mr Rievaulx?"

"Business is running smoothly. Grimfern Botanical Garden is in order. Peace reigns in the glass forest."

"No, *you*, sir. And maybe Mr Sandys. How are things? You know what I mean." Jenny really wanted to touch his elbow but refrained.

"I do not."

"Blimey, sir. You think you're operating on some invisible plane of existence! You think us normal folk don't understand the unspoken energies of things. Well, sir, I'm afraid you're quite wrong. We ordinary people have an uncanny sense for when things are tense, for when important things are unsaid. And that's why—Lord preserve me—I'm speaking my mind now. Please harken to me now, Mr Rievaulx, I know when you're angry at Mr Sandys. Perhaps I know better than you do."

There, she'd said it, it was out there now. She did hate all of the insinuations and second-guessing that went on between her masters. Quite honestly she hated how it made her feel herself, caught between. She scanned Mr Rievaulx's face for signs of a reaction, but there were none. After a while he looked up and saw her, as if the last few minutes of conversation had never happened.

"One last thing," he said, with an eerie brightness, "I want you to have this."

Building up suspense like a morbid ringmaster, he revealed his present: a taxidermy squirrel in a pretty yellow dress, not unlike the one Jenny had worn when she first came to Grimfern. He presented it to her as if it were some holy relic. She winced slightly, trying not to let her disgust read on her face. The piece was much heavier than she expected—it nearly dragged her down. It was unnaturally rigid, and its dusty smell reminded her of the few times she had attended church. But the tail—oh, the fur on the tail was incredibly soft.

"And look—tiny flowers in her hair. Heuchera, are they?"

"Oh yes, a dry and dainty spray. And there's heather, and gorse, and that one there is—"

"I don't know what to say, this is too kind, Mr Rievaulx. This is too, too much—"

"Nonsense. Some people think of squirrels as rodents. I think they're perfectly charming. This one has such maddeningly auburn curls, it reminded me at once of you! I'm sure you won't mind me saying: a gift like this trumps a couple of weeds that Gregor could give you, I'd wager!"

Jennifer thought of the living blooms in the greenhouse above and compared them with the dead squirrel and dried flowers in her hands.

"Thank you. But regarding our previous conversation about Mr Sandys: don't you think you two—"

"Well now," he said loudly, "once you're done dusting in here you can clean the central workstation, which seems to have gathered some soil. That is all, Miss Finch." With that he whisked out of the basement.

Jennifer stood dumbfounded, staring deeply into the squirrel-Jenny's glassy eyes. She may have looked like her human counterpart once, but now the poor creature was stiff and unmoving. Nailed to its plank, garlanded with grave flowers… Jenny knew Mr Rievaulx meant well with his gift, but she couldn't help interpreting it as a threat, or at least an ill omen.

She took up a little coping saw from the workbench and separated the squirrel from its mahogany pedestal. Under a conker tree, a little out of sight from the greenhouse, Jenny dug a little hole and interred her effigy. The dark wood panel served as a coffin lid, and she covered the grave with dusty earth and a cross of twigs. Nobody should lie in an unmarked grave.

# Thirteen

The summer wore on, and an overly generous sun continued to scorch the earth. The greenhouse boilers hadn't been lit since May, yet the temperature was such that Gregor's tropical specimens were thriving while his alpine displays withered. Even the indigenous plant life was struggling in this unnatural summer—leaves were yellowed and petals were brown. The rolling, landscaped grounds of Grimfern Estate were dusty and dry. All the groundskeepers could do was stand about and tut. The lawns were merely hay. Gregor was obliged to turn off the rustic-style artificial beck, and he used a long hose and hand pump to draw water from the lower reservoir to slake his parched flowers.

Once he had completed his rounds, Gregor used the hand pump hose to fill his elegant long-spouted watering can and his copper spray pump. These special utensils were reserved for scientific specimens, and for now that meant they were reserved for use on Chloe.

She was lying in state at the very centre of his laboratory glasshouse, covered with a light cotton canopy to protect her from the vicious sun, as well as from prying eyes. Even under the canopy she was burgeoning from the stream of morning-time sunlight in the west wing. Gregor had become used to pruning her excessive growth, lest her limbs fuse with the twisting of fronds. The growth of plants, most notably ivies, has a disconcertingly exploratory quality. If there is a small nook in a wall, some weed will find it to cling to. The plant kingdom's will to life is at least equal to our own.

Gregor used his long-spouted watering can to send bolts of water deep into the substrate—which now had the appearance of mossy soil held together by fine roots. Distressingly, a fair amount of the water cascaded right through her and ran in rivulets off the workbench. This indicated that the substrate was compacted.

From a tool drawer, Gregor withdrew a pair of chopsticks—gaudy enamel chinoiserie he had picked up in a Soho emporium—and set about poking her all over, loosening her roots. Like with the pruning, CHLOE showed no sign of displeasure at the procedure. She wriggled slightly, but only like a cat when it deigns to be petted. Gregor thought of doting mothers playfully teasing their infants by pulling at their feet or pinching their cheeks. Instinctively checking that Simon wasn't nearby, he formed words with his mouth but did not dare voice them: *Coo-coo, there you go, coochie-coo!* Gregor, ever the rationalist, was not accustomed to talking to his plants. But he was beginning to entertain the idea they might be up for a chat.

After the loosening, he found she was able to hold much more water. Finally he took the hand-pump spray can and set the nozzle to a fine mist. This would keep her foliage damp and clear of debris. To start off, he sprayed a thin cloud into the air above her. Her thirsty xylem sensed the moisture and her chest heaved towards the cloud. Another spritz, another yearning reaction. Gregor smiled and sprayed the entire space under the canopy with fine mist—CHLOE was enthralled. The rain man called forth clouds, and the earth child thrilled and danced.

Faster he spritzed and wilder she danced—he was beginning to enjoy himself. Gregor's waistcoat was quite damp. Water ran from his hair down the side of his jaw. He was laughing—laughing more heartily than he had in years. CHLOE jiggled and flailed, catching the airborne dew. She reached out, then shivered, then shook her head, and then—

Then she opened her eyes.

The dance immediately ceased. Gregor just stood there sopping wet, his spritzer digging into the palm of his hand. CHLOE's eyes were wide open, staring straight ahead. Neither she nor her maker took a breath. The final cloud of water droplets sank silently to the workbench.

Gregor felt as if invisible thread were holding him upright in fear. His rational faculties were overpowered by the repeating thought: *this is impossible*. That phrase attacked him from every angle, raiding his brain. Constance had been dead now for many weeks. Plants and fungi—even very clever ones like the Sumatran mycelium—did not know how to operate human eyes.

A new thought allowed Gregor's rationality to return: just because her eyes were open did not mean that she could necessarily 'see'. The plant system may have opened her eyelids whilst exploring the mechanical properties of its host. But then—why did she instantly stop dancing?

Taking care not to brush against any of her sensitive leaves, Gregor leaned over her face to peer directly into her eyeballs. Simon had removed the lenses which had clouded after death and replaced them with thin glass. He had then injected the eyeballs with preserving fluid to slow the decaying process. Now, examining the insides of the optical chambers, Gregor found them strangely discoloured. He scrambled around his laboratory for a candle, found one and lit it, then prepared himself to once again enter the linen canopy. Holding the candle towards her eyes, he saw her retinas light up—a flickering but bright algal green.

On a hunch, he moved the candle to the side of her head. Slowly, CHLOE moved her head so that her green-eyed stare was once more fixed on the light source. Gregor could hear her disused neck bones creak, twisting through wet soil. He moved the candle to the other side and she tracked it, unblinking. He set the candle down and ran his fingers through his hair.

Through the glass and arbours of the greenhouse, Gregor heard music. Simon was playing the piano in the atrium—the muffled sounds of early Beethoven on the ill-tempered grand. It was a rare event, Simon's playing. Unlike Gregor, whose music was wild, expressive and somewhat slapdash, Simon's playing was an exercise in precision and elegance. Scalic passages were nimbly executed and tempo was metrically perfect. What was lacking was soul—perfection tends not to induce an emotional response. And it was certainly not to Gregor's taste. Gregor would prefer a few improvised passages, or a sudden harmonic detour. He much preferred Beethoven's work *after* all the syphilis.

The smell of burning broke his musical reverie. CHLOE had grown fixated on the candle and reached out to touch it, singeing her fingertip *Mimosa* in the process. Gregor pulled her hand from the candle, fiddled with his spritzer and doused the burned digits with a few sprays. It wasn't clear if CHLOE could truly feel the flame or its effects on her body, but it was reasonable to conclude that she could in fact see it. How she could do that though was anybody's guess. He blew the candle out with a studious huff.

CHLOE's countenance was grim—wide-eyed as if in fear or fascination, unblinking as if deceased. Whose eyes were these that thirsted for light? CHLOE's perhaps, since the algal growth on the retina surely used photosynthesis for some rudimentary sight. But Gregor couldn't shake the fear that Constance had re-emerged from the root-bound soil, asserting ownership of her body. Which was preposterous, of course. But Gregor still felt it.

Simon's perfunctory performance ended on a perfect cadence. Gregor needed to tell him of this latest optical development, but Simon was being such an obstinate, dour little... *well*. Simon was being Simon. Perhaps enough had changed that the senseless impasse between them could be broken? Gregor was certain of this, so stroked CHLOE's ivy-hair and kissed her gently on the forehead. Some instinct caused her to close her eyelids and settle into calm repose. Gregor squelched in his wet clothes to find Simon at the piano.

Jenny finished her dusting as she always did, now that Mr Rievaulx had allowed her into his work-basement. She spread her elbows wide on the side counter, resting her chin in her hands. This way she could look the kitten-bride in the face directly on her level; eye to glassy eye. Poor thing didn't have a proper funeral like the squirrel-Jenny did. The stuffed cat continued on with her eternal wedding. She had not changed at all in the few weeks they had known each other, but Jenny now knew so much about her. So what if it was all her own personal fiction? She had a deep appreciation for the kitten's short life and interminable death.

In the silence of her own stillness, Jenny could hear the congregation muttering, waiting for Kitty's entry to the church. Grandfather Kitty would be giving her away, since her father had perished at sea on a clipper from India. The groom was doing a good job of seeming calm, but Jenny could tell from his too-frequent tongue-cleaning that he was anxious to get the ceremony started. A hush fell upon the crowd. A hundred heads twisted to ogle the figure in white, supporting the old grandfather tomcat in top hat and tails. They began to make their way down the aisle, when a horse—ginormous relative to this cathedral made for cats—crashed through the stained-glass window above the altar. The hamster-vicar, with uncanny instinct for self-preservation, screwed himself up into a ball and rolled behind the pulpit. The groom, however, displayed a valiant streak and brandished his walking stick at the equine aggressor. The stallion whinnied demonically, bringing down recently repaired tiles and arches from the church roof, reared and *stamped, stamped*. Blood ran down the steps of the apse, and stained the kitty's white dress…

Jenny became aware of music—real music—floating on the air. Her eyes focused back onto her actual surroundings—the wedding scene was once more physical and unmoving in front of her. Reality was a pale imitation of her fantasy. The music was coming from the piano in the bright greenhouse, far above the workshop, which felt like it was in the bowels of the earth. Jenny was used to Mr Sandys playing the piano in his peculiarly stormy manner. She didn't know much about music, but she could tell that the measured and soothing strains upstairs were not being played by Mr Sandys, leaving Mr Rievaulx as the only suspect. His music was precise and calm—*brown*, somehow. Jenny repolished the sideboard where she had been leaning and made her way up to hear Mr Rievaulx's performance.

It was another hot day inside the Grimfern greenhouse. Jenny was glad she had spent the most sweltering hours deep underground, underneath even the boilers and pipes, in Mr Rievaulx's cool, earthy sanctum. Up here under the glass roof Jennifer could see the air bending. She could hear the heat as pressure on her eardrums. She could feel condensation brushing onto her cheeks from the waxy leaves and fronds of the garden. Drawing closer to the piano, Mr Rievaulx's music seemed all the more exquisite for the strange echoes of the crystal rafters. The cut-glass brilliance of the notes fluttered around the room like a clutch of nightingales.

Jennifer dallied by a glistening begonia, lost in the murmuration of the melodies, when a tramping on the gravel made her start. It was Mr Sandys, no doubt—rushing towards Mr Rievaulx from his laboratory. She hadn't spoken to the great botanist since his argument with Mr Rievaulx, so she slunk behind a Spanish moss and hid like a startled faun.

Mr Sandys stamped to a halt by the grand piano, standing with one hand on its side as if he were about to deliver a blustery aria. He mumbled a few terse words which Jenny did not catch.

*Here we go.*

They would be arguing about her again—she couldn't take it. If she didn't need this job so badly she'd quit to avoid feeling the guilt. She used one finger to widen a gap in the mossy drape, peeping through to watch the fray. Mr Rievaulx did not react to Mr Sandys' utterance and continued with the sinuous strands of a particularly tricky development section.

Some more pained words from Mr Sandys, some more smug Classical music from Mr Rievaulx. Eventually Gregor's good grace eluded him and he turned away with a violent swish.

"Do you not understand what this means?"

Mr Rievaulx kept playing his elegant piece, but it was quiet and sad. He was seeing it through for the sake of completeness, even though his heart mustn't have been in it. It seemed Simon always had to defend Jenny to Mr Sandys. Mr Rievaulx was a strange old stick but she was grateful for his continued commitment to her. He polished off his lacklustre performance and held the silence.

Mr Sandys broke it with a harsh whisper, which Jenny still couldn't hear. It must be really bad this time, but she couldn't think of anything she'd done which would make Mr Sandys this angry. Perhaps the build-up of pressure from Mr Rievaulx's silence, and the incredible heat, had simply come to a head. If it was all going to come out now, she wanted to be around to hear it. She edged through the hanging moss, crept down along a bristling hedge, and took up a new hiding spot behind a potted plant which seemed to be made of green knives. Through the pointed, waxy leaves she could see the gentlemen's lips, and she could catch the majority of their speech. Mr Sandys was still in his apron and gloves. Mr Rievaulx was staring with uncommon intensity at the sheet music in front of him, his hands folded in his lap. He still hadn't said a word.

"She's *wonderful*, Simon. I wish that you could see that."

Jenny was taken aback. This was not how she expected their argument to play out. Usually the boys would spar without landing a direct hit, battling through inference and implication. What Mr Sandys had just said was direct—and what's more seemed to be in Jenny's favour. After all, there were no other 'she's in Grimfern. Unless he was referring to Florence, the grey mare? But surely the two gentlemen's affection for that horse was beyond doubt. Had Mr Sandys changed his mind about his housemaid?

"She's more alive than we'd ever imagined."

Jennifer beamed behind her knife-plant. This was so true—she was overjoyed to be recognised as a living, passionate person, not the faceless hedge-peasant who quietly toiled out of sight.

"No, Gregor."

Jenny frowned and widened her view through the potted plant's spiky leaves. She could see Mr Rievaulx's jaw muscle clenching and unclenching.

"She is precisely as alive as we have discussed. Of course she is alive, everything living is alive—and what of it? She doesn't *hope*, she doesn't *desire*, she doesn't know right from wrong for goodness' sake. She should just exist, not requiring any special attention from us. She's a function of the house, no more."

Jenny's lightly freckled cheeks were flushed red. Her eyes were hot. She gripped the knife-plant's stone pot, feeling its weight to keep her grounded. How could Mr Rievaulx betray her like this? Luckily for Jenny, Mr Sandys exploded on her behalf.

"How dare you! You know full well *what she is!*"

Gregor was tearing around the piano, waving wildly. His outburst was uncontrolled and often muttered, but always accompanied by spittle. Like a bank of heavy cloud descending from the Highlands, his mother's influence came out in his accent—his vowels grew wonky and his 'r's began to roll with Caledonian thunder.

"—into our very home! Into your workshop! And yet you *refuse* to take her into your heart. I thought—I thought she could be our *daughter*."

Mr Rievaulx had been sitting passively, still observing the

book of sonatas lying open on the piano. There was no doubt that he was taking in all of Gregor's ravings, but also was there no outward sign of his opinion on them. That is, until he took in a deep sniff of air through flared nostrils, his eyes suddenly furious and bright—

"She is no child of mine!" Mr Rievaulx took his fist and brought it down roundly on the body of the mildewed grand. Its poorly dampened strings rang out like mad church bells, buzzing around the bizarre roof, bouncing back and forth off panes of indifferent glass.

"She is not like us, Gregor. She is a creature of the dirt!"

Mr Sandys was clearly chastened by the outburst—it was a rare occasion that Mr Rievaulx showed any emotion stronger than ennui. Jennifer, however, was incensed. She had given her life and her labour to these gentlemen for two months, thinking she could dwell in this secret garden—an escape from the tattle of the village. But now she saw that she could never truly belong in this place, no matter what platitudes the men had given her. Because she was deemed a race apart. Less than them, those lofty men. Yet she knew in her heart that her strange yearnings made her belong here, in the queer forest of botanical oddities and human misfits. It hurt so much to be pushed away even from such a special sanctuary.

"I have one further point to make," said Mr Rievaulx, now speaking as delicately as ever, pausing for extreme clarity, "and it is this. We need to protect ourselves from her, Gregor. We need to protect our house, our work, and our very souls from infection with feeling for the sub-human."

"What the bloody hell did you just call me?" Jennifer cried, standing up with such force that the green knife-plant toppled. Its stone pot cracked and the floor was strewn with soil. Mr Rievaulx jumped to his feet and both men held their hands in front of the other. It was a very British standoff. For a moment Jenny's anger faltered, but she summoned it back soon enough.

"There is no part of me," she continued, face wet with tears and saliva, "not one part of me, that is less than human. I am human *and more*, sirs. These blistered hands are honest. These knees are tired but strong. There's never a false word passes through my mouth and never an ill wish in my heart. So yes, I am a creature of the dirt, a daughter of the heath and twisted briar. And I may be less than you in standing, gentlemen, but I am never 'less-than'. My name is Jennifer Finch and I *feel things*—and I am alive!"

The two men dropped their mutually protective pose. They shared a glance, but just barely.

"Jennifer," said Mr Rievaulx, "please believe me. Both of us hold you in the highest regard. You are a fine housekeeper, and we appreciate your flexibility and your discretion. We are eternally lucky to have you—and eternally grateful."

"But Mr Sandys resents me," she said, wiping her cheek.

Gregor shifted his weight and looked at his boots. "Miss Finch—Jennifer—I do not resent you. I regret that you have become a pawn in our own petty squabble."

"But still—Mr Rievaulx, you said I was sub-human, not like you, a creature of the dirt? How can you think of me like that?" Her voice was a hoarse whisper.

"We were not speaking of you, Miss Finch," said Simon, taking a step forward, "but of… some other girl."

Mr Sandys glowered at his companion, who winced at his own words.

"What other girl?" asked Jennifer, her words a quiet dagger.

"You—you don't know her. She's from the village. No wait, she's from abroad. Both, I suppose. Mr Sandys knows her from the East Indies."

"And you think she's dangerous?" Jenny squared her shoulders. "I'll keep my eye out for her just in case."

Mr Rievaulx reached out to touch her arm but seemed to think better of it. Instead, he gestured for her to walk with him.

"Yes, thank you, Jennifer. Now, I think that will be all for today. Here's a small advance on your pay. Send my regards to your father."

Jenny held the coins in her palm. They were the only things right now she knew to be real, so she clutched them tight. Mr Rievaulx escorted her all the way to the front door of the greenhouse and waved her off awkwardly. Glancing back at Grimfern, Jenny could still see the taxidermist steadying himself against the ornate glass doorframe, head in his hands.

# FOURTEEN

[Extract from Gregor Sandys' experimental jotter, Thursday 1st August 1889]

*The social context of my experiment has become extremely precarious. Simon is as unpredictable as he is vindictive. It is perhaps fortunate that he no longer wants anything to do with* CHLOE. *He claims she is unthinking, unfeeling—such a hypocrite! It is he who is failing to demonstrate the softer qualities of humanity. And now his feeble prattle leaks information to the housekeeper! Jennifer must not learn anything of* CHLOE, *lest she come closer to seeing the ghost of Constance upon her. But neither can she be sent away, having seen so much of us…*

*My senses are stretched to the limit. Of course I do not believe in ghosts, or even traces of ourselves after death. I am brittle and sensitive though—springing like a frog at the slightest rustle or rattle of the greenhouse.* CHLOE *is no danger to me, as Simon accused. No—it is the outside world which is a danger to the plant-girl. Discovery now would be her undoing. I shall have to close the grounds to all comers. The groundskeepers will have to be let go. Regrettable, but I can't risk their coming into contact with* CHLOE. *It is incumbent upon me to protect her in any way I can.*

*To the science of the matter.* CHLOE's *sight is developing at a prodigious rate. With careful examination, I can see the growth of fantastically detailed patterns in the algae of her retinas. Whilst examining the ocular bloom, we stare into each other's eyes—quite literally in to them—and perhaps some part of ourselves is transferred to the other. Once the sun sets, I tie a silken blindfold over her blossoming face to keep her settled and sedate.*

*Now that* CHLOE *has rudimentary sight, I intend to encourage controlled movement in her, possibly leading to ambulation. In hopeful anticipation of this, I have reinforced her legs with a frame of braided living hazel, planted into her feet. Time will tell if the mycelium will be capable of operating its leafy limbs.*

———

In the haze of late-morning, Jennifer arrived at the gatehouse of the Grimfern Estate. Strangely, all the groundskeepers were sitting by the roadway, slouching about despondently, some with their heads in their hands. Jenny didn't really know any of them to talk to them, much less in times of distress, so she edged by to the gatehouse and whistled her customary greeting to Will. He didn't whistle back. She stuck her head round the door, finding him standing there, scratching the back of his head through his cloth cap.

She whistled her part of the greeting right at him. He turned to her and only shrugged.

"He's let everybody go—Mr Sandys. He's fired the whole ground staff."

Jenny blinked.

"It were just this morning, out of the blue. No word of reason, only like, 'here's two weeks' pay, good luck with your life,' kind of thing."

"But you're alright, right? I mean, you've still got your job?"

"Yeah, but I'm to stay at the gate. No one's ever to enter the grounds now, unless Mr Sandys says special-like. No one goes in, 'cept him, Mr Rievaulx, and…"

"…and me. I don't get it, Will. He's just impossible. I'll see if I can have a word. Not that I have any say in anything, but it might be worth a try."

Will smiled sadly and went to open the great gate for her. One of the former groundsmen, already red-faced from the early sun and an emptied hip flask, stood and jeered at them.

"Here. In't it funny how little madam still trots off to the glasshouse. Her who'll never touch a man from the village still shacks up with the flowerboys up the hill. How strange it is. How *queer.*"

The other men cheered and laughed, some staggering to their feet. Jenny sauntered right over to him, nodding grimly at the taunt.

"It's true, I've never touched a man from the village. Would you say I'm missing out?"

"Yeah, love, you should try touchin' *me* sometime!"

"Y-you shut your mouth, there, you," said Will, unconvincingly. Jenny let the bawdy laughter simmer down.

"Alright, then. Time for you to feel a woman's touch."

She drew her arm back and laid a fist square on the jaw of the lecherous drunkard. He swung around and toppled. Will ran over and bear-hugged Jenny clear off the ground, dragging her away from the braying mob. He dropped her on the Grimfern grounds and closed the gate behind her.

"Hop it, will you?"

"I better had. Thanks, Will." She sped up the driveway to the greenhouse hedge, shaking out her punching hand.

Mr Sandys was still stalking around up there, with a look of wild distraction. Jennifer squared her shoulders and straightened out her dress.

"Mr Sandys, sir. You once told me that on certain matters the correct time to speak is 'out of turn', and that around here I was free to speak my mind."

"I did say that. And I meant it."

"Then let me say now that what you've done is *wrong*. You've let a dozen men go wanting for work, which means wanting for bread. Sure they can be louts and idiots, but they need their jobs to live just as surely as I do. And it makes no sense, the grounds are shrivelling in the heat as it is! Why, Mr Sandys? Why have you fired all those men?"

"If the grounds are shrivelling we have no need of groundskeepers."

Jennifer made no effort to conceal her disdain.

"Oh—don't try and fob me off with that, Mr Sandys. Is it

money? Are you hard up for it? 'Cause if so, you should fire me first. Those men know nothing other than tending lawns. I could find other work somewhere else, I suppose. If I had to."

"You could leave the garden so easily?"

Jenny surprised herself with the answer to this, which caught in her throat.

"It would break my heart."

Mr Sandys fixed her with that inescapable stare of his. "I wouldn't fire you now, Miss Finch. I'd never let you go. As it were. No, no, no. We need you close by—you have become invaluable to us. Plus, you have seen inside my great greenhouse. You know all our little secrets! Well, most of them."

Jenny did feel pride at this, and not a small amount of relief—she had become invested in the crucible of this queer ménage, seeing herself reflected in the many panes of glass. The awkward girl who was no use to anyone in the village could be a pillar of this tiny community. She doubted she would ever chance upon such a place again, if she had to leave.

Mr Sandys' face grew grave once more.

"Only… let me say this to you also. You must be extremely careful around the garden. Watch your step. A summer greenhouse can seem like a sanctuary, but you cannot imagine the dangers. The shadows behind the leaves."

Unsure of what else to do, she nodded. Mr Sandys hurried her under the topiary arch, locking the gate furtively behind them.

[Extract from Gregor Sandys' experimental jotter, Saturday 3rd August 1889]

*Each and every benchmark I set for* CHLOE's *success she surpasses. My pride at this is tinged with unsettling feelings—I hesitate to truly claim 'fear', but something akin to a parent's apprehension at their child's precocious development. The more adventurous she becomes, the less I can control her surroundings, the more danger she might encounter. Not least that silent vulture, Simon… but also his pet, Jennifer. I must look at ways to fortify the laboratory.*

*To elaborate on* CHLOE's *progress—I have encouraged her to sit up on the workbench. The rhizomes emerging from her back will soon have to grow down to her waist like a maiden's long, flowing hair.* CHLOE *takes a keen interest in her surroundings. Such a curious child! Her eyes flit about, absorbing information like other plants absorb sunlight for photosynthesis.*

[Extract from Gregor Sandys' experimental jotter, Tuesday 6th August 1889]

*On entering the laboratory this morning, I found* CHLOE *already sitting up, the roots of her hazel-toes reaching towards the floor. She cocked her head and stared at me with her inquisitive but unsmiling face. I confess she is beautiful. The morning sun graces her plush green cheeks. The ivies of her hair waft of their own accord.*

*It may have been unwise, but I advanced and took her hand. Like a gentleman helping a lady out of her hansom carriage, I encouraged her from the bench to the floor. Her weight lurched forwards and*

*I caught her with my shoulder. Soon she was bearing some of her own weight even as she relied on me for guidance. Together we slow-waltzed around the laboratory until the sun scorched at noon. I placed her gently down on her workbench-bed, covered her with soft linen, and she fell into an exhausted slumber.*

*Am I father to this creature? I am not its master, but I am its protector and teacher... I put her to bed and I check she is watered. Do I hope she is well? Do I want what's best for her? Dash it all—this sweet lack of objectivity will be my undoing. As she sleeps I watch her respiring. A green angel.*

## [Extract from Gregor Sandys' experimental jotter, Wednesday 7th August 1889]

*Please forgive my shaking hand as I put this record to paper—it is my scientific duty to report it, even if I would prefer to pretend it never happened. This has been an extraordinary summer. Even now, this storm that is coming has not broken, and everything in my garden that doesn't prefer tropical conditions has wilted. CHLOE—the experiment—continues in her unrelenting flourishing.*

*I spent the evening clearing my mind with a ridiculous novel and several glasses of port outside in the cool night air. Having nodded off in the moonlight, I picked up the book and drinks tray and trudged back inside the sweltering atrium. Recovering from a profound yawn, I heard—or felt—a movement in the corner of my eye. Turning slightly, I tried to focus on the source of this disturbance. It was coming from the birdcage, which was no surprise, since the birds often get flustered for no discernible reason. Turning back towards our sleeping* area I heard another, fouler noise from the birdcage—a crunch. My hands involuntarily released their load, and the port glass and bottle reduced themselves to shards on the brickwork floor. It was dark, and I padded over to the birdcage. I lit a nearby oil lamp—

CHLOE was behind the cage with her fingers through the bars. Her moss-green eyes shone brightly in the lamplight, piercing the dappled shadows of the garden. Vines were extending from her fingers— sturdy, fresh green shoots which wound their way around our birds of paradise. The poor creatures were quite dead. Asphyxiated perhaps, or hopefully they died suddenly when her crushing tendrils snapped their delicate spines—that sickening crunch in the darkness.

I unlocked the horrid cage and teased the bird corpses from CHLOE's elongated fingers. I led her back to my laboratory, and I think my feet were more unsteady than hers. Although inexperienced, she is now entirely capable of self-propelled movement. Settling her down for 'sleep', I carefully affixed her blindfold. With a heavy heart, I swaddled her in linen so tightly that she would not be able to wander again until morning.

I gave the bird corpses to Simon, on the proviso that he wouldn't ask how they died. He did not seem best pleased.

# Fifteen

Gregor considered himself to be 'not very good at answering mail'. This wasn't strictly true: he was entirely capable of writing letters. He even had a lively style, excellent accoutrements, and passable skills at calligraphy. What he lacked was the desire to sit for an hour or two answering the day's drudge of correspondence. Why write if you have nothing to say? Why burden the postal system with fripperies in ink? Why not just meet face to face, which is after all a much better forum for said fripperies? Better yet—why not just have thoughts about each other, fond or otherwise, and not feel compelled to share them? Gregor knew Aunt Muriel thought of him often and fretfully. Aunt Muriel knew Gregor did not care a fig for her opinion. Aunt Muriel still insisted on writing to him weekly. Such correspondence, unopened, became mulch.

Today, a whole pile of letters lay on Gregor's writing table. He was studiously avoiding looking at it while he went about his ministrations with CHLOE. Her skin—Constance's skin—was showing in places where certain of the surface plants hadn't taken. What she needed was coverage, so Gregor re-purposed some bedding plants which had been destined for a lusty hanging basket. Making an incision in the surface of her withered skin, he pressed the root balls of nursery plants into her loam. Hart's tongue fern added a queer roughage to her coat.

Gregor eyed the mound of letters. A deep green envelope was poking out of the pile. He knew what it meant. He didn't want to read it.

What CHLOE needed now was some colour other than deep green. Soon she was bedecked in silvery *Lamium* and black-purple *Ajuga*. He also added a wrist-corsage of vivid pink decorative kale. He checked her over for more gaps in her foliage. There were none left. Damn.

Gregor removed the emerald envelope from the pile and threw the rest into the mulch bucket. With a sharp breath he tore it open and removed a single-sheet letter and an embossed calling card.

Dear Gregor,

It is with great regret that I note the lack of correspondence between us these last few years. What could my previous letter possibly have contained to irk you thus? Really, Gregor—I thought I meant more to you than that! Still. In a great show of magnanimity I shall swallow my pride and write to you twice consecutively—albeit now nine years since my previous letter.

I can only imagine the reasons as to your silence. Perhaps you have been abroad all this time—perhaps you have died from some elaborate and desperately fashionable disease of the jungle. That would be your style. Perhaps your line has died out with you there in Siam. That would certainly be your style.

Another possibility of course is that you have devoted yourself to your research. Maybe you have developed some new and fascinating specimens for display. But please, Gregor, I say this with love: *no more mushrooms*. No more mould, no more lichen. No more fungus—there, I said it.

If it is the case that you have sequestered yourself in pursuit of botanical brilliance, then I may have some good news for you. The Duke of Buccleuth has died. As such, I have been elected President of the Royal Horticultural Society. It does not embarrass me to say that I intend to shake up the Society so that it can be ready for the end of the 19th century. I think, then, it would be time to set the cat amongst the pigeons and (gulp) *readmit you*. Enough years have passed since the incident— what did you call it? Oh, that's right, the *Bouquet Fongique*— that polite company will have moved on to gossip about some other scandal.

*Bon et bref*—the only thing for it is for me to visit Grimfern. I am sure you will have all kinds of wonders to show me. And who knows, maybe we can *catch up*?

Devotedly yours,
Julian Mallory, Esq.
President of the RHS

Gregor folded the letter and placed it back in its envelope. Julian had kindly provided him with a calling card for his desk at the RHS. So—the old enemy had landed himself the top job at the Society. Pretty soon he'd be angling for a knighthood. He always had been a social climber—horrid little man.

Julian was one of those people who always seem to pop up unbidden when you are at your lowest ebb. You never truly choose to be around such a person, but through force of attrition they become part of your life. Encounters with them reverberate through the years, punctuating your time on this earth with a dismal knell, making each fresh meeting worse than the last. Julian and Gregor had been schoolmates at Ampleforth, had attended rival colleges at Oxford, and had become competitors at that blasted garden show nine years ago. Mallory won. Gregor, with his *Bouquet Fongique*, was disgraced. He didn't like to think about it.

Despite a rather intense hatred for each other born of jealousy and resentment, Julian's most egregious crime against Gregor was not professional, but romantic. Mallory was one of those Uranian men who had swallowed whole the idea of the 'primacy of respectability'. Despite eternal vigilance to propriety, and denials both public and private, Julian Mallory could never shake the trace of queerness. A homosexual heart beats as tellingly as Poe's. Thus, with the heat generated by a decade of social friction, Julian and Gregor had once or twice carried a torch for each other. That period of Gregor's life was well and truly over now—Simon possessed a kind of predictability that led, in most cases, to stability. Julian was a foppish turncoat—

an agent of chaos. Stability is worth more than golden hair, or eyes of lapis lazuli. Or dress shirts which are slightly too tight, or larking about in spring on the Balliol lawn…

Or that radiant smile. Simon never smiled like that.

Gregor rubbed his finger along the embossed 'RHS' on Mallory's card. He dug around for his most moisture-damaged letter paper—that way it would appear that he was extremely busy and didn't care a jot about Julian Mallory's new position. He leaned back in his chair, licked his nib, and allowed himself a little grin.

Dear Jules,

I was surprised to receive your letter. You always did have a way with words, and now I see you've had your way with the old dames and Marys of the RoHoSo. Well-played, Mallory. Well-greased, I'm sure.

I am enjoying my time away from the Society. You have no idea how liberating it is to be away from all the poo-pooing—the smell of horse manure and deceit. And now I hear you have planted yourself firmly at the top of that compost heap! The fairy atop the Christmas dunghill! Jolly good show, old sport. You really are the prize shit.

As you correctly assumed, I am buried in my work, furthering the science and art of botany. In fact, I am on the cusp of a discovery so far beyond our current understanding—alas, there's no time to elaborate. You'll simply have to read my paper when it comes out. Forget the RHS, old boy; I'm aiming for the RS itself!

Therefore it is incumbent upon me to expressly forbid you from visiting. I fear that our *catching up* would shatter my sanctuary and quite imperil the experiment. You understand, Mally. You always did know to keep your gaiety far away from home.

Reluctantly yours,
Dr Gregor Sandys
Botanist and Apostate

# Sixteen

The principle of 'waste not want not' is a core tenet of taxidermy. Simon hastily designed and constructed a brand-new piece to make the best out of this bad situation— the unexpected situation being three fresh corpses. The three birds of paradise perched on their own private pedestals but were designed to reflect each other's sinuous curves to be taken as a single piece. The one in the centre, bursting with fiery feathers of yellow and red, was reaching wide with outstretched wings—its head hanging down like the suffering Christ's. The birds on either side mourned the martyred innocent.

For Simon, an improvisatory approach to taxidermy represented a kind of working-through of his feelings. Slip the meat out of the skin, acknowledge your grief. Scrape out the brain matter with a tiny scalpel, accept your sadness. It helps to have a task to perform. Anger, though, that was more difficult. He knew he must be furious, but that emotion simply didn't register. It was too far and too long suppressed. No amount of mortification of the flesh could bring Simon into communion with that emotion. Instead, Simon placed a lustrous glass eye into its socket with a tiny pair of tweezers. It was the sixth eye of six, and the final element of his avian triptych.

Nobody would buy this piece. Maybe playful Rosalinda would take it to offend her dreary husband. Simon stepped back to admire his work and heard a sound of rushing far overhead. Removing his magnifying headpiece, he set off upstairs to investigate.

Reaching the ground floor, Simon was treated to an awesome sight. The heavily clouded sky was bruised purple and bright yellow in the early sunset, and rain—real, heavy rain—was falling at last. Thick droplets struck the glass roof, bursting helplessly. Rivulets cascaded down the panes and drains. The air was so dense with water that the entire sky seemed to be made of it, and the barrier between the yonder water-world and this palace of glass and flowers was implied but immaterial.

There was a figure standing outside, under the ropes of rain. Simon approached a French window and peered at his partner through the glass. Gregor was standing with arms outstretched, not unlike the central bird in Simon's religious display. His grey waistcoat was dark with rainwater, his white shirt translucent.

Although it was a strange thing for a normal person to be doing, it wasn't such a strange activity for Simon's bizarre beloved. After a long, hot summer, it felt poetically natural for Gregor to be communing with the weather's release. The bursting of the dam was welcome and worth celebrating, but Simon was glad to be *inside* on a day like this, thank you very much.

The sopping-wet scientist let his wide arms fall to his sides, leaving a trail of droplets which fell to the floor in resignation. He stared up at the burnished gold clouds and sank to his knees, head in his hands. Simon touched his fingertips to the windowpane—if Gregor wasn't careful he'd catch a terrible cold. Simon began rustling around the atrium, trying to find an umbrella. It was a difficult item to locate, given that it hadn't been used since May.

By the time Simon tracked down the umbrella and bustled his way back to the patio, Gregor had vanished. Simon clutched the umbrella close and peered through—quite through—the house of glass. Gregor was nowhere to be seen. Simon stood there, rotating this way and that in the waterless column under his umbrella. He must have ventured out further into the landscaped garden. Simon had a pretty good idea where Gregor had gone.

He stuck his head back through the door of the atrium and shouted for Jennifer. Her head bobbed up like a meerkat's.

"I think I shall take a turn around the grounds. If I have not returned by the end of your hours, feel free to lock up after yourself."

"A pleasure walk, in this weather, sir?"

"I am off to locate a missing botanist."

Simon cricked his neck and ventured out into the sodden garden.

Grimfern Estate had been carefully designed by Capability Brown at the height of the fashion for naturalistic landscaping. There was a cultivated wildness to the place—sloping prairies, irregular copses, stony creeks. It was, of course, entirely artificial. Nature is natural, but this nature had been corralled by humankind into an aestheticised version of itself. As such, the country park of Grimfern was carefully arranged so that from any given landmark you could see every other important feature. The lower lake with the boating house; the upper lake with the Grecian folly; the glasshouse; and of course the manor itself, or the ruins thereof. Taking care not to leave the protective confines of his umbrella, Simon made his way hurriedly to the old manor.

Humankind's mastery of nature is sometimes thought to be absolute. That singular landscape gardener Capability Brown managed not just to tame the earth under his hand, but to cause it to resemble itself. Perhaps he cast his eyes upon his work and taunted the gods that made him, that he could perfect their flawed creation. Eden was not for him, but Arcadia. His nature would be more naturalistic than Nature itself. When Grimfern Manor burned to cinders, Gregor had instructed the groundstaff to cease maintaining the paths and planted beds immediately surrounding the ruins. Hedges became wild and lawns became groves—statues were overtaken by moss, and topiaries lost their precision. The hill upon which the House of Sandys formerly perched had become a wild wood. Mother Earth has entropy on her side. Nature had reclaimed her territory.

Simon feared that, given Gregor had now fired the entire groundstaff, all of Grimfern would soon suffer the same fate.

Simon arrived at the empty doorway of the manor. Yellowed vines clung to crumbling brickwork, cradling that which remained upright. The upper floors and roofs had collapsed in the great fire of Gregor's youth. Blackened debris lay all around— Gregor had never had the place cleaned up, let alone restored. For most, the inclination is to leave our troublesome memories at the bottom of the garden, where they can be forgotten amongst the weeds. For Gregor it was the other way around—he had hidden *himself* at the bottom of the garden, leaving his memories to smoulder in the ruins of the manor. Simon picked his way gingerly through the rubble of the entranceway.

The large hallway of the house must have been quite magnificent in its heyday, for now it was a whole grove unto itself—a secluded glade of tender saplings, slender and tall. With the abstractive power of rainfall, it was hard to tell where the fresh canopy ended, and the distressed Gothic gestures of the surrounding architecture began. The carved stones were blackened, but the leaves were sweet and vibrant in the strange light of this summer downpour.

Simon pressed through the trees, using his umbrella to part the branches, to reach a clearing formed by the absence of growth where the grand chandelier had fallen in flame. Simon had only been here once before, six years ago—the last time the great botanist had hit a rough patch. The trees were higher now, fuller. It was harder than before to reach this inner sanctuary. Sure enough, though, Gregor was there in his sodden woollens, perched on a piece of twisted iron.

"You'll get wet," said Simon, proffering the umbrella.

Gregor turned round to look at Simon, incredulous. A small spray of rainwater spun from his fringe. Rivers ran down his

". . . a few years since you've been out here."

"I know," replied Gregor, "and look how tall the trees are now. Look what happens when I leave plants the hell alone!" He leaned back against the twisted metal and gave a tight-lipped smile. The two men grew sodden in silence.

"This chandelier must have been quite a sight when it was lit," said Simon after a while. "What—sixteen, twenty candles?"

"Thirty-two, in fact. A fortune in tallow."

"I'm surprised they never got it plumbed in for gas?"

"Father wanted to when the rest of the house got fitted up, but Mother wouldn't hear of it. She said it would *impair the drama*, meaning in the Shakespearean sense. It's not Glamis if the lamps don't flicker." Gregor scuffed at the rubble with his heel.

"Something of a Romanticist, your mother?"

"Something of a Medievalist—she preferred her beauty with a side of dark mystery. Probably what drew her to my father, and to this place. She had this thick dress, basically a tapestry wrapped around her, and black as shadow. But if you saw it in just the right light—candlelight, of course—you could see it shimmer with all sorts of colours. It was black on black, you see:

itself. She was like that, a beautiful tinderbox.

Simon carefully looked away, allowing Gregor time and privacy to cry without embarrassment. Around them lay the remains of the Sandys family seat. Moss had nestled between broken banisters and slender trees, forming a carpet of green over the cracked parquet. The undulations in the moss implied human figures underneath—here and there an arm would poke through, or a face. These broken statues were the traces of Gregor's ancestors, abject and greening with time.

"I've been a contemptible fool," said Simon, "I've been so caught up in this quarrel that I failed to see the central issue. That's what this whole experiment is about, isn't it?"

Gregor did not appear to understand. Simon knelt before him so he could look him in the eyes. He'd heard people like it when you make eye contact. It sounded improbable to him, and rather frightful, but he deferred to the popular opinion.

"Legacy, family, it's all tied together in this place. You're trying to create a real family for yourself again—*that's* why CHLOE is so important to you. Well, far be it from me to make pronouncements of this type, but I would like to declare… yes." For courage Simon kissed Gregor's wet knuckles, which were terribly cold. "If CHLOE is a scion of the House of Sandys, your daughter to wit, then she is to me a child also."

Gregor squinted, considering. Whatever hesitation he had seemed to be vanquished by relief. He laughed a little, which released a wayward sob, and he kissed Simon on the forehead.

"A family! Simon, *of course!* That's what binds people together. If we can be a *family* then the contextual issue solves itself. Mutualism, homemaking, protection... and if ill-providence robs one of a birth family, one simply has to find another! Or make it from scratch."

Between every utterance was a flurry of kisses, until Simon was quite befuddled by the botanist's lurching mood. At least this time it was lurching for the better—Simon's declaration must have hit its mark. They embraced under the umbrella, the rain-soaked man doing so more enthusiastically than the formerly dry one.

Each raindrop made itself known as a sound, bright and crystalline against every leaf. The sky can play the earth like a glockenspiel. A distant roll of thunder signalled the thickening of the storm; Simon instinctively fretted, but Gregor grinned devilishly.

"Are you wet yet, Simon?" Gregor's eyes were beaming.

"I was doing well until you got my shirtfront rather moist!"

"Well let's remedy that then, shall we?"

Gregor leaped to his feet, grabbed the umbrella out of Simon's hand, brandished it like a rapier, and bounded out of the clearing. Simon struggled up, squinting and wiping his eyes uselessly. With even a few seconds of this heavy rain, his considerable fringe had flopped down to his nose. He shook himself like a dog and chased after the crazed gentleman.

Gregor skipped, ran, and bounded like a much-younger fellow imitating a gazelle; a wanton faun in the forest. Simon galumphed awkwardly, not because he was unfit, but because he was incredibly self-conscious. No amount of "see here"s and "that's quite enough"s could slow his quarry, however, and soon they were at the Grecian folly by the upper lake.

Is a dry lake still a lake? And is a dry lake still dry if it's raining? The hot summer had forced Gregor to turn off the mechanism which kept the upper lake filled with water. The lakebed had been exposed, and soon grew a lawn of leafy reeds. The Grecian folly, a kind of domed temple with Ionic columns, was normally surrounded on three sides by tranquil water, but now seemed lost in a rainforest. Gregor leaned against a faux-ruined pillar.

"Simon, I'm sorry, too," he said, chest heaving, "I've allowed this experiment to come between us."

"It takes two to sour a relationship," Simon replied, water running down his face, "and we've allowed that to happen with Jennifer as well."

Gregor slid down the column and picked at the ground. "Changing times can be disquieting enough, but if our fears grow silent they become ever more monstrous."

Gregor stared into nothingness for a while. Then he shot to his feet and grabbed Simon by the arms. His green glare shot through the other man like light through the luminiferous æther. Simon had some difficulty matching his gaze.

"You argued once that my experiment was unethical.

The circumstances with Jennifer, and the provenance of the substrate... You might possibly have not been entirely incorrect. But what's done is done, and now that the entity is coherent it is my—our—duty to sustain it. That is to say, there is a child now, and we must become a family for her."

"Yes. She is no longer your work, your experiment. Given that CHLOE is truly alive now, the only moral way forward is to look after her—to cherish her, even, as our child."

Gregor gave a kindly smile, then took his partner's hand and they ambled down to the lower lake.

"The very first work of mine that you ever saw was my *Bouquet Fongique*, which I entered into the RHS competition."

"In the *flower arranging* section, I believe?"

"That's the one."

"And which was laughed out for not containing a single flowering plant?"

"Well, quite." There was Gregor's charming evil grin again.

"With the greatest respect, that was a basket of mushrooms and mould. Of course the committee were scandalised!"

"They couldn't see the beauty in my creation! The delicate wisps and tender stalks contrasting with deep reds and bulbous browns... You saw the beauty, didn't you?"

"I did, but then again I've always had a taste for the bizarre." He kissed Gregor behind the ear.

"So I swore to myself that day I would show the world, and especially the yellowed-rhubarb nobodies of the Royal Horticultural Society, just how beautiful and sophisticated the fungal kingdom could be."

"And then I got in the way and ruined it."

"What? No—Simon, I want to be absolutely open with you…"

They reached the banks of the lower lake. The water levels had greatly receded, so that the boathouse was quite far back from the water's edge. Heavy rain caressed the lake's surface and washed its thirsty pebbles. Gregor was searching for words strong enough to express himself, and Simon was casually examining his diaphanous white shirt.

"It's all for you now. You remember when Rosalinda invited me to her salon after the disgrace? She was trying to rehabilitate me—and cause a little scandal along the way, no doubt. You came over and told me how much you liked my *Bouquet*."

"It was the first time we'd spoken."

"I thought you were just being polite, but now I know your ways I do believe that was your version of being *effusive*."

"Well, I—"

"That was the moment you dragged me out of the abyss. In all seriousness, Simon, I wasn't sure what I was going to do with myself. Since then I've been fuelled by twin goals: to prove the value of my work to the Royal Horticultural Society, and to make you proud."

He said the last bit very quietly.

Simon's social calculations became desperately convoluted—what did he feel? What should he say? In the absence of an obvious course of action, he decided to tell the volatile gentleman what he needed to hear in the moment. It wasn't a lie. And maybe he was speaking it into truth.

"You do make me proud, in everything you do. I love you, Gregor."

Gregor kissed him passionately, with hunger, tears, and rain. Every muscle in Simon's eternally nervous body released into pleasurable affection. In time, their raw emotion subsided and gave way to playfulness—soon Gregor's useless, see-through shirt was gone, and Simon kicked off his shoes. They bared themselves to each other; chests and souls and all besides.

Only when the clouds above condensed to thunderous rage did they leave the dancing lake. They traipsed their way back up towards the greenhouse without bothering to re-dress into their sopping clothes, since Jennifer would have gone home by now. Lightning joined its noisy lover and caused Simon and Gregor to pick up speed. On the patio where so often they had breakfasted tersely, Gregor brought his partner into an intimate embrace.

"Thank you, Simon, for everything."

Hands and mouths were everywhere over wet skin—physical touch is so often the culmination of emotional strife.

A crack of lightning revealed a spindly hand on a glass pane inside the greenhouse, and a mossy, curious face. A second flash showed several inches of burgeoning growth—twisted vines from its fingers, a contorted jaw… A third crash and she was gone.

The botanist and the taxidermist only saw each other. They slipped back into the sodden ruins of their respectable clothing, or at least what was strictly necessary, and lured each other indoors.

# Seventeen

The storm was a howler. Jenny's ears were being assaulted by the roar of the roof—it was as if she were a salmon cowering under a waterfall. Jennifer was in the central atrium of the greenhouse, cleaning up the debris of a potted plant which had taken a tumble. It was strange—every hour or so since the start of the bad weather, another plant had cast itself upon the brickwork. Perhaps there was a draught. Indeed, the countless panes of glass rattled monstrously against the wild wind. It was a tempest out there, and Jenny was not looking forward to rushing home through its vicissitudes. She stood up and stretched out her back before pouring the contents of her dustpan back into the shattered terracotta pot.

Some leaves bustling across the room caught her eye and she sprang over, but there was nothing there. Perhaps the floricidal culprit was simply wanton breezes. If the greenhouse had air leaks, Mr Sandys and Mr Rievaulx had better get it looked at. Lord knows it must cost them a fair bob to heat the place as it was—they couldn't be doing with holes letting out their precious warmth.

They'd be glad of the greenhouse's balmy temperature when they got back from being out in the rain. Soaked through, they'd be, she reckoned. Silly men, chasing their emotions across hill and dale. If Mr Sandys was in an ill mood, Jenny hoped that the soggy jaunt would cure it, for he'd surely gain a cold in its stead.

That bustle again, back where she just came from. Yet, when Jenny spun round it immediately ceased. To be sure there was a fair hurricane blowing outside—the trees surrounding the glasshouse were bending and the rain cast itself ferociously against the conservatory windows—but inside the glass cocoon was an unnatural stillness, with not a leaf out of place. Jenny scanned the sweltering room, pointing her hand brush to guide her eyes.

This time a flower bush definitely wobbled—she saw some petals flutter to the ground. Was it a fox from outside? How did it get in here? Or a bird more likely, but given how large the disturbance in the foliage—

A small aftershock made the heavy leaves of a small palm shudder.

*There is something behind that plant.*

Brandishing her cleaning utensils, Jenny made her way with careful steps towards the site of the disturbance. She steadied her breathing; waited. With a swift movement, she separated the dark green fronds of the palm with her brush. There was nothing behind the plant except for yet more plants and shadows.

Spanish moss billowed around her like a curtain, then the disturbance settled noisily by a yucca. There was no doubt—*there was* something in the greenhouse with her. The dull light coming through the ceiling carried shadows of raindrops hitting the glass, so that the entire space seemed to be the surface of a lake. The palm trembled once more. Did the disturbance want to be followed?

"Hello? Who's there? I won't hurt you." Jenny squeezed her brush and began to creep towards it.

At her first footfall, the thing darted away. The yucca tumbled, a large fern raised its arms like an octopus in the passing wind-rush. The disturbance made its way into a bamboo cluster, from where emanated a sound exactly like a child trailing a stick along a fence. The hollow thunk of the bamboo was somehow satisfying to the creature. Jenny thought it sounded *playful*, but that did not make her any less unnerved. The creature—if that's what it was—hit upon a particularly resonant bamboo chamber and paused. It began striking the stalk over and over, exploring its timbre. Oddly charmed by this, Jenny pitched herself to the bamboo tone and sang in her rough country alto:

> "*When I was bound apprentice in famous Lincolnshire,*
> *I served my master truly, for nearly seven odd year,*
> *Till I took up to poaching, as you shall quickly hear.*
> *Oh, 'tis my delight on a shining night, in the season of the year.*"

The thing played along for a while, but then paused to listen. Jenny could just about see a knotted mass through the bamboo. She raised the hand brush over her head and prepared to strike. Breathily she cooed the refrain:

"Oh 'tis my delight on a shining night, in the season of the—"

She burst through the bamboo and brought her weapon down hard. There was an awful scuffling as the creature fled unharmed. The thing travelled swiftly but with an uneven gait—galumphing along as if one of its legs was weaker than the other. Jenny whisked around to follow the trail of destruction it left. Potted palms toppled and trays of succulents went flying. She tried to give chase, but she got caught between two thick stalks of bamboo. She pulled herself through just in time to hear a small splash.

In the centre of the atrium was a pond dedicated to water-based plantlife. There were all kinds of elegant shooting reeds with fussy flowers, and giant lily pads jealously protecting the water's surface. This green and placid body of water must have provided the splash, and Jennifer could just make out the silver ripples dying away. No longer pretending to be soothing towards the beast, she stalked her way to the pond.

Looking in, she wondered if the thing had gone underwater. Would it be able to breathe? She could see nothing in the pond but her own reflection between lily pads. The splash seemed too small for the bulky creature she had glimpsed through the bamboo. What if this was a trap?

Jenny felt something entwining itself around her ankle...

Shrieking, she looked down to find a spindly vine tightening itself around her leg from behind, just above her clomping boots.

The splash must have been a distraction. Before she could look back to see the source of the vine, it pulled hard on her ankle. Jenny's feet came from under her and she toppled like so many potted plants had before her. She went right through a smug lily pad and into the murk beneath.

Jenny forced her eyes open underwater. There was very little light here—pale shafts came through the gaps between lily pads, implying their stalks. She became trapped in the drowned vines of this tropical pond—or were these the snares of the creature? She screamed underwater but only bubbles escaped. She tasted soil on the in-breath. Pulling herself tight into a ball, she then thrust her legs down with all her might, propelling herself back up to the surface. She leaned against the edge of the pool, spluttering, wearing the broken lily pad as a soggy ruff. Shadows of raindrops continued to dance all around the garden, cast by the glass roof. But now Jennifer was the only truly wet thing inside the greenhouse.

She rubbed the silt from her eyes. She was nose-to-nose with the horrendous creature. It had an almost human face but seemed to have grown spontaneously in some macabre bog. Fungal pods bloomed from its cheek. Its hair was a matted knot of vines and roots. It had a body almost that of a human girl, but terribly hunched and twisted. Its stick-fingers were unnaturally long. Jennifer took all this in on a slow inhale and felt for her dustpan and brush, but they had floated off.

The creature cocked its leaf-laden head—inquisitively? Jenny could see the thing considering her, perhaps as it had considered the bamboo. If it had been a rampant beast it would have been merely dangerous, but its curiosity marked it as truly insidious. Jenny could feel the muscles in her own face fighting to move away from the thing.

It extended its spindly hand, garlanded by soft green sprouts, and brushed Jennifer's sopping and gunk-laden hair behind her ear. Its touch lingered on her freckled cheek. Jenny felt as if she were tearing in two. Everything from her ribs upwards wanted to flee, but somehow, in the pit of her stomach, there was recognition... affection? The plant-creature's leaves quivered a gentle purr, and Jenny's abdomen responded with a yearning glow. She felt that, although the monster was bearing down upon her, their closeness felt... right. One twig-finger encouraged her chin forward, closer to the creature's face, and unconsciously Jenny's coccyx moved in sympathy...

A flash of lightning lit up the encounter. Jenny saw the back of the thing's eyes, its green algal retinas. She was being intently observed—consumed by these eyes, absorbed into its female gaze. She was horrified, and she was entranced. Without realising, she was also ensnared. Thin threads of plant matter were twisting through her hair and into the corner of her mouth.

Stamping, a thud, and a flash of light. The boys arrived from the outside, squelching and ruddy-faced. Seeing danger by the pond, they had armed themselves with a gas lamp and a letter opener. Mr Sandys held the small blade as if he was fencing, far too far away for any practical use.

"Oh, it's only CHLOE," he said, dropping the stance and casually flipping the letter opener in the air.

"No, Mr Sandys, it's me, Jennifer!"

"We understand, Miss Finch," said Mr Rievaulx in a strangely calming voice. "The being you see before you is CHLOE. She won't harm you."

"I… I know that, somehow. She's watching me."

"Just relax, we'll get you out of there."

Simon and Gregor crept up on the creature, who was still mesmerised by Jennifer's form. Simon brought the gas lamp round to CHLOE's face, which drew the attention of her rudimentary eyes. Like a moth she followed the light, and Simon drew her towards him. Gregor slipped in to free Jennifer, pruning back the tangles which had captured her face and hair with his letter opener. He braced his arms to allow Jennifer to use him to haul herself out of the pond. She stood there wet and shivering as Simon lured the creature back into Gregor's laboratory.

# Eighteen

There are several deficiencies which present themselves in households which contain only men. The principal one which concerns us here is the lack of women's clothing. Jennifer was thoroughly soaked from her encounter in the pond and wasn't drying in the damp heat of the garden. Simon and Gregor had snapped into an unusual protective mode, fussing over the housekeeper in a profound reversal of roles. The first issue, as mentioned, was Jennifer's wet clothes, and how to replace them.

Gregor manoeuvred Jennifer through to the bedroom, where he proceeded to ransack the wardrobe and chest of drawers. Menswear flung itself across the ivied room as Gregor discovered he didn't appear to own anything less formal than linen suits. Frustrated that he couldn't provide for the girl's needs, he picked up an arbitrary pile of ties and dumped them in Jenny's hands.

Jenny watched him as he stomped out of the plant-partitioned room, muttering away to himself. To protect her own mind from dwelling on her ordeal, she began to sort through and refold the clothes. She chose a tan three-piece suit to wear with a cream shirt. She didn't bother with the jacket but sported a black tie and rolled up her sleeves. She dried off her hair somewhat with one of her masters' towels—the softest she had ever used—and twisted it up into a loose knot. She caught sight of herself in a floor mirror which was partially obscured by a languid bush. The suit made her feel strong—it was thick, tight and protective. She squared her shoulders. Jenny was ready to stand her ground.

Mr Rievaulx and Mr Sandys were waiting by the piano when Jenny walked into the atrium. Both of them stood up as she entered, and Mr Sandys gestured for her to take a seat in a great leather armchair. The two gentlemen had never been particularly unkind to her before, but now their utmost deference to her was unsettling. Jennifer decided to play into it and adopted the airs and graces of a society gentleman, as far as she understood them. She put her hands in her pockets and tipped her head back so she could stare down her nose at them.

"It's been quite an evening," said Mr Rievaulx, pouring each of them a brandy.

"Yes, sir," she replied instinctively.

"Miss Finch," Mr Sandys said, swilling his brandy glass. "For tonight we want to ignore the strictures of the servant-master relationship. It's important that we openly discuss what we've seen here, without worrying about our station. So tonight we are Simon and Gregor, not Mr Sandys and Mr Rievaulx, and never 'sir'."

"As you wish," Jenny said with some nonchalance, before choking on his first name, the informality of which got stuck in her throat, "*Gregor.*"

A silence fell on the group. The rain overhead was less pronounced now, more a drizzle than a storm. Jenny took a sip of brandy, which she regretted. She took another sip, though, just to be sure. She regretted that one as well.

"Where is it now?" Jenny asked.

"I have put it to bed," replied Simon, "in the laboratory."

Although Gregor was fairly robust, his tailored waistcoat did not quite have room for someone of Jennifer's figure. As her chest heaved at the thought of such a monster being *put to bed*, the constriction placed on her was intolerable. She tried another sip of brandy and found it loosened her ribs somewhat.

"What is it?"

"Have you ever observed mushrooms growing on a tree," asked Gregor, his face half-lit by a gas lamp on the piano, "growing right out of the living trunk? Or have you seen lichen on an elm? Have you seen ivies winding their way up an oak to share in its vertical reach?"

Jennifer gulped down some more of the amber liquid. Now that she'd broken the back of the taste, she was becoming quite fond of it.

"In those cases," Gregor continued, "plants and fungi are working cooperatively for mutual benefit. The ivy brings all sorts of creatures to the wise oak. The lichen is itself a composite of fungi and algae. And consider the mutuality of mushrooms growing out of the root system of trees—the fungus coexists with the tree to draw in and share out nutrients, the roots and tendrils working as one!"

Jenny shuddered at the word 'tendrils'. She'd had enough of them for one evening.

"What Gregor is trying to say is that these plants are living together, making best use of each other's talents," Simon translated.

"Like the two of you?"

"In a manner of speaking, yes." Gregor blinked as he tried out the thought. "But I'd also include you yourself in that symbiosis. You rely on us for a wage, we rely on you for your housekeeping. Following?"

"Yes," said Jenny, "although I can't see what all this has to do with the creature."

Gregor's voice rose as he clinched his point. "So she isn't exactly 'a' single creature. She is a complex community of plants and fungi, working mutualistically. She is an experiment of mine which has been rather too successful. Her name is CHLOE."

Something clicked inside Jennifer. *So it was a woman.* Somehow she knew all along that this tangle of brambles and twigs was a person, and a *she*. Jenny was troubled by the not-unpleasant memory of being caressed by her spindles.

"CHLOE. She's a plant? Then why does she look like a girl?"

"She's less a plant and more… a *garden*," Gregor explained, scratching his beard urgently. "Less a girl, more an entity. She looks that way because… because that's how I made her. Sentimental sod that I am, I made her look human. I suppose I could have made her look like anything at all! But she does *look*, as you say, like a girl. Which might upset a certain kind of unimaginative person. That's why we need to keep her locked away and secret. To protect her, and us, from people who wouldn't understand."

"Which is why," said Simon, placing a hand on Gregor's wet shoulder, "we have decided to think of CHLOE as part of our family. Something… some*one* to look after and nourish. Like any precious child."

"Your precious child tried to drown me this evening. Wait— was it her what killed the caged birds? She's dangerous. We have to warn people about her!"

"No," Gregor roared, grabbing both of them by their shirt sleeves, "nobody else must know. Not yet."

Simon pulled himself free from Gregor's grip and straightened his cuffs. Jenny allowed herself to be held onto. She sensed more than anger in Gregor—fear, too, and the queasy anxiety of nearly reaching one's ultimate goal. His eyes were straining without looking at anything or anyone truly present. His gaze was fixed on permutations, not people.

Jennifer spoke with what she hoped was quiet strength. "Everybody else has a right to know she exists. The truth will out one way or another."

Gregor came around from his tense stupor. He looked at Jenny and his partner, really looked at them, and considered.

"I can see only one solution," he said, his whole demeanour returning to affable aristocrat rather than anxious villain, "which would allay all of our concerns. Jennifer, I beg of you, give me more time before we have to tell the world. I promise I will begin working on a scientific write-up of my findings tomorrow, and when it is done, I will present it to the relevant authorities. That is the proper way to introduce an entirely new species to the general public."

"But the village—"

"The people in the village would not understand. They would fear CHLOE, and would perhaps want to hurt her. We have come to think of her as our daughter, so none of us want CHLOE to come to any harm, do we? Of course not. So once again, Jennifer, I implore you, do not tell a soul what you saw here tonight. Not until I've completed my paper."

Jenny squinted at the scientist. "I'd better see you writing every day until that paper of yours is published."

Simon was slumped in a wing-backed chair. Nobody in this household was any good at sitting. He raised his pointed chin to speak, but kept his eyes closed with fatigue.

"You might actually get this one written, Gregor, with a taskmaster like the indefatigable Miss Finch."

"I mean it," Jenny said, threatening the botanist with one freckled fist.

"I believe you! I wouldn't dare cross you, Jennifer; and *thank you* for your dedication to my publishing schedule. But there is one further increase in your duties I must request of you. There will be many times when both myself and Simon will be working, slaving away at our desks and workbenches. We may not have time to give CHLOE, our child, the attention she deserves. That's where you come in, Miss Finch—*Jennifer*." He whisked around and took her hand, the madness back a little in his eyes. "I wish to offer you a promotion. CHLOE will need care from dawn until dusk, and, as you have seen, even overnight. I'd like you to move in as governess to our daughter."

A flood of opposing images coursed through Jennifer's brain. Her lonely father, the draughty mill, straw for a bed, her late mother's home. The sticky greenhouse, the perfect seclusion, the unusual gentlemen in whom she had grown invested, their life of private liberty. The algal eyes and tender shoots of CHLOE, the intertwining of fingers and vines... Perhaps the feeling of hazy recognition by the pond was a sign from Jenny's own soul that CHLOE's was important to her, or had been, or would be.

"I'll do it."

# Nineteen

The oblivion of sleep, however welcome at first, tends to linger beyond its usefulness. After rising late, somewhere around nine o'clock, Gregor padded through the greenhouse quite naked to fetch coffee and a pastry. Passing a small clearing in the thicket, where the piano stood surrounded by comfy seats, he spotted an unexpected bundle of linen sheets in a wing-backed chair. They had left their housekeeper—nay, *governess*—there last night with the wherewithal for sleeping, after she had begun dozing off with brandy in hand. Jennifer was just now stirring, blinking like a doe in a three-piece suit.

The naked naturalist darted behind a nearby plant, but unfortunately the palm in question was leafy at head height but narrow further down, and thus was of little practical use. Jennifer stretched and sat up in the chair, glancing around the garden in confusion. Perhaps she too had temporarily forgotten the events of last night. The palm trunk was just wide enough to obscure the prime meridian of the bare botanist, so Gregor stayed put—making sure to keep the plant between him and Jennifer.

"Who's there? Mr Sandys!"

"Ah—good morning, Miss Finch."

"Why are you behind that tree? What are you… doing there, like that?"

"Miss Finch, allow me to explain," Gregor began, thoughtlessly taking a step towards her. She jumped and drew the linen sheet up to her eyes.

"Mr Sandys, really!"

He shuffled back behind his palm. "I must say—I forgot you were sleeping here. We keep the greenhouse quite balmy all through the year, and it's so secluded here it has become my custom to go about *au naturel* before you arrive for work in the morning."

"I guess that'll have to change."

"Quite."

Gregor scuttled back to his bedroom to dress, feeling aghast, like Adam, at realising his own nakedness. Small liberties such as these would have to be censured now that there was a third actual human in the house. A shame indeed—but necessary if Gregor was to secure Jennifer's loyalty and secrecy. He needed her completely invested in the household so that there was no chance of her leaking knowledge of CHLOE to the outside world. The alternative to her devotion would be unthinkable violence. He straightened his jacket in the mirror and blocked out that dark impulse.

Gregor spent the rest of the day making practical arrangements around the greenhouse to adapt it for two extra people to live in, now that Jenny would reside here and CHLOE would be considered a member of the family rather than as an experiment. CHLOE's personhood was something that Gregor felt ambivalent about. He was fond of her in an uncritical sense, but his dreams for the girl involved a glory more scientific than paternal. The rigour of his materialist methodology did not allow him to see a mystical soul in his moving plant pot. In order to have enough time to maximise the success of the experiment, he had to secure the coalition of the household. Jennifer and Simon insisted on her *personhood*, so Gregor was happy to play along until such a time as CHLOE could truly live up to that identity.

First off, Gregor put on his waders and fished the broken lily pad from the pond. Aquatic pruning was always a little more complicated than its land-based counterpart, but more rewarding for it. He then spent some time modifying Simon's reading nook balcony above the atrium to be used by Jennifer as a bedroom. Simon usually brooded in it with his tea and his incomprehensible books. Now it would be a nest for young Miss Finch, a home for her in the rafters. Gregor replaced the wicker chair with a chaise longue and a pile of blankets and cushions. He hung light fabric from the greenhouse's painted white beams so that Jennifer would have some shelter from the sun. In some ways the bedroom was like a treehouse, rising as it did above the canopy, but it was also like a tent—soft and cosy.

Underneath Jennifer's nest, the moss dripping from the gallery's overhang created a small garden room, guarded by vines and trellises on each side. To turn it into a bedroom for CHLOE, Gregor set up 'her' workbench in there as a bed—she was used to sleeping on this, and probably would not appreciate soft furnishings since she was practically made of soil. It was dark and damp in here, just how a budding mycelial girl would like it.

Gregor also rigged a second shower for the household, hidden from view by a screen of living bamboo. This one would produce a fine spray so as not to damage CHLOE's compacted loam and save her the indignity of being manually misted by her 'fathers'.

So, the modifications were complete. Jenny's bedroom perched above CHLOE's, both spaces kitted out to their respective needs. Gregor brushed off his dirty trouser knees and put away his working tools. The sun was low in the early evening and Simon appeared from his subterranean domain. Jennifer was just finishing up her daily scrubbing. The three of them looked at each other across the sun-gilded garden, and at the impossible girl playing by the pond. She was the reason all three of them were tied here now. It was a ménage of implicit trust, and also one of implicit distrust. But they were all determined, for their own reasons, to make it work.

Jenny spent most of the first morning seeing to her usual duties around the greenhouse, sweeping and scrubbing, placing things back in their proper place after Gregor had discarded them randomly. All the kitchen utensils which had been co-opted by him as makeshift paperweights or gardening tools were returned to their proper drawers in the east wing. Now, though, she always kept one eye on CHLOE, who was for the first time allowed and encouraged to explore the garden freely. The leafy creature wandered about on tiptoes, drinking in the golden day with her algal eyes. Jenny observed her communing with tropical flowers, chasing ditzy butterflies, and sometimes just swaying in one spot, her neck and arms slack.

When Jennifer had finished the housework, CHLOE was draped over the edge of the pond, trailing her twig-fingers in the calm water. It was time to play at being the tutor. Jenny did not feel ready. She was not a natural-born governess. She had barely written or read a word since receiving her paltry schooling in the village. She simply had no need to. She was also one of the least disciplined people you could ever imagine, and therefore the least strict—she of the wild brooks and brambles, who would leave the schoolhouse on a whim aged eight to wander in the meadows. What could she teach this pile of plants?

Jenny breathed deeply into the waistcoat—she had decided to keep it on after yesterday, she felt protected by it—and strode over to the pond, which was laden with lotuses and waterlilies. There was a gap in the greenery where Gregor had removed the broken pad. The two young women perched on the pond's low wall, softly reflected in the mirrored surface of the water.

"What are you up to?" asked Jenny. She didn't truly expect an answer—she had spoken as one might speak to a kitten. CHLOE turned to her languidly and cocked her face to the side, further than a human head could twist. Jennifer recoiled slightly. She cleared her throat.

"I thought we could learn to… to sit up. Like a lady, I mean."

So saying, Jenny sprang to her feet. Gingerly she arranged CHLOE's limbs into an approximation of the severe, demure lines of a society woman—such as she had seen in newspapers and on chocolate boxes. She stepped back to view the effect, holding out her hands and saying "There!"—a gesture which CHLOE immediately and gleefully copied.

"No, CHLOE, I want you to sit…"

Jenny repositioned her ward, but now CHLOE had grown disinterested. Her head lolled back to watch the shimmering water. When Jenny cupped the vine-laden back of her skull to correct her posture, CHLOE instead imitated her by grabbing Jennifer's own head.

"No, CHLOE, ow…"

Simon approached from the kitchen. He was wearing a flour-dusted apron—to celebrate the household's expansion, he was making a pie. Or at least trying to.

"Miss Finch, wherever is the rolling pin?"

"It's where it's supposed to be," she said, patiently extracting her hair from CHLOE's twigs.

"But I've already checked Gregor's writing desk—"

"I mean it's in the second drawer in the kitchen, with the wooden spoons and potato masher."

"Oh," said Simon, taken aback, "that is where it is supposed to be. I hadn't considered that possibility after so many years with the botanist. My deepest gratitude."

"Don't mention it. Ow, CHLOE—"

The plant-girl was trying to help by fiddling with Jennifer's locks, making much more of a gnarled mess, pulling on her scalp. Simon leaned in and whispered.

"You might find it easier if you encourage her to emulate you."

Jenny held her hands up and CHLOE did the same. Simon quickly released the tangle and tottered off to the kitchen.

"You like copying, do you? Then how about we sit... like this."

Jenny pressed her knees together and pointed her toes. She straightened her back and placed her hands together in her lap, just so. To her credit, CHLOE copied admirably. Her spine and neck seemed to elongate—her head rose unnaturally high above her shoulders.

"Alright, CHLOE, that's far enough I think!"

The green girl reached her arms now up towards the ceiling—her reach was impressive since her fingers were so long—and wilted down balletically to lie prone on the bank of the pond.

"Oh, are you sleepy now? Well maybe let's have a look at this book Gregor gave us to read."

She fetched the tome and sat by CHLOE, blowing dust and soil from its hard cover. It was *Mycology in the Age of Steam* by a certain G. Sandys. She furrowed her brow. Reading was not one of her strengths, and this was hardly a nice fairy tale for her ward's nap. Still, if it was what the masters wanted, so be it. He who pays the teacher gets to set the curriculum.

Jenny let the heavy book fall open in her lap, leaning against the low pond wall upon which was draped the plant-girl. CHLOE was practically around Jenny's shoulders like a mantle of ivy. She began to read, pausing on the longer botanical words and taxonomic classifications to make sure she had them correct. Neither reader nor listener comprehended the biological and philosophical treatise contained in Gregor's work, but the sounds of the words danced between them. Soon CHLOE's tendrils wound softly around the nape of Jenny's neck, and both of them began to drift into slumber.

Jenny snorted awake to find Gregor looming over her with a pair of secateurs. The sun had set, and CHLOE had become so entwined with her that Gregor had to cut them free. He assured Jennifer that CHLOE wouldn't mind being trimmed. But secretly, on some level, Jenny missed the connection.

"Come on, CHLOE, let's show your fathers how we sit like proper women."

The whole strange family sat together to dinner, and CHLOE's posture drew polite applause. As did Simon's enormous pie—he enjoyed working with pastry, and this exquisite crust displayed his signature style, with decorative ribbons of shortcrust weaving in and out of little pastry skulls. CHLOE wasn't eating, of course, but she sat with them, slowly fusing with her seat. Jennifer cleaned her plate and polished off seconds before the two men even finished their initial portions.

Jenny requested brandy rather than the syrupy port Simon and Gregor were having. After everything was finished, Gregor showed her how he pruned the excess growth from CHLOE in order to detach her from the dining chair. He pointed out which stems were vital and which expendable, which plant-hinges were load-bearing and which were purely decorative. Jennifer watched with a morbid fascination. Garden pruning had never interested her before, but now it concerned such a wondrous creature as CHLOE… Jenny found herself hungry for this knowledge.

Once CHLOE was free, they led her through the twilight garden to her bedroom glade, where Gregor instructed Jenny on how to strap her down to her metal bench. It would be no good, Gregor said, to have her wandering about at night, hurting herself or the garden. Jennifer stroked her ivy-hair goodnight.

At the entrance to CHLOE's glade, Gregor paused. He presented Jennifer with the snippers he had used earlier on CHLOE. They were a small set of spring scissors, designed to be precise and sharp for clipping orchids.

"Just in case," he whispered, before withdrawing to his gas-lit laboratory.

Jenny clambered up to her perch and snuggled down into endless cushions. The floor of her gallery bedroom, which was also the ceiling of CHLOE's, consisted of an elaborate iron grille. Jenny peered past the soft furnishing, through the wrought-iron filigree, and through the natural filigree of vines and ivies, to see the sleeping form of the wood nymph. *Could this be real, she asked herself, or is this some bizarre other world where such strangeness could be so comfortable?*

# TWENTY

Later in that week, Gregor carefully prepared a pot of coffee—the first of the day—and, to his own exact specification, assembled the required concoction of bean juice, milk, and sugar. Just as he lifted the steaming liquid to his lips, Simon brought the novel he was pretending to read down to the table with a huff. It was the kind of huff, Gregor well knew, that meant that a grievance was about to be aired.

"It just won't do."

"What won't do?"

Simon's pause allowed Gregor to lift the cup once more to his lips, but yet again his caffeine intake was thwarted.

"It's CHLOE."

*Here we go.* Gregor had been pleasantly surprised by Simon's softening to his experiment. In the past few days, since Jennifer moved in, Simon had made several thoughtful gestures towards domestic affection. Gregor thought the social experiment was working. It was of course too good to be true—Simon must have been making an effort, and now that effort seemed to be rescinded. Gregor put the coffee cup down and braced against the table.

"What about her?"

"If she is to be a member of the household," Simon continued severely, "then she must be clothed as one. There are certain aesthetic standards here at Grimfern. She simply must have... a pretty dress."

Gregor smiled and frowned at the same time. It clearly caused Simon some discomfort to use the term 'pretty dress', and Simon's petty discomfort was always Gregor's pleasure.

"Do walking forests need pretty dresses?"

"No, but nymphs do," said Simon, pursing his lips. "It's a modesty issue."

"Very well, we'll have some made. The main problem is that we can't let the tailor see the client."

"I shall write a letter to dear Rosalinda." Simon wiped his lips with his napkin and made to leave the table. "I'll ask who does her dressmaking. Rosalinda is fuller-figured than CHLOE, but they are practically the same size when you account for fronds..."

Simon wandered off, leaving Gregor alone with his tepid coffee. *A dress for the flowerbed.* The anthropomorphosis was progressing apace. The thrill of his experiment's continued success was tinged with grit in his teeth—or was that the coffee dregs?

Gregor left the breakfast things for Jennifer to clean and went off to his laboratory to brood.

[Letter from Rosalinda Smeralda-Bland, Friday 16th August 1889]

Dear boys,
I feel sure I have mentioned several times—perhaps it slipped your masculine attention—that my exquisite gowns are designed by darling Wilhelm at the Savoy. He really is the top fellow for this kind of thing. I've called in a few favours from Arthur and W. S.—they wanted me for *Ruddygore* but alas! Mr Bland won't have me on the stage—and between them all they're sending through a suite of outfits from that deliciously dark operetta. I've asked them to send it 'care of' you up there in Grimfern so Mr Bland doesn't catch a whiff of the greasepaint. It's all very clandestine and exciting. Quite what you need three dresses for is beyond even me. I do so hope it's entirely improper!

*Gros bisous, mes p'tits,*
Rosalinda S-B

Some days later, Jennifer arrived at the grand gate at the bottom of the drive, as she did every morning before work. Will was already in the gatehouse, reading with his feet on a windowsill, chair leaning back at a precarious angle.

"If you break your neck, don't come crying to me," said Jenny.

"At least that'd be something to do," he replied, closing his Penny Dreadful and chucking it on a pile on a sideboard. "I'm so bored, I've read all these through half a dozen times. Not as fun when you know how they end."

Will wore his boredom on his face—he had a grisly look about him, dark of eye and sallow of skin. He hadn't shaved recently, probably because he had no cause to be around people. Jenny leaned against the open doorframe and tried to keep the tone light.

"Has the post come? The masters are expecting packages."

"Nope, no packages, papers, or post. Just late, I suppose. Here, I could fetch 'em up to the greenhouse when they arrive— stretch my legs?"

"No—don't do that," Jenny said quickly, "I'll be back for them later." There was no way Will could approach the greenhouse itself. Not while CHLOE was about. He just sighed and flicked through one of his discarded periodicals.

"So you're living with them, then? Up at the house?"

"I'm the housekeeper. They've needed one for a long time, I think."

"You look well, Jenny. Like you've grown into yourself."

Jennifer was taken aback by this. She was probably holding herself a little taller than usual. She felt less awkward in her body, more sure of her strength and suppleness. If she were a plant, then Grimfern was certainly the perfect pot for her—sheltered and rich. But it was CHLOE who was her sun, for whose warm beams she flourished.

"Are you off to see Constance?"

Will's remark snapped her out of her reflection.

"I am. It's been a while, since I've been living up here. I should get going."

"It's always nice to see you, Jenny. Best part of my day."

"I'll be back for the parcels."

Jenny swung off the doorframe and hurried away to the Wycombe Road.

Under normal circumstances, Grimfern was made impervious to visitors through layers upon layers of weaponised forgetfulness. Gregor would 'forget' to reply to the many letters begging him for access to his botanical menagerie—those dignitaries who requested visits would have to wait until his newest experiment was complete. Now that the groundstaff had been laid off, Gregor also 'forgot' to look after the area of the gardens around the gatehouse, which lent it a dilapidated air. Weeds grow quickly where gardeners cease to tread, and the gatehouse now appeared desolate and forbidding, surrounded by a cloak of brambles. Grimfern was protected not by locks or brick walls, but by the insistent sorcery of forgetfulness. Grimfern's inhabitants forgot about the world, and the world forgot about Grimfern.

Which is all to say, it was rather surprising—alarming, even—when Simon, who was breakfasting on the patio, saw somebody staggering up the long drive to the greenhouse. He ran back inside, leaving the butter knife spinning on his side plate.

"Gregor, we have a visitor," he shrieked.

Gregor came bounding from his workshop to the front door and scanned about. His eyes were unaccustomed to distance—he was rather short-sighted from long hours staring at tiny sprouts and the fine grain of soil composition. Sure enough, though, there was the figure of a young man—*the gatehouse boy, what was his name?*—making steady progress up the hill with a pile of parcels wrapped in brown paper. Just a delivery.

"Where's CHLOE? Where's Miss Finch?" Gregor enquired urgently.

"CHLOE is by the waterlily pond. Miss Finch, I believe, has stepped out. To the... to the twisted hazel."

"Take CHLOE down to the cellar, quick as you can. Don't come up until I say so, you hear?"

Simon nodded and turned on his heels. Gregor rolled up his sleeves and jogged out to intercept the unwanted visitor.

"Morning, sir," the lad wheezed. "Parcels for you, sir." The young lad was ruddy-faced from the rise, though he seemed to be filled with the childish thrill of being somewhere he shouldn't be. Gregor summoned up all the Caledonian granite he could muster. He enjoyed activating his Scottish side. It let him channel his furious mother.

"The gatehouse, boy. You must always stay in the gatehouse and keep the post there. This was agreed with you long ago!"

"Begging your pardon, sir," the boy stammered, "but Jenny, *Miss Finch*, said you was expecting parcels, and seeing as they're wrapped in paper and all, and with me fearing a drop of rain later, sir, I just thought I'd bring them..."

"Well, you thought wrong." Gregor took the parcels from the post boy and marched straight back up to the hedge arch. He shut the gate and glowered back through its many sinews of iron. The young fellow was still standing there, turning this way and that, not quite sure what to make of himself.

Gregor's capacity for meanness was quite considerable— words were his weapons and the very sharpest ones came to him easily. However, his barbs were often at odds with his heart, which on some level—hidden from all but the most dedicated investigator—was decent and kind. He sloughed off the packages and found his coin purse.

The gatehouse boy shrank back a little as Gregor approached again, such that Gregor held out his hands to call a truce.

"A small tip, for your trouble. Thank you for the delivery. Keep it in the gatehouse next time, eh?"

"Yes sir, Mr Sandys, sir." The boy sniffed and touched his cap.

Poor lad. Not his fault he tries so hard. Plus, it paid to keep the village folk on side. On side, but far away from Grimfern.

# TWENTY-ONE

Jennifer stomped along the rutted Wycombe Road out of the village. She had in her pocket a bunch of lavender Gregor had allowed her to pick from the herb garden. The ground was waterlogged from all the recent rain, and Jenny was cursing every clay-lined puddle. It gave her something to do along the way, so that she didn't have to think about her upcoming task—apologising did not come naturally to Jennifer Finch.

She clambered off the track at the boundary stone and stood before the twisted hazel. Its yellowed leaves were dropping, revealing the corkscrew bones underneath. All around, brambles were thinning and grasses were losing their lustre. Jenny placed her lavender on the ground and stared out at the wet horizon.

"I'm here to apologise, Connie," she mumbled to the hardscrabble earth, "it's been ages since I've visited. The boys at Grimfern have been keeping me busy, you know how it is. Oh, I wish you could see the garden, Connie, you'd love it. Such wonderful plants, and creatures… But that doesn't excuse my absence. I should always be there for you, like how you were always there for me. Connie—*I'm sorry.*"

The release of those words carried with it a flood of other things, old griefs which had gone ignored rather than healed. Jennifer's face clamped down on this outpouring—an instinctive reaction which protected her from emotion. Her features were screwed up to prevent strife from escaping through her nose and eyes. She sank to her knees with a woeful squelch.

Out of the corner of her eye, she saw something at the foot of the twisted hazel, glistening in the bracken. The brush was beginning to thin out with the onset of autumn, and here something precious was revealed. Jenny wiped her face on her apron and went to investigate. Sodden and muddy, and terribly cold between her fingers, the object turned out to be a pewter locket. Inside was a clutch of pressed yellow flowers— kingcups. An amateurish engraving on the inside read: *Connie Dearest, Forever Mine. J. F.*

Jennifer held the locket to her and cried out. This meadow-side tenderness of theirs, the brush of yellow petals and freckled skin, had soured when Constance's father came between them. He forbade them from ever seeing each other. Without naming it, he forbade their love. Of course they had their ways around that, but their time together was tainted by tales of the rows Constance had with her father, his rages and threats. But Jenny knew for sure that Constance had always kept the locket on her person, and always would—even in death.

She had been buried with it. Jennifer had witnessed that herself, though now the locket sat, small and firm, in her palms.

Then why—Jenny became dizzy with the thought—why was the locket just lying out in the weeds?

She stood up sharply, suddenly abhorring the treacherous ground, that would give up the treasures of its dead.

Blood began to roar in her ears; she could feel the throb of her heart. The echoes of its pounding mapped out her arteries—she could see the sound of her passion. Beyond this, and beneath it, she became aware of the hissing tendrils of the earth—the roots of the hazel which reached out and cocooned Connie's resting place. Those twisted roots held a secret. Jenny could taste the metal tang of it. *The locket.* Why wasn't it buried with its owner? What was the secret under the twisted hazel?

A low cloud rolled in, drenching the grim hillock and obscuring Jennifer's acts from the eyes of God. She began to tear at the dirt with her bare hands. She found the soil of the gravesite to still be loose relative to the surrounding sod. Once she had a hole for purchase, she began kicking at it from a lying-down position with her clodhopping boots. The earth was still singing to her, and her blood was in harmony with it. She held the tell-tale locket between her teeth.

After a time, her boot struck gravel-laden compacted soil. This was the very pit of the grave, a mere two feet deep, and totally cadaver-less. The rushing of blood and dirt ceased in Jennifer's ears. Instead she was struck by the ringing silence of clarity.

Connie's body had been taken.

Jenny was suddenly very tired and very cold. She had mud all over her arms and legs, and across her face where she had tried in vain to keep her fringe out of her mouth. She lay down in the shallow grave and clutched the locket. Jenny had been one of only two people who had witnessed the shoddy 'funeral' of Constance Haggerston since the village church refused to give a proper burial to a supposed suicide. Jenny was the only one to watch Constance's father dig a paltry hole and fill it with his child.

Her hands and feet were numb, but Jenny's brain was buzzing about like a dragonfly. She was starting to piece it together. The secret dalliance, intense and forbidden. The single-parent father, like her own, who would do anything to protect her. The blood-soaked scene of her apparent self-murder. How far would Mr Haggerston go to preserve his daughter's good name?

The shallow grave was slowly filling with rainwater. Jenny knelt there, not noticing the trench muck and cold. She clutched the wildflower locket, which was all that remained of *Connie Dearest, Forever Mine.*

Thick drops of rain began to hit the brown paper parcel, dampening and darkening its wrapping. Faster the heavy raindrops fell, until Gregor was running back inside the greenhouse. He shoved the door closed a little harder than he meant to with his hip. Why was the gate boy such an imbecile, why was Jennifer *not here* to enjoy the delivery? Why was everybody around him trying to *ruin* every little nice thing he tried to do *for this family?* He could hear that his breathing was growing shallow and laboured. His jaw was aching from clenching it so hard for so long.

Gregor peeled an envelope away from the sodden package and scanned its ink-bleed and scrawl.

[Letter from one 'Wilhelm', costumier at the Savoy, to Rosalinda Smeralda-Bland c/o Grimfern Botanical Gardens, Monday 19th August 1889]

*Liebe Frau* Smeralda-Bland,

It is with the greatest affection and consummate respect for your Art and Artistry in the Comic Opera that I enclose these humble garments as a gift from myself and the Savoy. The parcels herewithin contain amongst them a suite of garments from our recent triumph *Iolanthe*:

    – a fine gown fit for a princess

    – a Grecian robe for a faerie-nymph

    – a costume suited to a (forgive my lack of English) …
*Sumpfhexe?*

All are characters which are well within your considerable range. Oh, and Arthur and W.S. are still desperate to get you in for *Ruddygore*. You had better say yes at some point so they stop going on about it!

*Tschüss* and all that, duckie,

Wilhelm

*Destroy this bit when read, liebchen…*

    *Been a while, Rosie! What say me and you go down Wapping again, tear it up like old times, eh? That's if I can get you away from the old man for an evening?*

*I still remember Pinafore—that party after opening night! "The lass that loved a sailor", that was us both back then! And now I am Herr Wilhelm, and you are Mrs Smeralda-Bland. Funny the costumes we wear when we cease to be on the stage…*

Gregor smiled despite himself—Rosalinda was a complicated woman with complicated allegiances. Nobody got all of her at any one time. She gave herself freely in fragments, but the only person who got one hundred per cent of her was herself.

Gregor shook away his resentment and resolved to enjoy himself even though Jennifer wasn't here. The package had arrived.

"Chloe, oh Chloe! Look what has arrived in the mail. Come up here and see what your clever daddy has got for you from London."

The call was addressed to Chloe, but it was aimed squarely at Simon. Sure enough, the first head to pop up from the undercroft was the taxidermist's. He looked about with fluster and fear.

"Is he gone?"

Another head emerged from the cellar, this one gnarled but verdant. Chloe was facing the wrong way, absorbed in the intense beauty of Grimfern's sunbeams.

"Yes, it was just the gatekeeper boy with a delivery. He shan't be coming up again. Come on, everybody," said Gregor brightly, as if to children on Christmas morn, "we've got presents!"

Gregor handed Simon the note while Chloe began to explore the package. At first she just caressed it, then she tore through the brown paper wrappings, the pasteboard boxes, the crêpe paper lining…

Simon and Gregor shared a raised eyebrow in reference to the letter.

"What does the German mean?" Simon asked quietly.

"Swamp-witch, I think? Although my German does come from biological treatises."

"Whatever would we need a *swamp* costume for?" Simon whispered, nodding his head towards CHLOE.

"I think I shall look rather fetching in a bog-faerie outfit," Gregor declared, earning him a sharp dig. Gregor was trying his best to be pleasant and present, though his knee was bouncing away and his gaze fixed on the middle distance. *Why wasn't Jennifer back yet? What if she told someone, anyone, about CHLOE?*

Despite their request to Rosalinda, the gown was too tight for the plant-girl to wear without damaging her undergrowth. Instead, they draped her in the sinuous Grecian robe. She was quite pleased with the extra swish of the impossibly light fabric and began dancing around the garden.

Gregor put on the bog-faerie costume over his shirt and tweed suit trousers. It was essentially a loose cape of green and brown strips of fabric—he looked quite the smartest thing to have ever emerged from a swamp. Simon begrudgingly partook by affixing the laurels which came with CHLOE's nymph robe to himself, since there was no use adorning her herbaceous head with fake sprigs.

The rolling clouds above broke into squalls. CHLOE pranced

off between the trees and bushes, followed by Simon, who was beginning to enjoy himself.

Gregor watched them gambol off into the colourful underbrush. Then he swapped his costume for waterproofs and galoshes, himself disappearing out into the greying rain. Come what may, the governess must be returned to Grimfern.

Once wet, there is little use in escaping the rain. Jenny sat by the grave-puddle, near catatonic at the thought that Connie could have been torn from the earth. She lost the day, and herself, in these worries, as they bled like ink into the sodden hillside.

She only noticed the squelching footsteps when they were already close behind her.

"What the fuck is this?"

Jenny stiffened in shock—the voice belonged to Mr Haggerston, quiet but bitterly harsh.

"Constance isn't here," she said. "Her body's gone."

"What have you done, you little slut?" Haggerston's voice rose. A small in-breath triggered Jennifer's animal instincts and she hurled herself across the shallow grave to avoid him grabbing her.

"I've done nothing—someone's stolen Constance!"

Mr Haggerston blinked slowly. He was a large man, and blocked some of the thin rain-gusts as he towered over Jennifer, prone. Droplets were coursing off his close-cropped head.

"Grave robbing? Who in hell would—"

"I know who!" Jenny yelled. "Someone who needed to keep

a secret quiet forever. Someone who couldn't let Constance be found, not by anyone who cared how she died!"

"She killed herself." Haggerston's whole body flexed and bristled.

"I don't believe you," Jennifer said, wide-eyed, crawling backwards towards the twisted hazel. "I never believed you. She had everything to live for."

"You sayin' someone done her in?" growled Mr Haggerston, striding over his daughter's empty grave. Jenny had nowhere further to press back—the corkscrew branches of the twisted tree pressed against her from all their bizarre angles, and the great hulk of Mr Haggerston was bearing down upon her.

"I—I don't know. All I'm saying is that *someone's* taken her body."

"And all *I am saying*—is who the fuck would do that?"

Someone cleared their throat, approaching with light splashes from the Wycombe Road.

"I hope all's well here, George, Miss Finch?"

It was Gregor in his wet weather gear, his eyes hidden behind raindrops on his glasses.

"This stupid girl's fallen in a puddle. Come on now, Jenny. Up you get."

Jenny allowed herself to be roughly hefted to her feet, then hurried over to Gregor. She was wet and shivering, and tried to signal something to Gregor—something primal, something dangerous. Whether or not he picked up on this, his face remained impassive behind the soggy beard, glasses, and fisherman's hat.

"That is unfortunate, Miss Finch. Let's get you sorted out up at the house. Good day, George."

Mr Haggerston barely nodded an acknowledgement, and spat idly at the base of the hazel as they left. Taking Gregor's offered arm, Jenny tried to begin explaining, but he cut her off stiffly.

"I don't want to hear it, Jennifer. You should have been at Grimfern. We need you—CHLOE needs you—there at all times. I deeply regret your absence today, and now I see you have suffered plainly for it."

"But Mr Haggerston, he—"

"Silence. Not another word. We are not to speak of anything of import outside the glass walls of Grimfern."

They settled into a miserable return to Grimfern, in perfect resentful silence.

Approaching the botanical garden in the early evening rain was really quite something. Strafing clouds were picked out in bruise-blue and scarlet, and the rain gave the world metallic brilliance. Behind dark, protective hedgerows, the greenhouse gas lamps glimmered wetly, their sickly green light reflecting back and forth between glass panes and puddles. Reality was blurred and shimmering at Grimfern. Jenny shivered a little in her wet clothes, rushing to keep up with Gregor's determined strides.

He had locked the front gate with heavy chains. As Jennifer waited for him to fiddle with the hedge-gate, the jangle of keys and metal scraping seemed to her to emerge from the sound of rainfall, just as the smell of the wet earth emerged from the unkempt lawn. Gregor fastened them both into the patio, then the process began again to unlock the greenhouse door and close them firmly inside. Locks upon locks upon locks. Sometimes you are only truly free to talk once you are firmly locked away. Jenny kicked off her muddy boots and waited for the lecture.

"I can't have you running off like that, not coming back in good time, Miss Finch."

"I'm not your prisoner."

"You were supposed to be back to start your duties." Gregor began removing his sodden overclothes and left them in a pile. "We need you *here*, Jennifer, not gallivanting around the village. There's too much at stake. I must insist you remain at Grimfern at all times."

She pulled her hair up into a loose twist in a performance of nonchalance.

"So, what? I'm just supposed to stay in the greenhouse forever like a tree that's grown too big to fit through the door?"

"I thought you'd *want* to be here to look after Chloe. Apparently you don't care about her enough to be her governess."

Fury and flame. Jenny held back from thumping the wall, since it was made of glass. Instead, she began tearing at her buttons, trying to free herself from the strangling feeling of too much starched linen.

Gregor's trousers were wet at the knees, where neither his greatcoat nor galoshes could protect him from the weather. He had taken his useless glasses off and was using them to gesticulate.

"I worry when you don't come back, Jennifer. Who might you be shooting your mouth off to? You understand that our little arrangement here requires absolute secrecy—for Simon and myself, and for CHLOE's sake most of all."

*Do you think I don't know that? Do you think I'm stupid?* The bitter words caught in her throat. Rather, she asserted herself wordlessly by finishing off her buttons and stepping out of her dress. She stood there in her undergarments, otherwise clothed only in her rage. Gregor frowned and averted his eyes.

"For God's sake. What's got into you, Miss Finch?"

Jenny tried to keep up her furious defiance, but a pointed question always conjures its answer in the person asked. She recalled the twisted hazel, the locket, the exhaustion… and she briefly failed to contain a sob.

Gregor softened and even caught her gaze.

"Tell me, Jennifer," he murmured, "and we can sort it out. I want you to be happy here."

Jenny put a lot of effort into regulating her breathing. She fished the locket out of the pouch in her discarded pinafore and showed it to Gregor. He studied it carefully, clenching and unclenching his jaw.

"This belonged to Constance," Jenny muttered. "My Constance."

"Who was she?" Gregor whispered.

"My best friend. We grew up together. Do you remember— I told you she died. They said she did it herself, but somehow I was always sure that wasn't the case. I went back to her grave this afternoon, and by chance I saw this locket in the bushes.

I gave her these flowers inside. She was buried with it—I know she was. I was there. But here was the locket, on the ground by the twisted hazel."

Gregor inspected the flowers and ran his calloused finger over the inscription.

"So you think—" Gregor's eyes were dark as he spoke.

"—that someone's taken her body. I don't just *think* it, Gregor. *I know*. I dug up the whole damned hill. Empty. Somebody's stolen Constance from her grave!"

"Who would do such a thing?" asked Gregor, barely moving his mouth.

"Her father."

Gregor blinked heavily, genuinely surprised. "Mr Haggerston?"

"I think he killed Constance. Because of me."

"But why would he exhume the cadaver—excuse me, I mean: why would he take her body back?"

"I don't know." Jenny crossed her arms. "He was always mad with rage and fiercely protective of her. Constance hated him for his outbursts. Maybe he just snapped again? Maybe he was worried that someone would find out, and the body would be proof."

Gregor thought long and hard, replacing his spectacles upon his nose and rubbing his beard with a soil-laden palm. When he spoke again, his eyes were glittering.

"You loved the girl?"

"I did. And she loved me. I know now it was wrong—"

Gregor grabbed her by the arms.

"It wasn't wrong! Curse it all—a pox on everything else, but love is never wrong. The goddamned world is wrong. Jennifer, in my long life I have suffered terribly for my inclinations, and now I see even in your short one you have suffered even worse. The weight of such loss on such innocent shoulders! But you are not the guilty party in this, Jennifer. Your love for Constance— *hell!*—it consecrates this earth."

"You and Simon love each other like that, don't you?"

"Simon is an insufferable creature, stiff and uncaring one minute, fretful and snide the next. And I suppose I'm no cherub to be around. But yes, we love each other dearly. Society wouldn't understand, and neither would the constabulary. I think you share that unspoken love, Jennifer—that forbidden love?"

Jenny nodded and looked at the floor. How hard it is not to deny something you have spent your life hiding—even when you know it to be manifestly the truth.

"Then we have an understanding, Jennifer Finch," Gregor continued, "which surpasses all others. We know what it is to love 'wrong', and to lose for it. We're closer than family now. We are shield-siblings in defence of our lives and our loves. You say that Constance's father, Mr Haggerston, killed her over you, and even seems to have dug up her body. I say: I will not stand for it. Leave it with me. Justice will be served."

Jenny hugged Gregor tight with fists clenched.

"You're a good man, Gregor Sandys."

Gregor was unaccustomed to being embraced by semi-clad women, but eventually he reciprocated the gesture, his glasses squishing into her cheek.

Jenny took up her pile of clothes and hurried barefoot through the gas-lit garden. Gregor's words seemed impossible—what could he do to avenge Constance? Reservations aside, Jennifer was roused by Gregor's words; it seemed as if the greenhouse itself were glowing with possibilities. Through the undergrowth she saw Simon snoozing on a chaise longue, a book open in his lap. He must have been reading to CHLOE, who was now standing over him, idly swaying her hips from side to side.

Jenny raised her hand in a silent hail, waited for CHLOE's animal-gaze to focus on her, then closed and opened her fist—*hello*. CHLOE's head remained perfectly still, her face unmoving, but her green pupils focusing on her governess. Confident the greeting had been registered, Jenny carried on across the garden. As she traipsed through, CHLOE's head twisted unnaturally to follow.

Jenny dumped her stuff in her cloth nest on the balcony, wrapped herself in a towel, and slid back down to take advantage of CHLOE's mist-shower. It started off cold but was fresh and clean, so she let the spray fill up her hair before squeezing out the grime. Fiddling with the taps caused the pipes underfoot to groan and roil. Jenny could feel the gentle vibrations of the floor as it coursed with hot water. The boiler sat at the heart of the garden, a throbbing nub which spread its leaden tendrils throughout the greenhouse. The steam became too hot very quickly, but Jennifer endured it to scour herself of any residual grave-mud.

The shower was surrounded by waxy-leaved palms and ample ferns, which benefited from the airborne moisture and balmy temperature. In return, they provided the showerer with the illusion of shelter from prying eyes. No one in this garden would spy on another—that was a founding principle of the ménage. A sense of security is important for a person when they are naked, however, so this and the boys' shower in their quarters were jealously guarded by the undergrowth. But all walls have two sides, and in this case the price of being hidden came at the cost of being *hidden from*. A rustle went unnoticed. As Jenny bent a little to work on her stiff calves, a glimmer came from the shadows. It wasn't until she stood back up again that she felt a clutch of twigs brushing up against her spine, and by then of course it was too late. CHLOE was standing there in the shower with her, staring at her unblinkingly in the mist.

# TWENTY-TWO

Gregor was doing delicate work this morning. Grafting orchids took an awful lot of patience, a steady hand, and plenty of know-how. He was of course aided by his financial position—his laboratory was stocked with only the finest scientific equipment. The Astronomer Royal would be jealous of his lenses. If Gregor knew about one thing it was botany; if he knew about two things, they were botany and glassware. Not that he made any himself, but you know what they say: those who live in glass houses had better know a good glazier.

He was working away with his most delicate instruments, aided by a swivelling lens-boom. While he was craning over a particularly crucial grafting point, there came a faint tickle on his earlobe. He scratched it away, stuck out his tongue and peered back through the lens. The tickle again—this time stronger. He rubbed his whole ear hard with the palm of his hand, then shook himself to refocus. Just as he controlled his breath to steady his tweezer-hand, the tickle came once more, this time tracing down from his ear to his jaw-joint, round to the top of his spine, and down to his starched collar.

Gregor spun around, taking some time to adjust his sight to the room after focusing so intently on the precious petals of the orchid. There, wide-eyed and innocent, was CHLOE. Her new dress was already a little tattered—possibly due to the fact she was partially made of soil and sticks. The fabric was a little damp.

"You really mustn't wear your dress in the shower, CHLOE dearest. The water is good for your biological systems, not your sartorial ones."

She didn't respond, merely twisting her leg in idleness. How like a child she seemed. Gregor was never quite sure if she was taking in what he said. That didn't stop him chatting to her.

"What do you want, gentle petal?"

She took a step towards the main atrium, still staring at her creator. Gregor raised one eyebrow.

"CHLOE, what is it?"

She took another step away, hands clasped behind her, never taking her green eyes off him. Gregor sighed and removed his gloves. As soon as he started moving, CHLOE hurtled off into the main body of the garden, leaving Gregor to scamper after her.

She led him through his own unnatural garden. It was designed to emulate nature, and was even made out of it, but somehow it remained inescapably artificial. Gregor only caught flashes of his mossy quarry through the winding passageways of the steamy atrium. Finally, they reached a clearing—the one with the grand piano. She stood by it expectantly, stroking its peeling varnish. Gregor tried not to let himself think of the thing as so much dead wood. It was strange to see the plant-girl posing with her felled countryman—not that she understood any of this, of course.

If there were *three* things that Gregor knew, they were botany, glassware, and how to make a piano sing. If he could reanimate CHLOE from dead matter, so could he bring this tree-corpse to life with music. He sat down to play, still wearing his work apron.

CHLOE stood there as Gregor began his sarabande—a sumptuously-slow Spanish dance of courtly heartache. Her long fingers gripped the stick which held up the piano lid. As she started to sway, like she always did when listening to music, Gregor tried to discern her rhythm to no avail. She wasn't rocking with the pulse, or with the melody, or even on the emphasised second beat of each bar. Perhaps her sway had a higher mathematical relationship with the music—a fractal cross-rhythm; a Fibonacci fever-dream.

As a scientist, Gregor was perplexed. Using the limited brain-space he had available to him whilst also playing the piano, he tried to pinpoint exactly how she could 'hear'. It was theoretically plausible that her human ears were being operated by the mycelium. They were such delicate structures, though, any number of things might have caused them to cease functioning post-mortem. The deaf and hard-of-hearing were known to be able to *feel* music, even if sound was inaccessible to them. The very resonance of the notes, rather than their relative pitches, might be what CHLOE was responding to. *As a scientist*, Gregor had more delicious questions than answers.

As a father, Gregor glowed with pride at his talented daughter. No child's recital could bring more joy than this little girl's balletic sway. He made to scribble some notes in his jotter but thought better of it. This was a moment to enjoy. The data gathering could wait.

He started to show off. Little thrills of passing notes, scalic figures, nimble arpeggios. CHLOE's stems quivered with excitement. Gregor coalesced these tiny notes into tremolo chords—a shimmering spectacle of hundreds of infinitesimal notes creating a cloud of music.

CHLOE stopped dancing and straightened her back, neck arched. She stood on her toes, reaching as high as she could towards the crystal ceiling. Gregor was a little perturbed but modulated his tremolo to wilder and wilder harmonies. CHLOE rolled her eyes back into her head in ecstasy. Gregor watched as her spindle-fingers grew up along the piano lid-stick, wrapping around it like a vine; her hand never moved but her fingers themselves extended at a rapid rate. Her neck elongated beyond that of an ordinary human; her toes cast their roots down, propelling the rest of her upwards an inch or two. The ivies of her hair corkscrewed out from her, budding and blossoming. Gregor couldn't help but continue playing his maddening dance—was he the orchestrator of her extraordinary growth? His fingers felt powerful.

Gradually he noticed that the piano's upper register was muffled, and soon it was entirely muted. This dampening effect crept down from the high end towards the middle, so Gregor brought his impromptu performance to a hurried but graceful finish, ending low to avoid the dull sound up top. When he stood, he could see the cause—CHLOE's inquisitive tendrils had wound themselves around the piano strings, spreading out from her clenched fist at the lid-stick. Her feet—or perhaps rather *Constance's* feet—were now half a yard off the ground, supported by an outpouring of fresh roots. Tender shoots emanated from her fingers and head, suspended in the air as a person's hair might be underwater. If a photograph of poor Ophelia could have been taken as she floated outside Elsinore, it might have looked like this. CHLOE's facial mosses were 'blossoming'— sending out yearning buds from their bushy depths.

For once, Gregor was acutely aware of the presence of the plant-system, as separate from the presence of Constance's host-body. The 'substrate', as he had once called it, was quite discernible—a broadly human shape at the centre of this florid mass. The shoots, roots, and vines, however, coursed out from her—more powerful than any human body in its first life.

Gregor was reminded of a custom of scribes in the Middle Ages. When arrogant monks thought they had something important to write, they would simply scrape the ink from an old manuscript and write their ramblings on top. It saved on vellum—tightly stretched calf skin was a precious commodity. And hadn't Gregor done the same as these monks? Taken an old text and used its flesh-paper to compose a new story?

Now here stood CHLOE in her tree-like magnificence, the majestic story of a life written on the carcass of another, too quickly ended. Gregor owed a debt of gratitude to the raw material of his creation. He would avenge Constance's death, as he had sworn. He would do this for Jennifer, yes, but also for CHLOE. She had, after all, never stopped *being* Constance, no matter how hard he tried to think of her as the 'substrate'. No—the corpse was the vellum, and CHLOE and Constance were the two stories written on it simultaneously. Doing what was right for one meant doing what was right for the other.

Gregor whipped a pair of secateurs out from his apron and set about pruning CHLOE back hard. When he liberated her from the piano, she wilted in a dead faint. Gregor caught her and carried her back to her ivied bedroom to complete the trimming of her overgrown limbs.

With her swooning on the table, Gregor could see an arc of tight forget-me-nots bristling across her abdomen. He ran his trembling finger across this strange eruption of blue amongst the green. CHLOE's flowering traced out Constance's wound— and graced it with impossible beauty.

Gregor had a new clarity of purpose: vengeance it would be, in the name of Jenny, Constance, and CHLOE. The man who slew the girl would pay the ultimate price. Gregor stroked the plant-girl's mossy face and remembered how grim she had looked when freshly dug up.

*Plus—it would be a chance to tie up some loose ends.*

Gregor barely slept that night. He tossed and turned under the vine-laden canopy of his bed, until Simon's obvious displeasure became such that he withdrew to the central atrium to watch the dawn through the crystalline roof. The piano was pockmarked from CHLOE's burgeoning and was littered with her debris. She was a protean thing—a changeling. There was no way he could allow knowledge of her existence to escape these glass walls.

*So, who knew about her?*

He threw himself down into a wicker chair and rubbed his face 'til the capillaries of his eyes blossomed red. Simon, in the east wing—fond of her, even protective. Jennifer, high up in her perch—flighty, perhaps, a loose cannon. But she was devoted enough to CHLOE to keep her secret. And Gregor himself, of course—the spider at the centre of the garden. How he longed to reveal to the world his creation! But not yet. It was too risky.

*Then who knew about Constance's death, and the disappearance of her body?*

The aforementioned denizens of the greenhouse, all comfortably wrapped up in their unconventional domesticity. All of them could surely be counted on to keep CHLOE secret, if only for their own protection. But then what of that one truly chaotic variable—Constance's father? He knew of Constance's disappearance from the earth under the twisted hazel. What would he do about it? He seemed quick to blame Jennifer, as laughable as that thought would be. At what point would he go poking around to find his dead daughter, if only to secure her corpse for fear of anyone discovering her murder wounds?

Gregor poured himself a toddy, finished it and replenished. The night sky was bleeding dawn.

If Mr Haggerston found out in some uncontrolled way the whereabouts of his daughter's corpse, and its present state... not only would the experiment be jeopardised, but so too would

Grimfern, and Gregor's life of seclusion with the people he loved.

*All knowledge of* CHLOE *must remain at Grimfern. Her powers, and her provenance.* He developed this 'reasoning' over a very early coffee, fortified with whiskey. Rather than a thought based in 'reason', though, it became a fixed thought from which there was no escape—a circular mantra. Such thoughts are like inconvenient and perilous paths, which can still cut themselves into the mountain under repeated footfall.

"Morning, Gregor." It might have been Simon, yawning in his bedclothes. "You don't… you don't look well. Maybe try to get a few hours' sleep?"

Gregor shook his head and gathered his wet greatcoat and keys. He mumbled something about the village and locked his whole world behind him inside the greenhouse.

A morning is lurid and nauseating to one who hasn't slept. He veered around puddles as gravity took him down to the gatehouse. Will wasn't at his post yet—just as well. The boy probably did need firing. Or perhaps he, along with the gate he guarded, could be replaced by a simple brick wall.

Gregor scurried through the furrowed streets of muck around Hazlemere Village to a clearing of scrubland on the outskirts. He hopped a fence—poorly constructed, given that its owner was a woodworker—into Mr Haggerston's yard and crossed the door-less threshold into the carpenter's workshop.

The timber hovel was meagre to say the least. A raised section served as a bedroom, whereas the dirt floor was dotted with self-made woodworking spaces—a rudimentary lathe, a trestle table for sawing, a ruined tree trunk for chopping. All around were examples of his wares. 'Furniture maker' was too generous a term for Mr Haggerston; he was a purveyor of rustic slabs of cut wood for the absolute bottom end of the market in stools. His designs were aggressively boring, violently puritan, and ruthless in their economy.

The great hulk of George Haggerston blocked the dusty light coming in from a tiny window. He had been washing his face and pits with water from a dirty basin, and now stood with his braces loose and rag-towel around his neck. He folded his arms and glowered in the semi-darkness.

"I must be the unluckiest bastard this side of Buckingham, to see you again so soon."

"I have something you want, George," Gregor said softly.

"You've not got nothing I could possibly want," growled the carpenter, "so do what you're best at, and *bugger off.*"

Despite the importance of his mission, Gregor fumbled for his courage. He forced a tight smile.

"You've not heard what I'm offering."

"What can you offer me? Flowers? I bloody think not. Now do what I say and *sod off.*"

Haggerston strode slowly over as he spoke. Gregor had to crane his neck, given that the carpenter was head and shoulders taller than him, and not to mention twice as wide. Gregor removed his spectacles to wipe them.

"What I have… is *information.*"

The mountain of a man folded his arms and spoke with

infinite though effortless contempt. "What kind of information?"

Gregor replaced his glasses and blinked. His response was calm and measured, as if what he was saying was the most natural thing in the world.

"Information pertaining to the whereabouts of your daughter's body."

Haggerston's bravado cracked just a little. Gregor swore he saw his eyes flicker up to a beam in the rafters. Could this be the beam—the plank of wood that supported Constance in her final moments? Gregor became mesmerised by it. This was the place. The locus of evil, the source of such pain for his little girl—his CHLOE. No—for *Constance*. The scene flashed before his eyes, all fiction of course, based on the best guesses his and Simon's amateur pathology could afford them. Constance, struggling against her father's impossible grip—a sharp implement, there were plenty around—blood flowering on her pinafore—panic, a system of hoists, a faked suicide.

Any failure of his composure before was now overridden by hatred for the man before him. Fury evokes a strident form of bravery.

"Go on then. What d'you *think* you know about my daughter?"

"I thought there was nothing you could possibly want from me?"

Haggerston roared like a beast. He picked Gregor up by the scruff of the neck and thrust him against the hovel wall. A stool went flying and a number of saws fell from their hooks.

"Well, now, maybe this isn't the right time or place... How about you come up to Grimfern? Yes, that's it. Come up to

Grimfern"—Haggerston went to bash him against the wall again—"*tonight*, and I'll tell you everything you need to know."

"Why should I listen to you, little man?"

"Because, quite truthfully, you're in danger. I saw what happened to your daughter's grave, and I think I know the culprit. But I've already said too much. Tonight! Visit Grimfern tonight. I want to help you, George."

The carpenter released his grip all at once, causing Gregor to land inelegantly on unsturdy feet.

"Get out," Haggerston spat. "Get out!" He sent a trestle table flying with one rush of his massive fist.

Gregor scarpered and kept at a smart run all the way back to Grimfern. He couldn't help but feel elated at the thrill of the confrontation. He was sure his arrows had found their mark— Haggerston's shifty eyes betrayed his fears. Constance's father would be at Grimfern that night.

Will was just settling in for a hard day's nothing at the gatehouse when Gregor arrived. The lad shrank back visibly from the dishevelled but grinning botanist. Gregor smoothed down his hair but it might not have helped much, given the twitch in his eye.

"Mr Haggerston will arrive at Grimfern this evening. He is to be let in."

"G-George Haggerston? But—"

"That will be all."

Gregor fastened himself inside the grounds. The greenhouse shimmered atop his ancestral hill.

*All knowledge of Chloe must remain at Grimfern. Her powers, and particularly her provenance.*

# TWENTY-THREE

Sensibly, the other denizens of the crystal palace avoided Gregor for the rest of the day. There was a strange, sickly buzz about him. Nothing good could come from the botanist's jerky behaviour, moving furniture, pacing and disappearing.

There was so much to do. Gregor rubbed his jaw and scratched his head. Looked this way and that. *Decision.* The decision was… a pair of his heaviest secateurs. What'll prune a plant'll prune a person. He tapped his thighs, trying to will himself into being confident. The thought of the act ahead of him brought with it a certain rising horror: that bubbling tar, that anxious peat bog at the centre of each person. He refused to let himself acknowledge the murk. He had preparations to make. And besides, wasn't this beginning to be fun?

Gregor made haste preparing a space in the strange thicket. He arranged himself a kind of smoking room: two wing-backed chairs, his moodiest lamp, and an occasional table. On this he placed a silver cigar case and an ashtray. Revenge was a grisly business, but there was no reason not to be civil about it.

"Are we expecting visitors?" Simon enquired through tight lips.

"An important one, a final one. A certain Mr George Haggerston."

If there was an explosion of anger in Simon, it was buried deep.

"How dare you bring him here. To Grimfern."

"I shall invite whoever I want to my own greenhouse."

Simon stilled completely. After a long period of silence, Gregor left him, semi-hunched, eyes fixed. There would be no rousing him from his emotional petrification. When Gregor next came past that way with a clutch of forget-me-nots for the table, Simon had withdrawn to his basement sanctum. Gregor would pay for that outburst in vicious silences from his partner. But at least Simon was safely out of the way.

Gregor lowered himself into one of the chairs and gripped the arms. The sun was high, his trap was set. Blinking drowsily, his wondrous garden disappeared before him into the purple void of delayed sleep.

He woke from his unscheduled nap with a start—there was something moving in the bushes. His nerves on edge, Gregor cried out and pushed back into his chair. At the commotion, Jennifer, the loveable rodent, poked her head round an aspidistra. She was in her new uniform of a waistcoat, shirt, and suit trousers. Her hair never did quite stay in that up-twist.

"Anything I can do for you, Mr Sandys?"

"Wh-what time is it?" The sky had ripened into the fullness of evening.

"Just gone half-seven, I reckon, sir."

"Good, then there's still time. I want you to put CHLOE to bed."

"Of course, I do that every night."

"I mean now, Jennifer."

"But it's not even dark yet!"

"Do you think she cares? She is a plant. And once you've finished with that, I want you to make yourself scarce. Spend the night at your father's."

Jennifer did not like that one bit, judging by the size of her pout, but Gregor had already dragged himself to his feet. Stifling a yawn, he was off fetching some brandy and glasses. Only the best brandy, only the finest glasses. Everything would be perfect.

Gregor settled into pacing around the clearing in his forest. He practised conversations, mumbling both parts of an imagined exchange between himself and the carpenter. He practised laughing hospitably. He also practised his moves with the secateurs—a vicious lunge, a wild slash, a strategic snip.

"Mr Sandys! …Gregor!"

Jennifer came skidding once more around the aspidistra. She had changed into her pauper's wear—she couldn't very well turn up at her father's water mill dressed up to the nines like Gregor.

"It's CHLOE. She won't go to bed. It's only just sunset—there's light still streaming through the windows."

"Then we shall kill the sun, Miss Finch."

Gregor left his weapon with the brandy decanter and jogged off to CHLOE's bedroom. The nymph had tangled her twig-fingers up around a column to avoid being taken to bed. She shrank back to hide behind it as Gregor approached.

"There, there, little girl. It's alright." Gregor took a big forced yawn. "It's nearly time for bed! Can't you feel the evening's breeze?"

He wafted his arms and alternated his weight between his legs, mimicking the plant-creature's dance. CHLOE perked up a little but stayed by the relative safety of her pillar. Jennifer arrived, winded. Gregor swayed his way over to her.

"Blanket," he whispered harshly, but still smiling for CHLOE, "blanket, *now*."

Jenny disappeared up and down the ladder to her bedroom and was back again before Gregor could show off his three-step. He held out his hand to his daughter.

"May I have this dance?"

She took her time to entwine her fingers around his, but soon they were gently stepping and leaning in their irregular minuet. The dance grew wilder—a mazurka no less. Gregor saw the bristles on CHLOE's shoulder flourish, her lush ferns gave off spores in their wake. He didn't want her to get over-excited. He segued into a grand waltz—ups and downs and fluid movements. Her cloud of spores was settling on his tweed. He spun her into a graceful rise... but gave Jennifer a firm 'chopping' gesture. She threw the blanket over CHLOE, whose legs immediately gave way. Gregor took the momentum of their turn and swooped her up and around into his arms and onto her slab.

"Her eyes aren't as sophisticated as ours," Gregor panted, "she probably only sees patches of light and dark. And when it's night time she consumes oxygen but doesn't release any—it's a totally different state. She uses the lack of light to tell her that it's time to respire. Which is analogous to our sleep."

Sure enough, her wriggling gradually ceased in the swaddling cloth.

"Do we need to tie her down again?" Jennifer asked.

Gregor didn't catch her eye for his response. "Not this evening, Miss Finch. Now, goodnight."

He gestured towards the exit. There was so much running through his mind. He was going through his list of preparations, so was spending the very smallest amount of brain power he could on removing Jennifer from the garden. It was in the late stages of sunset when they reached the front door, and Jennifer stopped dead in her tracks.

"Is that—Constance's father?"

The silhouette of a brute was shambling up the long drive to Grimfern. The sun's gold was fading, threatening annihilation. The shadowed figure was bringing the dark with him. As well as his threatening heft, he had what seemed like a three-foot pole with a trigger.

"Why's he got a rifle?" Jennifer said under her breath.

"For shooting things, I'd imagine."

Gregor brandished a finger at Jennifer, then dashed off back to his clearing. He returned to where Jennifer stood with the secateurs in his hands—she regarded them with wide eyes. He secreted them into his cummerbund at the back.

"Sandys!" Haggerston roared.

Gregor straightened his cravat, took a deep breath and stepped outside, arms open wide.

"George! How good of you to come!"

Haggerston brandished his rifle and took a potshot at the glasshouse. The violent rupture shook the air of Grimfern and shattered a pane. A clutch of grouse sped away along the rolling lawn. Somewhere in the garden a delicate flower was showered in vicious shards.

Gregor made a sidestep to shield Jennifer from the confrontation, but she had already made the same gesture and had pushed her way in front of *him*.

"What the bloody hell do you think you're playing at, shooting at people's houses?" she declared.

"You stay out of it, Jenny, you don't know what this is about!" Haggerston grunted, approaching slowly, reloading his weapon.

Gregor placed his hand on Jennifer's shoulder. "He's right, you know, my dear. It's time to right some wrongs. I don't want you to be around for this."

She looked into his eyes pleadingly. Gregor didn't exactly seem like the kind of man who could take on the likes of the murderous George Haggerston.

"Don't worry, I've got a plan."

Jennifer clearly doubted that, but relented, touching his forehead with her own.

"Do what you have to do."

She set off with a chest-puffed swagger but gave George Haggerston a wide berth.

"Get home safe, Miss Finch," Gregor called after her.

"Now isn't that touching. A master what cares about the help." The carpenter strolled right up to Gregor, menacing him with his closeness.

"Welcome to Grimfern, Mr Haggerston. I thought we'd have a drop of brandy before we get down to business. Right this way."

A glass of brandy—a second—under the heavy weight of silence. Gregor sat awkwardly in the wing-backed chair— in the forced and false naturalness of his facial and vocal performance he failed to mask his perennial inability to sit properly. Each man kept his weapon close by—the rifle on Haggerston's lap, and the secateurs in Gregor's cummerbund. Each man pointedly avoided looking the other in the eye. Each man cradled a brandy glass, both obstinately refusing to acknowledge the brandy's excellence, or its effect on them. The twilight dissolved slowly in alcohol. There was darkness between each surrounding plant; a threat under every leaf.

Gregor made an overture towards the pressing issue.

"I was sorry to hear about your daughter."

Haggerston swilled his glass, which was tiny in his shovel-hand. "Not as sorry as I was."

"I'm sure. When Jennifer told me her grave had been tampered with I was beside myself with rage. And she had been laid to rest by the Wycombe Road? No wonder I hadn't seen her headstone in the graveyard."

"No headstone. Church wouldn't have her. Suicide."

Gregor let the lie hang in the air. He felt nothing but contempt for this man, who had let his daughter's name be ruined to save his own. The lie poisoned the atmosphere and caused the space between the foliage to swirl—was that the brandy?—or was there really a rustle? Nothing should have been moving in the greenhouse with Jennifer at home, and Simon underground… Perhaps the broken pane of glass was letting in a draught.

"Look, if you know something about Connie's grave you'd better spit it out," Haggerston growled, "'cause I am not a patient man."

"So I've heard. That temper has got you in trouble before, hasn't it, George?"

"You watch your mouth."

"Absurd indeed are the half-truths we tell ourselves as fathers. We claim to want what's best for our children, when really we can't distinguish that from our own self-interest."

Haggerston threw his brandy glass to the floor. "You don't know what it is to be a father. You, out here in your sad little greenhouse, you'll never know."

Gregor was taken aback by this outburst. He knew it to be false, of course. Gregor *did* know what it was to be a father, first-hand. He had brought CHLOE into the world, and though she was his experiment he was rather fond of her after all.

Furthermore, it stung to be reminded that people like him weren't *supposed* to bring up daughters. He brought his gaze to meet Haggerston's reddening face, spotting on the way a stray root by the large man's ankle.

That root had not been there when Gregor set up the smoking room. Gregor felt his blood rush in anticipation. The root was wriggling slowly, exploring Haggerston's trouser hem, reaching out and winding tight.

"I think I know why I'm here," the carpenter continued, oblivious to the strange growth. "You're gonna say I dug her up myself. Well, I never dug her up—and if you say I did we're gonna have a problem."

A vine appeared behind his ear, this one a tender shoot with fresh, wet leaves. It wound around the carved filigree of the chair and poised to strike at his temple like a cobra.

"You probably think it's me what killed her in the first place," Haggerston said, letting out a dark laugh and brandishing his rifle, "but if you ever so much as *whisper* that I killed my daughter—"

Behind him, in the undergrowth, a green pair of retinas caught the light of the gas lamp. Gregor stood up and the word left his lips—CHLOE.

Haggerston shot Gregor a dumbfounded, quizzical look. CHLOE used that moment to strike. She tightened her roots around his calf and threw the vine over his shoulder, latching on firmly under his other arm.

Haggerston staggered to his feet—the rifle fell, forgotten, to the floor. He threw his shoulder forward, pulling CHLOE sharply into the back of the chair. To Gregor's abject horror, she twisted her legs up and over her body, slithering her way over the chair. Once righted, she extended her bindings to envelop more and more of George Haggerston. Her vines were keeping his body facing away from her, but he twisted his neck to catch a glimpse of his assailant. It must have been a sight, spines and spindles and vicious leaves, like being attacked by a rancid hedge.

"Damn you to hell for this, Sandys!"

Gregor fumbled for his secateurs and held them out with two trembling hands… but who was his target?

"That's it, cut me free, then!"

Chloe had strong cords around all his limbs now, and around his chest and forehead. Haggerston strained with all his considerable might to remain standing, but she forced him to his hands and knees.

Who was this creature, who not long ago Gregor had danced with and put so sweetly to bed? This child of his with soft moss for skin and English ivies for hair? What he saw now was a knot of brambles, the deep rage of the earth. And yet here too was Constance, the only truly slighted party in all this, whose body was an unwitting host to a virulent mycelium. Was she finally exacting revenge on her appalling father?

The entity known as Chloe walked up Haggerston's back, digging her spikes into his spine. With all the grace of a ballerina, but with distorted and irregular angles, she bent at the waist and brought her face to the ear of her prey. Elegant moss-feelers reached out from her cheek and stroked his sullen eye socket.

"What *is* it?" Haggerston mumbled, his mouth crushed against the brickwork.

Gregor was filled with disgust, for the sight and for the man. He swallowed his bitter saliva.

"I thought you'd recognise your own daughter."

CHLOE stretched out her unnatural neck to bring her head into Haggerston's vision. He was presented with his daughter's face in all its necrotic greenery. His body twitched but CHLOE kept him in his place.

"Connie…"

Haggerston let his left flank fall to the ground, giving him a second's opportunity to reach for the rifle. It was just beyond his fingertips when CHLOE reasserted her control of his limbs—he shook helplessly against her binds, stretching out desperately for the weapon.

Gregor saw the soft flesh of Haggerston's wrist and knew what he had to do. He drove the pointed hook of the secateurs into a vein and dragged them up to his elbow. Haggerston roared as a crimson canyon erupted in his forearm, spraying Gregor and the garden with blood.

CHLOE capitalised on Haggerston's flinch by smashing his head sharply to the ground. The sound was less of a smack, and more of a crunch. He became quite still, except for his remaining eye. That one dark orb looked around, bewildered and furious.

CHLOE shivered in delight and sent out all manner of buds and tendrils. Her ivy-hair stood on end. She contorted her skeletal form in exquisite delight. A gossamer root system spread out over Haggerston's face, exploring his heavy features. It probed his crushed and bloody nose. It entered the corner of his vicious mouth. It dug the tips of its roots into the skin around his eye socket, forcing the lids open. His bloodshot eye darted this way and that. Presumably all he could see was a cage of fibrous roots threatening the sanctity of his eyeball.

There was a rustle in the forest that was the entity; a pulse in every shoot and stem of CHLOE, an exultation in every thread of mycelium. In every waxy leaf and in every human bone, she was ready. CHLOE added immense pressure across the entire new root system on Haggerston's face.

His eye burst. Blood and optical fluid ran down his cheek. His skin bulged under her grip, the cartilage in his nose twisted, and eventually his whole skull fractured in on itself.

There was a long silence. Gregor lowered himself down to the floor to prevent himself from falling.

It was hard to tell where Constance's body stopped and where her father's began, so profound was the overgrowth. It was as if a bramble patch had opened up its maw and eaten a man whole. Despite the twisted nature of the tableau, Gregor sensed that the entity was at peace. A forelock of flowers blossomed on CHLOE's brow—a constellation of daisies for the sweet plant-girl.

# TWENTY-FOUR

Simon had been cowering in his basement, idly working on a new tableau. But nothing came out right. There were noises upstairs—muffled words, footsteps? Simon shook them away and wrestled with his own adversary: a ferret supposed to look like it had just fallen off its tiny penny-farthing. Try as he may, Simon could not get the sinuous curves of the rodent to sit convincingly. Frustrated, Simon's hands refused to cooperate. A limb came unstuck from the poor cyclist. A patch of hide lost its fur. Simon put the piece to one side and tried instead to paint the scenery on the base—greens of various shades to evoke the sensation of myriad grasses.

Suddenly there was silence from above. Concerted, persistent. Simon added a tyre mark to the fresh 'grass'. The newfound silence proved to be more horrendous and distracting than the noises had been. Simon set down his paints and went to check on Gregor.

It was after two in the morning. The confrontation had left an intolerable burden on Simon—did Gregor truly think only he had the right to choose who came and went at Grimfern? Where did that leave Simon's standing—as that of a lodger? He dallied on the stone staircase. A large part of him did not want to see the landlord right now. But the results of his meeting with George Haggerston… that was another matter.

Gingerly Simon made his way through the dark green corridors of Grimfern. Pushing aside the heft of a palm leaf, he entered the fateful clearing. The sight that greeted him was awesome and terrible. Their side had clearly won—the brute was incapacitated. In fact, he was practically encased in the sinuous excesses of CHLOE. Gregor was still slumped on the floor, staring into nothingness.

"It seems you got your point across," said Simon. He stood there straight and smart, but his hands were balled into fists.

Gregor chewed the air but didn't shift his vacuous gaze. Behind those glazed eyes were a million frantic thoughts, Simon knew. It took him a good while to work out exactly which of his many questions would help shift Gregor out of his freeze.

"What do we need to do *next?*" was what he settled on. He chose the word 'we' in place of 'me' or 'you' to avoid the apportioning of blame. 'Next' was also important. In times of crisis, it's all too easy to lose oneself in the spiralling horror of dreadful possibilities. Simon leaned on the word 'next' in his delivery, so that he could bring Gregor back to his practical, analytical self.

It worked—Gregor cocked his head, finally noticing the world around him. God bless the tangible world of matter, into which we can go to escape our intangible fears. And God bless menial tasks, which are so much more powerful than unmenial ones for purging our darkest thoughts.

"Next. Next, next, next—" Gregor repeated to himself, clicking his fingers. He rose and spun around, breaking down the horrid situation into achievable tasks. Finally his revolutions took him all the way back to Simon, and he broke into a bizarre smile. "I say," Gregor chuckled, "it's time to give CHLOE a little trim, I should think."

Simon gave the slimmest of nods. He didn't like the mad gleam in his lover's eyes.

Gregor took his discarded secateurs and gave them a quick wipe on Haggerston's shirt. He then set about energetically pruning CHLOE right back to her substrate. Leaves and vines started flying about as the botanist continued his frenzy. Soon there were patches of skin—or what used to be skin?—showing beneath the underbrush. Simon delicately placed his hand on Gregor's twitchy shoulder.

"Let me do that, Gregor. It's still CHLOE in there—our daughter."

Gregor dropped the secateurs and stepped away. With another twitch, he pulled out his jotter and scurried off, scribbling.

Simon summoned the infinite calm of the paediatric doctor and began to trim CHLOE. He left a little more 'seam allowance' on her coat of greenery. All the while he stroked her hair and bom-bom-bom-ed his way through a little ditty. His deep bass voice bounced pleasantly through the greenhouse. CHLOE stirred from her stasis.

With a sudden lurch she wrapped her long fingers round Simon's wrist and tried to wrestle the secateurs away. She was too drained from the recent growth to put up much of a fight, however, and Simon merely chuckled.

"Come now, little girl," he said, liberating her last sprig, "it's sleepy time for woodland faeries such as yourself. Hush now, the moon is calling you to rest."

He lifted her with some difficulty and carried her, knees wobbling, to her bedroom. He saw the fresh sweep of daisies across her face and traced them with his fingertip. He kissed her sweetly on the forehead, which caused her various *Mimosa* leaf-tips to shiver.

"Pleasant dreams," he whispered. "Oh, how I hope you do dream."

Back in the clearing, under the great arches of the atrium— under the still-greater arches of the sky—Simon found his partner inspecting the new corpse and making notes. He quickly hid the jotter when he saw Simon coming. He always was so precious with his note-taking. Gregor took every precaution to keep his records private. The hiding away seemed especially furtive tonight, for which Simon blamed the scientist's evident distress. Gregor looked as if he had a terrible hangover, and he seemed to blame everyone and everything for it but himself.

"Next," Simon repeated coaxingly, "we place the body in the lake where no one will chance across it."

"I don't want him down there," Gregor croaked. "Even if he's never found, *I'll* know he's under the water. He'd spoil the aesthetic."

"Burn him, then? That would get rid of any residual mycelium, too."

"No fires. I'll not have any bonfires at Grimfern."

"Well then, what do you propose?"

Gregor took a slow walk around the body of Mr Haggerston. He nudged it with his shoe, causing the brambles coursing from its back to jostle.

"There's only one place fit for this monster," said Gregor, his chest swelling, "and that's in a shallow grave under the twisted hazel."

Simon went to speak but thought better of it. After assembling his own thoughts a bit more, he tried again.

"I must say the poetic justice appeals to me, but we should also think about practicalities. If he's at Grimfern at least we know he isn't going to be found. And then what of all these branches, coursing with mycelium? What if it grows there by the roadside?"

"If he's at Grimfern then they'll know we did it, and we'll be reminded that we did it every single day. If he's by the twisted hazel he'll be out of everybody's way, erased from the village. That's what he tried to do to Constance."

Gregor lifted the corpse at the shoulders. Its desecrated head lolled to one side. He gestured for Simon to take the feet, which he did with great reluctance.

"And as for the mycelial growth," Gregor continued, "we'll simply have to salt the earth."

With great difficulty they bundled the body through the greenhouse, leaving a trail of darkly shimmering blood. They propped him up in their carriage, just as they had done with Constance some months prior. Gregor was looking vacant and droopy, so Simon set off at a noble trot to wake Florence. The grey mare was less than impressed to be disturbed at this time of night, but Simon gave his profuse apologies and eventually she agreed to be shackled to the carriage. Simon rooted round in the stable's storeroom for the big box of salt-lick. Florence licked her lips at the sight of it, but this salt was not for her. Simon packed it into the luggage trunk.

Gregor was being profoundly useless. It took as much effort to coax him into the cab as it had to set Haggerston in there. The pair of them sat slumped, one dead, one distant, heads flopping towards their respective windows. Simon rolled up his black velvet sleeves, clambered up to the driver's mount, and took the reins.

He allowed Florence to pick up some speed sweeping down through the Grimfern Estate. According to his pocket watch it was already past four, and they had to complete their grisly business and be back by dawn. Once out of the gates and into the countryside, the hedges and brambles either side of them became oppressive. Simon pressed the grey mare to make haste. Neither of the carriage's occupants would mind a bumpy ride.

Once they reached Hazlemere they were obliged to slow down so as not to wake the villagers. Still, they were far from silent as they trundled through—the horse's hooves, the creaky frame, the uneven road. Simon was alert like a wounded animal, fierce yet vulnerable. There was no candlelight flickering in the windows of the squat dwellings, no fires in their hearths, and not another soul made their existence known.

That is, until a heavy shadow appeared from behind a slumping wall.

Simon stopped the mare firmly, causing her to fret. The shadow was a man in a weighty coat and misshapen hat, hunched over with various ropes. From each one hung the silhouette of a woodland animal. There were many corpses in Hazlemere tonight.

"Curtains, Gregor," Simon whispered. "Close the curtains!"

"Who goes there," cried the shadow, "with horse and carriage on such a queer night?"

Simon heard the flutter of the curtains and prepared himself to speak.

"It is Simon Rievaulx," he stuttered. "And who, sir, are you?"

The shadow man swung his animals over his shoulder and removed his cap. "Oh, Mr Rievaulx! It's just me—John Finch, Jennifer's father!"

Mr Finch lumbered over to the carriage. Simon sat very tense and stiff.

"Mr Finch, my regards."

"Jennifer was back this evening, popped in just before I 'eaded on for work. Didn't say owt about it, either," said Finch. "Don't get me wrong, it's nice to have her, but is everything alright up at the estate?"

"Everything's quite fine, I'm sure Jennifer simply wanted to spend some time with her doting father."

"Well, I suppose," Finch said.

His eyes were level with Simon's boots. Was he scrutinising the dirt on them? And was there more than dirt? Simon crossed his legs.

"Where are you going at such a time, and with a carriage?" asked Finch.

"We are going to London," said Simon in an unnaturally high voice, "to collect some taxidermical supplies which can only be purchased from specialist establishments."

"You say 'we'…"

"Yes—yes, yes. Mr Sandys is in the back, dozing off of course. He is no friend of the larks, but we like to set off nice and early to really… make the most of the day." Simon trailed off. In the pre-dawn gloom he couldn't quite read John Finch's expression.

"Well, hie thee hence, sir. Safe travels. I'll let Jennifer know not to expect you until later in the day."

With that he returned his cloth cap to his dirty head and trundled off towards the old water mill. Simon nudged Florence onwards, replaying the conversation in his mind, analysing every element, and wincing at his own stupidity.

Simon found the boundary stone by starlight at the edge of the village. The twisted hazel loomed over the gravesite—a great spiral blackness against the sky, only implied by the absence of constellations. He took a shovel and tested the ground, finding it thoroughly mauled by the prior excavation. He took some time to dig even further down—though it was more than Haggerston deserved—then dragged his partner out of the carriage. Together they crumpled up the salt-licks, casting some into the bottom of the grave, and saving one intact for Florence.

With a general air of emotionless dignity, they heaved the corpse into its pit. Haggerston was the first person to dig this hole. Now hopefully his body would be the last thing to fill it. They covered him with dirt, alternating soil with salt. Finally they trampled the earth underfoot to compact it as much as possible, and they sprinkled the remaining dust of the salt-licks over the surface. With any luck, nothing at all would ever grow in the shadow of the twisted hazel.

It was not yet dawn, but the darkness was lifting imperceptibly around them. The pair stood there panting, with mud up to their knees, salt on their hands and, in Gregor's case, dried blood on his waistcoat. Simon felt the exhilaration of a job well done.

Gregor lowered his head to Simon's shoulder.

"We did a good thing here," said Gregor, making to get back into the carriage. "Now, back to Grimfern."

"I should think so," Simon replied, kissing Gregor's thick brown hair. "We've got a lot of cleaning up to do."

Simon swung himself up onto the driver's seat, and Gregor clambered up beside him.

"Thank you, Simon," Gregor said. "Thank you for everything."

Simon only smiled and geed the horse. They rolled out over hill and dale towards the burgeoning dawn.

# TWENTY-FIVE

Once he was back at Grimfern, Simon had itchy fingers. He got changed into his nightclothes, trying to summon sleep with that routine, but ended up just sitting on a wicker chair in the bedroom. He tried to close his eyes but they refused. They had seen too much tonight. They seemed to insist upon staring into the emptiness of the early morning sky.

Gregor had kicked off his shoes and just about fainted into bed, lying diagonally under the vine-canopy. Giving up on the hope of sleep, Simon swivelled off the bed and descended to his workroom. He rummaged about in the cold storage for a fresh piece upon which to practise his art, but his stocks were damnably low. Only some miscellaneous limbs remained, and these would not do for his purposes.

They would not do at all. He tapped a piano scale on the cold-storage door. Surely there was no way he could present himself at the poacher's today—not after the elaborate and slightly fumbled lie about visiting London. But then again, there never was a day when he so urgently needed the perfect specimen, to soothe his wild mind.

Grabbing his satchel, he set off down the winding pathway back out of Grimfern. Florence the grey mare deserved a rest, poor thing, so Simon resolved to make this journey by foot. An excuse for the poacher would hopefully come to him with a spot of constitutional exercise. And the brisk walk and the various late summer wildlife would keep his conscience distracted, even if his wide eyes betrayed a sense of guilt.

One or two silly butterflies, poppies in the grass verge, a ruby dragonfly by the brook—everything was bathed in the sickly honey of dawn. Simon named everything he knew, muttering their taxonomies like exorcistic rites.

*Lepidoptera, Papaver, Anisoptera! Crux sacra sit mihi lux!*

Simon came to the wooden gate of Mr Finch's water mill. He wriggled with the latch to no avail—it was rusted shut. Judging by the splattered footprints on either side, the Finch family had taken to hopping the fence rather than wrestling with it. Simon tried to raise his leg up to shimmy over, but the lack of give in the fabric of these particular trousers severely reduced his manoeuvrability. He gave a feeble *what ho* which failed to rouse even the birds. Finally, he pressed his sternum into the top of the gate and topple-rolled over with his legs and arms perfectly straight. It was at times like these that Simon's lankiness made itself abundantly clear, but fortunately this morning only the larks bore witness to it.

Inside the mill, lit only by a meagre unglazed window, Mr Finch was preparing last night's catch over a bucket. Simon took care not to peer inside the grisly vessel. All around were signs of Mr Finch's work—traps, nets, carcasses—but very few signs of his *living*. Where did he eat, or sleep, or find a modicum of comfort? Surely not on that blood-stained stool where he was currently shucking the eyes of various woodland animals out of their sockets.

The poacher raised his weather-beaten face to squint accusingly at Simon.

"Well, as it happens—" Simon began, but Mr Finch shushed him furiously. He nodded up to the rafters, where a collection of planks constituted a hayloft of sorts. On closer inspection Simon could see a flopping, freckled arm and some frizzled hair between the bales. He felt himself suddenly attuned to Jennifer's breathing, which caught in her throat as she snoozed with her mouth open.

"To reduce a considerable saga to its proper brevity: we did not go to London."

Mr Finch stuck his knife into the gap between a fresh eye and its socket. He nodded dismissively and popped the eye out into his bucket. Simon followed its wet trajectory with his own firmly socketed gaze. A dozen bright pupils stared back at him from the congealed slop. Eyes like his own which had seen too much.

"I have come to purchase… something. I haven't exactly decided what to work on…"

He remained transfixed on the bucket. Its contents were globular stars in a crimson firmament. He could see himself in there: ensconced like Orion in his constellation of gristle.

Those were his own eyes down there, opening up like mouths from the effluent.

"Mr Finch? I should like to purchase your bucket." Maybe if he made this monstrous slop his taxidermy project, his own eyes would become unseeing. This would be preferable to clawing them right out.

Mr Finch of course acquiesced—there was no part of his life that wasn't for sale or loan—and quickly finished off filling up the bucket. Jennifer dropped down from the rafters like a squirrel, caught sight of Simon, and gave a wheezing *yurp*. She tried to cover as much of herself as possible, but Simon was not interested in her diaphanous night-blouse—he was focused on his precious bloody slop.

"Is everything alright, Mr Rievaulx? Up at the greenhouse?"

"Ah, Miss Finch. Yes, yes, yes. We are… *back from London* and in need of your services again today. At your leisure, of course. But as for 'everything', it is indeed alright."

Jennifer nodded and glanced over at her father, who only shrugged in eternal indifference.

Once it was all prepared, Simon traversed the rusted gate by raising himself to sit on it side-saddle and kicked his gangly legs over. Then he set off with the grisly pail and a ratty dishcloth with which to carry it.

A holy silence reigned at Grimfern, save for the splutter of the sprinklers. Gregor must be up to have set them going, but he was surely still in the coffee-and-sulk stage of his morning, or may even have taken himself back to bed after the morning rounds. Simon processed into the undercroft unnoticed. From his supply of glassware he withdrew an old barber's cylinder—the kind used to disinfect their various blades.

He pulled the ocular globs from their chum bucket, rinsing them carefully and arranging them on a tray in order of size. With scant regard for the danger of the chemical, he injected each gelatinous profiterole with formaldehyde. It had been his intention to arrange the eyes precisely in their vat, but with a frisson of nihilism he 'poured' them into the glass cylinder, enjoying each satisfying plop. To complete the grisly sacrament he topped up the barber's glass with ethanol and secured the lid.

*Kyrie eleison.*

He lifted the specimen to the paltry gaslight. Weak radiance drizzled through and gave each eye its own distorted halo. He carried the piece to his reliquary cupboard as if he were transporting the urn of a hated aunt to a dreadful mantelpiece. The movement caused the eyes to jostle quite alarmingly.

*Christe eleison.*

He found a space on the shelf alongside his previous exorcisms—the rabbit's brain, the pheasant's entrails, and the sheep's heart. As he struggled to place the new specimen on the top shelf, the top-heavy barber's glass toppled towards him. He caught it just in time before it hit his face, but all the eyes rolled around to glare at him accusingly.

*Kyrie eleison. Now I won't see last night when I close my eyes.*

Jenny arrived at Grimfern in her crumpled dress and her clodhopping boots a little after eight. Late summer was giving way to autumn, ripening into deep red and gold. There was the beginning of a chill in the air, which she didn't mind at all. What she *did* mind was the long walk up the hill to the greenhouse with the evening's events still fresh in her thoughts. Gregor had insisted he'd sort everything out, but what could he possibly do faced with Constance's brute of a father?

When she finally reached the greenhouse, it was Simon who solemnly let her in through the many locks and chains. The skin of his face was sagging away from his prominent bone structure—he clearly hadn't slept a wink last night.

"Are you alright, Simon?"

"I'll live, Miss Finch."

He was carrying a mop and a bucket and set to work on the brick floor in the entranceway. To Jenny's horror, the mop turned brown-red with blood and suds. Bringing her hand to her mouth she set off at a jog, following the dried blood trail. Fearing the worst, she approached a clearing.

There was Gregor on his hands and knees, sporting a pinafore and gloves. He was scrubbing the brickwork in much the same manner that Jenny usually would. It struck her as strange to see Gregor doing such labour, but then it struck her as strange that it had struck her as strange. Of course the great botanist should do his own housework.

"Where is Connie's father?" she blurted out.

Gregor sat up and considered his answer. "He is—"

"Mr Haggerston has mysteriously vanished," Simon finished, entering the clearing with a strange gleam in his eyes.

"So he's gone for good?"

"I said we'd take care of it, Jennifer," said Gregor, returning to his scrubbing, "and he got no more or less than he deserved."

Jennifer had no idea how they might have done it, but it was clear that the soft gentlemen of the Grimfern Gardens had done the carpenter in. She saw them as strangely powerful, even with their domestic garb and limp demeanour. She felt powerful too—she had requested action, and on her word a man had been killed. This terrible power must never be used again.

"I shall go and see to Chloe," she said. Gregor gave the slightest of nods as he scrubbed.

It was easier to speak once she had turned away from them.

"Gregor, Simon—thank you." She turned back to face them, in defiance of her emotions. "*Thank you.*"

Simon stepped forward and squeezed her arm. He squinted a little at her and tightened his lips. This was the closest he ever came to a smile and a hug.

Jenny hurried off to wake Chloe. Her dappled bedroom was festooned in sweet-smelling climbers, and there she lay serenely, covered in a soft blanket which was stained with potting soil.

Jenny pulled back the covers, revealing Chloe's fresh face. The new crop of daisies across her temple were striking against the vibrant green of her moss. The plant-creature opened her eyes.

"Good morning, precious girl," said Jenny, "what lovely flowers you have today!"

Chloe smiled and wriggled under her covers in sheer comfort.

"I had a very good friend once, who used to wear daisies in her hair just like that," she said, passing her fingers through the unassuming stalks. "Unfortunately a bad man took her away. But your fathers have done a wonderful thing! They fought the bad man, so that my good friend can be free at last. And now you have beautiful daisies in your hair, just as if Constance had put them there herself."

CHLOE bore her algal gaze straight into Jennifer's. As she did so, the plant-girl lowered the covers slowly. Leaf by leaf, her body was revealed in its supple verdancy, until there was a sudden splash of blue across the abdomen.

"Wait, more flowers?" Jenny asked. The plant-girl guided Jenny's freckled hand to her torso. The blue spray of buds was springy to the touch. "Forget-me-nots. Oh, CHLOE, how could I ever forget you? You are beautiful."

Later that day, Simon was raking up the first fall of autumn leaves on the patio. Gregor seemed to be happy to let his partner do this menial work, as he sat nearby with a book and a pot of coffee. It had been a long day for both of them, but only Simon seemed keen on continuing with daily tasks. He tried gentle huffing and tutting but couldn't draw the botanist's attention.

Inside the glasshouse, Jennifer was developing CHLOE's motor skills by encouraging her to copy various movements. She would stand on one leg or reach high with a particular arm. CHLOE could understand the general gist of 'up' or 'down' but wasn't very good at choosing the right limb to move.

"I want you to know that I have the greatest respect for your bravery last night."

Simon damn near dropped the rake. Gregor hadn't looked up from his book but he was the only person who could have said those words. Words which Simon would never have expected to hear.

"Excuse me?"

"Your bravery." Gregor closed the book but still didn't look at Simon. "I respect it."

As a couple, they weren't very good at giving compliments. It felt unnecessary to praise when success was already self-evident. But still, for Simon it was always nice to have the great scientist acting a little humbler than usual. Simon's reflex was always to deflect attention, however.

"It was all for CHLOE," he said, shaking his head to refuse the compliment, "or for Constance's memory as a part of CHLOE. She's our little girl. I guess we'd do anything for her."

"Our *little girl* has strength beyond our comprehension."

"Don't be silly. She helped you take down Haggerston, yes, but that was merely a function of her biology."

"Is revenge a biological function? From where I was standing it seemed as if she took pleasure from destroying the man."

"What are you accusing my daughter of?"

Gregor stood, tying off his dressing gown, which he was wearing over his suit.

"She is not your daughter. She is my experiment. And I am observing that my experiment is displaying a tendency towards violent retribution."

"This is hardly a fair experiment, Gregor," said Simon with furious spittle. "You're projecting your own desire for vengeance onto the results. CHLOE is our *child* and last night we did right by her."

Gregor tidied the coffee things and his book onto a tray. "She is no child of mine. You are the one projecting yourself onto her. I regret encouraging your idle fancy that CHLOE is a member of the family, a child. I see her now for what she is. A threat."

Simon stood there, wounded. He scoured his memories, trying to work out if what Gregor said was true: had the scientist manipulated him into paternal affection? Gregor turned and carried his things back into the house. Simon eased his worries by reminding himself of the botanist's megalomania and pathological need to be always right. Through the many panes of Grimfern Simon could see CHLOE attempting to mimic Jennifer, with little success.

Gregor was wrong: she was no threat. She was a darling princess, a cherub.

# TWENTY-SIX

Dear Gregor,

Alas—I am wounded. Why must you hurt me so? I am Saint Sebastian, slain by your twin arrows of slander and desire. Somebody fetch a Florentine to paint me, or a Roman to carve me in marble. Giovanni Antonio Bazzi of Siena would create an ideal rendering of your crimes against me—and what was his nickname again?

I debase myself by appealing to our former fondness, but here we are. Gregor—I would be *ever so delighted* to receive you into the Society. Someone of your calibre could really make a difference to our shared passions. Please, Gregor. It's so dull here. As I write, my secretary is sleeping at his desk. I have a long list of meetings with withering dowagers lined up for the rest of the week. Having you around would add a little healthy irritation to my bureaucratic ennui. *Ohimè!*

And yet, to go by your letter, you think of the RHS as a

cesspit. I think of it as fertile ground. Fair warning to you, Gregor: *muck spreads.*

Beatifically yours,
Julian Mallory, Esq.
President of the RHS

P.S. Gregor—I imagine your reluctance to have me visit stems less from your aversion to my presence and more from your fear that I shall find your botanical endeavours entirely devoid of merit?

Gregor thumped the breakfast table. The cutlery and crockery jumped. So did Simon.

"What? What is it?" Simon stuttered in repressed fury.

"That bastard. Sly, malicious, oily—"

"There's no need for language," said Simon, re-smoothing the jewel-red preserve on his crumpet.

"There's every need of language, civil and otherwise. This is a letter from—"

Here Gregor paused, knowing the likely reaction from his partner. He briefly considered measures to contain the situation. A small white lie? He could not think of anything; Simon was staring at him as if he could see the workings of his brain, the pulsing of his blood, the construction of a fable. Gregor sighed and surrendered the letter to Simon.

"It's a letter from Julian Mallory. We've had a back-and-forth, but I swear to you, Simon, I've been pushing him away at every opportunity."

"So I see," Simon said, perusing the insouciant letter, "and now he's the President of the Society. The little shit."

"That's what I said."

"I don't want him to come to Grimfern. There's too much at stake. CHLOE, and—"

"And what? And me? Simon, don't you trust me with Jules after all these years? After what he did?"

Simon folded his napkin and placed it over his crumpet in the manner of an undertaker covering the face of a corpse. He kept his gaze trained firmly on the tablecloth.

"There is trust, and then there is specific, contextual trust. I trust you to do everything in your power to further your goals. I assume, even after what they all did to you for your *Bouquet Fongique* you are in fact desperate to return to the Royal Horticultural Society."

Gregor made to deny it, but Simon held up his hand.

"I trust you to hide CHLOE from prying eyes. I trust you to keep her safe—she is your *greatest experiment*, after all. But do I trust you with Julian Mallory?"

"Well?"

Simon's huge eyes were dark and pained. For a long time the men held a dangerous silence between them. How common it is to doubt! How normal to fear! And yet it remains difficult to admit that one's opinion of one's lover is not always exactly positive.

Simon blinked several times. He tested out an answer with

his tongue on the back of his teeth. He thought better of it and hurried swiftly away.

~

Dear Jules,

I see my arrows have found their target—*mea culpa*. It was not my intention to wound, but merely to fire a warning shot. Pre-emptive self-defence, you know. I really cannot receive you at Grimfern. The balance of the experiment is extremely precarious, and its social context—I'm sure you can imagine. Julian, I am on the verge of something great. I am standing upon a precipice, with infinite possibilities stretching out before me. Please allow me time to prepare for the leap.

You have me imagining our potential future encounter. What a golden day our dream together is! Maybe we are taking a turn around the grounds here at Grimfern, or perhaps we're strolling around a London park. We are catching up, of course—no doubt there is gossip to be shared which cannot presently be put to paper! Perhaps, in this dream of a *rendez-vous*, we're idling by a lake; perhaps there are boats upon it; perhaps there are swans and statues—and secret places amongst the blossoms. Perhaps I turn to you there in the bushes, look you straight in the eye— your hair is all tousled from the romp, how charming!—and I ask: "How in the damn hell could you ridicule me like that, and in front of the whole assembled Society? You absolute worm. You destroyed me—and all for your personal gain." At least, that's what I would perhaps be saying... in my dream of our theoretically-possible-if-we-have-to future *catching up*.

So, with regret and some firmness—and, I think I'm quoting you here, *I say this with love*: the interdiction remains.

Reverentially yours,
Dr Gregor Sandys
Botanist and Iconoclast

P.S. A warning of my own, Mr President: in the end I believe the Romans threw your man Sebastian into the sewer. *Sic transit gloria mundi.*

# TWENTY-SEVEN

Simon stewed over the Julian issue for the rest of the day. Once again a dark cloud hung over Grimfern, not only above its glassy arches, but within the transparent walls, and between the two men of the house. Gregor shut himself off in his laboratory wing. Lord knows what he was doing in there. Simon, for his part, had made a special point of spending as much time with CHLOE as he could, watching Jennifer give her lessons. He was good at almost smiling even whilst his insides roiled. He sketched both of his girls with the softest of pencils, and what a sight they made—lifting limbs, waving, sitting grumpily on the floor.

At the last light, when CHLOE had grown entirely uninterested in the dance class, Simon took it upon himself to put her to bed. She held his wrist close to her daisy freckles as she snuggled down to repose.

"Emeralds and jades are quite exquisite, but a leafy companion is greener and more dear to me."

He gently removed his arm from the sleeping creature's embrace and hurried off towards his basement. Seeing Jennifer en route he gave a curt good-night and left her in his wake. He had the most marvellous idea, but where had he put the equipment?

In his cellar he shifted some furniture to get at a great pile of crates and trunks. He had to displace a good number of non-functioning lamps and once-read books, not to mention a fair few discarded taxidermy projects, to get at the containers themselves. One after another the crates were prised open, until he found what he was looking for.

In a smaller box, with soft lining, resided a series of silver plates. The various cartons he found nearby contained all the paraphernalia he needed to create a daguerreotype. It was a gently outmoded process these days, but no new-fangled paper photography could compare with the celestial glimmer of Daguerre's silver wonder.

With the lights as dim as they would go, Simon spent the rest of the evening polishing and buffing one of the back plates. There could be no speck of dust or other residue. It was a rather fiddly procedure, daguerreotyping, but if anything that meant Simon enjoyed it more. He buffed away until he quite dozed off, then scoured it with nitric acid before putting himself to bed. Gregor wasn't there, even though Simon went to sleep at one in the morning.

Simon woke with the dawn, noting that Gregor had slumped on top of the covers still in his shirtsleeves. Stubborn old man. Even he couldn't fight sleep altogether. Simon dashed down to his workshop to continue his preparations.

In near-total darkness and protected only by a flimsy screen and a Chinois silk scarf around his mouth and nostrils, Simon exposed the silver-coated plate first to iodine fumes, and then to bromine. The stench was unbearable, but worth it for the incredible photo-sensitivity of silver halide.

There was a spring in his step as he rose once more from the crypt to set up the scene for his picture. It would be a *tableau vivant* of sorts—Gregor would play Pygmalion and CHLOE would make a fetching floral Galatea. They would use the central atrium for the staging, near the grand piano. The piano was placed there for the acoustics, but the high roof also provided Simon with what he needed: plenty of natural light. He turned over a wash tub and placed several decorative ferns around it. CHLOE would look as if she were emerging from the very earth at Gregor's command.

Once everything was in order, he set up the camera and carefully ferried the silver plate, protected from the sun in its velvet box. All that remained was to position his models.

Pygmalion was not amused. Gregor had only recently emerged from bed, still wearing yesterday's garments, sans socks. His face still bore the creases of sleep. Simon found him in the modest kitchenette, nursing a cup of coffee.

"Gregor, I would be *delighted* if—"

Gregor shook his head. His saggy jowls flopped slightly. He waggled his finger and tapped the rim of his coffee cup. *Whatever it is: not right now.*

Simon pursed his lips and turned on his heels to find Jennifer and CHLOE. The human was feeding the plant-child nutrients directly into her substrate using an elongated watering can with a sharp spout.

"Good morning, ladies. When you're done here, Mr Sandys and I require your presence by the piano. Jennifer, if you would be so kind as to help Miss CHLOE into her Grecian outfit?"

"Yes, Mr Rievaulx!" Jennifer cried, mugging an excited face for CHLOE's benefit. Things were finally abuzz in the greenhouse, even if Gregor was being an under-caffeinated ogre.

Eventually the strange family was assembled around the piano. CHLOE stood on her tub-podium, swishing the diaphanous veils of her toga. Jenny attended to her, fussing over the drapes of her costume and the nonchalant curls of her ivy-hair. Gregor slouched where he had been told to stand, wearing a fez and smoking jacket, clutching a second cup of coffee.

"Are we all in position?" Simon sang. "Jennifer, come behind the camera, please. Gregor, get that cup out of the tableau. We'll go for a trial run. You'll have to hold the pose for ten seconds. Do you think you can do that, CHLOE?"

The wide-eyed plant-being dropped her ear to her shoulder.

"Gregor, hold your arms like Prospero," Simon said, demonstrating the gesture by reaching forwards with palms heavenward and fingers tensed.

Gregor sighed and adopted the pose at half-energy. It was as if he were holding two imaginary bowls he didn't particularly care for.

"Now, Jennifer, adopt the statue pose so that CHLOE might mimic. Gregor, give it a bit of *oomph*, will you, my dear."

Simon dashed behind the camera and under its velvet drape

to check the inverted image created by the lens. Gregor rolled his shoulders and gave a slightly more emphatic rendition of carrying imaginary bowls. Jennifer puffed out her chest and lifted one arm high above her head. CHLOE, to her credit, tried to imitate Jennifer as they had practised. She raised herself by stretching out the root system emanating from her feet and shins. Her head however stayed at the same height, forcing her to buckle at the neck. All the while her eyes were wide, her face placid.

Simon saw Gregor's position falter and fall. The tiny upside-down image of the botanist shook its head and walked out of shot. By the time Simon extricated himself from the camera, there was nothing but a pile of robes on the floor. Gregor was nowhere to be seen.

Simon clenched his fists. He felt as if thick cords were pulling him to the floor.

"I try to do something *nice* for this family," Simon said through gritted teeth, "and he has to ruin it."

Jennifer patted him on the shoulder. CHLOE copied the gesture in the air.

"He's in a mood right now, it's not your fault. You just have to wait it out."

"I can't *breathe* when he's like this."

Jennifer put her hands on her hips. CHLOE's mimicry failed slightly—her hands were placed higher, on her ribs. She was leaning over quite precariously. Fortunately, her temporary root system kept her anchored to the podium.

"I know it's uncomfortable for you," Jennifer said, "but you can't insist he be happy all the time just for your benefit."

Simon pulled himself out of his downward spiral and shook himself. He padded about a little to remove the last dregs of the impulse to shut down. CHLOE—bless her—was strangely beautiful in her grotesque arabesque.

"What shall we do instead?" asked Jennifer.

"We need a new Pygmalion. And look—Galatea has fashioned herself in your image, Jennifer."

"What, me?" Jenny blushed. She hated being looked at. The thought of her image being captured on this device filled her with dread.

"Yes, Miss Finch. In the absence of her creator, let me record CHLOE's relationship with her very best friend."

Jenny blushed harder. Her neck was retracting into her shoulders. The thought of CHLOE's gentle finger-twigs tempted her. Soon she was wearing the toga—with a few modifications for modesty—and the scene was ready to be constructed.

CHLOE was getting very good at mimicking Jennifer. Too good, in fact. When Jenny reached up towards her like Gregor had, CHLOE also reached up and away. Simon stroked his chin and in a flash of inspiration removed the podium. It made more sense for the ladies to be equals. They stood holding hands at arm's length, like two nymphs gambolling in the forest.

"No, no, it still won't do," cried Simon from the camera, "you're not quite in the picture and I get no sense at all of your relationship. Stand right next to each other."

"Like this?" Jennifer stepped in and placed her hand on CHLOE's nearest shoulder. Bosom friends. As close as sisters.

"No, ladies, it still isn't—"

Just then, CHLOE copied Jenny's approach, which shoved her own torso quite into her governess's. They were now touching from ankle to armpit, both of them wearing only robes and veils. Jennifer could feel CHLOE's moss on the flesh of her own thigh. It was too awkward to keep her hand on CHLOE's shoulder, so she lowered it to her leafy waist. With CHLOE's various tendrils and both sets of limbs, the two were soon thoroughly intertwined. They rested their heads against each other's. The tiny petals of a daisy brushed Jennifer's cheek and she took in a shuddering breath.

"That's exactly right," said Simon, "stay right there. Even with the bright light we need a long exposure! Three, two, one… it's open!"

Oh sweet paralysis of ecstasy. If you'd have asked Jennifer to move right now, she couldn't. CHLOE's fronds and feelers were exploring her body. Jennifer's own flesh was alive not with flora but with passion. How much longer would the picture take? Something long and stem-like was emanating from CHLOE's moss and tickling the very top of Jennifer's thigh. It was all she could do to stop herself leaning in to it…

"And that's it! The shutter's down, the exposure is complete. You can relax now, ladies."

"Uh, Simon…"

The taxidermist popped up from behind the camera and saw Jennifer's predicament. Her clothes and her hair were trapped in CHLOE's winding growths. Simon fetched a pair of scissors and pruned her back enough to liberate the governess.

In the darkness of his cellar, Simon developed the image with fumes of mercury, taking little care to protect himself from the miasma. Then, to stop the plate from reacting to further light, he used hot salt water to remove the silver halide. He placed the plate into a protective sleeve and slowly increased the brightness of his gas light.

The image of the two young women shimmered in the gloom. They were formed out of crystal moonlight—both tangible and immaterial all at once. This holographic quality brought out the deep strangeness of the image. Two good friends in a sisterly embrace, except one sister was sprouting vines and leaves—a true nymph captured in the reflection of a limpid pool.

A single tear dropped down Simon's face. His daughter was truly beautiful. A woman more than a girl now, he realised. And it was so nice that she had such a supportive governess in Jennifer. On the daguerreotype Jenny's lips were slightly parted, her face wide with gentle shock. He smiled. Jennifer was such a wonderful friend for his precious daughter.

# TWENTY-EIGHT

Several days later, Gregor received a long-awaited package. Some time ago, while he was laid over in Zanzibar before sailing on to Ceylon, he had encountered a lively young fellow who showed him a most unusual orchid. Its flower had six sharp points in a star-burst pattern, hence its name: the Star of Bethlehem orchid. Most intriguingly, it boasted an impressively long spur which seemed to render pollination practically impossible. The orchid had been discovered one hundred years ago by a French botanist, and even the great Charles Darwin could only give conjecture as to how it was pollinated: 'Good Heavens what insect can suck it!' Of course, though it was only discovered by the *Europeans* in 1798, the native Madagascans knew of it long before the French claimed 'discovery'. What is more, this bright-eyed young chap in Zanzibar, Mijoro, hailed from that forested island, and could show Gregor the orchid's natural habitat and method of pollination.

The botanist had taken a diversion from his trip to Ceylon to explore Madagascar. His guide showed him an elusive moth as big as a fist with a proboscis at least a foot long. This was the monstrous beauty that pollinated the Star of Bethlehem. Gregor and his guide Mijoro had spent several weeks collecting samples of the orchid and the moth, as well as generally pollinating each other. Gregor paid him handsomely before he left and set up a system with the British officials in Zanzibar whereby Mijoro could send larvae of this special moth on any passing clipper bound for Britain, with Gregor returning cash by the same method. If letters were passed between the two of them, barely a trace of them remained. The larvae were keen Romanticists and would literally devour the most ardent parts of this correspondence.

Gregor carefully opened this new package in his laboratory. The larvae had pupated, and one was ready to hatch—in fact it was halfway out of its casing. A tattered letter with many chunks missing was lying in the bottom.

"—in the moonlight of our excesses—long to reach out and—just one taste of your—"

Those larvae were voracious.

Gregor brought the box to the steamiest part of the greenhouse—right by the gents' shower. The creatures' biological processes would speed up now they were back in tropical climes. And there, guarding the entrance to the shower, were the Star of Bethlehem orchids, clinging tightly to a trellis arch. The spurs of their flowers pointed out lewdly across the path of any would-be showerer.

Gregor set the pupae down under the arch and went to find CHLOE. Recent events had given him a certain distance from her emotionally. He wouldn't describe that distance as 'fear'... But he still felt an impulse to nurture her, to encourage her wonder at the world. It would be so wonderful for her to see the creatures emerging.

He searched in all the usual places, but Gregor could not find CHLOE cavorting with the flowers or sunning herself by the piano. He came across Jennifer, who was lounging in a wicker chair, looking at pictures in a volume of botanical illustrations.

"Where is CHLOE?"

"I haven't seen her," Jenny replied, not paying much attention.

"Isn't it your job to look after her? I thought we paid you for that?"

Gregor stamped off, looking this way and that amongst the foliage. His eyes fell upon an innocuous nightmare. The French doors to the patio were wide open.

They were to be shut at all times. He had made that perfectly clear to everybody in the house who could be made to understand him. The doors were to be shut at all times to keep the heat in, yes. But this year they had to be shut to keep the *plants* in.

"These doors are to be kept *shut,*" he bellowed, slamming them on the final word. But what if CHLOE had already escaped? He opened them again and trudged outside, quite numb. On the other side of the patio was a large rosebush. Within the rosebush—inside it, absorbing it and absorbed by it—was CHLOE.

Gregor roared and slipped a little as he set off for the rosebush. CHLOE was truly embedded. Perhaps, childlike, she had sat down and hugged the body of the bush close to her own. Now it seemed like the rosebush *was* her torso—green head, rosebush belly, and mossy rump on the ground.

Gregor tried to prise her from the bush but she was so entwined he could not move her. He gave himself several nasty thorn wounds for his trouble.

"Simon! Bring the secateurs!" Glass panes rattled at Gregor's insistence.

CHLOE seemed to be wincing—the small leaves of her face were flattened down, her daisies had closed their petals. The thorns which had drawn blood from Gregor must be damaging her as well, leeching her sap and keeping her tangled. Despite himself, Gregor stroked her ivy-hair to comfort her. Damn this experiment and its ability to evoke in him such feelings.

Eventually Simon wandered out onto the patio with arms full of different secateurs. When he saw the commotion he picked up his pace and rushed the implements to the botanist. Gregor chose the largest ones and lopped off the thickest rose branches. He earned himself a number of new cuts up his arms and on his face as he reached for the most awkward bits.

Once she was free of the strongest snags, Gregor pulled CHLOE from the rose thicket, tearing the bush asunder and ripping holes in his shirt. He lay her on the wrought-iron garden table and Simon set about removing the fiddlier thorns with smaller secateurs. Gregor paced the patio, seething but also fretting. He hated that he cared about CHLOE. For now, he would channel that into hating the fact that the doors were left open.

"But who would have left them open? Who would have been so careless?"

Simon glanced over to where Jennifer was watching the operation, mouth covered by a shaking hand.

"It doesn't matter who it was," said Simon with a bolt of twine in his mouth which he was using to stitch together CHLOE's larger wounds. "What matters is that it *won't happen again*."

"Too right it won't," Gregor thundered, "I'll lock every door and keep the only key. Let's see if anything can escape then—animal or vegetable."

Simon pulled his stitching tight and stepped away from his patient. He had removed the woody branches and thorns and sutured her wounds. He left some of the more deeply embedded roses, styled as a corsage across her verdant breast. At a distance it was a floral sash; on closer inspection you could tell it was a thorny bandolier.

"Take her inside," Gregor muttered, "and let those roses be a reminder to all of us. This is what can happen if the mycelium gets out. It will envelop everything and anything it sees. CHLOE might be an innocent, but the mycelium within her is not."

He shut the doors behind them and placed a chair to block the exit. Simon held CHLOE in his thin arms. Jennifer was still shaking. There was scarlet blood from Gregor's untreated wounds on the white door handle.

"Nobody and nothing leaves this house without my say so. Clear?"

Gregor's Scottish brogue was strong. The spectre of his furious mother manifested in his tortured vowels. Both Jennifer and Simon felt the malign presence and nodded hurriedly.

The botanist stalked off to look at his moths. The one that was trying to emerge had taken too long to do it and had expired in the attempt. He pulled the overripe moth out of its chrysalis. He should probably keep the specimen pinned to a piece of card. Instead he cast it to the ground and crushed it with his heel.

# TWENTY-NINE

Jenny spent that night not quite sleeping—her chest high, her eyes resolutely open. She had really made a mess of things this time. All she could see was a bleak future for herself: cast out of Grimfern, forced to live once more in her father's attic, alone and miserable. To lose the freedom and protection of the greenhouse, to lose her irritable masters, after everything they had done for her, to lose her deep connection to CHLOE... No. She couldn't let that happen. By the time dawn broke through the drapes of her bedroom-tent she had made up her mind.

She rose and dressed smartly, with her now-habitual waistcoat and a special cravat. She tied her hair up in a plait laced with chamomile flowers from Gregor's garden. Then she set about preparing her first overture of repentance: a lavish breakfast.

Simon got up not long after and nodded gravely when he saw Jennifer cooking eggs. This tacit acknowledgement seemed like a good sign. Simon went off to prepare CHLOE for a formal breakfast, and Jennifer served up the kedgeree, toast, and extra fried eggs. She usually left the food preparation to the boys, since she couldn't provide for their refined palates. But Gregor had such a taste for seafood and spices, he had taught her gruffly how to season the kedgeree to his exacting specification. She set the table *just so*, then removed everything and set it again, angling and re-angling the silverware. She cut some lavender and arranged it in a thin vase in the centre. A rich burning smell came from the kitchen—the coffee. She thumped the table, causing the silverware to bounce out of alignment.

"Stupid, stupid," she said, using the words as weapons against herself. "Come on, Jenny. Let's do this. The coffee."

When she returned with a fresh pot, she was met with a radiant sight. CHLOE was luxuriating in her chair, leaning back to stretch out her ample blooms. She glowed from root to tendril and was covered in a fine dew from her morning misting. Simon was also there, possibly reading, Jenny didn't notice. Everything other than CHLOE seemed hazy and unreal.

Jenny's grip loosened on the coffee pot, which she was holding through a tea-towel. She caught it by the body with her free hand, saving the pot but scalding her palm. The resulting spasm caused her to pour coffee all down her front, spoiling her shirt, waistcoat, and special cravat. The pot clanged against the floor and rolled over to a pair of brown leather shoes—Gregor's.

"Good morning, Jennifer," he said, "get yourself cleaned up. I shall make the coffee."

Jenny trudged back to her bedroom. *Stupid, stupid, stupid.*

None of her nice clothes were clean, so she slipped on a rough blouse over trousers, taking care not to dislodge the chamomile in her hair.

Back at the table, the formal breakfast commenced. Simon only moved the food around his plate, as was his wont. Gregor attacked the kedgeree with some ferocity—this was a good sign for Jennifer. She herself wasn't eating. She was too anxious to impress the boys. And of course CHLOE was just sitting there, sweet and luscious, interested in everything except for what was happening at the table.

"Is it alright, then?" Jenny asked.

Gregor frowned and nodded, helping himself to another fried egg. Jenny sighed in sheer relief. Suddenly ravenous, she set to work on her own plate. Out of the corner of her eye she could see CHLOE dancing in her seat, swaying and twisting. Gregor was throwing the plant-girl dark looks and Simon tensed at her impropriety. CHLOE's fidgeting grew more rhythmic, until the table pulsed with her rocking.

"No dancing at the table, CHLOE dearest," said Simon, speaking with a forced levity of tone. CHLOE, to her credit, ceased swaying. She sank low into her chair.

Jenny chewed slowly. She couldn't help but scrutinise Gregor for how he was taking the situation. He was indeed stealing glances at the plant-girl, but for now seemed more interested in his plate. There were small flakes of haddock in his beard. Another good sign.

Just then the vase with the lavender tinkled over, spilling its contents across Simon's breakfast plate. CHLOE had poked her ganglia through the wrought-iron filigree of the table, possibly trying to reach the pretty flowers.

"It doesn't matter a jot," said Simon, at an even higher pitch than earlier, "I was quite finished already, in fact."

Gregor, in contrast, made no attempt to hide his disdain. He tutted and sighed pointedly, which just about boiled Jennifer's blood. The furnace inside her fought against her need to win the boys over. She had stuffed things up the other day and was trying to make amends. In the end, though, she just couldn't contain the flames of indignation.

"She can't help it—she can't say what she needs."

Gregor's chin sunk into his chest. He spoke extremely slowly.

"What was that, Miss Finch?"

"You can't expect Chloe to just sit there like an ornament. She can't express herself. I mean, what if she was hungry?"

"She doesn't have a mouth," said Gregor.

"What Gregor is trying to say," Simon stuttered, "is that Chloe doesn't eat like us, she takes in nutrients from her soil, and uses water and sunlight to…"

He looked at his partner, who himself was focused on the spilt lavender.

"Photosynthesise."

Jennifer was unimpressed.

"Look, I don't care what the botanical word is. She still can't say what she wants."

Chloe sat herself back up again. She had found some interest in the breakfast and entertained herself by playing her mimic game. She gave an abstract balletic performance of eating breakfast: placing her hands on the table, bringing them up to her face, and repeating. The three humans watched her oscillations in silence. A squall of rain passed overhead. It was a meaner, colder rain than they were used to—autumn was announcing her presence. First a drip, then a trickle came down from the glass roof, which still had a broken pane from Mr Haggerston's warning shot. The trickle was soon a stream, which cascaded down directly onto Gregor's breakfast plate. He remained motionless whilst being splashed by rainwater hitting the kedgeree and the china. His eye glasses were soon splattered, his shirtfront dampened. Jennifer and Simon watched, aghast, fearful of the scientist's reaction to this latest inconvenience.

Gregor's nostrils flared as he took in a long, slow breath. Suddenly moving with great haste, he drained his coffee cup and placed it under the leak.

"You're right of course, Jennifer," said Gregor, watching his teacup fill with rainwater, "she cannot express her own needs. What do you expect from her? She is a collection of plants and fungi."

"She's not a plant," said Jennifer under her breath, "she's a person."

Simon caught her eye and shook his head, clearly trying not to be seen doing this by Gregor. Jenny squared her shoulders and stood by her words.

"She is neither a plant nor a person," said Gregor, wiping his glasses on his shirtsleeves, "she is an experimental holobiont. She is a creature of immense and unknowable power. But wait…

in that case, if she could truly communicate… there would be incredible value in subjective data…"

He returned his glasses to his face, and they immediately became speckled with rainwater once more. Jenny didn't care for the scientific babble. She often felt the two men used fancy words purposefully so that she wouldn't understand them, or even to put her down. Well, she might have a limited vocabulary, but she knew how to use words to her advantage. She saw a way to steer this argument towards a 'win' for CHLOE.

"You've had tremendous success with your experiment so far, Mr Sandys. I can't imagine that this practical problem would stump you. It's just talking. Even children can do it. But I guess your experiment isn't all it's cracked up to be."

"Dash it all. You might be on to something, Jennifer. To let the experiment speak for itself…" Gregor emptied the rain-filled cup into the coffee pot. "Yes, it can be done. I shall find a way."

With that, Gregor disappeared into his laboratory. Jenny stifled a grin and hurried to tidy the breakfast things away. To her surprise, Simon helped her with solemn decorum. He wasn't particularly useful at the task, his mournful movements were much too slow, but Jenny appreciated the gesture. Once the crockery was washed and dried, he spoke to her by the locked door to the patio.

"I'm sorry for Gregor, Jennifer. You poked at a bruise there, by suggesting his experiment was deficient. He can get rather wild when he feels like he's not succeeding."

"But he is succeeding! Look at CHLOE, see how beautiful— I mean, how *impressive* a feat of botany she is."

Simon smiled and shook his head. He placed a hand on the rain-soaked door. "For men like him, no objective measure of success will ever be enough. He has to always be better, to be more than he ever was. And if one day is glorious, then the next day is all the more pitiful."

"Be that as it may," Jenny said, "I don't need you to apologise for him. I can take it. In fact, I could weather any hardship if it gets CHLOE a voice."

They turned to the æthereal plant-girl, who was investigating the leak. Having observed the stream from all angles, she put her head directly under it. Rivulets cascaded from her ivied hair and down her chin. Her grassy sternum coursed with fresh water, and her soil became rich and dark.

[Extract from Gregor Sandys' experimental jotter, Friday 30th August 1889]

*So I enter a new phase of my experiment. Why should my travails end once successful? I shall endeavour to improve always upon my creations, and any achievement shall be increased ten-fold by the subsequent one. Let it be known to posterity that Gregor Sandys was never satisfied with mere excellence.*

*It occurred to me that the entity should be able to express itself to display ordered thought and higher function. Therefore I have decided to provide her with a mouth, a pulmonary system, and a voice box. Here follows an overview of my proposed intervention.*

*Amongst humans and certain other primates, meaning in sound is created by careful manipulation of the mouth.* CHLOE *does possess a human jaw, but much of the important physiological elements for speech have been removed in favour of horticultural elements. I shall reinstate her mouth by separating her lips and providing them with dexterity with* Mimosa, *not unlike the pads of her fingers. Once the oral cavity is prised open, I will be able to check the state of her original teeth. I may need to replace these with dentures, although I would prefer a plant-based alternative. In lieu of a tongue— Constance's will have long since deteriorated—I will graft on the fruit body of a spongy fungus, namely* Clathrus ruber, *known as the latticed stinkhorn.*

*Regulated airflow is required to make sounds we would recognise as speech. The problem is that* CHLOE *herself does not 'breathe'. I propose a mechanistic solution to this problem. Within her thoracic cavity I will place a bellows, connected to her windpipe. The mycelium will be trained to squeeze the bellows to pass air through said windpipe. She will not be mortally required to take in air as a human breathes to respire, but she will pump the bellows to pass air out to speak.*

*The air will have to pass through some kind of voice box in order to produce pitched sound. Given* CHLOE's *taste for music I feel it would be appropriate to turn to existing musical instruments to provide her with timbre. A series of woodwind options present themselves: panpipes, reeds, double reeds, whistles. To streamline the system, I could use banks of double reeds for lower tones (I have an oboe d'amore lying around somewhere) and rudimentary recorders for whistle tones. The mycelium would be able to choose which pipes are played by the bellows by opening them in a manner similar to a human epiglottis. The overall system would resemble a pipe organ, minus the manuals and pedals.*

*Mimicry has proved to be a useful teaching strategy so far and copying our speech will be the best way for her to learn. But at the very beginning of the training, the abstraction of music shall be a useful intermediary between muteness and rhetoric. First we shall teach her to sing like the birds, then to sing like a woman.*

Note to self: fix that blasted roof. In fact, start sealing the whole greenhouse, with planks if need be. We cannot have another escape attempt.

# THIRTY

"I'm sleepy, it must be bedtime," said Gregor, yawning unconvincingly. Simon frowned at his partner, who nodded towards CHLOE. It was a few days later—everything was perfectly planned and implements procured. She, the innocent, was turning circles in the garden, round and round and up and down. Simon cottoned on and sprang into the performance.

"Oh yes, dreadfully tired, dreadfully late." He yawned and stretched high to the ceiling—a gesture which CHLOE copied vaguely. Jennifer looked around pointedly at the plentiful light of early evening and glared at the men.

"It's time now, Jennifer," said Gregor, "time *for bed.*"

Yawning and rubbing their eyes, the boys encouraged CHLOE to follow them. They did not lead her to her luscious bedroom, but instead they padded their sleepy way down the stone stairs to the undercroft. Jennifer followed with arms crossed, refusing to partake in the bedtime pantomime. CHLOE was to her a woman now, and she resented how the gents treated her like a young child.

Once safely past the brassy boiler, the men settled CHLOE down on Simon's workbench. The relative coldness and darkness of his taxidermy workshop would slow down her biological processes, encouraging a deep sleep of sorts. That way the procedure would be less stressful on her physiology—and her speculative psychology.

"Goodnight, sweet pea," said Gregor, stroking her forehead from her hairline down to the tip of her nose. CHLOE succumbed immediately to oblivion, becoming nothing more than a spring bulb over winter.

"Let's make a start," said Gregor. "We've got a lot to do."

Simon and Gregor donned protective aprons while Jennifer merely stood aside, feigning indifference. All pretence of tiredness was gone, and the air was as serious and alert as in an operating chamber.

"The time is thirty-three minutes past eight o'clock, on Wednesday the fourth of September 1889," Gregor announced. "Let us begin."

He loomed over CHLOE and prodded her clavicle with two fingers. He poked his way down her mossy cleavage until he found the metal clasp which kept her rib cage together at the sternum. With some difficulty—it had rusted a little with frequent waterings—he unlocked the clasp. Simon stepped forwards and opened the doors as if her chest were a Kievan icon: a gilded triptych to be revealed only on the holiest days of the Orthodox church.

Seeing the interior of his daughter broke Simon's funereal reserve. Inside was soil, yes—mulchy and dark. But there were also millions of white, wisp-like roots; and thicker, throbbing veins of mycelial hyphae. The smell was ordurous but sweet. Simon grimaced and turned away.

By the staircase, Jennifer covered her mouth. So often ruddy-faced, she was now pale as undercooked egg white.

Gregor inhaled sharply. "The substrate appears to be infested with earthworms…" he said.

Jennifer ran up the stairs, limbs flailing. Gregor pressed his fingertips into the spongy surfaces of CHLOE's chest cavity.

"…which appear to be aiding moisture absorption. Even the innermost mycelial conduits are wet to the touch."

With a nod to each other, the two men began their appointed tasks. Gregor continued working on the thorax, reasserting the windpipes which had been overtaken by roots, and clearing space where the lungs had once been for the bellows. He had to be careful not to place too much stress on the roots, nor to remove any vital element of the ecosystem.

To the left of her thoracic cavity was a particularly dense rootball, pulsating calmly in the gaslight. This was CHLOE's plantbrain, the mycelial centre which served as a locus for her consciousness. Many weeks ago, Gregor had introduced the Sumatran mycelium to Constance's heart so that it could use her veins and arteries as its nervous system. Now, that fungal blob had become a sophisticated cortex. The component parts of CHLOE—the mycelial network, the various plants, and the cadaver—had become a single entity. Gregor felt nostalgic for those optimistic times when the science of fungal consciousness was still brand new. Well, now they had a chance to propel this nascent field still further.

Simon set to work on CHLOE's mouth. With a tiny pair of hooked scissors he separated her lips, which had fused through disuse. He massaged her jaw apart. Opening her mouth reminded Simon of taking a root-bound plant out of its pot. He had been careful when preparing Constance to remove the fleshier bits of her—the tongue, the soft palate—so he was actually met with a fairly orderly cavity. But across every blackened surface was a crazed frieze of rhizomes, and the stench was incredible. Before continuing, he tied a handkerchief around his mouth. This way he wouldn't have to smell *hers* as he scraped it clear of debris.

Perhaps worse than the stench of rot and the queer pattern of roots—her mouth was littered with loose teeth. Back in early summer he should have probably removed them, lest they fall out due to the deterioration of her gums. Now, he took them out and arranged them carefully in a tray to reflect their positions in Constance's mouth. Then he replaced them with an ad hoc set of 'dentures'—actually the sawn-off top part of a mahogany jawbone borrowed from an anatomical model—fastened directly onto her own jawbone with medical-grade screws.

This preparation phase took them a good hour. Then they swapped places to make best use of their individual talents. Gregor would perform the botanical grafting required to attach the stinkhorn fungus to the base of her mouth. Simon would do the joinery work required to attach the array of pipes which would simulate the voice.

Whilst rooting around in his box of flutes and whistles, Gregor had found a precious relic. On one of his trips to the Far East, he had come across a gentleman playing a *sheng*, a small tower of reed pipes connected to an air chamber at the base. He blew or sucked into a single mouthpiece and with his nimble fingers manipulated which pipes were engaged. His skill and dexterity meant that he and Gregor had passed an extremely pleasurable weekend together in Peking. However, even the full force of Gregor's charms couldn't persuade the musician to part with his instrument. Instead, Gregor had picked one up in Hong Kong for a very reasonable price.

The *sheng* would be fitted into CHLOE with a few extra appendages—Gregor wanted her to have access to purer wind timbres as well as the *sheng*'s natural reediness. So he replaced the lower-pitched reeds with a series of tin whistles in different keys. The instrument now looked like the youngling of a monstrous pipe organ—or a fungus of the species *Flammulina velutipes*, known as *enokitake* in Japan, which is formed out of many long, thin stems.

Simon felt the weight of it in two hands, then placed it with infinite dignity into CHLOE's chest. He took great care not to tear any roots or mycelial nodes. After he had eased it into position, he felt a slight tickle by his left wrist. A fat earthworm had escaped from the substrate and was exploring his shirt cuff.

Simon's peripheral vision faded away. All that existed for him was this earthworm and his left hand. The worm was thick with the innards of his daughter—indeed his own hand was smeared with her soil. He retched as he saw the body on the slab for what she really was: *his child*. He had prised her open and rummaged inside her chest with his own hands, and now he had pieces of her all over him. He shuddered violently, sending the earthworm flying into the air. Simon let out a cry of anguish and staggered backwards.

"Simon, whatever's the matter?" Gregor had his whole hand in CHLOE's mouth, trying to embed the ganglia of the stinkhorn down where the base of her tongue used to be.

"She's all over me, I've seen inside her, my little girl, and now I have bits of her all over my hands."

"Stay calm, Simon, *breathe*," Gregor said. It had been a while since he had talked his partner down from a spiralling nervous episode, but the script was eternally fresh in his memory. He took a moment to check all the mouth components were firmly embedded, then approached his shivering partner. "You're safe, I'm here with you. We can just wipe your hands clean, see?"

Simon let Gregor clean his hands with a rag.

"That's all better now. You're safe. You're calm. Everything is fine and you are in control."

Simon didn't feel in control. There were worms all over the backs of his hands, running through his veins and munching away at his tendons. He felt their creeping all over his body. He knew they weren't there, but he could *feel them*.

"I can't do this, Gregor. We have gone so far, *so far*, down this path together. But I cannot go any further."

"Oh, Simon. You're right. We've gone so far. Further than I ever dreamed. But we're so close now, we only have to be strong a little longer and then our beautiful girl will be able to talk.

Hell, she'll be able to sing! Imagine that—CHLOE will sing so sweetly the earth itself will weep and the nightingale will pack her bags and move to America."

"But I'm so tired."

"Then imagine her saying in a still, small voice: *I love you*."

Simon's eyes refocused. Those words were like smelling salts to him. Gregor saw the reaction and repeated himself incessantly, with each *I love you* more persuasive than the last. He began kissing him on the forehead, the cheeks, and the soily knuckles. Soon Simon was back on his feet, and with great ceremony Gregor handed him the ornate bellows which were re-purposed as CHLOE's lungs. With his taxidermical skills, Simon joined one of the wooden paddles to CHLOE's spine, and the nozzle to the *sheng*. In effect, taxidermy is an esoteric form of carpentry.

Gregor was then free to 'train' the mycelium on its new equipment. He teased goopy tendrils from CHLOE's heart-brain out to the *sheng*'s finger holes. He diverted a larger ganglion to the handle of the bellows. After a period of trial and error, the Sumatran mycelium would work out that sound was produced when it tensed that appendage.

Simon closed her mouth using one loving finger under her chin. Solemnly, he closed up her ribs. Her bone-hinges squeaked and squelched. The clasp was fastened tight, and with that she was hermetically sealed once more.

"You did a great job, Simon," said Gregor, looking at his partner with warmth as they assumed the position to carry CHLOE back upstairs.

"I was only following your excellent plan!" Simon insisted. He took her ankles while Gregor had her by the shoulders. They carried her up through the entrails of the boiler system and through to Gregor's orderly laboratory, where the heady atmosphere would help reassert her organic chemistry.

She was laid upon yet another workbench, but this time the pair endeavoured to make her as comfortable as possible, with rich fabric drapes and sumptuous cushions. Gregor removed his apron and leaned against a counter with a heavy sigh. It was approaching daybreak, but Simon wasn't the least bit sleepy now.

"You head to bed," he said, "I'll watch over her."

"She's fine," said Gregor, rubbing his hands down Simon's flanks and kissing his neck, "come to bed."

Simon stepped out of Gregor's embrace.

"I'd like to be here when she wakes up."

Dawn made itself known in the softening of the sky's darkness. Gregor screwed up his apron and tossed it aside as he left. Simon settled down on a stool with CHLOE's hand in his. She seemed entirely inert. He hoped they were doing the right thing for her—for his precious CHLOE. He fell asleep holding his daughter's hand.

Unbeknownst to him, Simon's sleep-laboured breathing was joined by a much stranger sound: the unstructured wheezes of a mushroom playing a *sheng*.

A crash—a tinkle—a disc spinning to rest. Simon woke with a start. Groggy and disoriented, he noticed CHLOE was missing from the west wing workbench. He spun around—there she was. A terracotta pot, or what was left of it, lay at her feet. Soil and roots were strewn all around. The girl was standing on tiptoes, but every vine-ligament in her body was tense. Vicious thorns were bristling from the side of her forearms and her shoulders.

*Oh, poor* CHLOE, *my sweet pea.*

Her shoulders were up by her ears and her fingers were twisted and roiling.

"Shh now, CHLOE," Simon began, "it's—"

With a great squeeze of her thorax she let out a dissonant roar. It frightened Simon no end. It sounded as if someone had punched an accordion. The plant-creature didn't seem to like it either—she tore off around Gregor's workspace, thrashing about, leaving a trail of broken equipment behind her.

"Now, CHLOE, this is perfectly natural," said Simon, ducking to avoid a flying tray of seedlings, "you're simply getting used to your new voice box. Soon you'll be laughing and talking and singing, and you'll be jolly glad you have it then!"

He placed his hand on her mossy arm. For a moment she was calm—the roar of the wilds had abated. But when she turned her face to his, Simon could see that there was water streaming from her algal eyes. Her sensitive *Mimosa* wreaths were closed off for protection—even her daisies were hiding their petals.

"What's wrong? Tell me."

CHLOE opened her mouth and warbled a mournful ditty, so intricate, so piteous, and so thoroughly disquieting that Simon quite forgot himself and withdrew from her in terror. This caused her to fly once more into a rage, and a fresh batch of orchids were victims this time. Simon grabbed a beaker and started ringing it with a glass stirring rod, as if for an after-dinner speech.

"Gregor, G-Gregor!"

Jennifer was the first to respond to the summons. Entering the lab, she stood there surveying the carnage with one hand over her mouth. Not long later, Gregor came skidding into the west wing in his nightshirt. He sank to his knees.

"My laboratory," he whispered.

"Stuff your laboratory," said Jennifer, "something's wrong with CHLOE."

The poor girl was stuck in a vicious cycle of roaring in anger, being angered by the sound of her roar, and roaring again. She brought a bark-encased wrist down onto a workbench and a series of tiny sproutlings jumped and fell. Her tendrils lashed about, tearing through the waxy leaves of various experimental samples.

"A season's work," Gregor croaked, "*gone.*"

"Look sharp, Gregor, or it'll be more than a season's worth that you lose," said Simon, but Gregor was despondent on the floor, his arms limp.

"Mr Sandys," Jennifer cried, "your sludge!"

The wild squall that was CHLOE had paused in front of a glass dish containing a mucus-like substance. This ugly mush with an iridescent sheen wound up some spindles like a rose climbing a trellis, reaching out for a sugar-water well at the top. This was Gregor's initial experiment with the Sumatran mycelium, the same life form which was now coursing through CHLOE.

She seemed transfixed, like Jenny had been, with the thing's oily sheen. The three humans used Chloe's calmness to creep towards her, careful not to distract her and send her back into a rage. Did she simply enjoy the rainbow glimmer of the substance? Or did she recognise the fungus as an intrinsic part of herself? Gregor gently brought himself into her view.

"Chloe, I know you're frightened. We can help you. Come with us now, let's get you misted."

He reached out with a shaking hand to touch her elbow. She batted his hand away, catching his skin on a thorn. She sang a dissonant rebuke—so mournful and so bitter that Gregor found sorrow blossoming in his own chest.

"I want you to understand something," he said, smiling for Chloe's benefit even as he avoided her bristling thorns. "This remarkable organism in the glass dish is your brother."

Chloe brought her face down close to the mycelium, leaning this way and that—possibly to witness the purples and yellows of the iridescent fungus. She parted her lips as one desperately parched.

"*Vrasha*," she trilled.

"That's right," said Gregor, cheeks moist in exhausted pride, "your *brother*!"

Her various weaponised thornbanks retracted and she snuggled down to embrace the glass dish. "*Vrasha*," she cooed.

# THIRTY-ONE

There was a twitch in Gregor's eye as he tore around the greenhouse, blocking up any little holes with wax. He tried lifting his spectacles and rubbing the offending eye to no avail. It *must* be hayfever—although it was very late in the season for that, and he'd never suffered before.

He boarded up the worst-offending windows and then those with even the slightest of hairline fractures. He barred the French doors to the patio, sealed them with grouting, and dragged a pot and trellis over to block it. His eye was causing such a twitch in the side of his face that he kept it scrunched shut.

The three living humans would need access through the front door, so Gregor merely locked this with a heavy-duty padlock and thick chain. There were three hefty keys for the lock, and he gave one to Simon with a mutter before scurrying away. Something kept him from presenting Jennifer with the third, and instead he placed both on a string around his neck, hidden by his cravat.

The final hole to block was the trickiest of all—the bullet wound in the great glass roof. Gregor fetched his longest ladder and set it up on the gallery against an iron rafter. He shimmied up the ladder and along a florid girder with a hammer in his hand, a board under his arm, and nails between his teeth. He kept his twitching eye firmly closed to prevent an unexpected spasm, although this made navigation quite difficult.

As he reached the offending pane, he stopped to marvel at his garden. Even in the early autumn Gregor's paradise was lush and verdant. His artfully nonchalant pathways curved this way and that, winding between tranquil clearings. In one such glade, Gregor could make out Jennifer's messy mop of strawberry hair. She was playing with CHLOE, developing her diction and vocabulary by parroting words back and forth. CHLOE's cooing was still hauntingly irregular as she sang her strange exercises back to her governess but given the short time since actually having a mouth the progress was astonishing. "Yes!" she sang, trilling upwards. "No," she near growled on a low note. "Jennifer," she warbled, with joyful melisma—a sweet chuckle in her throat.

Gregor's firmly closed eye managed to spasm through his face's vice-like grip, expressing itself more like a judder of his whole head. He made haste to cover the broken pane and nail the board in place before shimmying back down, his hair and shirt quite ruffled.

Waiting for him on his desk in the west wing was the usual pile of correspondence—nine-tenths of which went straight into the compost. He reserved and tore open two vibrant envelopes: one a deep mauve in colour, the other one being aggressively emerald.

Dear Gregor,

I find myself writing this letter under some duress. Darling, whatever have you done to Mally? Right now he is sitting across from me in the parlour, a ball of pent-up frustration, quite insisting that I write to you this very moment! I may have made something of a scene. But at least now he daren't read my actual words for fear of my wailing! Julian thinks he has a certain scandalous leverage over me, but I assure you he is sorely mistaken. I must however *appear* to be affrighted by his threats, to maintain the careful equilibrium of my Bohemian reputation. So here is the message he wishes me to send, which I implore you to ignore entirely.

Oh goodness! Isn't it such a long time since we've met up with that nice man Julian Mallory? He is a devil and a rogue and I do so love him for it. You two used to get along so well! I hear on the chaise-longue circuit that he has been making waves as the President of the RHS after that ghastly affair with your *Bouquet Fongique*. What a fellow, that man, whom I admire and respect for his integrity!

Wouldn't it be *topper* to have him over to Grimfern? You simply *must* invite him. I shall come along, too—it's been an age since we saw each other. I'll have to bring Mr Bland, of course, which is good because he'll hate it. I shall have to leave before sunset but ~~Julian tells me he~~ I imagine Julian would like to stay a little longer.

"Dot-dot-dot," he says. I pretend to laugh with all the sauciness I can summon.

"*Ellipses*," says I, "are the last recourse of the cowardly lecher." (He presumes to dictate the content of a lady's correspondence, the wretched little man.)

Careful there, my love.

—*Sua Rosalinda mais linda.*

P.S. I haven't told him about the you-know-what you showed me—(chrysanthe)mum's the word!

Dear Gregor,

I just happened to bump into Rosalinda the other day—my, my, how time has flown! And yet she never seems to age. She always was the third person in our relationship, wasn't she, Gregor? The erstwhile fulcrum of our friendship, and sometimes the referee of our pugilism. This chance encounter led me to remember that you still haven't invited me to Grimfern—wouldn't a get-together with Rosalinda be such a perfect occasion? It would be just like old times, before all that unpleasantness with the *Bouquet Fongique*.

It was Rosie's idea, of course, to assemble at Grimfern. She also said you're cooking up something spectacular in that little greenhouse of yours. Why not have us both over, then, if you're so intimidated by my solo presence? That way you'd have a chaperone to protect whatever virtue you consider yourself to still possess. And if the sickly spectre of Rievaulx were banished for an evening, so much the better. I simply cannot tolerate his cloying, deathly presence. Really, Gregor—you need some fresh air and bright sunlight on your Caledonian visage! Simon keeps you trapped in that dark green world—it must be rotting your brain. You need to spend some time on pursuits less morbid, and with companions less cadaverous...

Vivaciously yours,

Julian Mallory, Esq.
President of the RHS

The thick paper began to twist itself between Gregor's contorted fingers. Small holes appeared, then larger tears, along with large patches of semi-translucence from his sweaty hands. Gregor was stuck in apoplectic paralysis—tense in every fibre of his body.

Gradually a hiss of air escaped his clenched teeth, which led to a squeak, then a moan, then a guttural roar. Freed, he shoved the letters with the rest on the top of the compost, forcing them right down into the muck—clawing and punching at the decomposing slop until Julian Mallory was right at the festering bottom.

Hunched and filthy by the bin, Gregor caught his breath and planned his next move. No equivocations this time. He had to frighten Julian away or risk him coming back into his life. Gregor couldn't allow that. Gregor couldn't allow himself to begin thinking about that. His brain slipped right off the idea without entertaining it.

He made a round of the glasshouse, once more making sure all the doors and windows were locked and sealed. Using the key under his cravat, he let himself out of the front doors, locking them firmly behind him.

*Drat—Simon still has a key.*

Gregor moved a stone planter with some difficulty from its position flanking the entrance to stand right in front of the door.

Gregor felt a twinge of guilt but soothed himself by rationalising that he wouldn't be gone long. The likelihood of a terrible act of God, say a grand conflagration, was minuscule. The likelihood of a terrible act of CHLOE, however, such as an escape into the charming wilds of Buckinghamshire, was quite considerable. He set off down the drive, fighting away the oppressive thoughts which flickered and smouldered all around him.

Will jumped to his feet when Gregor stormed into the gatehouse. The master's hand and sleeve were covered in compost, and some had made it to the side of his unkempt beard through mindless scratching.

"You don't look well, sir," Will stammered.

Gregor's rage at such idle drivel made him look a hell of a lot worse, adding a real glow to his haggard demeanour. Will staggered back and almost tripped on a discarded Penny Dreadful.

"Two telegrams, boy. Extremely urgent. Don't you dare tell me the price."

[Telegram to Rosalinda Smeralda-Bland, postmarked Thursday 5th September 1889]

```
33 2.30 HAZLEMERE 26
R. SMERALDA-BLAND

DEAR BOTH COMMA I SEE YOUR LITTLE GAME
STOP STOP STOP PLEASE STOP COMMA I SHALL
NEVER RELENT STOP
KIND REGARDS
G. SANDYS
```

[Telegram to Julian Mallory, postmarked Thursday 5th September 1889]

```
33 2.31 HAZLEMERE 25
MALLORY, RHS. PRES.

DEAR BOTH COMMA I SEE YOUR LITTLE GAME
STOP STOP STOP PLEASE STOP COMMA I SHALL
NEVER RELENT STOP
REGARDS
G. SANDYS
```

Later that day, and after a shower, Gregor brought CHLOE to the grand piano and placed her hand on its lid. Since she showed such a natural affinity for music, he would provide her with formal singing lessons that might help bridge the gap between pure melody and true speech. And *that* would certainly be a parlour trick to show the old RHS.

"CHLOE, I want you to repeat after me." He played and sang, "*Do re mi fa so.*"

Having practised with Jennifer, she knew it was her role to respond. She did so with a fair approximation of the 'lyrics', but her notes were a long way away from Gregor's Western diatonic major scale. Her warble was heavily ornamented with chromatic grace notes and weird resonances, more at home in an exotic call-to-prayer than in a *bel canto* singing lesson.

"No, CHLOE, that is wrong," Gregor insisted, "let's start with simply *do.*"

He sang the tonic note at her over and over, with increasing severity of tone. She crooned back a myriad of alternate harmonisations—a flattened 6th, a sharp 4th rising to the 5th, even a flattened 9th trilling to a minor 10th. None of these would satisfy the maestro disciplinarian, who slammed the keyboard lid closed in anger.

CHLOE shrank back, thorn-hackles raised. Once the percussive strike had subsided, the metal strings of the ill-tempered piano continued to ring around the greenhouse. She delighted in the dissonant resonance and tried to sing all the notes she could hear, like a child trying to pop a cloud of bubbles one by one.

This gave Gregor an idea. He stood with his foot on the sustain pedal, causing the inner dampeners to rise. Sticking his head deep into the beast, he declaimed "CHLOE" with a great boom. The thunder of his voice caused the strings to quiver, adding an otherworldly resonance, and many extra notes for his daughter to play with. She danced a little and echoed "*Ker-oh-ee*," over and over. She repeated each sound in endless combinations, until Gregor was quite sure she was singing more than one note at a time. It was as if a dozen voices sang in chorus, her mouth a sumptuous basilica.

They continued this way for some time, with Gregor amplifying the richness of his voice with the piano, and CHLOE exulting in a shower of music. She enjoyed learning 'father' and 'pater' for Gregor and Simon respectively, and 'piano', and 'music'. But it was 'Jennifer' that really set her imagination soaring with ecstatic cadenzas, at the end of which she fell quite asleep in her father's arms.

Gregor put her to bed and stroked her mossy face. *Sleep well, my precious—my singing pear tree.*

After a moment's hesitation he swaddled her in linen and strapped her to the workbench with two leather belts.

That night, Jenny was roused from sleep by a series of plaintive sighs. In her half-dreaming state it seemed to be the song of a forest nymph—one who lives under a lily pad and lures travellers into her peaty depths. Dream-Jennifer hitched her skirt and dipped her toes into the shimmering lake, whereupon they were seized by the creature and kissed and caressed mercilessly in the living murk.

Jenny fully awoke with a convulsion and gasp, as if coming up for air. To her surprise, the siren song continued even here on dry land. Of course this must be CHLOE—her sonorous snoring was wafting through the fabric of Jenny's nest-tent. Listening intently to the sound, however, Jennifer could hear distinct vowels and even consonants. She lowered herself from her bed in her nightgown and pressed her ear against the iron floor. It simply must be CHLOE's muffled warblings—her pipes were pure even if her diction was strained. And strained it most certainly was—her words were distorted and barely intelligible. There was a sob to her voice which fired all kinds of fear and fury in Jenny. Hitching up her hemline and baring her feet for real this time, she crept down to CHLOE's verdant bedchamber.

What she saw down there lit the fire of Jenny's indignation. Her beloved CHLOE was strapped to her bed, struggling hard against the coarse swaddling to no avail. She strained against the too-tight belts and used what little movement she had in her neck to try and brush the fabric away from her face. Poor CHLOE whimpered all the while in evident discomfort.

"What in the name of… Hold on, CHLOE, I'll get you out of there."

Jenny attacked the belt buckle with shaking fingers, but it was affixed so tightly she couldn't get purchase to unclasp it. CHLOE was getting more and more uncomfortable, so Jennifer caressed her leafy face and tried to distract her.

"CHLOE, what is this?" she said, pointing to herself.

"*Jennifer,*" she sang, in between what seemed like sobs.

"What is this?" Jennifer asked, this time pointing at the plant-girl.

"CHLOE," came the faltering response. "*CHLOE sad.*"

Jennifer let out a guttural sound of devastation before she managed to control it. She fiddled some more with the first belt and managed to undo it, freeing CHLOE's arms somewhat.

"Well then, my darling," she continued, struggling to maintain a smile, "I think it's your turn now."

Jenny made a start on the second belt while CHLOE looked around the bedchamber. Her long green neck twisted this way and that as she surveyed her world unblinkingly.

"*What this?*" she said, pointing to the glass wall on the edge of her domain.

"That's a window, pumpkin." The belt loosened, and Jenny rushed to remove the fabric which shrouded CHLOE like an Egyptian mummy.

"No," said CHLOE, rising to point and ogle, "*window no. What this?*" She gestured at everything beyond the window—a clutch of trees, a hedge, the clouds picked out silver by the moonlight. She meant all of that—the other place—the dark green yonder.

"CHLOE, that's the outside."

As soon as she said the word, Jennifer's heart flooded with memories of dashing madly through wildflowers, scrambling up a beck, wading through a bog to retrieve a prized throwing-stick. Spending time away from her father's misery and in the company of her wonderful friend Constance. The outside had been the most precious thing to her back in the day. How ugly, then, was Gregor's insistence that CHLOE could never experience this. How dare he keep this bundle of Nature itself prisoner in a glass cage?

"*The—out—side?*"

"CHLOE, the outside is the most wonderful place. It's where everything is. I don't know how to explain it to you. It's where I'm from. And it's where we both belong."

CHLOE rose and pressed herself against the glass, wishing herself through the panes.

"You want to go there, don't you?" Jennifer thought long and hard. Finally she scrunched up Gregor's belts into a ball. "I'll see what I can do."

# THIRTY-TWO

*L*ate the next morning, after a silent breakfast between the two gentlemen on the patio, Simon announced that he had something to say with a gentle cough. It was the kind of cough which does not serve any physiological function. An *ahem*. No mucus was dislodged by his decorous epiglottis. Gregor glowered at the taxidermist, who placed his napkin back on his plate.

"I need to go to London. For mahogany, you see. I shall probably go on Monday."

"Can't you have it sent here?"

"I need to select the pieces."

"You'll stay put. We need to look after Chloe."

"I'm going to London on Monday, Gregor." Simon did not raise his voice, but in an act of extraordinary defiance he did stand up as he spoke. "I do not require your permission. I shall probably stay with Rosalinda that evening. You can expect me back first thing Tuesday morning."

"I expect you," Gregor snarled, although Simon was already hurrying away, "to do right by this *family* and stay right here! Simon!"

Gregor retreated to his workshop to begin the clear-up operation. Jennifer saw that the men were separated and took her opportunity, when Simon happened to be as far away from the laboratory as it was possible to be, to sidle up to him with CHLOE in tow.

"Mr Rievaulx—Simon? Miss CHLOE here has something she wants to ask you."

Simon tried to beam at the pair, although his large eyes were strangely shiny.

"To ask me! Well, that is delightful. Your English must be coming on leaps and bounds, CHLOE, no doubt due to your diligent tutelage, Miss Finch. Well then, let's have it. What was it you wanted to ask me, sweet pea?"

CHLOE looked to Jenny for reassurance, who smiled and shooed her forwards.

"CHLOE—*pater*—*outside.*"

Simon shrank back, his jaw stretching even as he kept his mouth pursed. "Y-yourself, myself, and outside? You want to go… out?"

"*Jennifer—outside.*"

The plant-girl wove her fingers between Jennifer's, entangling her fronds around the governess's freckled wrist. Simon stood there stammering.

"I'm sure that you'd never deny your daughter her deepest wish," said Jennifer with the slightest twinge of guilt. No—

she was doing this for a noble cause.

"It's not quite that simple. Gregor doesn't think it's safe, and he has locked the doors."

"Am I to believe you don't have a key?" Jennifer was pressing hard on the stuttering gentleman, but he needed a little persuasion.

"Yes, well, but…"

"Am I to believe that Mr Sandys decides who goes into and out of the garden?"

"No, well, I'm sure I—"

"And am I to believe"—she swelled herself up to deliver the final blow—"you would deny CHLOE's request, when she has learned to speak specifically to make it?"

Simon looked aghast. His neck was tense and he blinked a lot.

"Meet me at the door f-f-f—"

"Yes, Mr Rievaulx?" Jenny smiled encouragingly.

"—forthwith!"

He swished away, leaving the girls to celebrate silently, hand in peaty hand. They dashed around to assemble things for a picnic—well, Jennifer dashed, coaxing CHLOE hither and thither, stifling her laughter lest they arouse Gregor's suspicion. Jenny rummaged in the linen closet and found a hamper with a cloth of striped Manchester gingham. In the kitchen she prepared sandwiches; none of those pale, delicate things favoured by some gentlemen she could mention, but her own hearty cobs of bread with healthy slavers of cold meat and cheese. Finally she added a bottle of one of Gregor's homemade botanical beverages to the wicker hamper, and a slim volume of verse from the boys' library.

Her own reading was sub-par, but she would enjoy posing with this little 'Byron' book as her masters had so often done during that summer. She dressed the part, too—pale cream trousers and a tweed waistcoat over a billowy white shirt.

The three assembled silently by the front door. Outside waiting for them was an overripe morning, quivering in the sun after a light shower. Simon withdrew the iron key from his wrist sleeve but could not bring himself to undo the padlock.

"Quickly, Simon, quickly!" Jennifer whispered.

"I cannot—for fear of the noise announcing our departure!"

"Gregor's probably head-deep in a hydrangea right now."

"Still... you must distract him. Use your womanly ways—say something irritating. I shall listen for his rumbling and use it as cover to undo the chains."

Jennifer puffed herself up, ready to retaliate for the slight on her 'womanly ways', but merely glared at Simon and saved her ire for Gregor. She stomped off into the west wing where Gregor had been distracted from clearing up CHLOE's rampage with a long-forgotten (and now irreparably damaged) experiment where he meticulously varied the pH balance of the soil of various hydrangeas, to compare the effect on their flower colour.

"Gregor," said Jennifer, swallowing a sudden pang of fear, "I hope you're nearly finished."

"Finished?" enquired Gregor, with such uncanny calmness that it betrayed his inner anguish. "No, this ericaceous experiment will last for several seasons to come."

"I mean with the write-up of CHLOE's experiment. You remember—you said that when you'd finished your paper you would send it out to all the cleverest botanists of the world and then we wouldn't have to live in secrecy any more. So, then. Are you nearly finished with it?"

"Not quite yet, Jennifer."

"Well, how long will it take? How often do you work on it? Can I see the bits you've written already?"

A blousy blue hydrangea head came right off in Gregor's hand.

"You have no idea what you're talking about. In fact—to ruins with this." He threw the flop of petals to the floor. "You ridiculous and thoroughly cretinous girl! You seem to have forgotten that you know nothing about anything. That was the express reason we hired you—you were too stupid to pose any threat to my research. Then we gave you wildflowers for your hair, and new clothes and responsibilities. You became more meddlesome but no less stupid."

Jennifer stood her ground but screwed her face up against hot emotion. With effort, she feigned nonchalance.

"You might search yourself, Mr Sandys. For all your intelligence you lack the vision to see CHLOE for what she really is. A woman not of flesh and blood but of soil and sap—yet a *woman* nonetheless. You lack the humanity to see her as human. You lack the humility to set her free. But worst of all, Gregor, you lack the guts to stand by your work."

"Get out," Gregor whispered, before roaring, "get out!"

The hydrangeas bounced as the wild-eyed scientist slammed the table.

"I shall."

Jenny had hit her mark—but at what cost? She hurried out of the west wing with a backward glance to check the botanist wasn't following her. He leaned against his workbench for support, before slumping down to rest his head against the petal-strewn surface.

Jenny felt awful but focused herself on the glorious prospect of a day out with CHLOE. There she was—finally on the other side of the open door where she belonged. Radiant in the light of midday, she rotated gracefully; caressing the breeze and soaking in the peculiar nature of sound out there. Simon hurried Jenny over the threshold so he could shut the door in such a way that it wouldn't immediately appear unlocked. Then he took up the picnic hamper in one hand and CHLOE's arm in the other. The three of them set off towards the lake by way of the guilty pathways and leering hedges of Grimfern.

"What was all that commotion back there?" Simon asked in passing, as if he didn't really care.

"Just an experiment that Gregor ruined."

They found a spot on a small rise looking out over the boating lake—that artificially naturalistic body of water in the Grimfern Estate. The earnest summer was easing into its first flushes of gold and red. The picnickers spread their cloth under a beech tree, which Simon remarked was turning to bronze just as Gregor was turning to silver.

"He'll have a few more grey hairs than that even if he finds out we've escaped," said Jenny.

"We haven't escaped as such, ladies," he addressed the group while hitching up his trousers to sit down. "We are merely stretching our legs."

CHLOE pointed her bare toes as far as she could from her spot lying on the cloth, which was considerably farther than a normal human. She luxuriated in the golden air, raising her ribcage up to the sky. Jennifer watched her intently as she unpacked the luncheon things.

They ate more than was reasonable and drank sparkling water with elderflower. CHLOE only pretended to eat in her graceful way and poured the flowery fizz straight into her bosom. Both Simon's and Jennifer's eyes widened, but only Jenny blushed. After food they settled down to leisurely pursuits— Jenny opened her book of poems, but found herself restless, so she wandered a little with it and leaned against the tree, using the book as a prop over which to observe the plant-girl. Simon sketched a few ideas for taxidermy projects, and CHLOE sang a duet with an autumn robin.

Were there always dahlias on CHLOE's torso? Was she always so glossy and shimmering? Jennifer thought she knew every visible inch of the creature, but at the height of the afternoon she spotted new buds and fronds all across her verdant body. Jenny had never seen her looking so lovely and so rich. There was something comfortably familiar about the girl today, as if she had known her form for years, rather than weeks. Against the tree, the governess continued pretending to read her poetry book. Glancing over the crisp pages, Jenny noticed something unsettling—CHLOE's corkscrew curls of ivy, which usually barely reached the bottom of her neck, were stretching out and exploring her shoulders.

*Good for her.* It's always nice to change one's hairstyle, and the longer style was most becoming of her. She was less the girl of summer and more the woman of autumn, or so it seemed to Jennifer anyway. Simon had fallen asleep over his technical drawing. CHLOE's song tuned into the low humming of the golden grass. Jenny's book heaved on her chest.

From the direction of the glasshouse a storm cloud came raging. That thunderous front was Gregor, striding with shirt cuffs loose and greying hair unkempt.

"Mr Rievaulx! Miss Finch! What the devil do you think you're doing?"

Simon jumped to his feet and spun around three times, looking for ways to minimise the damage but finding none. Jenny also rose, but with an obstinate huff.

"How dare you trick me," Gregor near spat at Jennifer. "You snake in gentlemen's clothing!"

"Now here, Gregor—" Simon began.

"And you, do you realise you have betrayed me totally?" Despite his fury there was a falter of emotion in Gregor's voice. "I told you all… we have no idea what she…"

"You keep acting as if she's some great mystery," Jennifer cried, "when she is quite simply a woman."

"It is not a woman. It is a collection of plants with the heart of a mushroom. It is an ungodly experiment—and one which I thoroughly regret."

CHLOE wilted a little. Her recent growth now seemed premature, giving her a leggy appearance so abhorred by gardeners.

"I won't have you talking about CHLOE like that," said Simon, without meeting the botanist's eye.

"CHLOE is not our daughter," Gregor roared, "she is an aberration. The Promethean fire which drives each of our human souls does not flicker in the creature. Her black spark was given to her from the bowels of the earth—her animation is chthonic, not divine. Bloodless, only tendrils creep within her. Heartless, she thinks only of the survival of her fungal core. Soulless, her only yearning is for retribution!"

He grabbed her mossy arm a little roughly and tried to yank her towards him, but she did not budge. He took her wrist in both of his hands and tugged, but her body refused to leave the rug. On closer inspection, CHLOE had sent out thousands of exploratory roots from her back. These various thick white threads had forced their way through the blanket and were gripping tightly into the dark soil of the hillside. In amongst these fresh roots were tendrils of grey-green, pulsing with a mucus-like lustre...

"Great Lord below—the sinews of the earth..." Gregor muttered.

He sprang into action, whipping his secateurs from his holster—they gleamed in the sun. Jennifer saw their sharpness and grabbed Gregor's arm. Their scuffle resulted in imprecision in Gregor's swing, and he caught his own bicep with the blade. He roared and cast Jennifer off him so firmly that she landed square on the small of her back. Gregor sat panting, his glasses barely on his nose, and a crimson rose blossoming on his shirtsleeve. His mutterings were indecipherable as he undid his cravat one-handedly to use as a bandage. Simon wisely kept his distance, tending instead to the toppled governess.

Gregor rolled CHLOE over with his feet as much as her attachment allowed and wielded his secateurs as a Russian rustic wields a scythe. Once freed from the ground, he scooped her up as she cried out in panicked resistance.

"Stupid, stupid girl," he groaned. It wasn't clear whether he meant CHLOE or Jennifer. He deposited her in Simon's arms. "Put her to bed in your undercroft. Securely."

"I hardly think—"

"Tie her down, Simon! Shoulders and legs! Put a sack over her head if it makes you feel any better."

"It does not."

Simon balefully trudged back to Grimfern with his daughter mewing in his arms.

"You are a monster," said Jennifer, still lying on the ground.

"Miss Finch, one day you will see," said Gregor, taking a trowel and digging out a circle around the picnic blanket, "that I am not the monster here. The only monster is the mycelium which flows within CHLOE—and it is manipulating you as if it had its very tendrils through your freckled nose. Now, bring me the sack of salt from Florence's stable."

"Salt?" Jenny blinked.

"We must destroy any trace of the mycelium which escaped from CHLOE. We must salt the earth."

Gregor carved his bizarre sigil into the hill—a criss-crossed circle christened with salt and his own blood. He was ashen-faced and delirious from the blood loss. Once he was satisfied that there was no risk of contagion, he pointed his trowel accusingly at Jennifer, then to the broken earth.

"Never again."

She acquiesced with a bow of the head, and he staggered back to the greenhouse. He thought he saw flames in the reflections of the glass, but it was only the jerking of sunbeams as he stumbled home. He donned an apron and gave his hands a maniacal scrub before descending the stone steps to Simon's workshop.

There she was, tranquil and resplendent even as she was tied to a taxidermy table. Simon had done as he was told before withdrawing to their bedroom to hide, but he had not obscured his daughter's face. *The specimen's face*. Gregor rooted around the undercroft for a sack but had to make do with a handkerchief. He brought it to her face but hesitated. She was such a pretty girl. Her forehead was a miniature glade of buds and shoots, ripe from her day of excitement. He couldn't help himself; he caressed it with a trembling hand.

She batted her eyes open.

"No, no, CHLOE, it's bedtime now." He went to place the cloth over her.

"*Bedtime:* not," said CHLOE with a thousand voices.

"Y—yes it is. I can control you. You are my creation."

"*Not! CHLOE not! CHLOE outside—CHLOE outside* please."

CHLOE began kicking and screaming, fighting against her considerable restraints. Her voice was dark and dissonant like someone was burning a church organ. Gregor held her down with his weight and shoved the kerchief into her mouth, but that didn't stop the screaming from the instrument within her.

Still fighting her convulsions, he found the metal latch on her sternum and opened up her ribs. Her voice became shrill like a factory whistle before softening into the sound of mewing sobs. Gregor reached into her mould-covered thorax. CHLOE pushed the cloth out of her mouth with her elongated fungal tongue.

"*Poor CHLOE, Father,*" she said falteringly.

"It's for your own good. You have to be kept apart from the world, and we… we can't be trusted."

"*Poor CHLOE, please—*"

He gripped her slimy windpipe and pulled it firmly out of the *sheng*.

"*Father…*" The last wind escaped from her instrument with a sad wheeze. Her hyphal threads kept pumping the bellows, but the only sound was the rush of air as she formed empty words with her mouth. CHLOE lay back, unmoving and defeated.

Gregor stood for a while watching her face. Sweet child, and sweeter success. He couldn't keep her hidden forever. Soon enough he would show her to the world, just as soon as he could work out how to contain the mycelium within her.

# THIRTY-THREE

The sun was setting as Jennifer paced around her nest of a bedroom. Cushions and drapes were strewn everywhere—she picked them up but found that once she had an armful she didn't know where to put them. She dumped them right back on the chaise longue again.

Gregor had insisted that CHLOE be taken to the basement. The cruelty of hiding a plant-creature from the sun! What would he do to her? The men were nowhere to be seen and judging by the mad gleam in Gregor's eye, CHLOE could be in grave danger. Who knew what he was capable of in such a condition? Jenny worked herself up to such a point that her abdomen cramped. Her tongue was parched, her bruised coccyx wouldn't let her stand still. Eventually she burst out of her quasi-tent on the balcony and went in search of her precious companion.

The floral patterns in the ironwork of the gallery pressed into her bare feet as she roamed the greenhouse. Her view was excellent across the canopy, but she could not tell what shadows lingered beneath the leaves. Jennifer descended into this weird glade and stalked through it—a panther in the jungle.

The gentlemen were entirely absent. Jennifer had the glasshouse to herself, though it gave her no thrill. She checked Gregor's laboratory, littered with debris from CHLOE's chaos the day before. The botanist hadn't bothered to tidy up, and now had seemingly scarpered. Unless he was still with his daughter, down in the undercroft, performing whatever unspeakable experiments—or, worse, *punishments*—upon her? Jennifer crept down the stone steps and passed the grotesque contortions of the boiler and pipework—currently not in use. She hated that metal contraption with its groaning and its creeping tentacles. Below her, in Simon's sanctum, she found the two men having a terse discussion. Jennifer pressed herself against the archway to listen in.

"And if she should escape?"

"There is no escape. I shall see to that—"

"Gregor!"

There was a scuffle and a clatter. Jennifer rushed into the room to find that sure enough Gregor had collapsed, bringing one of Simon's dioramas down to the floor with him. He was still just about conscious. Furious but white as a sheet, he brushed off the fake moss and so many dead animals.

"Your wound, Gregor," Simon urged, reaching out for his partner. "I don't think it's healing properly."

"Get off me," Gregor grumbled, staggering to his feet.

Jennifer could barely breathe in the dusty tension of the basement. The air was thick with soil and sweat, but cold as a sepulchre. CHLOE was laid out like a corpse under the arches of the crypt, a corpse that was bound fast to its resting place.

Gregor squinted to focus on Jennifer but turned away in derision.

"Very well. Simon, you may go to London tomorrow. Miss Finch, you are free to return to your father's home. Get out of here, the both of you. I'm better off alone. I shall remain here and guard the *beast*"—here he began shouting, with great clouds of spit glistening in the lamplight—"since I'm the only one who cares about protecting this *family*!"

Simon took Jennifer by the arm and hurried her away to avoid the worst of Gregor's ravings. The botanist hobbled over to CHLOE and held the back of his trembling hand against her face.

"Now look what you made me do. You're losing me the few friends I have in this world."

The pressure against her feelers triggered a venus flytrap to close harmlessly around his finger. CHLOE slumbered on.

"Perhaps you're hungry? Poor girl—poor *specimen*. I know just what nutrients you need to flourish."

～

Dear Julian,

I need you, Jules. I hate it, but I do. I am so close to the realisation of my incredible experiment, but I cannot seem to clear the final stretch. I admit it: you are the only one who can help me.

Please do not spurn me in my hour of need. Simon has gone away to London, and if you were to visit within a few days I am sure we would be uninterrupted. We could work together on

the culmination of my fungal enterprises. And yes, I do so hope
we can *catch up*.

Desperately yours,
Dr Gregor Sandys
Botanist and fool

P.S. Apologies for the haste of my letter and for my shaking
hand—the inkblots provide me with no end of embarrassment.
You understand the provenance of my tremor, as well as you
understand yourself.

Gregor sat awkwardly scrunched in a wingback chair, biting
his nails to the quick. He had made more than the usual effort
at dressing, although even his finery was looking crumpled
and mud-smeared. The sun was low—sullen and brooding.
Simon had ridden off to London without a backward glance,
ostensibly to buy mahogany, but also to escape the crucible of
Gregor's hot house experiment. All that remained now was for
Jennifer to be dispatched and for Julian to take the bait. Gregor
felt like the spider at the centre of a complex web. Of course, he
wasn't really the spider—just a turncoat fly.

"I'm done for the day," said a voice—the girl. Gregor did not
turn to her but continued staring at the shadows.

"Good. Now get out."

"But CHLOE, Gregor: I won't let you keep her chained up like
that. Let me look after her while she's up in the sunlight at least!"

"She won't be chained up forever. Contained, yes, but hopefully unchained. Now, Jennifer, pretty girl, run along home to your father, who must miss you terribly."

Gregor rose disgracefully, performing a pantomime of civility. Jennifer had the horrifying impression that his body was a dead one, operated as a marionette by an unseen puppeteer. She took a few steps back.

"I don't want to leave CHLOE," she stammered.

"Run along, dear heart, across the wildflower'd fields to your father's home. He must be wondering where you've got to!" Gregor ushered her towards the door, entirely oblivious to her protestations. Once she was through the ornate portal, Gregor locked everything up and the governess became to him nothing more than a muffled yammering.

Gregor prepared a drawing room in the clearing by the piano, just as when he entertained Mr Haggerston. There was brandy, of course, and cigarillos, and a pair of secateurs. He checked himself for presentability in a standing mirror. The last few months had aged him terribly. His eyes were puffy and awfully dark, his hair wiry and grey. His arm was leaking blood and pus into the bandage, growing new skin around the fabric. Gone was the blind optimism of his youth—that simple self-assurance of a man who still believes he can achieve his dreams for free. Gregor now knew in his soul that greatness came at a price, and *true* greatness is paid for by the hour.

The clamour of a horse heralded Julian's arrival. On with it, then. It was time to pay another invoice.

"Sandys! My good man, how the devil are you? Surprised to see me?"

Julian Mallory was a dashing fellow, even after all these years. Smooth of face and sleek of hair, he had a grin which some might describe as ingratiating, but which Gregor would describe as coprophagous.

"Surprised? No. But tired—very tired."

There was a moment of an embrace, second-guessed by each gentleman, barely a bumping-together of cravats and a pat on the arm. Gregor winced horribly.

"You look as pale as a Scotsman," Julian said, taking off his riding gloves. "Fancy a wee dram, for auld lang syne?"

"Aye, my jo. Let's."

It was hard to look Mallory in the face—he was too much like the sun to a cave-dwelling creature. Gregor gestured into the darkening greenhouse, where gas lamps flickered and secrets clung to the foliage. The pair meandered around the atrium, arm in good arm, as they had wandered in their youth around Balliol. Gregor took up Julian's air in his weakened baritone:

> "We twa hae paidl'd in the burn,
> frae morning sun till dine;
> But seas between us braid hae roar'd
> sin' auld lang syne."

They reached the piano clearing and Julian put Gregor, now coughing and spluttering, into a chair.

"Spot of brandy will sort you out. I have to say, Gregor, I was hoping to find you in a better state of repair."

"I am perfectly well, thank you," Gregor croaked, "although I have rather been burning the candle at both ends."

"You always were the consummate scientist. Come on, then, out with it. What is this incredible discovery you're working on?"

"You shall see soon enough," Gregor said, draining his glass and reaching for the decanter. "All in good time."

Julian looked around the greenhouse appreciatively. His eyes were less those of an aesthete, more those of an appraiser. His inner monologue was practically numerical. He knew the price of everything, but the value? The intrinsic value?

"You know the value of *nothing*," Gregor spat, out of nowhere.

"Come now." Julian laughed. "You're practically delirious, old fellow! But here—what's this? Ah, your floral displays are quite something to behold."

Julian crossed over to a stone urn which was overflowing with bedding flowers. He ran his fingers through the blooms, stroking each petal, feeling the leaves bounce back into position. Gregor walked over, focusing very hard on appearing *compos mentis*. His wounded arm was tingling and numb. He refused to look weak in front of Mallory.

"The scent of the flesh of geraniums," said Julian, holding his palm for Gregor to smell, "how I adore it. Dark and enchanting, like your glass forest here."

Julian's pout made it quite clear to Gregor that he was being played—or at least, Julian thought he was playing him. Little did Mallory know that it was he who was being played. Still, Gregor allowed himself to enjoy the compliment.

"But I thought you had dedicated yourself purely to fungal enterprises?"

"A mushroom does not a garden make, didn't you say to me once?"

"Still harping on about that silly competition, are we? God's blood, Gregor. You went out on a limb, and your gamble didn't pay off. I won out that day, and rubbed your nose in it, as was my right."

"You destroyed me, in front of the entire Society."

"I mocked you, yes. I don't remember half of it. You seem to have committed every word to memory."

"It is etched on my skin. Every day since then has been a day closer to—"

He stopped short and slumped onto the piano bench. Julian drained his glass and made a great show of sinking to his knees.

"Gregor, I am truly sorry for whatever it was that I said. If I'd known you'd be so tetchy about it... I would have let my victory speak for itself. The better man won, after all."

Gregor felt for the secateurs in his cummerbund. "Would you excuse me for just one moment?"

He left Julian Mallory in the clearing and scurried down the stone steps, past the gnarled boiler, to the undercroft. Wielding his secateurs at last, he snipped away at the plant-monster's bindings. She stirred and slowly began to rise, the low temperature in the crypt having slowed down her metabolic processes. She blinked like the little lamb Simon considered her to be.

"Don't play coy with me," said Gregor, limping back upstairs, "you know what this is."

CHLOE made as if to speak, but only air rushed out—putrid, rasping air.

Back in the clearing, Gregor found Julian by the piano. He played a plodding scale which clanked and clicked against the vines still throttling the strings.

"Your beast is in need of a good tune-up," Julian said, breaking into a poor rendition of some Mozart frippery.

"She does alright for it," said Gregor, joining Julian on the piano bench. "Are you going to tell me about that ring on your finger or am I to make fanciful assumptions?"

"Ah yes—I was going to tell you. Gregor, I am recently married. Early this year, in fact, not long before I got the position at the RHS. It looks good, you see, to be a *family man*."

"And aren't we all family men?" said Gregor with danger in his tone. He closed the lid to the piano keys.

"Well, no, Gregor. Come off it. You've opted out of that life by hiding away here in Grimfern. I have married Charlotte—who is very beautiful, by the way—and I get to continue participating in high society."

"And where did you tell her you'd gone tonight? Some extraordinary meeting of the RHS catering committee?"

"Vol-au-vents don't order themselves from Claridge's."

"And you're happy with that life, are you? Happy with the trade-off you made between living your dream and living your truth?"

"I consider you lucky, Gregor. Your dream and your truth coexist, if a little unconventionally, here at Grimfern. I have all of London at my feet."

"All of London's rentboys, more like. You're the latest in a stream of proper gentlemen who can't bear the fact they are attracted to men. Indeed, you can get married and have children, but you always come crawling back to get what you need. And where does that leave the rest of us, eh?"

"The rest of you? Gregor, there is no 'rest of you'. There are the people like me who do what it takes to survive, and people like you who buy their freedom—the price of which is silence. And don't forget how fortunate you are, safe here at Grimfern. What about the lower classes you so often bleed your heart over? They can't just throw up a conservatory in the country when the Peelers come knocking. What about the common homosexual?"

"I'm sure he'll be very grateful for your frequent acts of charity!"

They were very close now, shouting into each other's faces. Mallory paused to wipe a speck of spittle from his cheek. He spoke very quietly to emphasise their physical proximity.

"I do it all the spirit of almsgiving, I assure you."

He kissed Gregor hungrily on the mouth, but the botanist screwed up his lips and pushed him away. Mallory lurched back at him and the two became entangled in a scrappy wrassle. Gregor won by viciously kicking Julian's shins. He left him on the floor, red-faced, with his hair mussed across his forehead. Gregor straightened his shirtsleeves and went to pour another brandy.

"I need this, Gregor," the pathetic gentleman murmured.

Gregor leaned against the drinks trolley and wished he wasn't prevaricating. He had chosen Simon. All those years ago he chose the austere and distant creature of the night. But here was Mallory—creature of day and conventional success—throwing himself at him. Enmity is the strongest aphrodisiac. Gregor fumbled with the glassware.

"You need something, Mallory, but I can't give it to you. And I don't think your new wife can, either. In fact—"

Gregor stopped short as he turned around. Chloe had crept up on them and had Julian in a bind—his eyes were wide with horror as the creature pulled his cheeks back with tendrils like a horse's bit. It was all he could do to grip her branches to relieve the pressure and moan unintelligibly.

"Chloe, wait! I'm not sure—"

She was gradually extending her spindle-fingers to ensnare Mallory's arms and legs, keeping him quite immobile despite his protestations.

"You think he was attacking me," said Gregor softly. "You've identified a threat and intervened to protect me. Clever girl."

Julian Mallory was crying with fear and writhing ineffectually against his binds. Gregor stalked slowly up to him.

"Sorry about this, old chap, seems my experiment here has got the wrong end of the stick. Have you met Chloe, by the way?"

He hitched up his trousers and crouched to inspect his new captive. Chloe twisted Mallory's head round so he could see her face—impassive as always. He whimpered slightly.

"Or maybe she sees things more clearly than I. She has an uncanny knack for sensing the dark deeps of a person, Julian. And she seems to have taken a disliking to you. You came here to break my home, Mallory, under the guise of reviewing my experiment. Well, here she is! My myco-horticultural auto-ambulatory holobiont—or didn't you learn much biology in floristry school? She's sentient, Mally. And you've annoyed her."

Julian shook his head feebly under CHLOE's grip and writhed about with his last burst of self-preserving energy. In the mad struggle he struck Gregor under the chin with his elbow, causing him to crash to the floor, dribbling blood. Gregor was dazed but heard a rising wind-rush as CHLOE bristled—then a wet tearing of flesh signalled that Mallory's face could no longer take the tension. CHLOE had prised the flesh of his lips and cheeks quite away, along with half the cartilage of his nose. Dreadfully, Julian Mallory had not yet expired.

"Once again, so sorry about this, old chap," Gregor stammered, trying to sound off-hand while avoiding looking at the destroyed face before him. "This, I suppose, is the spiritual successor to the *Bouquet Fongique* which you derided so mercilessly nine years ago. Now, CHLOE, it isn't fair of you to leave a pathetic animal to die a long, agonising death. You should finish the job quickly and—if you please—painlessly."

The plant-girl looked up at her master, cocking her head innocently, like an enquiring cherub.

"Go on," Gregor coaxed, "have at it."

To Gregor's horror, the childlike creature withdrew from her prey and scuttled off into the rich and verdant garden. Gregor was left with a body and *that* face.

"I can't help but feel responsible for all this. But maybe it's no more than you deserve. And you never thought much of my mycological research…" Gregor unlocked his secateurs and positioned them around Julian's neck. "Maybe it's time for you to take a more active part."

He squeezed the handles together. On the other end of the gardening tool, the blade met with its anvil, with Julian's windpipe and several arteries in between. Blood shot from his pulverised neck and streamed from his mangled face. Gregor cried despite himself, tears running clear down his bloodied cheek. Already drenched, he cuddled up next to Julian and they lay together in crimson peace. Once the body had bled out entirely, Gregor flung it unceremoniously in the composting tank—the one rich in woodchip for use with fungal specimens. Of the two of them, the better man had finally won.

# ~PART III~

## PROPAGATION

# Thirty-Four

Days passed, and Jennifer did not see sight nor sound of CHLOE. In her absence, Jenny's duties returned to the mundane housework—cleaning, mostly, as meals were scant. Simon returned from London in high spirits and with a carriage full of mahogany and teak.

"Whose horse is that, Gregor?" he enquired.

"Horse? Oh, I don't know—it just turned up one day." Gregor caught a sight of Simon's incredulity and doubled down with bluster. "Jennifer, do you need a horse?"

This was the first time he had addressed her since sending her off to her father's. No she bloody well didn't need a horse, thank you very much. She needed her best friend in the whole world. She needed CHLOE. *Stuff your damn horse.*

"Oh, Mr Sandys, I couldn't possibly accept…"

"You shall, or it's the knackers, which would be a shame. Such a fine horse—so much rendering."

"I'll take the horse, Gregor. Thank you."

Jenny returned to her roaming around the greenhouse. She had long since covered every square inch of brick and iron, searched under every leaf for her lost love. Chloe wasn't in the basement workshop, neither in the west wing laboratory. She wasn't hidden in the boys' quarters, or anywhere she could see in the main atrium, or even in the pond. Jennifer was beginning to entertain the possibility that Gregor had released her into the wild. Jenny's imagination ran away with itself, conjuring the dangers as well as the excitements of a woodland adventure as a nymph.

One night, when she couldn't sleep, Jenny heard a strange knocking. It wasn't the sound of knocking on glass, or on bamboo—this was somehow further away, and seemingly coming from everywhere all at once. She crept around the moonlit glade in her nightgown, tracing the source of the strange percussion. Eventually she descended the stone steps towards Simon's workshop, but paused when the rapping became smarter somehow—sharper. It was coming from the grotesque profusion of pipes that made up the heating system. Perhaps Gregor had turned it on in anticipation of a chill, and that was the source of the sound? But there was no light or heat coming from the machine. Although Jennifer didn't understand the numbers and dials, she could see that they weren't *doing* anything. And yet there came a knocking from the huge brass boiler.

She fiddled with the clasp and swung it wide open. There, in the great metal drum of the thing, lit now by a moonbeam, was a grove of twisted greenery.

"Chloe," Jennifer gasped. She fumbled a gas lamp from the wall, lit it with a shaking hand. The amber light bounced off the metal and cast the mound of plant matter into sharp relief. On closer inspection—or was this since she arrived?—CHLOE had sprouted hundreds of mushrooms. Fruiting bodies, as Gregor would call them. They were long and thin, incredibly pale, and capped with perky, squishy bells. They were sprouting from all over CHLOE, with the greatest density at her chest.

"What have they done to you?"

She put the lamp down and gathered CHLOE into her arms. As the echo of gaslight faded from her eyes, Jenny could see an eerie glow from CHLOE's mushrooms. She carried her up from the boiler level and laid her out under the stars at the top of the stairs. CHLOE was rousing and moving her lips, but no sound came out.

"Your voice, CHLOE, I'm so sorry. I should have protected you."

The mushroom-clad lady shook her head and pointed languidly to her chest.

"Oh, CHLOE, yes I love you! I love you deeply, and madly perhaps, but oh so tenderly, my sweet petal."

CHLOE tapped with more insistence on her chest, and Jenny saw beneath the thicket of mushrooms the metal clasp. Feeling foolish, she reached between CHLOE's breasts and with sensitive fingers prised open the latch. Inside was all of CHLOE—her bellows for lungs, her woodwind voice box, and her mycelial heart. The smell of wet soil and rising damp was overpowering. CHLOE took hold of Jennifer's hand and brought it to the disconnected windpipe.

"You want me to reattach everything?"

The severed hose was tattered at the end; Jenny wasn't sure it could ever be repaired. But CHLOE squeezed her hand so reassuringly, and looked at her with such affectionate eyes, that Jenny couldn't help but try. She connected everything back up—it just wouldn't stay in place.

"I can't make it stay, CHLOE—I don't know how."

Even in the time it took to say those words, CHLOE's inner tendrils had set to work sealing the gap. A thousand threads of fungal goop arranged themselves around the tear and squeezed themselves airtight. With a splutter, CHLOE blew some debris through the *sheng*.

"*Outside*," CHLOE choked.

"What, my love?"

"*Outside. Outside!*" she repeated again and again, with the same insistent musical flourish over and over.

A list of reasons why they shouldn't run away flashed in Jenny's mind. But beyond these reasons why not, and beneath them, and through them, she felt the rise of excitement and purpose. This is what she was here to do, after all. The solution to CHLOE's captivity wasn't simply to give her more petty freedoms, but to free her entirely—once and for all. And better still, they could escape together, and be fugitives together, and live together, forever, in their own Grimfern which they would make for themselves.

"Alright, CHLOE." She kissed her on the side of the mouth. "Outside it is!"


Jennifer left CHLOE to gather herself on the floor while she dashed back up to her room. She packed a cloth bag with essentials and changed into her finest gentleman's attire. She raided the kitchenette for bread and cheeses, and also packed a watering can and a hooded cloak for CHLOE. She took a shiny apple from the fruit bowl and slipped through Gregor's enchanted forest to the side of the greenhouse which bordered the stable.

Here, Jennifer got her new horse's attention through hissing and careful rapping on the glass. It looked at her with infinite disdain and turned its rump to her. Florence, the grey mare, however, was enticed by the sight of the apple and ambled around the greenhouse to near the front door, which had once again been heavily padlocked.

Jenny encouraged CHLOE and Florence to be either side of the door and dressed the plant-girl in the hooded cloak. Gregor had seen to it that this front door was the most impermeable part of the greenhouse. But he had forgotten that every other part of the house was incredibly fragile, given that the walls, as well as the doors, were made of glass. Making sure her ladies were out of the way, Jenny took an aspidistra by the lip of its pot. She carefully aimed, then swung herself around. The rootball, being the heaviest part of the object, described a satisfying arc in the air, dragging the foliage behind it as if it were its fletching. The whole thing, plant, soil, and pot, crashed right through a glass pane to the left of the door.

The clatter took everybody by surprise, even Jenny, who had been expecting it. She shook herself and grabbed CHLOE by the hand.

"Come now, we have to get out of here!"

They raced through the aspidistra-hole, taking care not to get any of CHLOE's fronds snagged on the jagged glass. There were noises off in the east wing as Simon and Gregor woke at the crash, but Jenny put CHLOE on the mare with such speed that the men hadn't even arrived as she swung herself up behind. She took the reins either side of the plant-girl and geed the three of them off down the drive.

Turning back briefly, Jennifer saw the outline of two men in silhouette, raging against the liberty of darkness.

Simon and Gregor stood by the gaping hole in their glass home. A kind of devastation fell upon them, as joy fled from their lives. Simon clutched his robe around him and Gregor wiped sleep and ink from his face.

"We have to follow them," said Gregor.

"On foot? We have no chance."

"Where do you think they will have gone?"

"It's Jennifer with the reins, she could be anywhere. She loves the openness of the moors and meadows."

"She has the reins to the horse, but CHLOE has the reins to Jennifer. The party will go wherever the mycelium demands."

"And where, pray tell, will the mycelium demand to be taken, O newfound fungal phrenologist?"

"You know I don't know that!" Gregor brushed through the broken pane, causing shards to drop to the floor. He hated it when Simon pointed out gaps in his knowledge. Shouting at him usually shut him up—although Gregor used that power sparingly.

This time, to Gregor's great surprise, Simon shouted right back.

"You do know that!" Simon thundered. He bent his considerable spine to shimmy through the gap and took Gregor by the shoulders. "You do know that," he continued, "you stupid, stupid genius. *Think*, Gregor—what does the mycelium want now, most of all?"

Gregor scratched his greying hair. The lamplight shuddered.

"It wants to expand," he suggested. "I think it has become entirely root-bound inside the substrate. That's why it is expressing a yearning for the outside. It needs more room for growth, more nutrients."

"And if the picnic is any model, she can find that anywhere within nature. Lord—that's all of bloody Buckinghamshire!"

"But wait—Jennifer would never stay out in the open. Her love for the creature, like ours for each other, dares not conduct itself in plain sight."

Simon thought about this for a while. "So she loves CHLOE, then?" he whispered.

"I've seen the way she looks at her. It's the same expression you used to have when looking at me. Shock, I suppose, but with an uncanny certainty in its ardour. And more than that, Simon, your 'daughter' loves her in return."

"So the question becomes—where would the two women elope to?" Simon's breathing had quickened, and he couldn't help but smile.

"Simon, are you *happy* for the couple?"

"All love is sacred, Gregor. What God has joined together may no man cast asunder."

Gregor stared, dumbfounded by Simon's saccharine sentiment. Such a sweet conceit—such a dangerous lie. The mycelium's love was no gift from heaven. It was a curse unleashed from the cold earth, roiling and festering...

"And what an incredible success for you, Gregor," Simon said, his face unnaturally flushed, "what a glorious feather in your cap! You have created spontaneous affection! You have generated artificial love!"

Yes—it was all his fault. At every step of the way, if Gregor had simply decided enough was enough he could have prevented this. And now, what had he unleashed upon the world? Gregor cradled his wounded arm and pretended to smile at Simon's flattery.

"Save the plaudits for luncheons at Kew. Our first priority is to get CHLOE and Jennifer back in the greenhouse where they belong."

"Agreed," said Simon, "we need them back here to let them know that we support them and cherish them so dearly. Now then—if I were Miss Finch, I would take my lover to the water mill. It isn't too far away, and her father is out all night poaching. She will reckon that it is a fine spot to prepare for a longer journey."

"Then we need to get to the water mill at once!" Gregor set off at a jog, but the previous day's loss of blood got the better of him and he keeled over on the path after a few steps. Simon ran up to him and cupped Gregor's face, stroking his cheek with his thumb.

"We have to prepare ourselves, too, silly owl."

Gregor blinked up at Simon's smiling face—such a rare sight. He was clearly in a rapturous mood.

"Simon, what the devil is wrong with you?"

"After talking it over with Rosalinda, and seeing this latest catastrophe, I have realised one thing. You are a fool, Gregor Sandys. Quite possibly the most intelligent fool ever to have wielded a trowel. For a decade now I have shrunk back into the shadows, scared to damage the delicate balance of your ridiculous sense of self. Your pride is monstrously huge, yet your self-belief is laughably tiny. Your inner life must be like an elephant balancing upon a Fabergé egg. And now that I have Jennifer and CHLOE to care for, I can't be worrying about that egg, as fragile and as precious as it may be. So do continue your improbable circus act, by all means, while I get on with the actual business of running this household."

It came out stronger than he intended, but he stood by it. Simon kissed the bewildered botanist full on the mouth and hurried back into the greenhouse to prepare, leaving Gregor prone on the ground.

He sat up and nursed his damaged arm. Simon had never been like this—assertive, even defiant. All the careful balances they had set up for themselves—yes, Simon's reading of Gregor's emotional equilibrium, but also the balance of the relationship, the mutual dependencies of all four in the household, Gregor's status as lord over all he surveyed—all of that was falling down around him. Gregor had lost more than his experiment tonight.

Florence the grey mare hurtled down the country track as bramble hedges hemmed them in on either side. Both women leaned forwards in the saddle to protect their heads from the thorny roof—this route had become a holloway in time for autumn's blackberries. CHLOE's thighs pressed into Jennifer's as they bounced and clung tight. Sinuous roots tangled themselves around Jennifer's belt-buckle. Fronds caressed her legs from her waist to her boots... Jennifer took this as a tender hug from her beloved, so she kissed her leafy shoulder.

"We'll turn up this lane. It might be too obvious to hunker down at my father's house for the night, but I reckon Mr Sandys and Mr Rievaulx will assume we've travelled further afield. We'll have to be gone before father gets back, though."

CHLOE sang merrily in response. Despite the danger, Jennifer grinned. They picked up speed approaching the water mill and jumped the rusted gate. They did a few laps around the yard to slow Florence down, then disentangled themselves from the saddle and from each other.

"This, I suppose, is my house," said Jennifer, scratching the back of her head. "It's where I'm really from."

CHLOE, on tiptoe with wide eyes, examined the shambling cottage. There were roof slates on the floor, weeds in the brickwork, and no glass in the windows. In fact, there was no glass in the entire house.

*"Jennifer—house,"* said CHLOE.

The first person who had ever visited Jennifer at the water mill was Constance. As young girls they were too preoccupied by chasing games to pay attention to their surroundings. When they grew into teenagers, and the world began to have meaning for them, on rainy days they had sat about in each other's homes, discussing the traces of their absent fathers. An empty stool, dirty dishes, various sharp and serrated implements.

The last time someone visited Jennifer at the water mill, it had also been Constance. She had near staggered through the door, aimless and distracted. Jennifer had peered down from her hayloft bedroom. *What's wrong?* Connie had shaken her head unconvincingly. She had made to speak but the emotion broke through and she sobbed loudly. Jenny had jumped down and held her. *Whatever it is we can make it better.* Obviously, that had not turned out be true, and all too soon she had attended Constance's hasty funeral by the twisted hazel.

Now, Jennifer felt the guilt for having let Constance slip so far from her mind that summer. She had devoted herself instead to CHLOE, which was so much easier than thinking about Constance, and the endless summers of wildflowers and gorse which were now all gone.

CHLOE climbed up to the musty hayloft. Hearing Jennifer stifle a sob, she poked her head out above the ladder.

*"Jennifer—sad?"*

Jennifer was overwhelmed, but wiped her eyes and tried to smile. CHLOE extended herself down to where Jennifer was standing at the ladder and entwined her feelers around her waist and her pink ear. She held her so tenderly and softly—Jennifer could feel rich soil against the nape of her neck.

*"Whatever it is,"* said CHLOE, singing some buried quotation, *"we can make it better."*

Jennifer looked straight up into her algal eyes.

"You can't know that."

*"Maybe* CHLOE *can?"*

"No—you can't know those words."

*"Maybe* CHLOE *can!"*

Their lips locked, with the taste of roots and soil disgusting Jenny for a moment. But when she became accustomed to the petrichor, she kissed with hunger and need. The unspoken words and imagined conversations of a whole girlhood of longing were suddenly real for her—she had Connie back at last, and finally in her arms.

Simon near ran on his spindly legs back through the broken window and into the east wing. He rifled through his wardrobe, not caring where the discarded clothes fell—such was the freedom afforded him by mad ardour. Once he was dressed in a slim suit of black with tails and jaunty frills on the shirt, he looked at the mess he had made. He tried for a moment to leave it, out of gay spontaneity, but thought better of it and tidied his clothes away neatly.

He descended into his taxidermy crypt, casting his gas lamp this way and that amongst the columns and cadavers. From an immaculately organised zinc stand he retrieved his thinnest leather gloves. These would give him maximum dexterity with significant protection. Then he took his array of scalpels, which were arranged in a cloth sack which could be rolled up, tied, and affixed to his belt.

All around him were his creations. They were minions of minor stature, but they cast grotesque shadows. That ridiculous owl, done up to resemble a scholar with a master's cap and gown. It could pass for a caricature of Gregor. All the pieces seemed so cloying to him now, so sentimental—what did those bridal kittens know of love? Nothing—their stuffed matrimony was false and self-important. True love was all-giving, destructive, and desperate. Simon loved Gregor. Jennifer loved CHLOE.

Ah—CHLOE. Simon's greatest creation. She was the pinnacle of his artistic output. Gregor may have invented her processes, but Simon had sculpted her from flesh. He had stitched her skin and sawn her timbers until she was beautiful and perfect. He had given her aesthetic beauty, Gregor had given her vigour, and now in return she had given them passion. This was a gift the stifled taxidermist never thought he would receive. He had lived his life in the dust of private schools and secret workshops, always under the thumb of some overbearing *other*. Now CHLOE had freed him to exist as himself—to feel for himself—and he was experiencing the last thirty-some years of feelings all at once, with euphoria and giddy grief.

His eye fell upon the cabinet of preserved body parts.

"Oh pathetic juvenilia, work of an unripened mind. This glassware contains my true feelings, my joys and my revulsions. Yet I gouged them out and trapped them, as if in ante-mortem canopic jars."

He ran his gloved hand across their shimmering surfaces. There was the meagre rabbit's brain, which had removed his capacity to think about his misdeeds. The entrails of a pheasant had 'cured' him of that heavy feeling of dread. The sheep's heart was supposed to stop him loving—how foolish that seemed to him now! And the myriad eyes in a barber's glass… they were supposed to rid him of the luminous daguerreotype behind his eyelids: the memory of a murder. Each one of these jars was a relic of a ritual self-exorcism.

"Symbols of my self-entrapment. I hate thee!"

He blew out the gas lamp, and allowed a moment for himself to get used to the darkness. Then he took the scholarly owl by its lacquered feet and crashed it against the cabinet. Glass shattered and preserving fluid poured down over him, drenching him in ethanol and eyeballs. Simon breathed the fumes in deeply, laughed a little, and cried. He felt thoroughly liberated and alive—he was suddenly aware of his own brain, guts, beating heart, and burning eyes. Simon scampered up the stone steps like a boy. He was wild and glad, his hair flopping quite undone.

"I'm coming, Gregor!"

# THIRTY-FIVE

*J*ennifer stepped back from the kiss. CHLOE was radiant, bright and shining, with rapid shoots securing herself to the ladder and roof. Looking at CHLOE was like looking at herself in a way—like looking at her own desire. So this was it: this face, these eyes. This was what Jennifer had always wanted, and what she would always need near her. She had the uncanny knowledge—lovers always have such certainty—that CHLOE felt the same way looking back at her. Their mutual need was overwhelming. Their faces touched from forehead to nose tip. CHLOE's spiral feelers wound their way up Jennifer's wrists.

*"Come into the rafters, my love."*

Jennifer made to climb the ladder, but CHLOE shushed her into stillness. With a hundred points of contact, CHLOE's ganglia lifted Jennifer lightly off the floor and up into the hayloft. Jennifer didn't have the power to resist, but didn't have the desire to, either.

They lay amid irregular beams—facing each other as adults in Jenny's childhood domain. They were lit only by moonlight through the broken roof, but their eyes were as bright as any constellation. Jennifer ran her fingers through CHLOE's ivy-hair. It had become even longer than before, and partially obscured the curves of her torso.

With slender fingers, CHLOE began to undo Jenny's many buttons. Rather than removing each garment in turn, she undid all the uppermost buttons until Jennifer's clavicle was exposed, then proceeded down along her cleavage. Jennifer's breasts were released from their waistcoat corseting, and though not yet exposed they were liberated.

Buttons flew and constrictions eased. There was the sliding of fabric, and the sensation of bark against skin.

Discarding the clothes which had been ceremoniously unbuttoned by her lover, Jenny was left in her bloomers. She felt thoroughly exposed, and more than a little self-conscious. CHLOE lay there, head cocked, happy to just observe. There could be no guile in the creature, no malice. Jennifer was ashamed, not of her nakedness, but of her clumsy un-nakedness. She shimmied out of her bloomers and kneeled, prone. Being unclothed together was more honest somehow.

Jennifer climbed across and leaned over CHLOE on all fours. She put her head to her chest—sensitive foliage tickled her ear. But she heard no heartbeat, no vital pulse. Jennifer had seen inside CHLOE's chest once before. In there amongst the bellows was a throbbing core of sinews and soil. When plants become too large for their container, their growth takes on the shape of the pot, blocking absorption of nutrients. CHLOE was at that point, Jennifer felt sure. Hers was a root-bound heart.

"You should be free," said Jennifer. "There is so much more of you than can be contained in your body."

CHLOE shivered and thrilled. Her sing-song voice dropped sweet and low, and in a spurt she sent out a network of white roots all across the hay bed. Jenny was buffeted by the release of joy from CHLOE and their abdomens rubbed firmly.

Jennifer leaned in for another peaty kiss. She had developed a taste for it now—the rich and dark tang of dirt and mould, spores perhaps, and lichen. She began to work her way down CHLOE's front with hungry lips.

"I may not have your knack for buttons," she said between kisses, "but I can do this instead."

She wanted every taste of CHLOE on her tongue: her leaves and her petals; sweet nectar and bitter pollen; the mud and the moss, and the rusted metal clasp. At the bottom of her torso there was a grove all of its own, a burgeoning garden of ferns and mosses. Jennifer's tongue tasted it all. When she resurfaced, CHLOE's ivy-hair had taken the form of a halo—she was an emerald saint in some forbidden icon. Across her head was a crown of roses.

CHLOE rose like an ocean wave rolling over Jennifer, casting a spray of petals and perfume. Still attached to the hay and timber, she looked benevolently over her former governess. CHLOE was an amorphous mass of nature, with only the suggestion of a woman at the centre.

CHLOE's spindle-fingers and fronds explored Jennifer's naked body—the underside of her breasts, the inside of her thigh. Jennifer lost track of the innumerable tender stems rubbing against her. A tendril caressed her lips and explored her mouth. The song—that impossibly sweet lilt—seemed to come from far away.

A fern's feather touch stroked Jennifer's labia, and she gasped a faltering breath. A thick, soft root about the size of a finger pressed more insistently. Jenny could not help but lift her pelvis, leaning into the protrusion.

The scents of jasmine and hay mingled in the heavy air. Every part of Jennifer was explored by the cooing plant-woman. Soon Jennifer could see nothing but knotted stems and brambles. Was there blood on the thorns? She was being filled and stretched, done and undone. From the green darkness appeared CHLOE's mossy clitoris—misty wet and all-encompassing. It became Jennifer's entire world. CHLOE was doing so much for her right now, at every conceivable point of pleasure. Jenny surely had to do something in return. She leaned forward with difficulty, given that CHLOE's bonds were tying her down, and she licked the partition. Hungry for her loam, she strengthened her tongue and parted her. It was as if a breeze blew through the rafters as the two women entered each other fully. Deeper and deeper they pressed into and received each other. Something deep inside them both erupted, and all they could see was beauty, and each other, and iridescent algal green.

# Thirty-six

Gregor tried as he might, but he could not get Julian's horse to settle down enough to let him saddle her.

"Must be missing her master," said Simon, arriving at the stables.

"What do you mean by that?"

"She's all of a dither—never mind, we'll have to walk!" Simon set off at a fair run down the sloping drive, leaving Gregor to hobble after him.

The two men hurried out of the Grimfern gates and along the muddy path to the old Finch mill. There was a crisp mist in the silver hours before dawn. Simon was several paces ahead, and to Gregor he seemed to be a dream of himself. He vanished here and there into the first chill of autumn, then rematerialised in turn. His long black coat caught the infinitesimal water droplets and swung them around. Gregor blinked hard and struggled to keep focused. His wound had gone untreated overnight, and its sharp pain was transforming into something much darker and deeper. Gregor sweated even in the cool night air.

Simon had a spring in his step. Gone was the stiff taxidermist, sharing so many morbid traits with his creations. Here in front of Gregor was a new man, younger than his years, determined and devoted. Layer upon layer of self-hatred landed on Gregor, suffocating him as he staggered along. He hated that he had clearly repressed Simon for so long. He also hated that he had now lost whatever power he had over him. And he hated that it was the insidious tendrils of the Sumatran mycelium that had upset the order of things.

Gregor arrived at the boundary of Mr Finch's crumbling mill. The great waterwheel, which hadn't been attached to its mechanism in decades, was so battered that it seemed to be made out of driftwood. A common English ivy clung to the shambling cottage, but Gregor was intrigued to spot some unusual species poking through the stonework—*Tillandsia dyeriana* 'Cancun orange', fronds and crosiers of non-native ferns, and a spray of Gregor's own proprietary orchids. The morning mist was deeper here; thick and pernicious.

Simon crouched by the rusted gate, face flushed and long hair wet with dew. Gregor staggered up to him.

"She's here," he growled. "We'll move quietly. Help me with the gate."

"Don't be silly; it's rusted shut. We'll have to climb over." Simon made to limber over the stubborn gate, his arms and legs moving with a freedom Gregor had rarely seen from him.

"Wait," said Gregor, struggling to articulate need. "I can't. My arm."

Simon slinked back to the gatepost against which Gregor was slumped. He kissed him on the forehead and provided a foothold with his interlocking hands.

"Have at it, then!" Simon beamed.

Gregor scrambled over and fell to his knees on the other side. Soon he was joined by Simon, who gracefully dismounted.

"See, not so hard. Now come on."

Gregor grunted a bitter acknowledgement. Perhaps there was such a thing as too much assertiveness from Simon. Having tried out this version, Gregor wished for the reserved and predictable gentleman of yesteryear.

In the corner of Mr Finch's yard stood the spectral figure of a horse. The men recognised it as their grey mare, Florence, but her bearing and posture implied great fear as she cowered against the dry-stone wall. Simon and Gregor crept towards the open doorframe of the water mill cottage.

The air was heavier inside, thick with condensation. The mist seemed to roll out of the cottage like a storm front in the jungle. The splintered doorframe was wet to Gregor's touch.

"Halt! Who goes there!" a shout came from behind them. "Get out of here, you bleedin', why I ought to—"

It was the lumbering silhouette of John Finch, laden with fresh bodies from the hunt. He swung himself over the fence and came clattering across his yard. Simon hailed him urgently.

"Mr Finch, it's Messrs Sandys and Rievaulx from Grimfern."

"I don't right care who it is, come to think of it. I can't have you creeping around my home at all times of the night. What the devil are you up to?"

"John—your daughter may be in danger. We're here to make sure she's alright."

"Whatever mal-deeds there are here it'll be you two making sure of their occurrence, I'll wager. Why I let her gad about with you odd fellows I'll never know. What kind of trouble have you brought to my door?"

"Mr Sandys here is a botanist," Simon tried to explain, "that is to say he is an acolyte of the science of plants and fungi—"

"John, there is a great risk to your daughter. The whys and wherefores are to be left 'til later. I say this to you: we are here to save Jennifer from an unspeakable occurrence. Help us, John." Gregor reached out uneasily and grabbed the poacher's arm.

Whatever moral calculations John Finch made then were unrevealed to the universe by his constant frown. He sloughed off his catch with a squelching thud on the cobbles and took his rifle in hand.

On Mr Finch's mark, the three fathers burst into the mill cottage.

Once the wisps of fog had settled, their faces fell. Simon grabbed his heart and fell back; Gregor steadied himself against the doorframe. John Finch held his gun close.

"What damned root is this…"

There were leafy creepers across the roof beams. A cascade of vines hung like a waterfall from the hayloft, dripping wet with dew. Orchids sprang from wooden columns, and the air was sweet with the scent of exotic nectar. It was as if Gregor's carefully controlled garden had been mixed up and spat out in a riotous explosion of foliage. At the centre of the bloom were the shapes of two women intertwined. CHLOE was implied only by the sinews of rubber plants and creepers—she was a living death mask of herself, the imprint of Constance in this spontaneous wood. Jennifer's skin was mottled blue-green, with visible dark arteries. She was cocooned by a lattice of mycelium bristling with slender mushrooms. The two botanical daughters were locked in an embrace, bedecked by flowers from Gregor's garden: roses, and daisies, and bindweed. Jennifer seemed so peaceful; only resting. Gregor knew from the fruiting bodies erupting from her veins that she had been taken by the mycelium to be a new heart for the holobiont.

John Finch was aghast.

"Jennifer!" the old man sobbed, stepping forwards.

Gregor held a hand out to stop him, but John Finch shrugged him off. He had lost the last precious thing to him.

"This is your doing," he rasped, pointing a stony finger at Gregor, "you and your sordid ways. This is an unholy grove planted by your hand!"

"John, this creature..."

Gregor's explanation was ignored by the poacher. A burly man despite his advanced years, John Finch staggered about the cottage, trembling with rage.

A deep murmuring came from the hayloft canopy. It was as if a thousand voices were singing blasphemous curses far below the ground. It was as if the rustle of a forest's trees were intelligible to humankind. Every limb of the ecosystem rose gracefully in a grand inhale before breathing out: *Father*.

John Finch regained his focus. "Jennifer? It must be her. She's still alive—I'll cut her out!" He cast aside his rifle, brandished his hunting knife and made for the heart of the fungus.

Gregor leaped forwards and shoved Mr Finch's knife arm so forcefully he spun to the ground. "We must keep the specimen intact!"

CHLOE's leaves rattled menacingly all across the mill house. She shot out vines to hold back Gregor's arms, preventing him from hurting one of her many beloved fathers.

*Fathers! Fathers all.*

"I am not your father!" Gregor bellowed. "I am your maker, your cultivator, your inventor. I conceived you not of body but of mind. You are not my child. You are my greatest success and my gravest error. You are my monster!"

CHLOE screamed. The high-pitched scream of the *sheng* was joined by ear-splitting reeds and the scratching of thorns against stone. She picked Gregor clear off the ground and thrashed him about before driving a root head deep into his festering wound. He contorted and roared.

"Hush, CHLOE, my sweet pea," said Simon, stepping into the centre of the misty chaos. In CHLOE's sudden silence, you could hear the steady drip of moisture from her hanging moss. "We love you dearly. We want to help you. And we want to help Jennifer. You want us to help her, don't you?"

A cluster of black tendrils extended their proprietary grip over Jennifer's pallid cheek.

*We are all. We are Jenny, we are* CHLOE.

In Simon's confused silence, John Finch reached for his rifle and made to load it, crouching low at the back of the room.

"Simon! The gun—" cried Gregor, hearing the rifle's action.

"You dare point that weapon at my daughter!" growled Simon.

Mr Finch's hands were shaking, but he brought the gun to bear. Simon whipped his scalpel out of its pouch. The poacher scoffed at the tiny weapon.

"I'll do anything for my daughter, Mr Rievaulx," John Finch said, "even die."

He shot the musket well wide of his target, but it struck CHLOE's foliage and brought down a roof tile. Her vines retracted in fear, more a flinch than a retreat, quite dropping Gregor from two feet or so onto the stone floor. He did his best to prop himself up against the shucking stool.

"You will not harm my daughter!" Simon roared. "You know nothing of fatherhood, Mr Finch. You have destroyed your own daughter day by absent day and night by lonesome night. And now you have hurt my precious CHLOE. What do you have to say for yourself?"

"Burn in hell like so much kindling, the lot of you!"

John Finch made to aim once more, but Simon hurled himself at the poacher, sliding the scalpel firmly into and across his throat. The poacher slumped over and twitched as he bled out, spluttering crimson through his whiskers. Simon was splattered head to toe. He panted, animal-like, before stepping back and wiping his scalpel on a handkerchief from his cuff. He stiffened a little with every small move, until he was quite still and thoroughly clenched once more.

*Pater...*

"No, CHLOE," said Simon, addressing the rafters, "nobody here is your true father. This man wanted to hurt you—what parent could do that to a child? Gregor and I assembled you, yes. But, when all is said and done, we are not your parents. I regret to say you are fatherless. But you are not an orphan— you are an immaculate entity of your own creation. As for myself and Gregor, I promise that we will protect you and cherish you always. We may not be your fathers, but we owe you that much."

CHLOE's tendrils embraced Simon, and she wove a spray of anemones through his long black hair.

*Family...*

Simon chuckled. "Yes, if you like. We can be one unconventional family."

"One unconventional *holobiont*," Gregor muttered. Simon flared his nostrils at him. It was in their best interest now to keep her calm, keep her close, keep her contained.

They buried John Finch in his yard while Florence kept her vigil.

"We have ended the Finch line," said Simon simply once they were done.

"The Finches will never die, as long as CHLOE is alive," Gregor replied.

Anxiety subsides when there are practical steps to be taken. Sometimes busywork is the only thing holding back existential dread. Dawn bronzed the mist over the millpond, and the two men set about their minutiae. Gregor found some curing salt in Mr Finch's store and one-handedly cast it about the orifices of the house to slow CHLOE's expansion. Simon took a saw and dismantled the rusted gate. They were now to take turns guarding the building and making sure CHLOE did not escape into the Buckinghamshire woodland before such time as they could move her back to Grimfern.

Simon helped Gregor up onto the grey mare. "Go straight to High Wycombe, and have the doctor see to you."

"Yes, Simon," said Gregor with great tiredness. "I think... I think it's done."

"It's done."

Gregor leaned down and kissed his partner on the mouth. "I love you, Simon. No grave loss or unfathomable gain would change that simple fact."

"And I love you, you impossible man. Now go—before gangrene gets you." He patted Florence on the thigh and sent them both off. He rooted around in John Finch's tool shed and found a battered pair of shears.

"Right, my sweet pea. Let's see what needs a little trim."

# THIRTY-SEVEN

Throughout autumn they took turns at the water mill, trimming away new growth, boarding up the windows and cracks, and generously applying sodium chloride to the environs. With pruning, wood, and salt, Simon and Gregor were able to contain CHLOE inside the cottage.

The only time they saw each other was at the changing of the guard, when one of them would bring supplies from Grimfern or the village and relieve the other of warden duty. Sometimes they tarried, drinking in the season together, but often the labour was too much and they acknowledged each other with a kiss on the cheek and a weary goodbye.

The cold of autumn encourages mushrooms to sprout— they are the fruiting bodies of networks of mycelium running through the ground or through the trunks of trees. Visible mushrooms are only the berries of the great fruit bush hidden from sight. By October, CHLOE's prodigious fungus erupted into bell-cap mushrooms in the dank cottage. They emitted a slight luminescence, which, given the sheer number of them and the density of the fungal thicket, caused the room to glow like the night sky. On clear nights, Simon would open a roof hatch to drench CHLOE in the light of the moon, so that the constellations below might mirror the Milky Way above.

CHLOE could not stay there forever. As soon as he could, Gregor hired architects to construct a new greenhouse to the north of the central atrium at Grimfern. It would be unconnected to the main space, though warmed by the same subterranean boiler. Plumbing it in was the devilish bit, but once the floor was laid the iron frame and glass went in relatively quickly.

Once the delicate work was done, Gregor hired a different set of contractors—entered as Croft & Son & Son on his ledger, these being country folk with traditional knowledge—to build a full-size replica water mill inside the greenhouse. They built it to a vague design Simon had scribbled down based on the Finch residence, complete with millstream. It slowed them down greatly to have to pass every brick and beam through the single slide-out window of the glasshouse, but with no expense spared on materials and extra labourers the construction was finished by Christmas.

In the first frosts of November, CHLOE died back considerably. The tropical elements of her ecosystem were not fit for British seasons, and Simon and Gregor spent the early part of winter managing her decline. The flowers died off quite early and were swiftly deadheaded. Thick leaves grew brown and shrivelled and were disposed of. Frond by frond, they worked their way back towards the rafters where Constance and Jennifer lay embracing.

On a dull and blustery January morning, Simon arrived at the cottage to take over from his partner. Gregor was standing and staring at the forlorn plant. The Constance substrate had been majorly depleted by CHLOE's fruiting season. She was gaunt like an Egyptian mummy, her leaves quite skeletal, her roots exposed like an old lady's hand-veins. Jennifer by contrast was jewelled with moss and winter foliage. Cyclamen were bursting from her neck, although they were distended from the lack of sunlight.

"The building work is completed," said Simon, placing his hand on Gregor's shoulder.

"Good. Then it is time."

Gregor took a hoe, felt its weight, then severed the major tendrils from the daughter cortex to the rest of the system. Simon performed the more delicate work with his taxidermy implements. Soon they had excised the root-brain—that is, Constance and Jennifer—from the attic. They carried their emaciated corpses out to where Florence was waiting with a carriage.

Gregor withdrew a box of matches from his greatcoat. His hand trembled. He hated fire. He hated how it made him remember.

"I can't. Simon—you do it."

"I think you're ready now. You do it."

Gregor stepped inside the doorway to shield the match from the wind. All around the mill cottage was dead, dry brush from CHLOE's winter recession.

"After the fire comes new life."

He struck the match and placed it in a straw pile. The flame caught quickly and was blown about on the choppy wind.

Gregor jumped onto the back of the carriage and watched as they left.

The conflagration was horrifically vicious, tearing through the cottage like a tinderbox. The waterwheel caught fire in the intense heat, burst at the centre and fell into the millpond. Gregor thought of a time a decade hence, when saplings would grow within the ruined walls, and reeds would sprout from the waterwheel. He shuddered and hoped the fire would cleanse the area fully of the mycelium.

They lay the substrate onto a bed of damp woodchip in the basement of the newly constructed mill cottage. From there, agar-treated twine was strung out to connect the bed to various elements of the house—the doors, the window shutters, sprinklers in the roof, and a series of bells scattered throughout the building. It was Gregor's hope that the creature would be able to achieve homeostasis through aeration and hydration. Plus, it might be able to commune with him via the carillon. CHLOE's singing apparatus had degraded terribly over the autumn bloom and winter fade. Bells would provide a coded alternative—one incomprehensible to outsiders. And it was for *outsiders* that Gregor was preparing this pastoral scene.

Over time, CHLOE gained mastery of the new mill cottage. She allowed the artificial brook to flow at her will, turning the waterwheel in a delightful manner. She opened her shutters just enough to keep her insides cool and dark, and flung them open at night to drink in the moon.

[Letter addressed to the desk of President of the Royal Horticultural Society, dated Sunday 6th April 1890]

Dear Mr Mallory,

I am writing this letter with considerable consternation at not having received word from you regarding our previous correspondence—really, Jules! I had rather hoped I was higher in your affections than that, but still.

I am assuming, dear letter-opener, that you are not in fact Mr Julian Mallory, but someone hired to read his business mail in his absence. I also assume that Mallory is indisposed on some extraordinary voyage in search of vol-au-vents around the seedier parts of Istanbul. Perhaps he has fallen into some social disrepute. Regardless, it is to *you*, dear reader, that I extend the following invitation.

There is to be a gala at Grimfern—an Exhibition, if you will. For many years I have laboured in secrecy, and now I am ready once again to reveal my botanical achievements to the RHS and the general public. I can assure you that the trip will be worth your while, and the Society grandees will be astounded by my mycelial discoveries. Also visiting will be Rosalinda Smeralda-Bland and her fashionable salon, along with dignitaries of the theatre, and various other socialites.

So I trust I will see you on Whitsun of this year. If Julian himself cannot make it, I am sure he will be with us in spirit.

Yours most humbly,

Dr Gregor Sandys

Botanist

# THIRTY-EIGHT

On Whitsun of that year, the good and great of Britain's horticultural set converged upon Grimfern for Gregor's exhibition. The greenhouses were decked out with yellow and white bunting. Simon and Gregor had matching boating jackets in stripes of the same colours. Simon's basement was firmly off-limits to guests—a velvet rope was all the security needed against the gentler classes. He had set up a bazaar of sorts under a grand arbour, displaying his taxidermy masterpieces. When each was sold discretely to yet another minor royal or major poet, he would tie a red ribbon around its head like a blindfold. Soon he had a whole menagerie of sightless creatures.

The new greenhouse stood behind the main one as you approached it from the main entrance. Rosalinda had arranged for Herr Wilhelm to arrive early and set up a vast theatrical drape, on loan from the D'Oyly Carte Company. This would hide the mill cottage from the guests until such a time as Gregor could perform the grand reveal. The costumier was a smiley man, but his smile carried no warmth. He was composed entirely of spheres—the various roundnesses of his head, his fists, and his gut were mathematically perfect. Despite his heft he was incredibly poised and nimble—it seemed as if he were suspended from the sky like a marionette. His face was graced by a pair of tiny pince-nez, which he used exclusively for glaring over. Gregor was pleased to meet him in person, even if he didn't believe his 'Austrian' accent.

Gregor himself was in performance mode. His beard was freshly trimmed and he wore his straw boater at a sickeningly sly angle. He fluttered around the room, never stopping with one group long enough to have a whole conversation. Eventually he came across the contingent from the Royal Horticultural Society. He could tell it was them from the way they huddled together, dressed all in black despite this Sunday being the traditional start of summer. They were like a flock of Emperor penguins, each one haughtier than the last, but all relying on each other for security. Gregor inserted himself into the middle of the gaggle, forcing them to split. Divide and conquer.

"Welcome, Horti folk! So glad to see you," he said, making a great show of looking around. "But I don't see Mallory—I assume he's still in Istanbul?"

"If he is, he never said anything to us," said a mousy man with a grating voice.

"Be quiet, Harold," said a handsome woman dripping with black ostrich feathers. "In his absence, I am acting chair of the Society. Lady Caryll Sydenham—I trust you're aware."

"It'll come to me," said Gregor, making as if to kiss her over-sized opal ring but not really touching. "Listen, chaps, I have something in the next greenhouse the likes of which you have never seen. You'll go quite mad. Trust me—and try the vol-au-vents!"

Then he was gone, tactically whisking into the hubbub of visitors nibbling cucumber canapés and quaffing cucumber gin. Gregor lifted a champagne flute and a gin tumbler from two servers, combined them, and downed the concoction. He climbed up to the gallery, where Jennifer's bedroom used to be. This now was his podium—his stage. From this vantage point he could see Lady Sydenham pouting. She struck the mousy gentleman viciously with her fan.

Gregor tapped his empty glass against an iron column.

"Friends," he began, opening his arms wide, "and enemies. It's so good to see you! I have missed this. But sometimes as a scientist you have to experience a long dark night of the soul before you can return to the glittering gas lamps of respectable society. So, apologies for my absence. But I trust you will find my most recent achievement worth—*as they say*—the wait."

Gregor let the crowd build up a murmur. He signalled to Simon across the atrium, who disappeared into the cellar. Imperceptibly under the muttering, the boiler thrummed as it diverted maximum heat from the main house to the mill. Wilhelm took up his position by the curtain's drawstring, standing bevelled like a chorus girl.

"In a phantasmagorical admixture of East and West, using materials and specimens collected from as far away as Sumatra, and from as close to home as this very village, building upon my *success*"—he said the word very loudly—"with fungal specimens *as witnessed* by the RHS, built by the sweat of my brow and with no small part of suffering, brought to you today to dazzle and amaze but also to educate, I give you—the Living Machine!"

Wilhelm pulled the curtain with a flourish and a low bow. The fabric fell heavily to the floor, revealing through Grimfern's many-panelled windows the greenhouse extension. The mill cottage inside the glass seemed like a captured world—a terrarium of delicate mosses, or an orchid under a bell jar. But it was on an entirely full scale, which staggered the guests. The heat pumped into the annex caused CHLOE to flap her shutters and run her waterwheel double time. She threw spores into the air; golden clouds glittering around like in a snow globe. You could almost see the vines of tropical creepers spreading across the brickwork.

"Marvellous!"

"Astonishing!"

"Surely," shrieked Lady Sydenham, "there must be some sort of pneumatic automaton at the heart of this. After all, what seems to be magic is always revealed to be science."

"You are very right and very wrong, Lady Sydenham," said Gregor with glee. "Science is indeed at the heart of all magics. But this science is botanical, not pneumatic. Biological, not metallurgical. The mycelium, that is the fungus, carries information—information!—through the building, joining up the various plants and mineral elements. They then act together as a single organism. A holobiont! I have breached the biting point of macro-sentience! The idyllic tableau you see before you is in fact a single creature. We call her—"

An involuntary twitch stopped him, and he was glad of the chance to correct himself.

"We call *it* the Living Machine. Please, do go out and take a look. But of course you may not enter the other greenhouse, which you will find to be hermetically sealed."

The excited throng rushed through the French doors leading out of the atrium and round to the mill. In the crush, many ladies' bustles were lightly ripped. The highfaluting socialites of London and the Home Counties crowded around the greenhouse, faces pressed against the glass, gawping at the fungal wonder.

Once the excitement had simmered down and people began to think how they would explain the spectacle to those back home, the party settled into that late period all parties have, where the music is more luscious and the gin brings a blush to satisfied faces. Leaning on the grand piano, Gregor drained his glass for the umpteenth time that evening. Through the departing crowd, Rosalinda wandered languidly towards him with a slim glass of champagne.

"Bravo, Gregor darling," she murmured, "you have done it again: all of the *jardiniers* from here to Canterbury love your work and hate your guts. A toast to the Royal Horticultural Society, green with envy."

She went to clink glasses, but Gregor held his upside down to show it was empty.

"Oh, boo. Have this one. I'll let you into a secret: I don't drink. I just like to hold it."

Gregor supped the flat champagne. Rosalinda must have been carrying it around since she arrived.

"I'm sure I've seen you tipsy on more than one occasion," he said.

"Tipsy on life, dear boy! Drunk on you. You are such a very clever clematis. Now *you* tell *me* an intoxicating secret. You know, it's a year to the day since you showed me that charming mush which could water an orchid."

"Then let me show you how it's doing now."

They were the last people left, other than the hired caterers and waitstaff. Mr Bland, Rosalinda's grey husband, was waiting for her at Simon's taxidermy stall. Like the many blindfolded animals, he could not see his wife's joy at being parted from him. They called Simon over, and Rosalinda instructed her husband to wait with the driver. Simon and Gregor held hands as the three of them ran like children towards the water mill conservatory.

"Are we going in? I thought you said it was hermetically sealed?" Rosalinda panted.

"Even thrice-great Hermes needed to water his plants," said Simon, taking an ornate key from the pocket of his boating jacket. This unlocked a sliding glass panel, which could be shimmied right out.

"I had to stop people trying to get in," said Gregor, "myself included." He took Rosalinda's hand and followed Simon through the gap in the glass wall.

The air was fetid and sweet, and very warm indeed. The planting might have seemed indigenous to Buckinghamshire at first glance, but on closer inspection the hedges were bristling with orchids and there were tropical lilies in the millpond. It was like a traditional English pastoral scene but completely drenched in colour, like some psychedelic John Constable. They stepped over mossy roots and parted drapes of woolly lichen to enter the cottage.

"Tell me, Gregor, is this something to do with the fungus you showed me last year?"

"You're correct, Rosalinda. It courses all around you. It controls the petals and leaves of every plant you see about you, as well as all the mechanisms."

"You impossible beauty," Rosalinda said, to everything and everyone.

Simon took a spray can from the vine-laden table and began misting CHLOE's ferns. Gregor ran his finger up a spray of sensitive *Mimosa*, and leaves all across the room shuddered in delight. CHLOE lowered a tendril to rest on Gregor's shoulder. A web of furry mycelium rushed out along the fabric of his garish jacket and fruited spontaneously into glowing mushrooms.

Gregor was overtaken by emotion.

"This is our daughter," he sobbed, "our botanical daughter."

Simon held him at the small of his back to stop the man sinking to the floor. Rosalinda, herself in joyful tears, embraced them both.

Bells started ringing—softly, as if far away. Below them all, in a dank cellar, the lovers lay in their root-bound tomb. Jennifer and Constance were intimately intertwined with each other, and with the mycelium. The entity CHLOE rang her bells for the part of herself that was them, those stolen girls, together again in death.

In every sinew of her being, CHLOE carried the nutrients of Julian Mallory. She knew his pride and blamed him for it and thanked him also. By his pride, she was nourished. CHLOE rang her bells as a feast day for him.

In the flashes of her pseudo-neurones, her brain plastered in root patterns on the soil wall, CHLOE remembered Constance's father, Mr Haggerston—how he flew into a rage at his daughter's wandering heart and stole her life from her. CHLOE rang her bells as a strident warning against him and his kind.

Here was her whole family—every green plant, every pealing bell, every dripping sinew of fungal excrescence, every person. All these were her family, but also part of herself: each leaf was an organ of her body, each living human was a limb. She had been a *family* since the beginning, a collection of souls, but now look at how she had grown!

Soon the carillon reverberated around the glasshouse, rattling windows and scaring the birds. Hers was a wild gamelan, played on church bells to a monstrous tune. From the corpses to the rafters, CHLOE sang once more through her ringing, in all its overlapping resonance.

For Rosalinda, so in love with the world, she rang Life.

For Simon, so ambivalent to the grave, she rang Death, and its beautiful transgression.

For Gregor, she rang Love. She rang love of knowledge. She rang love of gain. And she rang all laud and honour to him, the first and greatest of her component parts.

THE END

# ACKNOWLEDGEMENTS

Of all the things a person can choose to do with their time, writing a novel is perhaps the most foolish. That suits me just fine. The ridiculousness of the endeavour is actually what helped me start off in the first place, and a sense of pleasant bafflement has sustained me throughout. Those games of pretend—playing house with Simon and Gregor, or hide-and-seek, or scary monsters, or *being-a-writer*—gave me some escape at a time when my 'real' world was increasingly unmanageable. So these acknowledgements are for the folks who have helped me play the fool long enough to write the book, and for those who then pulled my nonsense together into the physical object you currently hold in your hands.

David-John—you were midwife to the monster, as well as its first victim. Whenever the business-end of publishing became too much, you had the right *questions* to coax me back to myself, back to Grimfern. Watching you read that early draft, wide-eyed and inquisitive, is one of my most treasured memories. If you'd have been the only person who read and enjoyed the book, that would have been enough. *I love you.*

A phalanx of two might not seem much, but it is more than enough when your shield-sibling is Ren Balcombe. I don't know what I did to deserve your agenting skills, but ever since you slid, Gandalf-like, into my DMs I had a strong sense that my destiny was already laid out before me. Thank you for multi-classing as both barbarian and cleric for this party.

Cath Trechman, Titan's editor-at-large, was that still, small voice of YES. Thank you for your YES, ANDS; for your YES, BUTS; and especially for your first YES PLEASE. I've learned so much from you on this project, and I hope I've repaid your dedication to this manuscript, and your belief in me.

To Jess Woo and Adrian McLaughlin, freelance copy-editor and typesetter respectively, thank you for jumping in with your skills and creativity—you've both added so much depth and detail to the world of Grimfern. To Julia Lloyd—your painstaking work on the cover produced an exquisite monster truly worthy of Simon and Gregor. It is at once sharp and soft, beautiful and strange. And so full of surprises—I am a big fan of the ants!

And to everybody else at Titan Books, especially George, Elora, and Kabriya, thank you for your expertise, passion, and patience as you shepherded me through this process.

To the authors who provided blurbs for the novel, I continue to be overwhelmed by your thoughtful and generous words. To be observed by such luminous peers as yourselves feels like having an x-ray. That you've set your laser-focus on my fleshy innards and found my bones appealing is both humbling and inspiring.

There's a strong impulse to thank everybody who has made my life better, or bigger, or brighter—since your kindnesses enabled *A Botanical Daughter*. Luckily for me there are so many of you, but here I will limit myself to naming just a few:

To those first readers who met my creature during its awkward adolescence, and who were imaginative enough to envision the monster it could become—David-John, Mum, Emma; thank you.

To Kate Beaumont, aesthete, who taught me more about living-out being an artist than any book or course—let's get dressed up and go for a coffee.

To Very Good Friends, who have always believed in and encouraged me. I think you were the first to spot that my nonsense life was something to be protected and nurtured— long before I accepted that myself. Thanks are not enough. I hope to be worthy of the support you provided unconditionally.

To the writing community, and especially the LGBTWIP folk I met in the halcyon days of Twitter, and who have waited as long as I have to get their hands on this book—thank you for your companionship. We were travellers on lonely trails, meeting to huddle around campfires, swapping stories of our treks. That bit of Twitter was always beautiful, and will continue to be wherever we are, on whatever platform or in person.

To my large and bonkers family, theatre friends and colleagues, Paul L. Martin, Louis Hartshorn and Brian Hook, Nik Briggs and everybody at York Stage, Southlands Methodist Church, and Dobbies Garden Centre York… in subtle and not-so-subtle ways, this is all your fault.

# ABOUT THE AUTHOR

**Noah Medlock** is a novelist and theatre musician living in York, UK. He writes vivid and off-beat stories which sit somewhere between Horror, Fantasy, and Historical. Noah plays piano and trombone for shows and teaches singing and performing arts in York. A passionate devotee of all musical theatre, but especially Stephen Sondheim, Noah is the kind of person who will happily start crying at the overture. He once worked as a horticultural advisor at a garden centre, which inspired the completion of his debut mycelial horror novel *A Botanical Daughter*. Noah can still be found shouting into the void on Twitter/X, as well as on TikTok and Instagram.

# BLOOM

## *Delilah S. Dawson*

Rosemary meets Ash at the farmers' market. Ash—precise, pretty, and practically perfect—sells bars of soap in delicate pastel colors, sprinkle-speckled cupcakes stacked on scalloped stands, beeswax candles, jelly jars of honey, and glossy green plants.

Ro has never felt this way about another woman; with Ash, she wants to be her and have her in equal measure. But as her obsession with Ash consumes her, she may find she's not the one doing the devouring…

Told in lush, delectable prose, this is a deliciously dark tale of passion taking an unsavory turn…

"A cottagecore dream turned nightmare, astonishing in its beauty and violence. Every page drips with delicious dread. This bite-sized tale is perfectly wicked."

Rachel Harrison, author of *Black Sheep*

"Sensual, smart, biting, and downright nasty, *Bloom* is a dizzying, heady feast for the discerning palate. I devoured this book in one greedy sitting."

Paul Tremblay, author of *The Pallbearers Club*

**TITAN**BOOKS.COM

# A LIGHT MOST HATEFUL

*Hailey Piper*

Three years after running away from home, Olivia is stuck with a dead-end job in nowhere town Chapel Hill, Pennsylvania. At least she has her best friend, Sunflower.

Olivia figures she'll die in Chapel Hill, if not from boredom then the summer night storm which crashes into town with a mind-bending monster in tow.

If Olivia's going to escape Chapel Hill and someday reconcile with her parents, she'll need to dodge residents enslaved by the storm's otherworldly powers and find Sunflower.

But as the night strains friendships and reality itself, Olivia suspects the storm, and its monster, may have its eyes on Sunflower and everything she loves.

Including Olivia.

"What has sprouted out from Hailey Piper's head is a fully-formed goddess of a novel, equal parts terrifying, awe-inspiring, and downright worshipful. I'm still scorched by *A Light Most Hateful*, even after closing its pages, blinded by its brilliance."

Clay McLeod Chapman, author of *Ghost Eaters*

# THE PALE HOUSE DEVIL

## *Richard Kadrey*

Ford and Neuland are paranormal mercenaries—one living, one undead; one of them kills the undead, the other kills the living. When a job goes bad in New York, they head west to wait for the heat to cool down.

There, a young woman named Tilda Rosenbloom hires them on behalf of wealthy landowner Shepherd Mansfield to track and kill a demon haunting a mansion in remote northern California.

As Ford and Neuland investigate the creature, they uncover a legacy of blood, sacrifice, and slavery in the house. Forced to confront a powerful creature unlike anything they've faced before, they come to learn that the most frightening monster might not be the one they're hunting…

"A thrilling, inventive, pulpy, bi-coastal romp with a bloody beating heart. The roguishly principled and endearing Ford and Neuland can kill for me anytime. I have a list ready."

Paul Tremblay, author of *The Cabin at the End of the World*

"*The Pale House Devil* showcases Kadrey's gift for gritty characters and snappy dialogue, but also his talent for eerie settings and lean, cruel horror."

Cassandra Khaw, author of *Nothing But Blackened Teeth*

**TITAN**BOOKS.COM

For more fantastic fiction, author events,
exclusive excerpts, competitions, limited editions and more

VISIT OUR WEBSITE
**titanbooks.com**

LIKE US ON FACEBOOK
**facebook.com/titanbooks**

FOLLOW US ON TWITTER AND INSTAGRAM
**@TitanBooks**

EMAIL US
**readerfeedback@titanemail.com**